A SCARLET WOMAN

THE FITZGERALDS OF DUBLIN BOOK ONE

LORNA PEEL

Chapter One

Dublin, Ireland. Friday, July 30th, 1880

Will blinked and fought to stay awake as the cab rattled along the dark streets. It was years since he had been this drunk. The night of their graduation, wasn't it? Fred, seated between Jerry and himself, was clapping his hands. Whether it was in an effort to keep warm or that it was because he was just as drunk but more intent on keeping awake, Will didn't know.

"Nearly there now," Fred announced.

"Eh, what?" Jerry slurred.

"Oh, you two are hopeless. It's my last night of freedom. We haven't had that much to drink."

"We have," Jerry stated firmly.

"Where are we going now?" Will wiped some condensation away and peered out of the window but couldn't see a thing. "Where are we, Fred?"

"My dear Dr Fitzgerald, we are about to have the night of our lives. My treat, to thank the two of you for being such good friends to me over the years. You don't get out enough, either of you. You with your swanky London practice,

1

Jeremiah. And as for you, William." Fred kicked his ankle. "The less said the better."

"Where are we?" Will demanded. He knew what Fred thought of his practice and didn't need to be reminded. "Fred?"

"Monto," Fred shouted triumphantly as the cab stopped. "Sally Maher's kip."

"A brothel?" Will straightened up, sobering a little. "No, Fred, I'd rather not."

Fred just laughed, irritating him. "Don't be ridiculous. I said I'll pay."

"You know damn well it's not that."

"I'm not listening. I'm getting the first pick of the girls, though. You two can toss a coin if you can't agree. Don't fall asleep, Jerry, we're here."

The three of them got out of the cab and Fred paid the fare. He and Jerry went straight inside while Will glanced up at the brothel. It was a commonplace terraced house if a little run down. Reluctantly, he took off his hat and followed them.

"Will?" Fred bellowed at him, and he jumped violently before turning away from the supposedly seductive red furnishings in the narrow hallway. "We're fixed up. What sort of a girl do you want?"

Fred, Jerry, and the brothel madam all waited expectantly. Will sighed. He hadn't a clue.

"I don't know... black-ish hair?" Cecilia's hair was blonde but he forced her face out of his befuddled mind. "Yes, black-ish hair."

"Good, you can have Rose." The madam turned away. "Maggie. Lily. Rose," she roared up the stairs.

Three young women appeared at the top of the stairs. The first was a redhead, the second a blonde, and the third his brunette. Will watched her come down the steps. She wore a red silk robe, her dark hair was loosely pinned up, and wisps fell over her face and neck. As she reached the foot of the stairs, Will also saw to his relief, that she was in her early twenties, tall, and quite shapely. Good. Cecilia was as thin as a rake and a year older than him. His brunette nodded to the brothel madam then gave him a little smile.

"I'm Rose."

"Will."

"Hello, Will." Taking his hand, she led him up the stairs, along the landing, and into a bedroom. "I hope you're not expecting anything too outlandish," she said as she closed the door. "Because you won't get it from me."

Again, he was relieved. He had never been very sexually adventurous and recently he had lived like a monk.

"No, I'm not," he replied, shrugging off then hanging his frock coat and his hat on a hook on the back of the door.

Glancing around the room, he noted that apart from a double bed, it housed a dressing table and stool, a wardrobe, a bedside table with an oil lamp and ewer and bowl standing on it, and an armchair upholstered in red fabric. A fire was lit in the hearth but the coal was producing more smoke than flames.

"Good. Shall I help you with your clothes?" she offered.

"I can manage."

He began to fumble with his cravat and collar, eventually managed to get them off, then set to work on his cufflinks. Minutes passed, he had made no progress whatsoever, and he swore under his breath.

"Allow me," she said softly. He stood meekly while she undid them before proceeding to completely undress him. "Celebrating?"

"Fred's getting married tomorrow."

"Are you brothers?"

"No. We were at Trinity College together. We're doctors."

"Doctors? I see. Are you married?" He hesitated before replying and she glanced up at him. "I won't mind if you lie."

"I won't lie," he replied tightly. "I nearly was married but I'm not."

"I'm sorry. There." She laid his clothes on the back of the faded and threadbare armchair then gave him a long look while taking the pins from her hair. How did he compare with the hundreds, perhaps thousands, of men who had passed through this bedroom? Cecilia had found him handsome. But ultimately not handsome enough. Thick dark brown hair fell down Rose's back and she slipped off her robe before throwing it over his clothes on the back of the armchair. He blinked a few times. She had a very shapely body and firm full breasts. This might not be such a bad idea after all. "Ready?" she asked, getting onto the bed.

Will nodded and followed her. Climbing onto the bed, and settling between her thighs, he pushed into her. Releasing all his pent-up hurt, frustration, humiliation, and anger at Cecilia, he pounded into Rose. She quickly reached up and, with both hands, held onto the brass bedstead as her breasts bounced and the bed squeaked. Ignoring her high-pitched gasps at each of his hard thrusts, he came a lot quicker than he would have liked, but that was down to far too many whiskeys.

He withdrew from her and lay on his back, catching his breath, pleasantly surprised at himself. He hadn't known he'd had that in him. That was what women did to a man. Beside him, Rose lay stock-still, the only sounds were her quick breaths. Her hands were still grasping the bedstead, her brown eyes were fixed firmly on the ceiling, but she was biting her lips hard.

"I hurt you," he said.

She turned to him, letting go of the bedstead. "A little, yes," she replied, and he flushed with shame. "You haven't been with a woman for a long time, have you?"

"No," he admitted. "I'm sorry."

Rose gave him a weak smile. "She must have hurt you deeply."

"She did, but I shouldn't have taken it out on you. I am sorry."

Rose shrugged. "It's what I'm here for. Company, comfort, advice, sex... Your friend, Fred, has paid for the whole night, by the way. So there's no need to go at it quite like that next time."

"I won't."

"You didn't want to come here, did you?" she asked him bluntly.

He expelled a long breath. "No. I wanted to get drunk but not—"

"Go with a prostitute? No, I don't blame you. We provide a useful service here, but the one thing we can't supply is love and I think love is the one thing most people need."

He frowned at her and she laughed kindly. "I think you're too drunk to answer that. Don't bother."

She slid off the bed, went to the armchair, and picked up the red silk robe. Across her back, he saw a long scar. She slipped the robe on, tied the belt, then pointed to a bottle and a jug on the mantelpiece.

"Brandy or lemonade?" she asked, but he was still staring at her back. "Will?"

He raised his eyes to her face. "Lemonade, please."

He got off the bed and went unsteadily to her as she poured the yellow liquid into two glasses. Gently, he lowered her robe and examined the scar. It ran diagonally from her right shoulder to her left hip. It must have been agonisingly painful but the skin had healed well, leaving the raised scar.

"Who did this to you?"

She pulled the robe up again. "Never you mind."

"Did you go to the police?"

"No. There was no point. Your lemonade." She held the glass out to him.

"Was it..?" he began as he accepted the glass from her.

"A client? No. Good health." She touched his glass with hers. "Why don't you put this on?" She passed him a green silk robe. "That fire doesn't throw out much heat."

"Thank you." Putting the glass down, he shrugged the robe on but didn't do it up. "Your scar isn't very old, is it?"

Sighing, she shook her head. "It dates from January if you must know."

"Who did it to you?"

"My father," she replied matter-of-factly, shocking him.

"Why?" he asked.

"He discovered I had been with a neighbour's son and was expecting a baby. He whipped me and threw me out. I came to Dublin and I heard that Sally – the madam here –

knew where I could have a safe abortion. I had the abortion and I've been working here to pay off the fee. Now," she added in a shaky voice, sitting on the edge of the bed. "That's more than enough about me. It's your turn. You were nearly married, you say?"

He nodded, and sat on the bed beside her. "My father is a doctor, too. Cecilia is the daughter of his recently retired practice partner. Everyone assumed I would join the practice once I qualified to bring in a bit of young blood. I did join but my heart wasn't in it. Rich people with more money than sense and too much time on their hands – hypochondriacs – so I left. I found a house in the Liberties and set up practice there. Everyone thought I'd only last a few months, the local people included, but I've been there four years now."

"And Cecilia didn't want to marry a doctor whose practice is in a poorer area?"

His face twisted bitterly. "No. Cecilia wanted me to move back to my family home and rejoin my father's practice. I tried to compromise with her and my parents agreed that Cecilia and I would live with them after our marriage, but I insisted on continuing to practice medicine in the Liberties. She said she would consider the compromise but, a few days later, she broke off our engagement by letter. A week after that, the announcement of her engagement to Clive Ashlinn – a rich barrister who lives only two doors up from her – was published in *The Irish Times* – only three weeks after our engagement announcement had been published there. She and Clive were married at St Peter's Church three weeks ago."

"I'm sorry," Rose said, actually sounding as if she meant it.

"We should never have become engaged," he went on miserably. "But I love Cecilia and I thought she loved me."

Rose put her glass on the scratched dressing table and he followed her, slipping out of his robe, and easing hers off her shoulders. She turned around in his grasp.

"I'd sit on the dressing table but it would probably collapse under us," she said, and they exchanged a grin. "The armchair?" she suggested. "We both need to keep a certain person off our minds."

"Yes." He gave her a grim smile. "We do."

He sat in the armchair, she placed her knees on either side of his thighs and sank down onto him. She began to rock her hips and he leant back with a contented sigh, closing his eyes.

"You're not going to fall asleep, are you?" she asked, and he reluctantly opened them. "Don't you like this? We can try something else?"

"No," he murmured. "I closed my eyes because I like it. Don't stop," he added, so she didn't, slowly bringing him to a grunting climax.

Stroking his hair, she allowed him to explore her breasts with his lips and tongue. "You really like them, don't you?" she whispered, and he nodded.

"It's not every day I get the opportunity to… you don't mind me doing this?"

"No. Just try not to bite."

He smiled and lowered his head to them again, circling her nipples with his tongue, and hearing her sigh.

"More lemonade?" Rather suddenly, she climbed off him and went to the jug. "It's home-made."

"No, thank you." He got to his feet, picked her up, and

laid her on the bed. Climbing over her, he found himself kissing her mouth for the first time. She responded for a few moments before turning her face away from him. "What is it?" he asked, and she turned back.

"I'm sorry, Will, but I shouldn't have let you kiss me. You are the first man to kiss me in that way since James."

"How on earth did you manage that?" he exclaimed, immediately regretting it.

"I'm not proud of what I am, you know?" she retorted. "But I have little or no money and no family now. You may as well kiss me again."

She pulled his head down and he kissed her mouth and breasts. Turning her over, he kissed her scar all the way from shoulder to hip before rolling her onto her back. He made sure he pushed into her more gently than the first time and slid in and out with an almost hypnotic rhythm. She lay on the bed, her arms above her head, and her breasts bouncing a little as he moved inside her. When she closed her eyes and began to produce little moans, he smiled, and gradually increased his thrusts until he gave way to his own orgasm, jerking hard against her body as he came.

Lifting his head from her breasts, he saw her turn her head back to him at the same time.

"That was better," she said. "You're good when you put your mind to it. I mean it. You are."

That was quite a compliment from a prostitute. "Thank you."

"Tell me about your practice," she added as he withdrew from her and lay on his back with his hands behind his head.

"I rent a three-storey house. It's very tall and narrow, Dutch Billy style, gable-fronted. The ground floor is given over to a surgery and dispensary, a hall which is used as a waiting room, and a kitchen. I live upstairs."

"Alone?" she asked.

"I have a housekeeper who comes in every day." He stifled a yawn. "Sorry. I'm not used to drinking a lot anymore."

"You'd better sleep it off."

"Yes."

Feeling her eyes on him, he crawled up the bed and got under the covers. He tossed and turned for a few moments to get comfortable in the strange bed then fell fast asleep.

She sat on the edge of the bed and watched Will sleep. He was a handsome man. Tall, muscular, and strong with kind brown eyes. She ran her fingers over his dark stubble, and smoothed tousled brown hair back from his forehead, before rubbing herself between her legs. He had been rough the first time but now she knew why, and it didn't really matter. He had apologised, and no-one had done that before. He'd also made her come – genuinely come – and only one man had done that before.

She got off the bed and picked up her glass of lemonade then turned to glance back at him. The last man to have made her genuinely come was James, and look where she had ended up – in a Dublin brothel – entertaining whoever walked through the door to pay off aborting his child. But she shouldn't be genuinely coming for any of them. She was there to be used, not to be apologised to, have her awful scar kissed, and then be brought slowly to orgasm. No, she shouldn't have enjoyed her time with Will, no matter how handsome he was. Enjoying sex only got you into trouble.

Hearing a squeal and a guffaw from the neighbouring bedroom, she couldn't help but laugh. Maggie was certainly giving Fred his money's worth. Maggie would do anything for money, so Fred would be having the night of his life. She sighed. What now? Will was sleeping peacefully. She may as well go to sleep now, too. She would be able to get up earlyish and go into town to look at the shops and the people. She got into the bed beside him and lay down. He muttered something and threw an arm around her. She grimaced, turned down the oil lamp, and closed her eyes.

She woke feeling Will stirring beside her. His brown eyes stared blankly at her for a moment before he smiled.

"You remember me, then?" she asked, fighting an urge to explore his now heavy stubble with her fingers.

"Yes, I do. Good morning." He rubbed his eyes. "Thank you for putting up with me last night. I don't often drink to excess. I hope I didn't pry too much and upset you."

"It was nothing," she lied, giving him as bright a smile as she could manage.

"I'd better go." Throwing back the covers, he got out of the bed and went to the chair and door for his clothes. "Any sounds from the other bedrooms?" he asked as he got dressed.

"I don't think they'll be stirring for hours yet."

"Well, I'm afraid Fred and Jerry need to stir right away. Fred's getting married in—" He took out his pocket watch. "Three hours." Putting his watch back in his waistcoat pocket, he went to the dressing table and bent in front of the mirror finger-combing his hair into place.

"Use my brush." She pointed to it lying beside a bottle of overly sweet scented perfume.

"Thank you." He reached for the brush, tidied his hair, then turned to face her. They observed each other for a couple of moments until she smiled self-consciously and pulled the bedcovers up to hide her breasts. "Why don't you—" he began, then stopped abruptly and flushed.

"Find more suitable employment?" She shrugged. "I'm all but unemployable. I was schooled to be a lady."

"But think of what you might catch here?"

"I am clean, Will," she replied tightly. "You needn't worry."

He flushed even deeper. "You could go into domestic service?"

"Yes, I suppose I could."

"I can only advise you to leave this brothel while you are still young and healthy."

"Thank you, Doctor." Getting out of the bed, she quickly put her robe on and went to the door. She lifted his hat down from the hook before opening the door for him. "Good morning to you."

"Good morning." Taking the hat from her, he went out. She closed the door, hearing him knocking loudly at the two other bedroom doors on the landing, ordering his friends out of bed and home at once.

Standing in front of the dressing table mirror, she opened her robe and surveyed herself. He was right. A few years of this and she would be as coarse as Lily down the landing and would probably have syphilis or herpes into the bargain as well. It was time to leave.

Pouring some cold water from the ewer into the bowl, she got washed and dressed, then pinned up her hair before going downstairs to the kitchen. Sally was seated at the table breaking her fast, seeming to thrive on as little sleep as possible.

"That tea in the pot is still hot," Sally told her.

"Thank you." Sitting down opposite Sally, she poured herself a cup and added milk, then cut a slice of soda bread.

"Your fella gone?"

She nodded as she buttered the bread. "Yes, he's just left. He's a doctor. All three are doctors."

"We did well out o' them. Hope they come back."

"Yes. Mine was nice."

Sally grunted. "So, what will you do with yourself today?"

She took a sip of tea. "I thought I might go into town and look at the shops. I haven't done that for a while."

"Do." Sally nodded. "You deserve a day out. You've worked hard of late. Here." Sally reached into the pocket of the white apron she was wearing over a gaudy yellow dress, lifted out some coins, and passed them to her. "Treat yourself to a bite to eat. But you didn't get this from me, all right?"

She smiled, trying not to stare too much at Sally's freshly dyed copper-coloured hair. "Thank you."

"Finish that tea and bread and be off with you."

In her bedroom, she counted the coins and dropped them into the small black leather handbag she had bought after seeing it for sale in a pawn shop window. Two shillings and sixpence ha'penny. Sally wasn't usually so generous.

Donning her best dress – a navy blue relict from her pre-Dublin life with a square neck and buttons up the front – and a fashionable hat in matching navy blue she had purchased from a second-hand clothes stall, she walked to St

Stephen's Green. It was the last day of July and the trees of the park, newly opened to the general public, were lush with leaves of varying greens. They reminded her of Ballybeg but she blinked a few times to banish the memory. For now, she was going to find a spot in the sunshine, watch the ladies and gentlemen parading past, and mull over what she could possibly gain employment as.

She found a suitable spot on the grass near the lake but found the ducks and pigeons far more entertaining. A little boy in a white sailor suit was throwing pieces of bread into the water for them and there were heated battles between the birds for possession. A little further along the lake shore, a gentleman folded his newspaper and got up, leaving it on the grass as he walked away. Immediately, she got to her feet and retrieved the newspaper. It was the previous day's *Dublin Evening Mail*.

Out of curiosity, she went through the pages until she found the Situations Vacant columns. Her eyes rested on one advertisement for a parlourmaid but her heart sank when she read that references must be presented. She bit her nails for a few minutes before twisting around and glancing through the trees at the imposing red-bricked facade of the Shelbourne Hotel across the street. She tore the advertisement out of the newspaper before closing and folding it, placing it on the grass, and putting the advertisement in her handbag.

Leaving St Stephen's Green, she adjusted her hat so it sat on her head at a jaunty angle, and crossed the street. She entered the hotel as if she knew exactly where she was going. Taking a quick glance around the foyer, she went to the reception desk. Scrutinising it, she saw just what she wanted. The concierge was dealing with a guest at the other end so she took a chance and grabbed a few sheets of notepaper and some envelopes. Hiding them in the folds of her skirt – trying desperately not to crumple them too much – she nonchalantly left the hotel, the doorman lifting his hat to her as she passed.

Her heart raced as she walked along the footpath towards the top of Grafton Street. She had never stolen anything before in her life. Retrieving the items from her skirt, she saw that she had three sheets of notepaper and two envelopes before halting. The name of the hotel was printed at the top of the notepaper and her heart sank. How stupid not to have realised that. Well, she wasn't going to go back with them now. She carefully folded the sheets of notepaper and put them in the envelopes before carrying on. Now to find a pen and some ink. A pencil was out of the question.

She wandered slowly down Grafton Street, passed a café, then turned back and peered inside. A young man was busily writing something in a notebook with a pen at a window table. She would have to part with some of the two shillings and sixpence ha'penny on tea or coffee. She went in, sat at the next table and ordered a cup of coffee, the young man only glancing briefly at her.

"Excuse me?" she began before he bent to write again.

"Yes?" he replied rather shortly, clearly not having liked being disturbed.

"I hope you don't mind, but could I please borrow your pen? I have an urgent letter to write." She pulled a sheet of the Shelbourne Hotel notepaper out of an envelope, laid it on the table, and he stared at it curiously. "Please? It is very urgent."

"All right." He passed his pen and pot of ink to her,

reached for a teapot, and poured himself a cup.

"You're very kind, thank you." She smiled at him and then up at the waitress who brought her coffee.

She dipped the nib into the ink, took a deep breath, and wrote a character reference in the nearest she could manage to her mother's handwriting.

> *The Glebe House*
> *Ballybeg*
> *Co Galway*

> *To Whom It May Concern:*
> *Maisie Byrne was a house-parlourmaid in my household from June 1876 to July 1879. During that time she proved to be a hard worker, good timekeeper and was always polite, tidy, courteous, and willing.*

> *I would have no hesitation in recommending Maisie Byrne for any future household position she may apply for.*
> *Martha Stevens (Mrs)*

She signed her mother's signature with a flourish and read the reference through twice. Maisie had left because her own mother had fallen ill. They had never seen her again and the chances of her turning up in Dublin were scarce.

She added milk and sugar to the coffee and sipped it, waiting for the ink to dry. The young man leant over, read the reference, and laughed.

"I hope you get the position."

She smiled and placed the envelope containing the unused notepaper in her handbag. "So do I. I really need it. Thank you very much for these."

"Not at all," he replied, taking the pen and ink back.

"Are you writing a book?" she asked, glancing at the pages of neat handwriting in the notebook, and he rolled his eyes comically.

"Trying to."

"I hope you get published."

"Thank you… Maisie."

Twenty minutes later, she stood outside a terraced Georgian townhouse on Merrion Square and took a deep breath to compose herself. She went carefully down the steep areaway steps and rang the bell. A maid, barely five feet tall, wearing a grey dress and white apron and cap, opened the door and looked her up and down.

"Yes?"

"I've come about the position—"

"Yes, yes, you're the ninth since it was advertised. Come in."

A little dejected, she followed the maid into the servants' hall. The cook, another maid, and a footman were seated at a long dining table and gawped at her curiously while the tiny maid knocked at then opened a door to her left.

"Good morning," she said politely.

"Morning," the cook replied, reached for a teapot, and poured herself a cup as the tiny maid returned.

"Mr Johnston will see you now. In the butler's pantry – there." The maid pointed to the door she had just opened and closed.

"Thank you." She walked to the door, braced herself, and knocked.

"Come in," replied a loud voice in a harsh Ulster accent and she complied. The butler and a woman, presumably the housekeeper, were seated behind a table. "Stand there." The butler pointed to a spot right in front of the table. "I am Mr Johnston, the butler. This is Mrs Black, the housekeeper."

"Good morning, Mr Johnston, Mrs Black."

Mr Johnston glanced up at her, then leant back in his chair. He was a gaunt red-haired man of late middle age, while the housekeeper was a little younger, her dark hair tied in a bun at the nape of her neck. Both were dressed in black. Mr Johnston wore a black coat, white shirt with wing collar, and a black cravat, while Mrs Black's dress was tightly buttoned almost up to her chin. She stood meekly as they noted her accent and their eyes took in her general appearance, face, figure, hair and posture.

"Name?" the butler asked.

"Maisie Byrne, Mr Johnston."

He nodded and held out his hand for the reference. Heart thumping, she handed it over and watched as he read it before passing it to Mrs Black.

"You have not worked since July 1879," he said. "That is a year ago. What have you been doing during that time?"

"My mother had consumption, sir, and couldn't look after herself," she told him, hoping she sounded convincing. "I left my position at the Glebe House and cared for her until she died a month ago."

"And where was that?"

"Gloucestershire in England. My mother had moved there to care for her sister. Aunt Mary also died of consumption. I have come back to Ireland because I now have no relatives left in England."

"Do you have relatives here in Dublin or in—" The butler leant over and peered at the reference in Mrs Black's hands. "Ballybeg?"

She shook her head. "No, Mr Johnston, but Ireland is my home, and I am more likely to find another position here in Dublin than in Co Galway."

"Number 68 is the residence of Mr and Mrs James Harvey, Maisie. Mr Harvey is a barrister. Mr and Mrs Harvey entertain frequently, their guests often not leaving until the early hours. Despite this, parlourmaids at number 68 are expected to rise every morning at six o'clock. They are expected to work very hard."

Six o'clock in the morning. She almost winced. Quite often, she didn't go to sleep until six in the morning. "Yes, Mr Johnston. I am prepared to work very hard."

"The wages are twenty pounds per year," the housekeeper informed her, passing the reference back to the butler. "There is one-half-day off per week and every second Sunday. Servants at number 68 are also required to provide their own uniforms. Parlourmaids wear grey for mornings, and black for afternoon and evenings."

Servants had to buy their own uniforms? Had she enough money for them? "Yes, Mrs Black," she replied all the same.

"And last, but certainly not least, parlourmaids – indeed, all servants at number 68 – must have no followers."

"Followers?" She was mystified and fought to stop herself grimacing. Had she just given her lack of knowledge of domestic service away?

"In your case, Maisie, men friends. Male admirers."

"No, Mrs Black," she replied quietly.

"Good."

The butler glanced at the housekeeper, who gave him an almost imperceptible nod, and he got to his feet.

"Come with me, Maisie. Mrs Harvey is in the morning

room and wishes to see each applicant."

"Yes, Mr Johnston."

Her heart thumping again, she followed him upstairs to the hall, and almost walked into him when he stopped suddenly.

"Wait here," he said and went into a room at the front of the house.

She gazed around the rather cluttered hall. Two narrow mahogany tables stood along one wall and a mahogany grandfather clock stood across from what she now knew to be the morning room door.

"Maisie." She jumped as the door opened and the butler held it open for her.

She walked into a large bright room. Two huge brown leather sofas stood opposite each other at right angles to the fireplace and on the walls, she counted four gas lamps. Before she could take in more of the room, a woman in her fifties with greying reddish-brown hair piled elegantly on top of her head got up from a writing desk at the window with the reference in her hands.

"I have never received a reference written on Shelbourne Hotel notepaper before," Mrs Harvey said, by way of a greeting.

"When I received the telegram from England telling me my mother was very ill, I left the Glebe House as quickly as I could so I wouldn't miss the Dublin train," she replied, hoping it wasn't glaringly obvious she was making the story up as she went along. "Mrs Stevens kindly told me I could request a character reference at a later date so, when my mother died and I was preparing to return to Ireland, I wrote to Mrs Stevens. That is the reference I received, Mrs Harvey."

"Probably in town visiting her dressmaker," Mrs Harvey murmured, smoothing a hand over a beautiful high-necked day dress of gold silk satin. "Well, Maisie," Mrs Harvey continued, folding the reference. "You begin on Monday. You may move in tomorrow."

She was so flabbergasted she almost forgot to reply. "Thank you, Mrs Harvey."

Mrs Harvey nodded and dismissed her from the morning room.

Her head spinning, she followed the butler back to the servants' hall.

"Mrs Black will be expecting you tomorrow afternoon or evening, Maisie," he told her, and all she could do was nod as she left the house.

Climbing the areaway steps up to the pavement, she walked away in the direction she had come.

Will was violently sick in an alleyway not long after leaving Sally Maher's brothel. It was just as well he hadn't hailed a cab. Strangely, vomiting cleared not only his stomach but also his head. He hurried across the city to Brown Street South in the Liberties, hoping he wasn't going to be late, as his housekeeper had his breakfast on the kitchen table at eight o'clock every morning. The kitchen was at the back of the house, and he could smell and hear bacon frying as he closed the front door and hung up his hat. Mrs Bell, a widow for many years and always dressed in black, turned away from the solid fuel range to look at him as he came into the room.

"Morning, Dr Fitzgerald," she said, one eyebrow rising a little. "Hungry?"

Surprisingly, he was. "I am, Mrs Bell, and a cup of tea would be lovely."

"The kettle's on the boil," she added, turning back to the range.

"Excellent." He sat down at the table and cut himself a slice of her exceptional soda bread.

"Enjoy yourselves last night?" Mrs Bell asked, putting a plate of bacon, egg, and sausage in front of him.

"Thank you, yes, we did."

"What you can remember of it." She smiled. "You need to go out more. A young man like you."

"I'll be out all day today."

"I mean properly out," she elaborated. "The pub, theatre, or whatever takes your fancy."

"I saw enough pubs last night to last me quite a while."

She harrumphed and stood back from him. "You know, you don't look as rough as I thought you would be. Did you get drunk at all?"

He laughed. "Extremely."

"No sore head?"

"Throwing up did wonders for it, Mrs Bell."

Chuckling, she returned to the solid fuel range and made a pot of tea.

Will ate a hearty breakfast, brought some warm water upstairs to his bedroom, and washed and shaved. He then put on the clean shirt, collar, and cravat Mrs Bell had left out for him, followed by a hired black frock coat in the latest style, waistcoat, and trousers. Mrs Bell nodded approvingly when she saw him about to leave and making a final adjustment to the cravat.

"All the ladies will be after you, dressed like that."

He immediately thought of Cecilia but managed a weak smile. "Once Fred's a married man, I'll relax."

As best man, he had to get Fred to the church with no mishaps. Hailing a cab on Cork Street, Will travelled to Fred's home on Ely Place Upper, hoping his friend was there and that he wouldn't have to return to the brothel and pull Fred out of bed. Luckily, he found Fred in the hall and surprisingly docile – the magnitude of what he was about to do was dawning on him – and by a quarter to eleven they were seated in St Andrew's Church beside Jerry waiting for Margaret Dawson to arrive. An hour later, Fred was a married man, and they returned to Ely Place Upper for a celebratory meal.

"One down, two to go," Fred roared after the speeches had been made and put arms around Will and Jerry.

"Perhaps." Will reached for another glass of champagne.

"Will?" Fred followed him outside to the garden. "Cecilia's gone. Married. Forget her. I'll wager you forgot about her for a while last night, eh?"

He nodded and thought of Rose. What a life she was leading. Had he pried too much into the origin of her scar? Had he been too harsh in his advice? She must know the risks of disease. His thoughts then returned to the scar on her back and how he had kissed its entire length... He glanced back at Fred. "Your cab will be here at five o'clock. Make sure you're both ready."

"Yes, sir," Fred replied, giving him a mock salute.

Destined for a honeymoon in London, Fred and Margaret got into their cab, which was to take them to the North Wall Quay passenger terminus and the express night service to Holyhead in Wales. The ship was due to depart at

7:30 pm and the newly married couple would be in London by 8:35 am the next morning.

Will heaved a sigh of relief as the cab turned a corner out of sight. His job as best man was at an end. He decided to walk home and bought an evening newspaper on the way. Sitting down at the kitchen table, he read it from cover to cover. The newspaper contained articles and commentaries on continuing agitation between tenant farmers and landlords in the west of Ireland, and on the Land League, who aimed to protect the tenant farmers from being evicted by their landlords and obtain reductions in their rents. But it was one tiny paragraph which caught Will's eye and held his attention. The paragraph mentioned a woman who had committed suicide by drowning after jumping into the River Liffey at George's Quay opposite the Customs House that morning. The body had not been recovered and was presumed to have been carried out to sea on the tide.

Low in spirits, as he was, he couldn't imagine ever being unhappy enough to jump into the Liffey. He closed the newspaper and went upstairs to change out of his hired clothes.

In a newspaper the next morning, as well as observations and editorials on Mr Parnell and the Home Rulers, who believed Ireland should have its own parliament while remaining within the British Empire, there was a short postscript of sorts on the bottom of the front page. The woman who committed suicide at George's Quay the previous day had been named as Rose Green, a prostitute from Montgomery Street.

"All right there, Doctor?" the newspaper seller asked anxiously, as Will lowered his edition, blood draining rapidly from his face, leaving him dizzy.

Good grief, was it the same Rose? Had she taken his advice and left the brothel, only to find herself unable to cope? What a waste of a life. He shook his head, cursing himself for not minding his own business.

"Yes… No… I've just had a bit of a shock. Thanks for asking, Brendan."

"You look like you've seen a ghost," Mrs Bell commented unhelpfully, as he sat down for his mid-day meal. "Mary Boyle hasn't..?"

"No. No, she's a little better, actually."

"Thank God. Oh, there's a message from your mother. Came about an hour ago."

The message was to inform him that he, along with his parents, were invited to dinner by their neighbours, James and Harriett Harvey, on Friday evening. The Harveys' neighbours on their other side, the Belchers, would also be attending. Will rolled his eyes. The Belchers had a daughter…

"I've been invited out to dinner," he told Mrs Bell wearily. "My mother is determined to find a replacement for Cecilia for me."

"I see."

"I wish she wouldn't." He groaned. "Amelia Belcher is pleasant enough, but I've been hurt more than enough for now, and I'm not at all interested in replacing Cecilia."

"Go, anyway," he was advised. "And tell your mother you're a grown man. You'll find yourself a wife in your own good time without her help, one who'll be lucky to have you."

He smiled. "If only you were my mother."

Mrs Bell's eyes widened, and she smoothed her hands over her greying hair. "I'm no way old enough to be your mother, Dr Fitzgerald. Sure, aren't I only forty-eight."

"You give sound advice, which I'm very grateful for." He made a helpless gesture with his hands then shrugged. "I'll go to the blasted dinner, and I'll tell Amelia all about my practice in the Liberties."

Sally Maher went to Mass every morning at eleven o'clock, rain, hail, or shine. So while Sally was out, and everyone else was still in bed, she returned to the brothel and prepared to leave. Finding a carpet bag, she went first into Sally's bedroom and took Sally's precious bible from the window sill. In her own bedroom, she packed her handbag and the meagre amount of money she had to her name, some respectable clothes, and a few other bits and pieces very precious to her.

She had to break all ties with Sally, there was no other way, especially as she hadn't paid off all the abortion fee yet. Leaving the brothel, she walked to George's Quay. She threw a hat into the river and left a few other items on the quayside, including her red silk robe and the bible, which had Sally's name written on the inside cover. She then raised the alarm that a woman had been seen jumping into the Liffey.

It worked, thank goodness. After spending all her money on two parlourmaid uniforms – which left her with little choice but to endure a cold and miserable Saturday night curled up in a doorway – she found a newspaper sticking out of a letterbox the following morning. The woman who committed suicide at George's Quay had been traced back to a brothel on Montgomery Street and identified. Rose Green was dead.

By four o'clock on Sunday afternoon, she was fit to drop as she arrived at the Harvey residence on Merrion Square. Mrs Black brought her upstairs to a tiny attic bedroom, which she was to share with the other as yet unnamed parlourmaid. She longed to simply crawl into the narrow single bed allocated to her and sleep, but she had to go back downstairs to the servants' hall to meet the other servants at dinner.

Mr Johnston sat at one end of the long dining table and Mrs Black sat at the other. Mrs Harvey's lady's maid, Edith Lear, Mrs Gordon the cook, Claire – the other parlourmaid – and Bessie and Winnie – the two housemaids – sat along one side. Down the other side, she was placed beside Frank, the footman, and Mary, the tiny kitchenmaid. She couldn't help but notice a large number of servants for what was actually a very small household.

They all seemed friendly, asking her where she had been born, why she had come back to Ireland after her mother's death, and telling her the Harveys' were a good and fair couple to work for.

As early as she dared she excused herself, and climbed the stairs to the bedroom with a small oil lamp. Unlike the rest of the house, Mrs Black informed her, none of the servants' bedrooms was lit by gas lighting. There was no rug on the bedroom floor either, only a small threadbare mat, and the window and door were draughty. She smiled all the same, as she unpacked her few belongings and ran her fingers over the two uniforms. She really needed two of each, but the others would have to wait until she received her wages. Being a parlourmaid was going to be hard work but it was infinitely better than being a prostitute.

She was sitting up in bed, plaiting her hair, when Claire came into the bedroom and gave her a smile.

"I'm glad I'm sharing again."

"What happened to the last maid?" she asked, as Claire began to undress.

Claire pulled an awkward expression. "She got pregnant by a footman across the square. Both had to go."

"Oh, I see."

"So, you were in England? I'd love to go to England one day…" Claire tailed off and watched her yawn.

"Sorry," she said. "I didn't sleep well last night. A bit nervous, you know?"

"You've nothing to worry about here."

"I'm glad. You'll probably have to give me a nudge in the morning."

Poor Claire almost had to pull her out of the bed. Used to not getting up until all hours, having to get up at six in the morning and being called Maisie, were completely foreign to her. Still half asleep, she washed in lukewarm water and got dressed in the dull grey dress and lace-trimmed white apron and cap, before following Claire downstairs.

In the hall, Claire explained the house to her. The morning room and breakfast room on the ground floor were for the Harveys' everyday use. The drawing room and dining room on the first floor were only used when the Harveys' had guests but still had to be attended to. The library – created when the drawing room was divided in two – also had to be attended to, as it was used each day by Mr Harvey. To escape his wife, Claire added with a grin. The lighting of the gas lamps in the house was one of the footman's tasks and, finally, the Harveys' bedrooms on the second floor were the responsibility of the two housemaids.

Mary, the kitchenmaid, had already removed the ashes from all the hearths, blackened the grates again and set new fires, so she and Claire only had to light them. She followed Claire's lead, only pausing for their breakfast after the table was laid in the breakfast room, the morning room had been done, and the serving dishes, milk, tea, and toast had been carried up to the breakfast room. They were placed on the sideboard as Mr and Mrs Harvey helped themselves at breakfast.

They continued on all morning, clearing away after the Harveys' breakfast, and setting the table for luncheon. Then, the cleaning, polishing and dusting in the hall, drawing and dining rooms, and the library had to be completed until, at last, they went downstairs to the servants' hall for their mid-day meal.

Claire was friendly and chatty and she warmed to her. Returning to the servants' hall after changing into their black uniforms, Mr Johnston informed them that Mr and Mrs Harvey were having guests to dinner on Friday evening.

On Friday morning, they set to their tasks with extra diligence. In addition to their usual responsibilities, all the rugs were taken up and brought outside to be beaten. The curtains were shaken free of dust, every single item of furniture and ornament was dusted and polished until it shone, and the table laid in the dining room. Mrs Harvey nodded her approval when she saw the finished result.

When the guests began to arrive, they were on hand to take hats, overcoats, gloves, cloaks and shawls. Returning to the hall, she heard a sharp intake of breath and risked a glance up at the tall male guest shrugging off a black three-quarter length overcoat. Blood drained from her face, leaving her light-headed. It was Will.

Chapter Two

Will stared at the parlourmaid in astonishment then did his best to disguise his reaction. It was Rose. Jim and Harriett Harvey clearly knew nothing of what she had been. The other parlourmaid stepped forward and took his hat and overcoat, while Rose extended a hand up the stairs without looking at his face again.

"This way please, sir," she said quietly, before turning away.

Will followed her upstairs, acutely aware of how he had done the exact same in the brothel, and into the drawing room. Despite his mother's machinations, he would try to enjoy himself this evening.

"Still in… where is it?" Jim asked, somehow always managing to forget, as Will nodded to Mrs Harvey, the Belchers, and his parents.

"Brown Street," he replied, having sat in the only empty armchair which was next to Amelia Belcher's, while Mrs Harvey signalled for Rose to come to her and she whispered something in the maid's ear. "Yes, I am."

Jim nodded. "How are you getting on?"

"Not bad. It's a challenge."

"I'll say. Like getting Fred Simpson to the church on time."

Will smiled then squirmed as Amelia Belcher unashamedly looked him up and down, admiring the white tie and tails he rarely wore. He crossed his legs then uncrossed them, missing the informal black morning coat he wore at home. Even the black frock coat he wore while making house calls and at his afternoon surgeries was more comfortable than this tailcoat.

"You are going to stay in Brown Street, Will?" she asked.

"For the foreseeable future, yes," he replied, noting her low-cut and short-sleeved cream gown. The colour was an unwise choice as it, together with her blonde hair and pale complexion, simply made her appearance seem even more washed out than usual. "There is a lot of work to be done in the area."

"Waste of time if you ask me," his father muttered. "Pretty girl," he added, and they all glanced at Rose as she left the room, closing the door behind her.

"Yes," Mrs Harvey replied. "She's new. Very satisfactory. Touch wood, we won't get the same trouble from her as we did with her predecessor."

"That was very unfortunate," Will's mother agreed. "Some girls just ask for trouble."

"Do they?" Will asked before he could stop himself.

"Yes, of course," Mrs Harvey cried. "The girl Maisie replaced, well, I take some of the blame. I should have noticed—"

"Maisie?"

"Yes, the girl just now – the dark-haired parlourmaid – I'll be keeping an eye on our servants from now on. A very close eye."

32

A stern look from his father told Will to mind his tongue. He decided to comply, feeling extremely relieved that Rose, or Maisie – or whatever her name was this week – was very much alive and well.

She assisted in the serving of the meal, keeping her head down, and not looking at his face once. She did hand him his overcoat and hat as he left the house but, again, did not look at his face. He'd liked to have wished her well but knew it was out of the question.

After turning down an offer of sleeping at home by his mother who didn't – or wouldn't – realise it wasn't his home anymore, he decided to walk back to Brown Street. Striding along the pavement in the chilly night air, glad he had worn his overcoat, he felt something in one of the pockets. Halting, he pulled out a sheet of notepaper, went to a street lamp and read;

Dear Will,

I'm very sorry if you were shocked at seeing me again this evening. I have broken all former ties in order to start again afresh and the only way I could think of to do so was by making it appear that 'Rose Green' committed suicide by drowning. Her 'suicide' was reported on in the newspapers so I know she is now dead to all who knew her. If it were not for you I would still be there, so thank you for speaking to me so frankly.

My name is now Maisie Byrne. Being a parlourmaid is a challenge, especially lighting the fires at six in the morning, but I am getting used to the hours and the hard work and I am happy and content here.

> *I have sneaked into the library to write this letter*
> *and I will be skinned alive if I am caught. Mr*
> *Johnston's tongue can be as sharp and harsh as his*
> *accent.*
>
> *Thank you again for your advice.*
> *Sincerely yours,*
> *Isobel Stevens*

Will stared at her name. Isobel. She must have signed it by force of habit. She had better be more careful in future. He folded the letter carefully and returned it to his pocket before carrying on back to Brown Street.

He brought the letter into the surgery and went to the bookcase. Lifting down Henry Gray's *Anatomy: Descriptive and Surgical*, he inserted the letter and replaced the book on the shelf. Mrs Bell dusted every morning but never moved any of the volumes, especially ones as large as Gray's. From what she told him, penny dreadfuls were more her cup of tea.

At five minutes past five in the morning, he was called out to a woman experiencing a prolonged and difficult labour. Ten minutes later he was on the third floor of a tenement house being watched both anxiously and suspiciously by the mother-to-be and two neighbours. Their eyes widened as he lifted his stethoscope out of his medical bag and placed it over the mother-to-be's abdomen. There was absolute silence from both inside and out as he listened for a heartbeat. The baby was most likely dead, poor little mite.

At a quarter past seven, the woman was breech delivered of a large baby boy. It was as he had feared – the child was dead. If only they had called him out sooner. If only…

Mrs Bell was cooking his breakfast when he returned to Brown Street and frowned when she saw his face.

"Delia Brennan's baby was born feet first and dead," he explained, and Mrs Bell crossed herself. "It was a boy and was dead before I got there. If only they had called me out sooner, but there's no point in saying that now." Lifting the kettle off the range, he poured some hot water into a bowl in the sink, added some cold water from a bucket and washed and scrubbed his hands.

"I was all set to ask you whether you had enjoyed the dinner last night."

He gave her a little smile as he dried his hands. "It was pleasant enough." And all the better for discovering he hadn't been responsible for 'Rose Green' killing herself, he added silently.

"Good. Now you sit yourself down and eat this." He sat at the table and she put a bowl of porridge down in front of him. "You can wash and shave afterwards."

"Thank you."

"That boy would have been Delia's seventh." Mrs Bell poured them each a cup of tea. "Tragic, but probably a blessing in disguise."

"I suppose so, yes."

"It's strange, isn't it?" his housekeeper mused, as he added milk and sugar to the porridge. "Delia's been married seven years and she's had a child every year. Maggie Millar, now, she's been married donkey's years and nothing."

"George Millar drinks like a fish."

"Could that be it?" she asked.

"It could be. It could be a lot of things."

"Do you want children?" she added suddenly.

He grimaced. Sometimes she could come out with the most probing questions when he least expected them. "One day," he replied. "I'm only thirty. I've plenty of time."

"But don't leave it too long, will you?"

"I need a wife first and they haven't exactly been queuing up of late."

"Did Amelia Belcher give you the eye last night?" Mrs Bell smiled.

"Yes, but I ignored it."

"You told her that you were staying here. Take it or leave it."

He nodded. "And she left it. And I'm relieved. I'm still battered and bruised after Cecilia."

He finished his porridge and two slices of soda bread and marmalade, drank his tea, and went upstairs with a jug of warm water. When he had washed and shaved, he went into the surgery and lifted some notepaper out of his desk drawer.

The following morning, the servants at number 68 were at breakfast when the areaway doorbell rang.

Mary, the kitchenmaid, went to answer it and returned with a letter. "For you, Maisie."

"Me?" She took it in surprise. "Thank you."

"Nothing wrong, I hope?" Mrs Gordon asked.

"No." She didn't recognise the handwriting on the envelope and put it in her apron pocket. "I'll read it later."

After the servants' mid-day meal, and between uniforms, she sat on her bed and opened the letter. The writing was an absolute scrawl but she glanced at the signature. It was from Will.

Dear Isobel,

I hope you don't mind me calling you that? I had read of Rose's death so I did receive rather a shock when I saw you. But a relieved one.

I'm sorry about the scrawl, but after the late night, I was up again at five to attend to a birth. These early starts! I'm glad you found a position and are happy there. I had feared that I had been a little too harsh in my words.

I am preparing to start my rounds. I have been here four years now. Fred will soon be replacing Cecilia's father, who has just retired, in my father's practice. I prefer a bit more of a challenge but we all agree to disagree.

I don't socialise a great deal but my mother had hopes for Amelia Belcher and myself. These will come to nothing. As I told Mrs Bell, my housekeeper, it is far too soon after Cecilia for me to be thinking along those lines. No doubt you understand. Does it get better? The pain and hurt, I mean. I hope so.

Yours sincerely,
Will Fitzgerald

He had signed off with a flourish and she frowned before reading the letter through again. The pain and hurt do ease but it takes time.

She got off the bed and opened the lower of her two drawers in the chest of drawers she shared with Claire. The bottom was lined with floral wallpaper and she slipped the letter underneath before changing into her black uniform and going downstairs to the servants' hall.

"Everything all right?" Mrs Gordon asked her.

"Fine, thank you."

"What are you going to do on Wednesday?" asked Claire. "You can't just go to bed and sleep again. It was such a waste of a half-day."

"I know, but I was getting used to the hours again. I hadn't thought about it. I might go and browse in the shops. I need new ribbon for my hat."

The sun shone on Wednesday afternoon so she spent as little time in the shops as she could. She bought another grey parlourmaid uniform – the second black uniform would have to wait until her next wages – and the hat ribbon before halting outside a stationer's. On impulse, she went in and purchased notepaper, envelopes, a pen, and a bottle of ink. At a nearby post office, she bought five stamps, then went to the café on Grafton Street. She sat at a window table in the sun, ordered a pot of tea and a scone, and replied to Will's letter.

Addressing the envelope, she hesitated. Should she really be writing to him? It was pleasant to have someone to correspond with, but what if he were only being polite? After all, she told herself, consider where and how you met him. And how he kissed your scar from top to bottom and made you come. Her cheeks flushed, she reached for the letter again and added a postscript.

When she returned to Merrion Square, she went straight upstairs and hid the pen and ink at the back of her lower drawer and the notepaper under the wallpaper lining. Nice as Claire was, she was incredibly nosey with it. How on earth would she be able to explain why she was writing to Dr Fitzgerald, the son of their employer's neighbours?

That evening, she sat at the dining table in the servants' hall adding the new ribbon to her hat. Claire put her own sewing down, came to the table, and admired it.

"That's a lovely shade of blue. I'd never have thought to match pale blue with navy blue. Was it expensive?"

She shook her head. "No, it was the last of the batch and not quite the length I asked for so I got a discount."

Claire pulled an exasperated expression. "That never happens to me." Pulling out a chair, she sat down next to Edith Lear, Mrs Harvey's very prim and proper lady's maid. "I heard Amelia Belcher shouting at you when she was here earlier."

"Miss Amelia was in a very bad mood today and took it out on me. Mrs Harvey asked me to remove a speck of mud from one of Miss Amelia's gloves. The mud turned out to be grease and you know what grease is like. I did my best but, of course, it wasn't good enough. Miss Amelia has finally realised that if she wants to marry Dr Fitzgerald junior, she'll have to up sticks and move to Brown Street because, after his debacle of an engagement, he now has absolutely no intention of moving back to Merrion Square. Somehow I can't visualise Miss Amelia Belcher on her knees scrubbing Dr Fitzgerald's front doorstep in Brown Street."

Claire and Mrs Gordon laughed but Isobel felt her cheeks burn at the mere mention of his name and bent her head lower over her hat.

"Dr Fitzgerald moved to Brown Street four years ago," Claire explained, and she warily raised her head. "His parents were appalled. Then he got his heart broken when his fiancée threw him over and married someone else. He wouldn't give up his practice in the Liberties and, having been born and brought up on Merrion Square, she simply wasn't going to be the wife of a doctor whose surgery is on Brown Street. I wouldn't have minded." Claire sighed. "He was so handsome in his white tie and tails at the dinner party."

"Have you ever been to Brown Street?" Edith demanded. "It is nothing more than a tenement-infested slum."

"Where is Brown Street?" Isobel asked curiously.

"Not far from Cork Street," replied Edith, which still left her none the wiser. "Whatever possessed him to go there, I don't know. If he wanted something different from life then he should have joined the army like his elder brother. Been promoted to major, last I heard. He's out in India somewhere."

"For Mrs Harvey's lady's maid," Isobel began, as she and Claire got into their beds an hour later, "Edith does seem to gossip a lot. I didn't think that was allowed."

"It isn't, but once she starts we can't shut her up. We all like hearing a bit of gossip, anyway. Don't you approve?"

"It's not up to me to approve or not. I just thought that Mr Johnston…"

Claire smiled. "Mr Johnston is rather fond of Edith, so she gets away with more than the rest of us."

"I didn't realise Dr Fitzgerald's former fiancée lived on the square, too."

"The Wilson residence is across the square from here," Claire explained. "And, unfortunately for poor Dr Fitzgerald, the new Mrs Ashlinn will still live on the square – in her husband's family home – just two doors up from her old home."

"Aren't Mr and Mrs Ashlinn going to move to a home of their own?"

"I don't know, but we can only hope for Dr Fitzgerald's sake that they do," Claire replied, as she turned down the oil lamp.

The envelope was leaning against the pot of marmalade. Will bid Mrs Bell good morning then tore it open. The letter was from Isobel, so he folded it and returned it to the envelope. He would read it later. In private.

After breakfast, he brought the letter into the surgery and sat down at the desk.

Dear Will,

Thank you for your letter. I am writing this in a café over a pot of tea and a scone. In Merrion Square, the walls have eyes and ears! It is my half-day, and I have just been to a milliner's and bought new pale blue ribbon for my hat. I got quite a bargain.

I cannot tell you how different my life is now. I work very hard but I haven't been this content and safe for a long time. I share a tiny attic room with the other parlourmaid, Claire. She is nice but very nosey!

The pain and hurt you mentioned do get better, believe me. It can take a long time but it does ease. After seducing me, James deserted me when I needed him most, and I used to continually wonder if he ever regretted what he did or felt any guilt. Now I can go for several days without thinking of him at all. It will be the same for you and Cecilia.

Are you kept busy in and around Brown Street? Forgive me, but I have no idea where Brown Street is. There is a map of Dublin in the library and I will look it up in the morning. I like the library. It smells of leather and Mr Harvey's pipe tobacco. It also reminds me of my father's study. He was always very strict. I was never allowed in there, especially when he was writing a sermon, but I used to sneak in to borrow books or to read the newspapers. He never once caught me!

I do not miss my father, as he was not only strict but a very cruel and vindictive man, too. I do miss my mother and brother, Alfie, dreadfully and I can only hope against hope that Father is not inflicting his anger and violence on them too much.

Father wanted Alfie to become a clergyman, but Alfie had his heart set on becoming a doctor. Poor Alfie, I expect he will never fulfil his ambition now. Do you have any brothers or sisters?

Here she signed off but it was followed by a hastily scribbled postscript:

Please do not feel obliged to reply. I will always be very grateful to you in spurring me on to change my situation and start afresh, but I would hate for you to feel under any obligation, or feel you must be polite and reply to this letter.

Will put the letter down on his desk. He did not feel in the least bit obliged to reply. He read the letter through again. Her seducer was called James. Her father was a clergyman, vicious and brutal, and she had always been closer to her mother and brother.

"Bad news?" Mrs Bell came into the surgery carrying a duster.

"News, but not bad news," he murmured.

"Good. It's just that you were sitting there with a deep frown."

He smiled and stood up. Mrs Bell had moved to the bookcase with her duster so he folded the letter, put it in its envelope, and placed it in his medical bag.

He returned from house calls to find an envelope on the table in the kitchen. Mrs Bell was at the solid fuel range, stirring the contents of a large saucepan, and pointed to the envelope with the wooden spoon.

"That was delivered about an hour ago," she said, and he opened the envelope, and pulled out a short note.

Will,

Just to warn you that Cecilia and Clive returned from Paris yesterday. So no apoplectic fit if someone mentions them or you see them. We must meet up before I go back to London.

Jerry

"This is bad news." He crumpled the note up and threw it into the fire. "Cecilia is back from Paris."

"Oh." Mrs Bell's face crumpled sympathetically.

"Oh." He smiled wryly. "I know. She's gone. Married. I should forget her."

"Yes, you should. Any woman who gives up a handsome man like you needs their head examining."

"Thank you." He kissed her cheek. "I can only try."

That evening, he walked to Merrion Square to visit his

parents. Going up the steps to the front door, the Harveys' door opened and a female acquaintance of Mrs Harvey's was shown out by Isobel and the footman, who helped the lady into a waiting cab. As the cab pulled away, the footman hurried back inside, but Isobel lingered at the top of the steps for a couple of moments. She looked up at the sky and closed her eyes, breathing in and out deeply. He couldn't help but stare at the wisps of dark hair blowing around her face and neck in the light breeze. On opening her eyes, she saw him and jumped violently.

"Maisie." He raised his hat.

"Dr Fitzgerald."

"It is a lovely evening."

"Yes, lovely. Please excuse me."

"Maisie?" He stepped closer to the railings which divided the steps of the two houses and she quickly closed the front door. "Isobel," he added quietly, and she bit her bottom lip. "Thank you for your letter. I don't feel obliged in any way, and I will reply to it."

She nodded before turning away and going inside.

His mother got up from the huge mahogany sofa upholstered in green velvet as Tess showed him into the morning room. Despite being in her late fifties, to Will, she was ageless and always elegantly dressed. There wasn't one grey hair on her dark brown head, and she was wearing one of her favourite dresses – a stylish purple creation with a narrow band of black lace at the square neckline and wrists.

"Will." She kissed his cheek. "How lovely. Some tea, please, Tess."

"Yes, Mrs Fitzgerald," the maid replied and left the room.

"How are you, Will?"

"Very well, thank you. You are blooming as always."

"Thank you." His mother frowned a little at his forced good humour. "Will, are you sure you're well?"

He shrugged. "Cecilia is back from Paris."

"Who told you?" His mother re-took her seat on the sofa.

"Jerry sent me a note." He sat opposite her in one of two matching armchairs.

"Try to forget her, Will. What she did was despicable."

"Like I told Mrs Bell, I can only try. Still," he added. "As we don't mix in the same circles any longer, I daresay I won't see too much of her."

"She and Clive are moving to Rutland Square soon."

"Well, good riddance to them both."

His mother smiled. "Your father is at a meeting, just in case you're wondering where he is. He'll be sorry to have missed you. How is Mrs Bell?"

"Fighting fit as always."

"Please give her my regards."

He nodded. "I will."

"I heard Frederick's wedding was a very grand affair."

"It was. Their mothers wouldn't have had anything less."

"Frederick being married is something hard to imagine."

He laughed. "It is. But Margaret has a firm hand and will be good for him."

"What about Jerry?" his mother asked.

"Oh, he's now stepping out with a Miss Lillian Parsons of Kensington. It is me who is completely woman-less."

The door opened and Tess, the head house-parlourmaid who doubled as his mother's lady's maid, came in with the tea tray and placed it on a side table. She was a handsome dark-haired girl, but not a patch on Isobel, and he quickly looked away in case she caught him watching her.

"Thank you, Tess, I'll pour." Mrs Fitzgerald reached for the teapot and tea strainer.

"Yes, Mrs Fitzgerald," Tess replied then left the room.

"Have you seen the new parlourmaid next door?" his mother asked, pouring the tea. "Oh, of course you did. Very pretty girl. Harriett told me a bit about her. An orphan recently returned from England. Good face, good accent, hard worker. Harriett was lucky to find her. Cake?"

"Thank you, yes. There's nothing wrong with Tess or Maura," he said, as his mother placed a slice of fruit cake on a plate and passed it to him.

"I know." Mrs Fitzgerald sighed. "But when you see what maids can be like, it makes you ponder."

Will bit into the fruit cake and didn't reply.

Isobel closed the front door and leant back against it. Will seemed quite adamant that he would reply to her letter. Hoping her cheeks weren't too flushed, she went down the steps to the servants' hall. The others were seated at the dining table enjoying a cup of tea, and she felt Claire's eyes on her as she lifted up a cup and saucer and went to the teapot.

"All right?" Claire asked.

"Yes, thanks. I'm fine."

"You look a bit preoccupied, that's all."

"I'm tired," she said simply, pouring herself some tea and adding milk.

"Well, you insisted on beating all the rugs."

"Yes, and you should have known better than to let her," Mrs Black scolded, and Claire immediately stared at the floor. "You are to share all the work. Do you hear me?"

"Yes, Mrs Black."

"And you, Maisie," Mrs Black added. "All those rugs are too much for one person."

"Yes, Mrs Black."

"Half and half next week. When you've drunk that tea you can go off early to bed."

"Thank you, Mrs Black," she replied gratefully.

Ten minutes later, she went upstairs to the attic bedroom. She got undressed, slipped her nightdress on, then pulled the pins from her hair and sat at the small window with one of Claire's penny dreadfuls. It truly was dreadful, so she put it to one side and gazed down at the square. A few minutes passed and her eyes were drawn to a man walking away from her carrying his hat. It was Will Fitzgerald, and she felt her cheeks glow with heat. She watched as he halted to speak with another man before moving on, the other man slapping his shoulder as if in sympathy, as they parted. Her eyes followed him as he put on his hat then disappeared from view.

"I thought you'd be asleep." Claire came in, making her jump, and closed the bedroom door.

"I'm sorry about Mrs Black earlier."

"It doesn't matter. Is that mine?" Claire nodded to the penny dreadful as she began to undress.

"Yes. I must save up and buy a book."

"A proper book?" Claire halted and stared at her. "Where are you going to find the time to read a proper book?"

"On my half-day. I'll find myself a sheltered spot in St Stephen's Green."

"You like reading, then?"

"Yes," she replied. "I used to read a lot. My first 'grown up' book was *Wuthering Heights* and I'd love to read it again."

"Oh." Claire was completely lost.

"Aren't the Harveys' going out tomorrow evening?" Isobel tactfully changed the subject and reached for her hairbrush.

"To a dinner, yes." Claire stepped out of her black uniform dress and hung it on a hanger on the hook on the back of the door. "It'll be a late night for Edith but we'll be able to relax, thank God." Claire pulled her nightdress over her head, got into bed, and extracted the pins from her hair. "Or we could ask Mr Johnston if we could go for a walk? Or you could ask? He likes you."

"What?" Isobel asked sharply, putting her hairbrush down. "He likes Edith. You told me he did."

"I just think he rather likes you, too."

Isobel pulled a disgusted expression. "Well, he's old enough to be my father."

"You've never had a man-friend, then?"

She sighed and got into her bed. "A long time ago."

"What happened?"

"It turned out we weren't suited," she replied. "What about you?"

Claire shook her head. "I've been here since I was twelve. What chance have I had? May – the maid you replaced – she was a complete flirt, all the footmen in the square were after her. I never stood a chance."

"But you must be relieved? May fell pregnant."

"I am about that bit. I'd just love to have someone to love me. A gentleman like Dr Fitzgerald."

"Senior or junior?"

Claire pulled an exasperated expression. "Junior, of

course. I'd move to Brown Street like a flash. That Cecilia Ashlinn was foolish to give him up."

"Is she beautiful?" Isobel asked curiously.

"Oh, yes, very. He worshipped her. She's tall with pale skin, blonde hair, brown eyes, always immaculately dressed. In looks, she is everything I'm not. But she's very cold. I don't think she ever loved him as much as he loved her. When she gave him up he didn't come near the square for weeks. She got married to an acquaintance of his a few weeks ago. Poor Dr Fitzgerald." Claire sighed, lay down, and turned onto her side.

The Harveys' left for their dinner party at seven o'clock the following evening and wearily, Edith prepared to wait up for Mrs Harvey until her return in the early hours. The joys of being a lady's maid, Isobel thought, as she broached the possibility to Mr Johnston of Claire and herself going for a walk in the evening sunshine.

"Be back before nine o'clock," he warned them, and she and Claire hurried upstairs to their bedroom for their hats and coats.

"Where will we go?" Isobel asked.

"I'll show you Brown Street." At Isobel's doubtful expression, Claire added, "It'll be all right with the two of us. Come on."

Twenty-five minutes later, they were walking along Brown Street. Most of the houses were two storeys high, but some were three storeys high, tall, and narrow.

"There." Claire pointed to one. "That's where Dr Fitzgerald lives."

The only difference between the grimy three-storey house and the others on the street were the clean windows and the shiny brass plate on the wall beside the front door with *William Fitzgerald M.D.* inscribed on it. Isobel felt uncomfortable and a little embarrassed at being there.

"Can we go now? Unless you want to go inside and make sure he's eating a good dinner?"

Claire flushed. "No. I just wanted to show you that it's not such a bad place."

"No, it isn't." Isobel thought of Montgomery Street where Sally Maher's brothel stood. "And if he's happy here, then good luck to him."

Claire nodded, and they retraced their steps back along the street.

"Maisie?" Hearing Mr Johnston's voice from the other end of the dining table at breakfast the following Tuesday, she glanced up from her slice of bread and marmalade. "A letter for you."

"Thank you." Isobel took it from him, briefly glancing at the envelope before putting it in her apron pocket. The handwriting was Will's.

"That's your second letter," Claire commented.

"My landlady." She thought quickly. "I stayed with her when I came back from England. She mothered me a bit."

"Why don't you go and see her on your half-day?" Claire suggested.

"Yes, I might. She was good to me. I was a bit lost when I came back to Ireland."

After the servants' mid-day meal, she changed her uniform, then sat on her bed and opened Will's letter.

Dear Isobel,

I promised I would write to you and I am writing because I want to. I don't feel obliged to in any way.

Writing to you keeps my mind off other matters,

50

such as Cecilia. I learned recently that she has returned to Dublin with her new husband. I felt a bit of pain at the news, but not as much as I thought I would. It must either be getting better, like you said it would, or else I am just resigned to the fact that Cecilia is now another man's wife.

It was pleasant to see you on the steps. You look well. I was on my way to visit my parents but only my mother was at home so I was given all the local gossip!

Did you ever look at the map in the library to find out where Brown Street is? It's not too far off the beaten track! In my four years here it took me a long time to win the people's trust. When they discovered I was a Protestant (and not a very devout one at that), it was all they could see for a while, unfortunately. But I've got to know the parish priest quite well, he's a good chap, and he seems to like and appreciate what I'm doing and that placated a lot of people.

Sadly, there are still those who do not call me out until it is too late. They have many cures, remedies, and superstitions of their own and only call me out as a last resort. So, mostly, I arrive at the same time as the priest or rector.

Your father is a clergyman, isn't he? You mentioned him writing sermons in his study. How a supposed man of God could do what he did to you baffles me.

I expect you have a half-day like Tess and Maura, Mother and Father's house-parlourmaids? What *afternoon is it? Do let me know and, perhaps, you would consider calling to Brown Street? It seems a little ridiculous in our writing to each other, not that I do not enjoy it, but as we only live about a mile or so away from each other. I would be happy to show you where I live, and also the surgery and dispensary. If you would rather not, I would understand fully.*

Isobel immediately went to her lower drawer in the chest of drawers, hid the letter under the wallpaper lining, and wrote him a note before going downstairs to the servants' hall.

"Mr Johnston, tomorrow is my half-day, and I've decided to go and see my landlady. I've written her a quick note to let her know. Can I run with it to the post box, please?"

"Don't be long."

"Thank you, Mr Johnston," she replied, and left the house, not bothering with either her hat or coat.

Will smiled when he saw the letter on the kitchen table and recognised the handwriting as Isobel's. He ate his breakfast then sat down at the desk in the surgery, tearing open the envelope, and pulling out the letter.

Dear Will,

Thank you for your letter.

I only have time to scribble a note. Tomorrow is my half-day. Would it be convenient if I called at approximately two o'clock? I did look at the map and I know the way. If it isn't convenient, please let me

know before I leave at one o'clock, as I need to run
some errands first.
    Sincerely yours,
    Isobel Stevens

Thank goodness he didn't have surgery this afternoon. He slipped the note into Gray's *Anatomy*, along with her other letters, packed his medical bag and shouted a cheery goodbye to Mrs Bell as he set off to make house calls.

There was a knock at the front door at ten minutes to three. Isobel stood on the step with a small black leather handbag and something wrapped in brown paper under her arm, a cabbage in one hand and a round tin in the other. She seemed a little flushed but gave him a smile.

"I found this on the step." She passed him the cabbage.

"Thank you. Sometimes I get paid in kind. Do come in. Can I take your hat and coat?"

"Yes, thank you. I must apologise, Will, I'm much later than I anticipated," she said, stepping into the hall. "I had to buy another parlourmaid uniform." He closed the front door and she put the package and handbag down on the floor beneath a row of hooks behind the door. She slipped off her black coat and passed it to him, along with her hat, and he hung them up. "This is for you." He took the round tin from her. "It's a cake from Mrs Gordon, the cook. You are supposed to be the landlady I stayed with when I came home from England. It was the only excuse I could think of."

"Never mind. Go through to the kitchen – it's along there."

She smoothed down her navy blue dress and he followed

her along the hall. He put the cabbage on a shelf in the larder then placed the cake tin on the kitchen table and lifted off the lid. It was a delicious-looking sponge.

"Lovely, thank you. Mrs Bell, my housekeeper, bakes delicious soda bread but you could build houses with her cakes."

"Is she here?" she asked.

"No, she'll be back at half past five to start dinner. She lives in rooms on Pimlico. It's a few streets away." He motioned to a chair. "Please, sit down."

"Thank you." She pulled out a chair and sat down at the table. "I enjoyed your letter."

He was relieved. "I thought it was rather morbid," he said, as he sat opposite her.

She shook her head. "You asked about my father. He is a clergyman. A rector, if you want to be specific. He wanted a large family but there was only Alfie and me. Alfie's twenty-three, a year older than I am."

"I have a brother, Edward. He's a major in the army. He's in India at present. Some of the places he describes in his letters…" He tailed off and smiled.

"Is he older or younger than you?"

"Older, by three years. He always wanted adventure, and you don't get many adventures in Dublin. Not the kind he was looking for, anyway."

"You were never tempted to follow him into the army?"

"No, I always wanted to be a doctor. I've been very lucky—" He stopped abruptly, flushing with embarrassment and anger at his gaffe.

She quickly reached out and squeezed his hand. "Don't be embarrassed. I was lucky to meet you. I'd still be there otherwise."

He felt her shudder at the thought. "Am I to call you Maisie or Isobel?"

"Oh, Isobel," she said. "Isobel, please."

"Isobel it is. I'll show you the surgery."

They got up, walked along the hall, and into the large room at the front of the house.

"You see your patients in here?" she asked.

"Yes." He pointed to the black leather couch. "For examinations. This." He unlocked and opened the door to the smaller room beyond, where shelves lined the walls. "Is the dispensary."

"You have it very well set up," she said, peering inside at all the medicines.

"Thank you," he replied, closing and locking the door, pleased she thought so. "Do you mind if I ask you something as a doctor?" he went on, sitting on a corner of the desk.

"No," she replied but frowned all the same.

"Your abortion." He ran his fingers along the edge of the desk. "Who performed it?"

"You want to know his name?"

"It was a man?" he clarified. "A doctor?"

"Yes."

"Good." He smiled with relief. "No, I don't want his name. I was just hoping it wasn't a handywoman, as they are called, who might either not complete the procedure fully, or be unhygienic and cause infection."

"No, he was a qualified doctor who lives near Sally's. Everything was clean and he said the procedure had gone smoothly. I couldn't have kept the baby, Will, not the state I was in. You hate me for what I did, don't you?"

"No, not at all. I'm not going to argue about the rights

and wrongs of abortion but if performed incorrectly you could have been left infertile, unable to conceive in future, or a lot, lot worse."

She nodded. "Sally told me of a woman she knew who died. That's why she always uses this doctor. He also certifies that Sally's girls are free of disease. Myself included."

"When was the last time?" he asked.

"The afternoon of the day you visited."

"How many men did you have sexual intercourse with after that?" he added. "Before you left."

She looked down at her hands. "One. You."

His heart pounded uncomfortably. "I was the last?"

"Yes." She raised her head, her cheeks crimson. "And I'm so thankful it was you. When I think of who it could have been, it makes me feel ill."

"Sit down." He guided her to the chair behind the desk and knelt down beside her. "It's over," he said gently.

She nodded tears in her eyes. "I think it's only beginning to dawn on me that it really is over. I still have the most awful dreams. I wake up perspiring all over. But I wake up in a house on Merrion Square and not in a brothel on Montgomery Street and the relief—" Her voice cracked, and she pulled a handkerchief from her sleeve. "I'll be all right in a minute."

"You can talk to me, you know? Even if you have to put it down in a letter. Everyone needs someone to talk to. Write it all down like you're talking to me."

"You'll do the same for me?" she whispered, wiping her eyes.

"I promise. Would you like to go for a walk? I could show you the sights of the Liberties? Then, we can come back here, have a pot of tea and some cake?"

She frowned. "You want to be seen out with me?"

"Why shouldn't I?" he asked, sharper than he had intended, and a little surprised at his reaction. "No-one here knows who you are."

"But you're their doctor. If they found out?"

"They won't from me."

"Thank you. Yes, then." She nodded, and they went to the hall for their hats and coats.

They walked to Cork Street, and she raised her eyes to the sky.

"It's nice here. I'm enjoying seeing more of Dublin."

"Is your half-day every Wednesday?" he asked.

"So far, yes."

"Would you consider calling again?" he added, very self-consciously. "Unless you have other plans?"

"No, I've no plans. Thank you. I'd like to call again."

"Good." He smiled at her. "I was hoping you weren't finding all this very tedious."

"This isn't tedious at all. It will give me something to look forward to each week. It's nice to have something to look forward to."

"I agree."

On returning to Brown Street, she helped him to make the tea. They then sat down at the kitchen table and devoured nearly half the sponge cake.

"Delicious," he proclaimed, before turning in surprise to the hall door as it opened and Mrs Bell came in.

Isobel stared in dismay at the stout middle-aged woman who came into the kitchen with a basket of vegetables.

"I'm early, I know, but stew takes a while." The woman

glanced at her, and Isobel saw Will flush.

"Mrs Bell, this is Maisie Byrne. Maisie, this is Mrs Bell, my housekeeper."

"Pleased to meet you." Isobel nodded to her.

"And you, dear. New to the area, are you?"

"A cup of tea and some cake, Mrs Bell?" Will leapt in.

"Thank you, yes." Mrs Bell seated herself at the table, while he got up and placed another cup, saucer, and plate in front of her. "It's just that I haven't seen you around here before."

"I'm not from this area, Mrs Bell," she replied.

"From the square, are you?"

"In a way, yes. I'm a parlourmaid at Mr and Mrs Harvey's residence."

"I see." Mrs Bell smiled at her before turning to Will. "Will Maisie be staying for dinner, Dr Fitzgerald?"

"Oh, I don't know," she began.

"Please, stay?" he asked her. "Mrs Bell makes enough to feed the entire street."

"Thank you, I shall, then."

"Off you to go to the parlour," Mrs Bell told them. "I'll help myself to some tea and cake then make a start on the stew."

Will nodded and she rose from the table. They went out to the hall and he extended a hand up the stairs. "The parlour is upstairs. After you."

She climbed the stairs with Will following close behind, acutely aware of how they had done the same in Sally Maher's brothel. But, instead of her leading him along the landing and into a bedroom, Will crossed the landing and opened a door to a back bedroom which had been converted into a parlour. A rather battered sofa in reddish-brown leather, two matching armchairs, and a writing desk were the main furnishings but, as he closed the door, a large bookcase straining under the weight of at least fifty books was revealed.

"The parlour had to be at the back of the house," he explained. "If I had slept in here, I couldn't be roused in the middle of the night. It is what you could call cosy, I suppose, but the surgery is the most important room in the house to me."

"I hope Mrs Bell won't ask you too many questions. Awkward questions, I mean. I think she rather assumed…"

"Mrs Bell assumes a lot of things. Won't you sit down?"

"Thank you." She chose one of the armchairs while sat in the other and crossed his legs. "You read a lot." She nodded at the bookcase. "I miss reading."

"What did you read?"

"Anything," she replied. "Thomas Hardy, Jane Austen, Charles Dickens—"

"Dickens?"

She nodded. "In secret. My father wouldn't have considered his works suitable for a 'lady'. Hardy neither. Claire reads – devours – penny dreadfuls. I must try and wean her off them and onto something better."

"Well, feel free to borrow any of those."

"Do they have your name in them?" she asked.

"Yes. Oh, I see." He grimaced. "Well, there are good bargains to be had second-hand."

"I'll have a look in the second-hand bookshops but I'm watching every penny I spend and saving as much as I can. I opened a bank account today."

"Good." He looked and sounded impressed.

"You never know when I might need the money. I never want to have to sleep in a doorway again."

"When did you sleep in a doorway?" Now he looked and sounded horrified.

"The night after leaving Sally Maher's and before going to Merrion Square," she said, shivering a little at the recollection. "It was cold and miserable. I don't know how I didn't catch a chill. I had a bag of my belongings with me, and I was afraid it would get stolen, so I didn't really sleep at all. That will be the one and only time if I can help it."

"If you ever find yourself in need of food or shelter, you come here," he told her sharply, leaning forward. "Do you hear me?"

"But—" she began.

"No buts. You come here."

"I will. Thank you," she said quietly, and he nodded. "You are being very kind."

"Kindness has nothing to do with it. It's friendship, I hope. If you'll allow?" He sighed. "I'm sorry. I'm being demanding. I always have been, I'm afraid. Sorry."

She smiled, reached out, and gave his hand a squeeze. "It's friendship," she agreed.

Three hours later, Will watched her walk away then closed the front door. The house felt empty as he returned to the parlour. He had been grateful to Mrs Bell when she had called up the stairs that the stew was ready before leaving them to it.

He sat down on the sofa and picked up a newspaper but couldn't concentrate on the words. He lowered the paper to his lap and rested his head back. Isobel must have thought him an utter fool for demanding friendship. Still, she had agreed to call again. At least he hadn't put her off that.

"Well." Mrs Bell smiled at him as he sat down to breakfast in the morning. "You certainly kept quiet about her."

"We're just friends, Mrs Bell."

"She's very pretty."

"We're just friends, Mrs Bell," he repeated. "It's far too soon after Cecilia."

"Put that one behind you. This girl's pretty, cheery, came to Brown Street…"

He smiled at that. "I know, but…"

"You're just friends, I know."

"You remember that I'm going to my parents' for dinner this evening?" he asked.

"I do. Give them my regards."

Reaching Merrion Square, he found a gate to the gardens ajar. He hadn't been in the gardens for months so he decided to make a circuit of the gardens in the evening sunshine. About half way around, he stopped dead when he saw Cecilia seated on a bench with a book open on her lap. As if sensing she was no longer alone she turned.

"Will?" she said, in faint surprise.

He moved forward reluctantly, taking off his hat. "Mrs Ashlinn."

"Please call me Cecilia."

"I would rather not. I am due to dine with my parents, so if you would—"

"You hate me, don't you, Will?" she interrupted.

"I wouldn't describe it as hate – more of a disappointment in

61

you for not having the decency to tell me in person that our engagement was over."

She flushed. "I have hurt you deeply and I can only apologise. You will find someone worthy of you, I'm sure of it."

"Someone who will be content with a husband whose medical practice is in the Liberties? I can only hope so. Please excuse me, Mrs Ashlinn." He put on his hat and walked away from her, his heart thumping.

His mother took one look at his face as he was shown into the morning room and got up from the sofa. "Oh, no, you've seen Cecilia," she said, putting a glass of sherry down on a side table then kissing his cheek.

"Whiskey, Will?" His father, dressed more like an undertaker than a doctor, in a black frock coat, trousers, and black cravat, was standing at the drinks tray in a corner of the room with a crystal decanter in his hand.

"Yes, please, Father," he replied, before turning back to his mother. "I hadn't been in the gardens for a while so when I saw an open gate, I decided to make a circuit. Unfortunately, she was sitting on one of the benches. She saw me before I could avoid her. Thank you." He accepted a glass of whiskey from his father. "When are she and Clive moving?"

"Tomorrow," his father replied.

"And I've ruined her last evening here. What a pity."

"You weren't too rude, were you?" his father asked as they sat down.

"No, just rude enough. Good health." He raised his glass and drank, noting the dark circles under his father's eyes. Unlike his mother's hair, his father's hair was now all grey and turning white at the temples. "You look tired," he commented, and his father's eyebrows rose and fell.

"I had a long night last night, Will," he explained. "I was sitting with a patient who died just after four o'clock this morning. She was briefly your patient at the practice – Miss Harris."

"Miss Harris…" Will tailed off and racked his brains. "Miss Harris – yes – good God – she must have been a great age."

"Ninety-nine," his father replied. "She put her longevity down to not being married, and she very much wanted to live to a hundred, but it wasn't to be."

"I'm sorry to hear she has passed away, I used to enjoy chatting with her," he said as his father stifled a yawn. "Have an early night tonight, if you can," he added, and his father nodded.

"You'll meet someone worthy of you, Will," his mother told him, and he fought to hide his irritation at her steering the conversation back to Cecilia.

"That's what Cecilia said, Mother."

"I hear Frederick and Margaret are back from London." His father swiftly changed the subject. "I cannot believe Frederick is married now. It seems like only yesterday when the three of you were starting at Trinity College. How is Jerry, by the way?"

"Oh, the same as ever," Will replied. "I showed him around Brown Street last week."

"And?"

Will smiled. "He wished me good luck. He said he would find a spot for me on Harley Street if I was so inclined."

"Except you are never going to be so inclined."

"I'm not in it for the money, Father, how often——"

"I know," his father interrupted. "I just don't want to see you struggling in Brown Street in ten years time, no better off in any way than you are now."

"You think I'm going to end up a poor and lonely old bachelor doctor, don't you?" he asked.

"Your mother is not the only one who worries about you."

"Edward has everything – army career – wife – and now a child. I have a medical practice in the Liberties and not even a fiancée anymore. Sorry about that, Father."

"Will," his mother warned. "Don't."

He peered down into his glass. "I'm sorry. Once Cecilia is gone from the square, and people stop commiserating with me, it will get better. I suppose it is getting better already. I faced her. I spoke to her. Not very civilly, I admit, but I did. Soon I'll be wondering what I ever saw in her."

Chapter Three

Isobel lay on her bed staring at the ceiling and didn't stir when Claire came into the bedroom. Will had more or less demanded friendship, and his horror at her spending a night in a doorway had taken her aback a little. Plus the house on Brown Street was more than respectable.

"So?" Claire broke into her thoughts and she reluctantly sat up. "How was your landlady?"

"Oh, delighted to see me. She doesn't receive very many callers."

Claire pulled a puzzled expression. "I thought she has a boarding house?"

"Personal callers, I mean. She's asked me to call again next week. Anything happen here while I was away?" she asked, getting off the bed, and beginning to undress.

"Not really, but I did see the new Mrs Ashlinn walking in the gardens earlier. She and the husband are moving from the square tomorrow."

"To live where?"

"Rutland Square," Claire replied. "She's a right cold fish that one. The sooner she's gone the better. Dr Fitzgerald didn't come near the square for weeks after she threw him over. Sorry, am I boring you?" she asked as Isobel stifled a yawn.

"No, I'm just tired. Go on."

"What was I saying?" Claire frowned.

"Something about Cecilia Ashlinn."

"Oh, yes. Well, she's leaving tomorrow and good riddance to her."

Two days later, Isobel received a letter from Will.

Dear Isobel,

I had to write and tell you how much I enjoyed the afternoon. Mrs Bell did ask some awkward questions but I told her we are just friends, which is what we are.

Last evening, I dined with my parents and I met Cecilia in the square's gardens. I wasn't too rude to her, I certainly wasn't going to stoop to pettiness to get my own back. Getting my own back would be pointless in any case. She is moving today, so I won't chance upon her again, I hope.

It was an odd feeling when I saw her. It was not hurt or pain but anger and awkwardness. I would have given a lot to have just sneaked away, but I am glad now that I did speak to her. But enough about her, it is finished.

I am looking forward to seeing you again. I do feel rather isolated sometimes. Mrs Bell usually leaves at around seven o'clock and for the rest of the evening, unless I am called out, I am alone. I talk to myself, Mrs Bell noticed one day. She knows very little about books, so being able to talk to someone who knows what or whom I am referring to is wonderful.

Isobel folded the letter and hid it under the wallpaper lining in her lower drawer. He had finally put Cecilia behind him and would probably only see her rarely, if ever, again. She found herself feeling pleased, yet wary at the same time, as she hurried downstairs to the servants' hall.

She counted the days until Wednesday and set off for Brown Street at one o'clock. As she neared Will's home, she could hear screams and shouts. The front door was wide open and she went inside, hearing Will's voice.

"Get out Mrs Dougherty. Your screaming and shouting won't help your daughter." Footsteps approached the surgery door and it was flung open. Will, in his shirtsleeves, stared at her in surprise for a moment then back at a woman whose hair was a striking mixture of red and grey. "Please wait in the kitchen, Mrs Dougherty – now."

The woman left the surgery and went down the hall, wiping her eyes with a corner of her apron.

"Can I do anything?" Isobel asked.

"Yes, come in here," he replied, and she went into the surgery with him without taking off her hat or coat. A little girl with curly red hair, about five or six years old, was lying prostrate over the middle of the examination couch. Her face was flushed, her mouth wide open, and her brown eyes wide with terror.

"Tell me what to do."

"Annie has a marble stuck in her throat and I can't hold her and release it at the same time," he said and, to her astonishment, picked the girl up by her ankles and held her upside down. "Hit her between her shoulder blades," he ordered, and Isobel did as she was told. "Harder, Isobel. With your fist." Isobel clenched her fist and struck the child again. Nothing. "Once more. As hard as you can." She hit the girl as hard as she could right between the shoulders and heard the marble drop onto the floorboards and roll away. Annie began to cough and Will quickly turned her the right way up. He sat her on the examination couch, clasping her cheeks in his hands. "Breath slowly," he instructed, and the little girl breathed in and out. "Slowly, Annie. Good."

"Will she be all right?" Isobel asked.

"Yes. She tried to swallow the marble but it got stuck. Didn't it, Annie?" The girl nodded. "Sorry about the shouting, but Mrs Dougherty panicked."

"Is there anything else I can do?"

"That oil lamp on the window sill, could you bring it over here, please? I need to take a look down Annie's throat."

Isobel brought the lamp over to the desk and removed the globe, while he retrieved a box of matches from a desk drawer and lit it. "Tell me where to hold it," she said, replacing the globe, and lifting up the lamp.

"A little higher, please. Good. Open your mouth, Annie, so I can have a look at your throat. Good girl." Annie did as she was told and Will peered down the girl's throat. "Mmm. Looks a bit raw. Sore, isn't it?" Annie nodded. "Thank you, Isobel, you can put the lamp down now."

"Would you like me to fetch her mother?" she asked, placing the lamp on the desk well out of the reach of the little girl.

"Yes, please."

In the kitchen, Mrs Dougherty was pacing up and down the floor. "The marble is out of Annie's throat," Isobel told her, and the woman rolled her eyes in relief.

"Oh, thanks be to God. I thought she was dyin'. Can I see her now, ma'am?"

"Yes, please come with me," she said, and Mrs Dougherty followed her into the surgery, where Will was lifting Annie down from the examination couch.

"Annie." Mother hugged daughter tightly. "Oh, thank you, Doctor."

"Not at all. Now, Annie's throat is quite raw and sore, so I'd suggest only liquids for the next few days. Things that will slide down. Bring her back in a few days and I'll take another look. Here's your marble, Annie. Don't put them in your mouth in future, will you?"

Annie shook her head then gave Will a hug around his waist. His first expression was one of surprise, then he gave the little girl a boyish grin, which transformed his rather serious face. He went to his desk and rummaged about in one of the drawers.

"There you go." He handed Annie a few boiled sweets. "Suck them," he advised, and she smiled and nodded at him.

"Thank you, Doctor, Mrs Fitzgerald." Mrs Dougherty shook both their hands vigorously and led Annie out of the house before either of them could explain.

Will closed the front door and turned to her with a weak smile. "Sorry."

"It doesn't matter. You were very good with Annie."

"Thank you. The marble could easily have choked her to death. I think the mother thought Annie was dying and was hysterical. I had to get her out of the surgery. Thanks for your help, Mrs Dougherty would never have hit her own child like that."

"I'm glad I could help. I'm not squeamish. I found a rabbit caught in a trap once. It hadn't been there very long and there was blood everywhere. I cared for it and released it a couple of months later with barely a limp."

He raised his eyebrows, clearly impressed. "I know who to call on for help, then."

"Thank you for your letter. I didn't get time to reply. Sorry."

"I wasn't expecting one, Isobel. As long as you came."

"I was glad to read that you saw Cecilia and were polite."

"Not polite," he said, with a crooked smile. "But not too rude either," he added, before leaning heavily on his hands on the desk. "I'm not in love with her anymore," he said quietly. "It feels so strange to look at the woman you thought you loved more than anything else, and with whom you hoped to spend the rest of your life, and feel anything but love. I hope I'm not going to get hard and bitter in my old age." Isobel fumbled for something to say and he shrugged. "I'll try not to. I don't want to lose you as a friend. Are you supposed to be visiting your landlady again?"

"Yes."

"And staying for dinner?" he offered.

"Oh—" She faltered. "I hadn't said."

"Well, you'll be most welcome?"

"Thank you. You're very kind. I hate lying to people but if they knew the truth…"

"What happened to James?"

She glanced out of the window at the street. Two boys were chasing each other with a little girl toddling behind them as fast as her fat little legs could carry her.

"James went to America," she said, struggling to keep her voice steady. "I told him I was going to have his child and I'll never forget the expression of horror on his face. I had no choice but to tell my father. Father went to James' home but

James was long gone so Father returned to the Glebe House. He stripped me and whipped me, and threw me out, calling me a trollop."

She raised a trembling hand to her forehead. "I was so naïve, so innocent. In the space of three months, I went from being seduced by James, to being whipped and thrown out of my home by my father, to coming to Dublin and having my baby aborted, to whoring myself to men for a pittance. After the first man left, I was sick. And having to be examined every few weeks to see if I had caught a disease… You cannot imagine how degrading that was—" She broke off and began to shake.

"Here." Clasping her shoulders, he guided her to the chair in front of the desk. He sat her down and crouched beside her. "I'm sorry, I shouldn't have asked."

"No, you should," she insisted. "If I keep it all in here," she tapped the side of her head, "I'll go mad." She peered into his face, the handsome but rather serious face, now contorted with sympathy. "I loved James so much."

"And now?"

"Now I hate him. He ruined me. Took away my innocence. Lost me everything. If it wasn't for you, I'd still be a whore."

He winced visibly at the word whore. "I wish I had never—" he whispered, but she held a finger momentarily to his lips.

"You were drunk that night and you were angry and bitter at Cecilia and you didn't fully grasp all of what had happened to me. I shouldn't have told you but no man ever asked about my scar before. Will, no-one except you knows both what happened to me and what my real name is. I wrote the letter to you the evening of the dinner party in such a hurry that I must have signed it Isobel Stevens by mistake."

"You had told no-one your real name?" he asked. "Not even Sally Maher?"

She shook her head. "I told her from the start I was Rose Green – Green without an 'e' at the end. Greene with an 'e' is my mother's maiden name. I was at the stage where I couldn't trust anyone."

"You were right. You can trust me, though. Nothing you've told me will go any further."

"Thank you, Will. You're a kind man."

"Why don't you go upstairs to the parlour while I make a pot of tea? I think we've earned it."

When Will climbed the stairs with the tea tray and pushed the parlour door open with his foot, he stopped dead. Isobel was fast asleep on the sofa, her head resting on the arm. He crept across the room and put the tray down on the writing desk. He poured himself a cup of tea and sat down in an armchair watching her.

She hardly made a sound as she slept deeply. He felt terrible for having reduced her to a shaking mess. What had happened to him seemed trivial in comparison with her experiences. She had barely given it a mention, but in his letters, he had gone on and on.

Ten minutes passed before she began to stir, rubbing her eyes and stretching, while he watched in fascination. She opened her eyes and looked blankly around her for a moment before remembering where she was. Her eyes widened and she sat up straight.

"I fell asleep? Oh, Will, I'm so sorry. That was very rude of me."

"Feel better?" He smiled and she nodded. "Tea?"

"Yes, please." She got up and joined him at the writing desk as he poured her a cup and added milk. "Was I asleep for long?"

"You were asleep when I came upstairs with the tea tray. Such snoring I could hear."

She stared at him in consternation before he began to laugh and she joined in in relief.

"Is that tea stewed?" he asked.

She took a sip and shook her head. "No, it's fine, thank you."

He saw her glance at the photographs on the desk, including a studio portrait of himself, Fred, and Jerry just after they graduated.

"That's Fred, there." He pointed to Fred with his newly grown moustache. "I was best man at his wedding recently. He and his wife Margaret live in the Simpson family home on Ely Place Upper and Fred has just started in general practice with my father. Jerry's medical practice is in London."

"You said Fred has been here, I think?" she asked.

"Yes, both of them have. We agree to disagree."

"It's good that you all keep in touch, though," she told him.

"Yes. There is no-one else you correspond with?"

"No," she replied quietly. "Claire has become a good friend. Another reason why I hate all the lying. She likes you," she added.

"Me?" he cried. "Little Claire?"

"She's twenty-one." Isobel laughed.

"Poor Claire."

"She'd be horrified if she knew that you knew. She'd move here in a flash."

He was silent for a moment. "So there was a lot of gossip about Cecilia and me? I should have known."

"Everyone was desperately sorry for you. They're glad Cecilia is now gone from Merrion Square and that you can get on with your life."

"I see," he murmured.

"I'm sorry. I shouldn't have told you."

"No, it's all right. I am getting on with my life."

"I'd hate to be gossiped about if that's any consolation?"

"Yes. Thank you," he replied, and she glanced at the photographs again. "That's my brother Edward and his wife Ruth," he said, pointing to the photographic portrait taken in London shortly after their wedding. "They're out in India now."

"Have they any children?"

"A little boy called John, after my father."

"Born out there?" she asked incredulously.

"Yes. He's two years old now."

"You've never wanted to travel?"

He shook his head. "I've been to London to see Jerry, but somewhere like India, I'll leave to Edward. I'd never stand the heat. You?"

"Oh." She sighed. "I've had my travels. My school in England was a very long way from Co Galway when I was twelve. And now I'm seeing Dublin. I don't think I'd like the heat in India very much either."

"You'll stay in Dublin, then?" he asked.

"I think so. I like Dublin."

"Good." He smiled at her in what he realised was relief and he began to fiddle awkwardly with the teapot. "More tea?"

"No, thank you. You should smile more," she said, and he stared at her before pulling a comical expression.

"If I smile more, people will think I'm an idiot."

"Smile at something or someone. Smile blandly at nothing and you will be locked up."

"I had better start practising, then," he replied, and she laughed. "Do you miss your brother?"

She nodded and smiled sadly. "Very much. Alfie and James were good friends so he must feel terrible about it all. I'm so glad I have you to talk to."

"I like talking to you. I never used to…" He tailed off.

"Talk to Cecilia like this?" she finished.

"No. It was always what she wanted to talk about. And I was a fool and complied. I realise now that I was a complete fool over her. I talk to you as if you were Edward. You could be the sister I never had if you'll allow?"

"You won't pull my hair or put frogspawn in my boots, will you?" she teased.

He laughed. "I don't think there is much frogspawn to be had around here, I'm afraid. I'll try not to pull your hair."

"Thank you." She smiled broadly, revealing lovely white teeth. "I'll remember that."

"There is someone you should meet." He went to a wooden box in a corner and lifted out a skeleton model. Her eyes widened. "This is Arthur," he said, hanging him up on a nail. "Arthur Skeleton because he's only Arthur person." She groaned at the terrible joke. "I was thinking of putting him in the hall as a sort of half-butler, half coat stand?"

"Maybe you should dress him first? A few clothes and he could be Mr Johnston's brother."

"My God, you're right," he gasped, realising how similar the thin butler and the skeleton were.

"Have you introduced him to Mrs Bell?"

"I have and, sadly, she thinks he's an 'awful looking yoke'."

"Pity."

"I thought so, too, but I do think he looks like me before Mrs Bell became my housekeeper," he said, and she laughed. "You are the first non-medical person not to find him revolting."

"I think he's lovely." She kissed Arthur's cheekbone. "And we're all skeletons underneath, aren't we?"

"We certainly are. But Arthur is definitely male."

"Male and female skeletons are different?" she asked, and he exhaled a comical groan.

"Oh, don't get me started."

"I don't mind."

"Well, there are a few things. Male pelvic girdles are different to women's because women's are designed to accommodate and allow a baby to pass through." Without thinking, he ran his hands down her body and over her hips. He felt her tense and straightened up feeling his cheeks burn. "I'm sorry."

She gave him a dismissive little smile. "It's true, though. Your body, the lower part, is straight, while mine definitely isn't. Look at poor Arthur compared to me. Stand next to him?" she asked, and he did while she compared them. "You are a much bigger man than poor Arthur ever was."

"That will be Mrs Bell's cooking," he said dryly.

"Oh, you're not fat." She laid a hand on his stomach before quickly lifting it off. "Not at all. You're just big-built, like me."

"But you're not big-built," he insisted, running his hands over her hips again, before straightening up in horror at what he'd done. "You're just… curvaceous…"

They stared at each other until she turned away and an awkward silence followed.

"I'm sorry," he said quietly. "That wasn't very brotherly."

"Perhaps you should put Arthur away."

"Yes." Arthur was returned quickly to his box in the corner and when Will stood up, he found her watching him intently. It unnerved him, and he extended a hand towards the door. "Come up to the second floor and see the view?"

They climbed the stairs and went into one of the empty bedrooms. From the window, he watched as she gazed over the rooftops then down at the street.

"Someone told me a lot of the houses in the Liberties are tenements," she said. "I don't know how true it is as she was being quite scathing."

"Some are and are crammed to the rafters with people. Sometimes up to twenty people in a room of this size. Two, perhaps three families. I have never seen anything like it. Coming here from Merrion Square certainly opened my eyes. Changed me, I suppose. For the better, I hope."

She nodded. "I don't know what you were like before but I think you are a good man."

"And you are too good to be a parlourmaid."

"No, I'm not," she said with a little sigh. "After what I've been, I'll never be too good for anything. But I'm content at number 68, and Mr Johnston says I'm a good parlourmaid."

Will felt a surprisingly sharp stab of jealousy. "You can't stay there forever."

"I'm not thinking about forever at the moment. I'm happy and content there for now. And I'm so thankful that I have you as a friend." Reaching out, she squeezed his hand, and he squeezed it in reply. "Being able to come here and talk to you is wonderful."

"I'm glad. You will call again?"

"You don't mind?" she asked. "I'm sure you must—"

"I don't mind at all," he interrupted. "You can fall asleep on the sofa here whenever you like."

The following Wednesday afternoon, Isobel found a note stuck between the front door and the door post.

> *6:00 am*
> *Attending to a birth.*
> *Will Fitzgerald*

She went inside, hung her handbag on the hooks behind the front door, then took off and hung up her hat and coat. In the kitchen, the solid fuel range was cold, and she busied herself in setting and lighting a new fire. The bucket at the back door was empty so she brought it out to the backyard where she found a water pump. Returning to the kitchen with the water, she half-filled the kettle from the bucket and put it on the range's hot plate to heat.

She went upstairs to the parlour and to the bookcase, pulling out *Wuthering Heights*, and bringing it back downstairs. She had reached chapter three by the time the kettle came to the boil. She made half a pot of tea, left it to brew, and went into the larder. If Will hadn't had anything to eat since at least six o'clock that morning, and probably not since the previous evening, then he would be absolutely starving when he returned.

She found bread, butter, and cheese and made two rounds of sandwiches before proceeding on to chapter four. She was half way through chapter five when she heard the front door open and close and she got up and put the kettle on the range's hot plate again. When the kitchen door opened, she was shocked when Will came in, his medical bag in one hand and a coat over one arm. His heavily stubbled face was grey with fatigue and his collar-less shirt and waistcoat were splattered with blood. He put his coat and bag down on the table and gave her an exhausted smile.

"Twins."

"Are they all right?" she asked anxiously.

"Perfect. Had to do a Caesarean, though, hence all the blood." He glanced down at his shirt. "Two enormous boys."

"Will the mother be all right?"

"Yes, she will," he replied, running a hand over his jaw. "Luckily, her mother-in-law is a capable woman and assisted me. I'll call back later this evening to check on them all."

"You look worn out. Go upstairs to the parlour. I've made you some sandwiches and the kettle is nearly on the boil."

"Thank you."

When she went upstairs with the tea tray, the door to his bedroom was ajar, and she saw him beautifully bare-chested and reaching for a clean shirt as she walked into the parlour.

She put the tray down on the writing desk and sighed. You're friends, she told herself. You agreed to be friends. Don't ruin the friendship by falling for him. A few moments later, he followed her into the parlour and joined her at the desk.

"They're cheese," she told him, passing him the plate of sandwiches.

"My favourite, thank you."

"Have you done many caesareans?" she asked, pouring the tea, while he bit into a sandwich.

"This was my fourth," he replied with his mouth full. "Sorry."

"I'll be quiet and let you eat."

"No." He reached out and squeezed her hand, and it was all she could do not to pull her hand away. "It was very nice to return home to someone. I'd pushed a note under Mrs Bell's door telling her not to come this morning."

"I thought you might have done that. The fire was out. So I set and lit a new fire, fetched some water, then read *Wuthering Heights*." She pulled an apologetic expression.

"I'd probably have put the water in the range and the coal in the water bucket."

"Why don't you have a nap for a couple of hours?" she suggested.

He shook his head. "I'll wait until later."

"You don't have to be polite because of me. I'll just sit here and read. It'll do you good."

He smiled. "All right." He finished the sandwiches, put the plate on the tray, and drank the rest of his tea. "Lovely, thank you. What time is it now?" He glanced at the clock on the mantelpiece. "Half past three. If I'm not awake by five o'clock, call me."

"I will."

She went downstairs to the kitchen and washed the cups and plate then brought the book back upstairs. On the landing she stopped, hearing him snore softly. Pushing the bedroom door open a little, she peered inside. He was lying curled up on the bed, his cheek cushioned in the palm of a hand. There was a rug folded up on a chair in a corner so she put the book down, picked up the rug, and covered him with it. He looked so peaceful, and she wished she could lie down beside him and fall asleep in his arms. But she couldn't, and she reluctantly returned to the parlour with the book.

Some hours later, she glanced at the clock on the mantelpiece. It was ten minutes past five. Closing the book, she went to Will's bedroom and opened the door. He hadn't moved and she went inside and put a hand on his shoulder.

"Will?" He jumped and opened his eyes. "It's ten past five."

He nodded and stretched, noticing the rug draped over him. "Thanks."

"Feel a bit better?" she asked.

"Yes, I do. This hasn't been much of a visit for you."

"I've read over half of *Wuthering Heights*. I haven't read so much in a very long time and I enjoyed it."

"Then, good." He threw off the rug and swung his legs off the bed. "You must be hungry."

"A little, yes," she admitted.

"I think there are some sausages in the larder. I'll concoct something for us."

"We will," she replied, and he smiled.

Will stood up, put on his morning coat, and they went downstairs. In the larder they found sausages and eggs and a few boiled potatoes on a plate left over from the previous day. All went into the frying pan and were devoured with thick slices of soda bread and butter and glasses of milk.

"Delicious," he declared, pushing his plate away, and leaning forward on his arms on the table. "Is there any gossip from the square?"

"None."

"At all?" he prompted with a grin.

"No." She smiled. "And even if there were, I couldn't tell you."

"That's a disappointment," he replied, his heart sinking as she pulled a length of thin black ribbon out from under her dress and opened a small silver pocket watch. "You're not going, are you?"

"I'll help you clear away and wash up, then I must go," she said, closing the watch and dropping it back under her dress. "I can't be back late or I'll have to think up more lies."

He nodded. "I enjoy you coming here, you know?"

"I do, too. Do you want to wash or dry?"

"You'll call again next week, won't you?" he asked.

She lowered her eyes. "Are you not tired of me calling here?"

"No, I'll never be tired of your visits. Didn't I just say—" He reached for her hand but, to his surprise, she pulled it back. "Isobel?"

"Don't, Will, please?" she begged. "You've been hurt badly once. I'd hate for it to happen again."

"But, Isobel?"

"No." She was firm. "Please, Will, I like being your friend very much. Don't ruin our friendship."

He sat back in his chair and ran a hand across his

stubbled jaw. "I like you, I can't help it. Do you like me?"

"Of course I like you."

"I don't mean just as a friend."

She shook her head. "Please don't ask me that."

"Why not?" he demanded.

"I didn't come here with the aim—"

"I know you didn't. And I didn't invite you with the aim… I chose dark hair at Sally's because Cecilia's hair is blonde and I wanted to punish her. But I haven't thought about her romantically in weeks – just you – just you."

"I'll go."

"I've made a complete and utter fool of myself, haven't I?" he asked bitterly.

"No."

"Then, tell me why you won't answer me?" he demanded, and she bit her lip.

"Because I don't want to even think it, never mind say it. Will, we met in a brothel where your friend paid for you to have sex with me. I was a whore and I'm now a parlourmaid in the house next door to your parents'. I've been lying to everyone—"

"Except me."

"Yes, except you. Will, I'm sorry. I was a complete and utter fool to think we could just be friends. Now, I'm going back to the square before I hurt you even more."

They got to their feet at the same time and he reached for her waist. He pulled her against him, sliding his hands up her body until he clasped her cheeks. Then he kissed her. He'd never kissed a woman in the way he kissed Isobel, he'd never had the desire to before. Thrusting his tongue into her mouth, he was astonished when, after a moment's hesitation, she responded with a little moan. Her tongue slid over and around his and her breasts heaved against his chest, betraying her arousal.

"No," she gasped, breaking away from him, and running from the kitchen and along the hall. He followed as she grabbed her handbag, hat and coat from the hooks at the front door, her hands shaking.

"Isobel, please?" he begged, turning her around.

"Don't, Will." She began to struggle and he let her go. "I won't be coming back and please don't write to me."

"Isobel—"

"Goodbye, Will." She flung open the front door and went out.

"Isobel?" he roared down the street after her but she kept walking.

Chapter Four

Isobel turned the corner at the end of Brown Street then sank back against a wall and burst into tears. She allowed herself to cry until no more tears would come knowing anything beyond friendship would be hopeless. Poor Will.

She found a tap and washed her face to try and disguise the fact that she had been crying then put on her hat and coat and trudged back to number 68.

Everyone fell silent in the servants' hall when she went in. Claire shot her such a look of hatred that she stared at her in astonishment.

"What on earth's the matter?"

"Edith has been dismissed," Mrs Gordon told her stiffly. "Mrs Black is with her now as she packs her belongings and will escort her out of the house. Mr Johnston has asked for you to see him as soon as you came in."

Warily, she knocked at the door to the butler's pantry.

"Come in," the butler called in his harsh Ulster accent and she opened the door.

"You wanted to see me, Mr Johnston?" She went in and closed the door then stared in surprise at the wretched expression on his face. Of course. He had been fond of

Edith, so no wonder. "Mr Johnston?"

"This afternoon, Mrs Harvey reported a brooch missing to Edith. Edith claimed to have no knowledge of its whereabouts so Mrs Harvey instructed Mrs Black that the entire house be searched. Each room was searched and that search revealed two shocking finds. The first was the brooch and a substantial amount of money hidden in Edith's bedroom and the second was these items found in yours."

Isobel stared in horror as Mr Johnston went to the table, opened a drawer and lifted out, not only all the letters from Will, but also her bible – grabbed as her father chased her out of Ballybeg Glebe House simply because tucked inside it were the only official documentation of who she really was – and which she had managed to hide even from Sally Maher's prying eyes.

"These letters and notepaper from the Shelbourne Hotel were hidden under the lining of one of your drawers," he continued. "And a bible with baptism and confirmation certificates tucked into the cover was found underneath the chest of drawers. The letters to you from Dr Fitzgerald junior are of a most intimate nature. Well?"

"My friendship with Dr Fitzgerald is over," she whispered.

"Friendship?"

"Yes, friendship. Nothing more."

Mr Johnston picked up one of the letters. "In this letter, he writes, *Dear Isobel, I hope you don't mind me calling you that? I had read of Rose's death so I did receive rather a shock when I saw you. But a relieved one.*" The butler put the letter down. "Who exactly are you?"

Isobel sighed and pointed to the baptism certificate. "That is mine and is genuine, I promise."

"So you are not Maisie Byrne, but Isobel Stevens, born November 17th, 1857, daughter of Edmund Stevens, Clerk in Holy Orders, and Martha Stevens, née Greene. This address – The Glebe House, Ballybeg, Co Galway – it is the same address given by Maisie Byrne on her reference."

"Maisie Byrne was our house-parlourmaid," Isobel explained. "She did leave us to look after her mother."

"But you wrote the reference?" he asked.

"Yes."

"On notepaper stolen from the Shelbourne Hotel?" he added.

"Yes."

Mr Johnston sighed. "What brings the daughter of a Co Galway clergyman to Dublin looking for work as a parlourmaid?"

"I was pregnant by a neighbour's son. He deserted me. My father threw me out. I came to Dublin."

"And the child?"

She bit her lip. "It died. I needed work. I was homeless and desperate for work. I am sorry for all the deceit, Mr Johnston."

"Are you."

"Yes, of course," she insisted. "I hated all the lies."

"According to this letter, a Rose Green is dead. Who was Rose Green?"

"The name I gave myself when I first came to Dublin."

"So why change it to Maisie Byrne?"

She shrugged. "I thought I would be more convincing if I pretended to be a real person whom I knew."

"Very clever of you. How did you come to know Dr Fitzgerald, then, Isobel?"

She frowned. Mr Johnston saying her real name sounded very odd. "He was very kind to me after my baby died. We became friends."

"So, Dr Fitzgerald is, in fact, your landlady?"

"Yes."

"But your friendship is now over. Why?"

She swallowed noisily. "Because he wanted more than friendship."

The butler's eyes widened. "You did not?"

"No," she whispered. "And I will not be seeing him again. Nor corresponding with him." She took a deep breath. "Mr Johnston, if I am to be dismissed, please tell me now."

Mr Johnston closed the drawer. "I will have to speak with Mrs Harvey on the matter. She will, of course, need to know all the details. Wait here."

The butler went out and Isobel sank down onto a chair. Oh, how she hated lying. Of course she wanted more than friendship with Will. She picked up his letters and stared not at the words but at his scrawling handwriting. She could hear his voice shouting desperately down Brown Street after her. She quickly turned the letters over before she began to cry again. She needed all her wits about her if she was to try and keep her position.

Over half an hour passed before Mr Johnston returned to the butler's pantry and told her to follow him upstairs to the hall.

"Wait here," he instructed, went into the morning room, and the door closed. A couple of minutes later the door opened and Mr Johnston held it open for her. "Mrs Harvey will see you now."

Her handbag in her hands and her coat and hat still on,

Isobel went into the room and the butler closed the door on his way out. Mrs Harvey turned away from the writing desk at the window and gave her a long look.

"Well, Maisie Byrne. Or, should I say, Isobel Stevens?"

"I'm very sorry, Mrs Harvey."

"And I for you."

Isobel frowned. "I beg your pardon, Mrs Harvey?"

"A neighbour's son?" she asked.

"Yes, Mrs Harvey."

"Seduced you, I suppose?"

"Yes." She forced James' grinning face from her mind.

"And the child died?"

"Yes, Mrs Harvey," she whispered.

"A blessing, of sorts. Here or in Galway?"

"Here, Mrs Harvey."

"And was that how you met Will Fitzgerald?"

"Yes," she replied after a slight pause.

"You must have received a shock when he arrived for the dinner party?"

She nodded. "I did, Mrs Harvey. I thought I would never see him again."

"I can imagine. Well, it has been an eventful day." Mrs Harvey smiled wryly. "Edith is a thief who has been stealing and selling my jewellery and you are a clergyman's disgraced daughter. Edith had been with me for eight years. I shall now, of course, need a replacement for her. Where did you attend school? Did you attend school? Or were you taught by a governess?"

"I attended school in England, Mrs Harvey. In Cheltenham."

Mrs Harvey's brown eyes bulged. "Not at Cheltenham Ladies' College, surely?"

"Yes, Mrs Harvey."

"Good gracious me." Mrs Harvey clapped a hand to her chest. "You are probably better educated than I am. Can you play the piano?"

"I could, Mrs Harvey, but I'm probably very rusty now."

"Cook? Sew?"

"Only sew, Mrs Harvey. I lived with a private landlady until the school introduced its own boarding facilities. She was an excellent seamstress who taught me to sew."

Mrs Harvey shook her head in clear disbelief. "You could probably run this house better than I."

Isobel moved awkwardly from foot to foot. "Well, I did observe how my landlady ran her house but I have never put what I saw into practice, so most likely not, ma'am."

Mrs Harvey smiled. "I am willing to offer you the post of lady's maid all the same, Isobel."

She was astounded. "You're not going to dismiss me?"

"You will be on trial for the next three months. It is hard work, Isobel, as you saw with Edith. I am hard work as you can see." Mrs Harvey indicated her exquisite high-necked sapphire blue silk satin day dress with white lace at the cuffs. "I demand perfection. One false step and you will be dismissed immediately. You accept?"

"Yes, I do, Mrs Harvey. Thank you very much."

"Good." Mrs Harvey gave her a satisfied nod. "Now, ask Johnston to come in, will you?"

Mr Johnston eyed her sharply as she went out into the hall. "Mrs Harvey would like to speak with you, Mr Johnston."

He nodded. "Wait here," he ordered, went inside, and emerged some ten minutes later. "You have done well for yourself, Miss Isobel Stevens. Move your belongings into Edith's old bedroom."

"Yes, Mr Johnston. May I have my letters, certificates, and bible back, please?"

He nodded. "Come to my pantry when you've moved your belongings."

She had a bedroom all to herself. No more having to wash, dress, and undress facing Claire so the other maid wouldn't see her scar. She retrieved her belongings from the old bedroom and placed them on the bed in the new room while she explored. Not only was the bedroom bigger, it had a dressing table, chest of drawers, and a wardrobe. She sat on the bed and bounced up and down on the good mattress. A faded brown rug lay on the floor, bigger than the mat in the old bedroom, and less threadbare. She smiled. She had a room all to herself.

In the servants' hall, the reception to her was frosty. Claire glared at her and turned away while the others stared at her in varying degrees of interest and friendliness. She followed Mr Johnston into his pantry and he closed the door.

"Don't expect them to be very forgiving," he said. "Here."

"Thank you." She took the letters, bible, and certificates from him. "I'm going to apologise."

"Good. I hope we can try and wipe the slate clean, Isobel. Mrs Black and I don't like an atmosphere."

"No. Thank you, Mr Johnston." Taking a deep breath, she went back out to the servants' hall. "I'm sorry," she began immediately. "I'm very sorry for lying and deceiving you all."

"You had your reasons, I suppose," Mrs Gordon said crisply.

"Claire." She turned to her. "I'm sorry."

Claire didn't reply, even when prompted to by a kick from Frank the footman.

Isobel sighed, accepted the cup of tea Mrs Gordon held out to her and went upstairs to her room. She put Will's letters, the bible, and her certificates in one of the dressing table drawers before sitting on the bed with her tea. Suddenly, a bedroom all to herself wasn't very appealing.

That evening, Will trudged up Brown Street on his way home from checking on Nellie Bergin and her twins. Nellie was over the moon, ecstatic at becoming a mother, and Will wished he could have shared some of her joy. Why did he make a complete and utter fool of himself over women? This was twice now, in only a few months.

He climbed the stairs to the parlour and saw the book on the sofa where Isobel had left it. Turning on his heel, he went straight to bed. He would block it all out with sleep. Or so he hoped. He tossed and turned before falling asleep but two hours later he woke and couldn't drop off again. He spent the rest of the night lying on his back staring up at the shadows the oil lamp cast onto the ceiling and got up feeling unrefreshed and very low in spirits.

"Late night?" Mrs Bell asked while he ate his breakfast.

"I hardly slept," he told her. "I've done it again."

"Done what?"

"Made a fool of myself over a woman."

"Maisie?" she said and he nodded. "Wasn't interested?"

He rested his head on a fist. "Yes, but wouldn't allow herself to be."

Mrs Bell frowned. "I don't understand you."

"It's a long and complicated story."

"It's a shame." Mrs Bell poured him more tea. "She was a nice lassie."

"She was beautiful."

Mrs Bell squeezed his shoulder, went to get the post from the front door mat, and put a letter on the kitchen table at his elbow. The letter was from his mother, who hadn't seen him for over a week, and was telling – not asking – him to call. He sat up as he read on. There had been some commotion amongst the Harveys' servants and one of the maids had been dismissed. His mother didn't know who yet but would find out more from Tess that evening.

"Bad news?" asked Mrs Bell.

"I don't know. After house calls, I'm going to visit my mother. You hadn't planned luncheon yet? I might be invited to stay."

"Might." She snorted. "No, it's nothing that won't keep until tomorrow."

Three hours later, Will turned into Merrion Square. The Harveys' house seemed quiet as he passed and his mother greeted him coolly in the morning room.

"Harriett Harvey has just been to see me."

"Oh?" He frowned as they sat down.

"Don't act the innocent with me, William," she retorted, and he winced. His mother only used his full name when she was in a great rage. "What exactly is Isobel Stevens to you?"

His jaw dropped. "Isobel Stevens?"

"Or perhaps you know her better as Maisie Byrne? What is she to you?"

"Nothing."

"I know when you are lying, William," Mrs Fitzgerald snapped.

He sighed. "We were friends but I made the mistake – again – of demanding too much. Isobel wanted simply to be friends. Now we are not even that. Has she been dismissed?"

"No, but she should have been, lying like that. Edith Lear was dismissed for the theft of one of Harriett's brooches and many other items of jewellery which she sold. During the search, intimate letters from you to Isobel Stevens were found, along with her baptism and confirmation certificates. She seems to be from a good family, her father is a clergyman, but she had a child—"

"The child died," he interrupted. "A miscarriage."

"Were you her doctor?" his mother asked. "Was that how you met?"

"Yes, I was." He lied again and was relieved when she didn't seem to notice.

"You felt sorry for her?"

"I was concerned. She had been seduced. Her father threw her out. The child died. She was in a very fragile frame of mind. I suggested that she try and find work. I had no idea that she would find employment next door."

"She is very beautiful." His mother looked straight at him. "And very different from Cecilia."

"I do not love Cecilia anymore," he announced.

"You love this girl?" Mrs Fitzgerald both looked and sounded astonished.

"She is not a 'girl'. She is twenty-two. And I don't know if I love her quite yet, but I am falling in love with her."

"She does not reciprocate your feelings?"

He looked away and grimaced. "Possibly."

"I don't understand?"

"She does not want anyone to know of her disgrace," he explained.

"But the whole square knows now," his mother told him and he cringed on Isobel's behalf, remembering how she had told him she would hate to be gossiped about.

"Are you telling me you approve, Mother?"

"No, not really." She gave him a little smile. "But I am giving up on meddling. Amelia Belcher will just be another Cecilia, I fear. She will not love you enough to accept a husband with a practice in the Liberties. Will Isobel Stevens?"

"I really don't know. Mother." He reached forward and held her hands. "If I pursue Isobel, you know what it will mean? Gossip. A lot of gossip. She is a fallen woman, thrown out of her home. She is a parlourmaid in your neighbours' home."

"She is now Harriett's lady's maid."

"Really?" His eyebrows shot up.

His mother nodded. "Harriett was very impressed with her education and was willing to give her a second chance. Will, I know there will be gossip. There would be gossip even if she were the epitome of virtue."

"I'm worried it could affect Father's practice," he admitted.

"Go and see him, Will. He's at the practice house all day today. You'll stay for luncheon?" she asked.

"Thank you, yes."

"Tell me one thing," his mother added, getting up, and ringing for a maid. "Are you really and truly finished with Cecilia? You have no feelings for her still? You are not trying to replace her too soon?"

"I am not trying to replace her at all. Isobel is completely different. I have no lingering feelings for Cecilia. I am really and truly finished with her."

"She hurt you so deeply," his mother said softly. "I do not want to see it happen again."

"I don't either."

After the meal, Will walked to the practice house on Merrion Street Upper. He went upstairs to his father's surgery and asked his father to please listen first and then question him if he so wished. His father complied then went to the window and stared down at the street.

"Brown Street has changed you," he said simply.

"Yes, Father, it has, but I almost married Cecilia while living there."

"So you are now setting your sights lower?"

Will clenched his fists angrily. "No, I am not."

His father turned to look at him. "I had such high hopes for you, Will. Now you live and work in a slum and wish to pursue a courtship with a fallen woman. Your mother must be delighted."

"Mother does not approve, but she does want me to be happy all the same. If you wish, I will conduct any possible courtship away from Merrion Square and cause Mother and yourself the least possible embarrassment."

"It could be the end of you in Brown Street, you know?" his father told him. "You don't know how the people there will react."

"I have been there long enough to know that they will be sympathetic."

"Come back to work here, Will? We need another young man in the practice. Come back?"

Will shook his head. "I'm sorry, Father, but no."

His father shrugged. "The girl is beautiful, I concede that. Oh, go after her if you must. I don't know what your brother will have to say on the matter."

"I'm not asking for Edward's opinion. Thank you, Father."

That evening, Isobel was summoned to the morning room. As she went, she felt Claire's eyes on her. Claire hadn't spoken one word to her since her deception had been uncovered and, knowing the parlourmaid's feelings for Will, Isobel couldn't blame her.

"You rang, Mrs Harvey?"

"I did. You may sit down, Isobel."

"Thank you." She sat on one of the sofas, thinking it highly unusual to be instructed to do so.

Mrs Harvey smiled at her. "I went to see Sarah Fitzgerald this morning. I felt she needed to be brought up to date on all the happenings. She was surprised, to say the least. She had written to Will telling him to call. He did so just before luncheon, after which he saw his father, and then called upon me."

"Oh." Was all Isobel could manage as Mrs Harvey rang the bell for a servant.

"Sarah does not altogether approve and neither does John but they do want Will to be happy and if that happiness includes you, well…"

"But, Mrs Harvey." Isobel found her voice. "I have told Will Fitzgerald I don't want to see him again. I don't understand how his parents could in any circumstances approve of me, considering my recent history."

"They wish to meet you."

Isobel's eyes bulged in horror. "I'm sorry, Mrs Harvey, but no."

"Why ever not? They know of your... troubles. They are expecting you."

"Now?" she gasped.

"Yes, now. Off you go. Use the front door. I will inform Johnston where you are."

In a daze, Isobel got up from the sofa and walked out to the hall. Mr Johnston gave her a puzzled glance as he was called into the morning room. She left the house and went up the steps to the Fitzgeralds' front door. Tess opened the door and smiled as if she had been expecting her. She was shown straight into the morning room and both John and Sarah Fitzgerald rose from their seats.

"Good evening, Isobel. Thank you for coming." Mrs Fitzgerald smiled. "Do sit down."

"Thank you." Isobel sat in an armchair while Will's parents re-took their seats on the large sofa opposite her.

"Well, it has been a most interesting day," Mrs Fitzgerald continued. "First Harriett Harvey called and then Will. You were the main topic of conversation on both occasions. Now, I do not care what you said to Harriett, you will tell us the truth. Is that understood?"

Isobel's head began to spin. "Yes, Mrs Fitzgerald."

"You will answer yes or no. Your real name is Isobel Stevens?"

"Yes."

"Born in Co Galway, your father is a clergyman?"

"Yes."

"Became pregnant by the son of a neighbour who abandoned

you. Your father threw you out and you came to Dublin?"

"Yes."

"In Dublin, you met Will in his capacity as a doctor when he attended you during and after the miscarriage of the child?"

Isobel's mind raced. Is that what Will had said? She had little choice but to comply. "Yes."

"Did you set out to deliberately entrap Will?" Dr Fitzgerald senior spoke for the first time.

"No, I did not," she replied emphatically. "I broke off our friendship because anything more than that is pointless."

"But we know everything now."

Cringing, Isobel looked down at her hands. "I do not wish to be an embarrassment to any of you."

"You would like your friendship with Will to progress, however?"

Isobel flushed. "Yes, but it cannot."

"This is a very unusual state of affairs but—" Dr Fitzgerald senior stopped speaking and Isobel's head jerked up as he glanced at his wife and she nodded. "We give our approval."

"You do?"

"Yes, but you will remain as Harriett Harvey's lady's maid for now."

"Thank you," she whispered.

Mr Johnston opened the Harveys' front door to her and had to steady her as she almost fell into the hall.

"Dr Fitzgerald's parents have given their approval for my friendship with him to progress, Mr Johnston. I honestly didn't expect it."

Taking one glance at her face, he nodded. "My problem,

Isobel, is that I do not know how the other servants will treat you now. You are in the rather unenviable position of being between stairs. You do not belong downstairs nor do you belong upstairs."

"I am sorry, Mr Johnston. Everything seems to have been decided for me."

"I thought I heard voices." The morning room door had opened and Mrs Harvey smiled at her. "Please come in, Isobel." Reluctantly, Isobel left Mr Johnston's side and followed her into the room. "Well?"

"They approve of me, Mrs Harvey," she said, closing the door. "And I really don't understand it."

"Are you not relieved?"

"I don't know what to think, Mrs Harvey," she told her truthfully. "But I cannot help but wonder that if I really was Maisie Byrne – a Catholic, and whose late father was a tenant farmer – and not the daughter of a Church of Ireland clergyman, they would not have been quite so approving."

"Well, it is up to you now, Isobel. Call on Will tomorrow morning."

"He will be doing his house calls."

"After luncheon, then."

"Mrs Harvey, I have to ask – why you are helping me?"

The older woman walked slowly around the room before coming to an abrupt halt. "Because you remind me of my sister. She also fell into disgrace. Her seducer also abandoned her. In her despair, she had an abortion. Not only did her child die, she died, too."

A shiver ran down Isobel's spine. "I'm sorry."

"Thank you. So you see, you have been very lucky. And if you have any chance of happiness you should take it."

"What was your sister's name?" Isobel asked.

"Millicent. She was younger than you when it happened, only eighteen. I do know what you have been through. Never think no-one else understands. If you have any feelings at all for Will, go and see him. He may never be rich and he may never move from Brown Street and I daresay such a life will not be easy for him, but I have watched him grow into the good man he is now."

"I know he is a good man."

Harriett Harvey nodded. "Don't tell anyone will you, but I was relieved when Cecilia gave him up. They would have only made the other unhappy. Will you call on him?"

Isobel nodded. "Tomorrow afternoon."

Chapter Five

Will had just finished his mid-day meal when he went to answer a knock at the front door. To his astonishment, Isobel stood on the step. He smiled but she didn't return one. In fact, she looked furious.

"Give me one good reason why I shouldn't slap you?" she demanded.

"Because I don't know what you are talking about?"

"Everyone in the square knows about me. I really—"

He quickly reached out and covered her mouth. "Mrs Bell is in the kitchen," he whispered. "Go upstairs to the parlour. I'll join you in a few minutes."

She rolled her eyes but complied and he returned to the kitchen.

"Was that Maisie I heard?" Mrs Bell was at the sink washing the dishes.

"Yes. Mrs Bell, I hope you don't mind…"

"You'd like me to go so you can speak to her?" she finished with a smile. "I'll leave the dishes to drip. She's a good lassie, Dr Fitzgerald. Don't let her go."

"I'll try not to. Thank you."

When he went upstairs, Isobel was pacing up and down

the parlour floor still wearing her coat and hat.

"How dare you." She rounded on him, shaking with rage. "How dare you go behind my back like that. How dare you deceive your parents and Mrs Harvey about me. You told them I had a miscarriage. That you were my doctor. It's all lies. I had an abortion. We met in a brothel. I was a whore."

"No-one need ever know."

"Will, I am not having the possibility of everyone finding out hanging over me."

"So what are you going to do?" he demanded. "Assume another identity? It will never work for you again in Dublin – the city is far too small."

That halted her rage for a moment. "Then, I will have to go elsewhere."

"Then, you will be moving on and moving on for the rest of your life. Do you really want that?"

She sighed. "No."

"What did my parents say?"

She pulled an incredulous expression. "They gave their approval. It's completely ridiculous. Now please just leave me alone."

"You really want that? You will be alone for the rest of your life, Isobel."

"It is for the best."

"No it is not," he insisted. "I don't want you to go. Please don't go."

"Goodbye, Will."

She began to walk towards the open door but he reached her before she could leave the room. He pulled her back and slammed the door closed. She began to struggle but he was the stronger by far and held her tightly up against the door.

"I will not let you go."

"Is this what you did to Cecilia?" she cried. "Suffocate her and make demands?"

Had he? Probably. And here he was doing it all over again. His hands slid from her shoulders to his sides.

"Yes, probably. I've always been too impulsive. Too demanding. I was willing to move back to Merrion Square for her but I insisted on keeping the practice here. She wouldn't accept that and I was so shocked I let her go. I am not making the same mistake twice. I am not letting you go, Isobel."

"Oh, don't be ridiculous, Will. Even Sally Maher didn't imprison me. I had a choice. I chose to be a whore. Try and explain that to your parents." He watched her fingers as she took off her hat and threw it onto the floor. She undid the buttons of her coat then her dress and he couldn't help himself and gazed down her cleavage as they fell to the floor, suddenly longing to touch, smooth his hands over, and hold her breasts in his hands. Cecilia had been as flat-chested as a boy. Whatever had he found attractive about her? Here was a real woman right in front of him. "This is what you really want, isn't it?" She gave him a humourless smile and unbuttoned his trousers.

"Isobel," he began, feeling her hands on him, and his control beginning to slip.

"It's what they all want," she went on in a flat tone. She unbuttoned his frock coat and waistcoat and eased them off his shoulders, along with his braces. "It's what it all boils down to, no matter how much of a gentleman you think he is." She pulled up her petticoat, letting her drawers drop to the floor, and he sighed when he saw her shapely stockinged legs. "Or when you are fooled into thinking he cares for you."

He found himself no longer listening to her as she took his hands and helped him to push his trousers and drawers down. He was desperate for her. He led her across the room to the writing desk and cleared all the photographs and utensils to one side. He lifted her up onto it, then pushed her petticoat out of the way.

He took her selfishly and savagely, unearthing a passion in him he didn't know he possessed. It was utter liberation, finally laying the ghost of Cecilia to rest once and for all. This was not revenge on her for not marrying him. This was him, Will Fitzgerald, for once acting with total abandon, with no reservations whatsoever. He wanted this woman, Isobel Stevens, like he had never wanted any other woman in his entire life.

Her generosity was a wonder he had not known existed. He didn't care that there had been so many others before him. He had lived alone for four years and, apart from the drunken night in the brothel, he had lived like a monk. Now he was stone cold sober and she was the release he had craved, reminding him he was a man as well as a doctor. She must stay.

He opened his eyes, hearing her moan a little. She lay back on the desk gasping for breath. He watched her breasts rise and fall then saw her watch him. He ran his hands up her thighs, up her body, and gently lifted her towards him. He bent his head to kiss her again but she turned away.

"I'm a whore."

"Don't say that."

"This is what I am good at, Will. You were only one of hundreds. How can you be sure I wouldn't go on whoring?"

"Stop it," he commanded.

"All you feel for me is lust. I'm good for sex, that is all."

"No." He took her chin in a hand. "I wanted you and you wanted me." She closed her eyes. "Look at me," he ordered, and she opened them. "Yes, you satisfied me. More than satisfied me. But I satisfied you, too. In Sally's, and just now. I saw you. I felt you. I heard you. You hadn't planned for that, had you? So don't you dare lie to me and tell me you have no feelings for me." She bit her lips. "You can't, can you?"

She began to struggle and slid off the desk. Quickly retrieving her clothes and hat from the desk and floor, she flung open the door, ran out of the parlour and down the stairs. A couple of moments later he heard the front door open then slam closed behind her.

Isobel got dressed in an alleyway then ran back to number 68, through the servants' hall – pausing only for an ewer of cold water – and up the stairs to her bedroom. There, she undressed and poured the water into a bowl on the dressing table. She stood in front of the mirror and stared at her body. Already, she could see faint bruises on her neck and breasts where Will had kissed and almost bitten her. She touched one of them then dipped a cloth into the cold water and began to scrub.

She dreaded being summoned but when the bell rang late that evening, she went to Mrs Harvey's bedroom and helped her to undress.

"Well?"

"I won't be visiting Will again, Mrs Harvey. But thank you for all you did."

The older woman's face fell. "But why?"

"It's for the best," she replied and went to the wardrobe with Mrs Harvey's dress.

In the morning, a letter from Will was hand-delivered for her. She sighed and brought it upstairs to her bedroom.

Isobel,

 There is no point in even trying to deny how you feel. I know and I know that you know. I know you want only me. I know there will not be anyone else. I know I can and I will keep you from straying.

 I have fallen in love with you, Isobel. Marry me? I want you here with me in Brown Street to share all this grandeur! And if anyone says a word against you, well, I'm six foot tall and twelve stones in weight.

 Please reply.

 Will

Isobel shoved the letter into one of the dressing table drawers. She had hardly been able to look at herself when she had got washed and dressed. Thank goodness she no longer shared a bedroom. How on earth would she have explained the bruises to poor, innocent Claire?

A letter from Isobel arrived on Tuesday morning with the rest of Will's post. He tore it open and read:

Will,

 How on earth can I possibly marry you? Please try and understand that I am a whore.

He quickly took the letter out into the hall and away from Mrs Bell's prying eyes.

You met me in a brothel, Will. A brothel. A kip.
A whorehouse. You may not have paid for me yourself
but you were still a customer. Please, Will, leave me
alone for both our sakes.
Isobel

He crumpled the letter in his hands then immediately began to flatten it out again. He went into the surgery, placed it in Gray's *Anatomy*, and went out to do house calls. When he returned, he sat down at the desk in the surgery and wrote to her again.

Dear Isobel,

I told you I was demanding. I don't give up easily either.

I know your intention was to shock and disgust me. Well, it didn't work, Isobel. I know it and you know it. A whore does not enjoy sex the way you did. Because that is what it was – SEX – between two people who wanted and satisfied each other. Not a means of disgusting me. Not what you had intended.

A whore can remain distant, it is a job to her. I've seen enough prostitutes to know. And I will admit that over the years I have been with a few. They do the deed with their bodies but their minds are elsewhere, you can see it in their eyes.

The look in your eyes was different. You wanted me. You could not keep up the pretence. You could not use it as a means of pushing me away. Besides, I wanted you, too. I cannot deny it. I will also admit that at first, I compared you with Cecilia. But now she means absolutely nothing to me. She has no figure, a broom handle has more curves than she does. Not like your body. I wanted to see your body, Isobel. Not through a doctor's eyes but a man's. And a selfish one that day. I wanted to see your body, kiss your body, touch your body. And you allowed me to use your body but you also used my body. You took great pleasure from it. I have the bruises, the bites, and the scratches to prove it. And whores do not do that unless paid to.

I love you, Isobel, and I want you to marry me. I will never be rich but I will make sure that I earn enough for us to live comfortably. If you love me the way I love you, which I am sure you do, then we will be happy here. Dr and Mrs Fitzgerald of Brown Street. How does that sound to you?

Please reply or visit as usual tomorrow afternoon. I want a response.

Will

He put his pen down and blew out his cheeks. Good God, he had never been so frank with a woman before. He had cramp in his side and he stood up and stretched. Without reading the letter through again, he blotted and folded it, put it in an envelope, addressed it and went out to post it.

Isobel did not call on Wednesday afternoon and, on Friday, his letter was returned unopened with Isobel's address crossed out and his address written beside it in her handwriting. He swore under his breath. He would deliver it personally after making house calls.

Just before one o'clock, Isobel was called by Bridget – her replacement as parlourmaid – to the areaway door. Her heart pounded when she found Will waiting outside at the bottom of the steps.

"Can you not read?" she demanded in a low voice.

"I could ask you the very same question," he replied, taking a letter out of his frock coat's inside pocket. "This is the most frank and personal letter I have ever written, so could you please be civil and read it?"

He held the letter out to her. It was the one she had returned unopened the previous day.

"Very well." She took it. "Anything else, Dr Fitzgerald?" she asked crisply.

A pained expression came into his eyes and she had to quickly swallow an apology.

"No," he said quietly. He put on his hat and raised it to her. "Good afternoon."

She brought the letter upstairs to her room, sat on the bed, and read it. Then she read it again. And again. When she finally put it down, she stood in front of the dressing table mirror and undid her dress buttons. There were still faint marks on her neck, chest, and breasts. She re-did the buttons and sighed.

He was right, of course. She had wanted to shock and disgust him. And she had failed miserably. The way he had touched her, held her, stroked her, licked her, kissed her – earning responses she had only given once before. With

James. But once James had got what he wanted he was off. Not so Will Fitzgerald. Even that very first night in the brothel and, despite him being very drunk, there had been something about him. The way he had kissed the entire length of her scar and thrusted into her with a soothing rhythm, making her moan, and come... She picked up the letter again. He had been with prostitutes before. Did it shock her? A year ago it would have. Things like that were simply not mentioned. But now? She just smiled wryly.

He had compared her body with Cecilia's. Not that he would have seen much of Cecilia's body, of course. A cold fish, Claire had called her and, besides, ladies like Cecilia went to their marriage bed untouched virgins.

Will Fitzgerald was demanding and stubborn. He said he loved her. He said he wanted to marry her. But could she trust him? He had got over Cecilia soon enough, so how could she be sure this wasn't just another bout of lust on his part?

She quickly lifted her notepaper, pen, and ink out of the centre drawer of the dressing table. She sat down on the stool, and put that down at the beginning of her response to his letter, and continued with:

Just how many women have you been in love with? How can I be sure that in another few months you won't have fallen head over heels in love with someone else? I cannot be sure. I want to be sure. I want to believe you love me but I need to be sure your love for me will not fade and all that remains is your shame at what I have been. Again, I cannot be sure. I have been so hurt in the past that I could not bear for it to happen to me again.

You have proposed to me, of which I am very flattered, but I will neither accept nor decline your proposal. I propose that we do not visit each other for a few months and see how we both feel then. You may write to me if you wish, but I will not be visiting Brown Street on Wednesdays for the foreseeable future. A testing, if you like, of those sayings such as 'absence makes the heart grow fonder' or 'out of sight, out of mind'. We shall see in a few months which is which.

>   *Sincerely yours,*
>   *Isobel Stevens*

She sealed the envelope, wrote Will's name and address on it, then stuck on a stamp. Before she could change her mind, she got permission from Mr Johnston and went straight out to post it.

When Will picked up the letter from the front door mat on Monday morning and saw Isobel's handwriting, he tore the envelope open and pulled out the letter. How many women had he been in love with? He grimaced. How many months were a few months? He sighed. At least they could write to each other. At least she had retreated from completely cutting him off. He slid the letter back into the envelope and stretched.

"Everything all right?" Mrs Bell asked from the kitchen door.

"Just a bit of cramp."

"I meant the letter," she added, nodding to it in his hands. "It's from Maisie, isn't it? I don't want to pry but it's clear to see how her letters affect you."

Will went into the kitchen and sat at the table. It was time he told her the truth.

"Maisie's real name is Isobel," he said and stood the letter up against the pot of marmalade. "Isobel Stevens."

Mrs Bell gave him a long, suspicious look, before pulling a chair out from the table and sitting down opposite him.

"Go on."

"Isobel is from Co Galway," he explained. "The daughter of a Church of Ireland clergyman. She was seduced by a neighbour's son and fell pregnant. Her father whipped her and threw her out. She came to Dublin and shortly afterwards I attended to her when she miscarried."

"She was one of your patients?" Mrs Bell exclaimed, and he spread his hands helplessly, hating having to lie to her.

"Very briefly, and I did not expect to see her again. But when I went to the Harveys' dinner party, there she was – now a parlourmaid called Maisie Byrne. She managed to slip a letter into my overcoat pocket thanking me for all I had done for her and we began to correspond. I have never become romantically involved with a patient and Isobel was no longer a patient when we did."

"And now?" Mrs Bell asked. "Are you still romantically involved?"

"Matters were moving too fast – it was my fault – and Isobel won't see me for a few months but she will allow me to write to her."

Mrs Bell grunted and got up from the table. "It's better than nothing, I suppose. What am I to call her? Maisie or Isobel?"

"Isobel. Mrs Harvey's lady's maid stole jewellery from

her and when the house was searched Isobel's baptism and confirmation certificates were discovered."

"So they know she'd been lying about herself?" Mrs Bell's eyebrows shot up. "It's a wonder she wasn't dismissed."

"Mrs Harvey took pity on her and Isobel is now her lady's maid."

"Your Isobel is a very lucky girl."

"She certainly is," he replied with a smile, got to his feet, and picked up the letter. He took an ewer of warm water from her and went upstairs to wash and shave.

That evening, he sat down at the writing desk in the parlour with the last of his notepaper.

Dear Isobel,

Thank you for replying to my letter. I will comply with your wishes regarding our not visiting each other for a few months. I am confident it will result in 'absence makes the heart grow fonder' on my part.

In response to your question regarding how many women I have loved, well, there was Mary, our head house-parlourmaid, but as I was only twelve and she was at least thirty, there was not much hope for us! As for real love, adult love, there have been only two women I have loved and they are Cecilia and yourself.

There have been prostitutes in the past, as I have mentioned, but I did not love them nor was attracted to them in any way. I did not visit Sally Maher's brothel willingly. It sounds feeble but I went in order to keep my friends happy, to keep the peace. A lot of the time I feel I have little in common with the two of them anymore as it is.

How can you be sure I won't fall in love with someone else over the next few months? You cannot. You will just have to learn to trust me, as I will have to trust you.

Trust him. Isobel sighed. There were times she thought she would never be able to trust anyone ever again. Even with Will, it would be difficult but she would do as he asked and learn to.

She read the letter through again. He clearly didn't remember her commenting in the brothel that he did not want to be there. So in that, she could believe him when he said he wasn't a willing participant.

She glanced up from her bench in St Stephen's Green. How could she spend the remainder of her half-day? She could buy a book to read. Nurse a pot of tea or coffee in a café for a couple of hours. Or she could visit the National Gallery. She chose the gallery. If she had time left later on she would look for a second-hand book.

She spent close to three hours in the gallery, savouring not only the paintings but also the peace and quiet. She had about an hour before the shops closed so she made a beeline for a second-hand book shop, coming away half an hour later with *Under The Greenwood Tree* by Thomas Hardy. She then made her way back to Merrion Square to reply to Will's letter and make a start on the novel.

Will received a letter in the morning, but the handwriting was Fred's, not Isobel's. Swallowing his disappointment, he slit the envelope open with a knife and pulled out the letter.

Dear Will,

Just a note to let you know that there is a lecture on tropical diseases in Trinity College on Friday 8th October at 8 pm. Food and drink afterwards. My father and your father are both attending so I thought of you so there would be two chaps there under the age of fifty.

Whether we are to expect a malaria outbreak in the not too distant future, I don't know.

By the way, what's this I hear about you and a certain very pretty lady's maid in Merrion Square? I want to know all the details, William.

All the best,

Fred

Tropical diseases? Whatever would they think of next? Still, an evening out would do him the world of good.

On the evening of the 8th, he changed his clothes and walked to Merrion Square. Maura admitted him to number 67, telling him Dr Fitzgerald senior was upstairs and would join him shortly. She showed Will into the morning room where his mother got up from the sofa and kissed his cheek.

"I saw Isobel yesterday," she announced. "She told me the two of you had spoken and that you had decided not to visit each other for a while."

"That's right."

"Why?" his mother asked bluntly, and Will grimaced. "Were you pressurising her, Will? You were, I can see by your face. Oh, why do you do it?"

"I don't know," he mumbled. "And it was Isobel who said we should not visit each other, not me."

"In that case, she is a wise girl. Good grief, Will, with what the girl has been through, surely you realise you must be patient?"

You have no idea of all she has been though, he thought but nodded. "I do now. I can't help being the way I am."

"Well, enjoy yourself this evening," she said as the hall door opened. "Here's your father."

"New tailcoat?" Dr Fitzgerald senior asked, looking him up and down.

"Only tailcoat. Doesn't often get an airing."

"Well, you look very smart. Are we set? We'll find a cab somewhere."

"Do we really need a cab?" Will asked. "Trinity's not that far."

"I'll pay." His father smiled.

Twenty minutes later, Fred winked at him as Will sat down in an adjoining seat in the lecture hall.

"Glad you could come, Will. You don't mind this spot?" They were seated two rows from the back. "But I thought if it was really dull, we could slip out."

"I don't wish to count all the lectures we've slipped out of," Will reminded him. "But thank you for the invitation."

"So, what about this girl?"

"Afterwards." He nodded towards the front, where the lecturer was preparing to begin.

"So?" Fred asked him the moment the lecture concluded, but Will got up and they filed out of the lecture hall, making their way to a function room where a large supper was laid out.

"Will?" Fred prompted as they stood in a corner with a glass of wine each. "Come on."

Will took a sip of wine. "Her name is Isobel Stevens. She is a lady's maid."

"Yes, but is it true what they say about her?"

"Say about her?" he replied sharply. "What's being said?"

Fred shuffled uncomfortably. "She's a fallen woman and all that."

"All what?" he demanded, and Fred frowned at him. "I want to hear what is being said."

"Well, that she's a clergyman's daughter but she fell pregnant, was thrown out, she came to Dublin, her baby died and that's how she met you."

It was the official version and Will nodded. "That's right."

"Does Jerry know about her?"

"No. Why?"

"Because we're your best friends, that's why."

Will sighed then nodded to the door. "Let's get some air," he said, and Fred followed him outside. "It wasn't long after Cecilia. I wasn't looking for anyone else, but Isobel was different. She had been through so much, so she wasn't looking for anyone either, but I could talk to her like I had never been able to with Cecilia."

"How did you manage to see her?" Fred asked.

"At first we wrote. Thankfully, her half-day was Wednesday and she came to Brown Street. She even helped me with an emergency on one occasion."

"Oh?"

"A marble which got stuck in a little girl's throat," he explained. "I held the girl upside down while Isobel hit her between the shoulders."

"Good grief. So what went wrong?"

Will walked to a bench and sat down. "I didn't give her enough time to try and come to terms with what she had been through. I told her how I felt about her too soon and put pressure on her. Exactly as I had done with Cecilia."

"So what now?" Fred asked, sitting beside him. "Is it finished?"

He shook his head. "At least I don't think it is. She doesn't want us to visit each other for a while." A stab of cramp, nearer to pain, shot down his side and he winced. "Ouch."

"What?" Fred looked him up and down.

"Cramp."

"You are looking after yourself, aren't you, Will? Mrs Bell is feeding you properly?"

Will nodded. "Yes, and, yes. Thanks for asking."

"So, how long has it been since you've seen her?"

"A couple of weeks. And, yes, I do miss her."

Fred smiled sympathetically. "You will give her time, won't you?"

"Yes, of course. I'm not a complete fool."

"Good. More wine?"

The following Friday morning he received a letter from Isobel and tore open the envelope.

Dear Will,

It is late on Wednesday afternoon and I am writing this letter over a cup of coffee this time. To the café owner, I am 'the girl who writes letters in the corner'. I suspect he longs to know to whom I am writing, but that is my secret!

I have become quite a regular in the National

Gallery, too. I love being able to just stand and stare and sometimes lose myself in the paintings.

Are you busy, Will? Do write and tell me if you are. I often think of the little girl who swallowed the marble. Do you ever see her?

Last Saturday evening, Mr and Mrs Harvey attended a dinner so I had to wait up for Mrs Harvey's return. She now knows I love books and gave me permission to read in the library if I so chose. Of course I did! I explored the library from top to bottom. I even found a couple of Mr Harvey's private photographs which, perhaps, I should not have seen. Compared to what I have seen and done, they were quite tame, but I wonder what would be Mrs Harvey's response if she saw them!

I also found a copy of this year's Church of Ireland Directory. My father is still residing in Ballybeg but is now a canon. I expect he will become bishop before long. If only I knew whether Mother and Alfie are both well.

I hope you are keeping well yourself, Will.

Write soon.

Sincerely yours,

Isobel Stevens

She's lonely but won't admit it. Will put the letter down and sighed.

"From Isobel?" Mrs Bell asked although Will knew she recognised Isobel's handwriting by now.

"Yes. She's lonely but I must do as she wishes." He got up from the kitchen table, winced, and massaged his side. "I'll see you later, Mrs Bell."

A dart of pain shot down his side as he strode along Brown Street on his way to begin house calls. He moved his medical bag from one hand to the other and massaged his side again. This was becoming a damned nuisance.

So Jim Harvey had dirty photographs. *Compared to what I have seen and done they were quite tame,* Isobel had written. But what to her was tame? Never mind Mrs Harvey, would he be shocked if he saw them? Had Isobel ever been photographed? He sincerely hoped not. Not just that he never wanted another man's hands on her ever again, whether on a photograph or not, but what if they fell into the wrong hands? He grimaced and returned the medical bag to his other hand.

When Mary, the kitchenmaid, passed her a hand-delivered letter that evening and she saw it was from Will, Isobel felt an acute pang of fear. Was there something wrong? She went upstairs to the library, where she was being allowed to wait for Mr and Mrs Harvey's return from a dinner party, almost tearing the envelope open.

> *Dear Isobel,*
>
> *This could not wait for the post. I need to ask you whether you have ever had photographs taken of yourself which are similar to those you found belonging to Jim Harvey?*
>
> *Forgive me if I am over-reacting but I need to know. My messenger, Jimmy, will be waiting outside number 68 for your reply. A yes or no will do.*

There were another two sheets of notepaper but she folded the entire letter, put it in her pocket and went downstairs to the front door, opening it quietly.

"Jimmy?"

"Yes, Miss?" The boy was sitting on the areaway steps in the dark but got up and stood on the front door steps in the light from the gas lamps in the hall.

"Jimmy, you can tell Dr Fitzgerald, no."

"No?" He both looked and sounded disappointed and she smiled.

"In this case, no, is very good."

"I'm glad to hear that, Miss. Dr Fitzgerald was very worried."

"Was he? Do you live in Brown Street?"

He shook his head. "No, Miss. Pimlico. Mammy and me live next door to Mrs Bell."

"I see. Well, you had better go and give Dr Fitzgerald my answer. Thank you, Jimmy."

"Goodnight, Miss."

She returned to the library, taking the letter from her pocket, and read on.

You deem these photographs tame, but how would you have reacted to them a year ago?

She just smiled wryly.

I have to confess that up to today I had never seen photographs of this kind and I was curious. So I made some discreet enquiries and I was directed to a photographer's studio on the north side of the city where I was shown some examples ranging from what even I would consider tame to photographs of a most disgusting kind. The photographer was most amused at my reaction and asked me whether I had come straight from a monastery. I did not share his amusement.

And neither did she. How dare the photographer laugh at Will. Compared to the vast majority of the men who had passed through her bedroom at the brothel, Will had been gentle, kind, and considerate.

I can only hope your answer is no. That other men could be looking at your body makes me feel ill because, as a doctor, I view your body as a unique machine and, as a man, I deem you far too beautiful to serve as cheap satisfaction for other men.

If your answer is yes, then, I am afraid I will have to break our agreement and ask that we meet.

I look forward to hearing your answer.

Will Fitzgerald

She returned the letter to her pocket, lit a small oil lamp, then hurried up the stairs to her bedroom to fetch her pen, notepaper, and ink. She sat at the leather-topped desk in the library and began her reply.

Dear Will,

Oh, Will, why could you not have waited for my answer instead of seeing such things? Sally Maher asked me to pose for photographs on two occasions but I pretended I was ill. I could never do something like that, Will. At least when I was in the brothel the deed was over quite quickly. A photograph is a lasting testament to it all.

I know for a fact that Maggie from Sally's brothel has posed for photographs because she showed them to me. Poor Maggie would do anything, and I mean anything, for money. Some of the photographs you would call disturbing, but I strongly suspect that the extra payments were insurance for when she can no longer work.

The one and only time I have lured a man into sex was that afternoon in Brown Street with you. I was trying to disgust you but we both know I failed dismally. I was ashamed afterwards because I felt as if I had whored myself again but I know now I could not have done that with any other man but you, yet it frightens me.

It frightens me because of what I have been. Should I have such desires, or am I damaged because of what I have been? An unmarried woman should not want men sexually. But I do. I wanted you that afternoon and I still do. You did satisfy me, Will, more than satisfied me. But what if it is not always the case? That terrifies me.

A year ago I would have been horrified. Horrified not just at seeing the photographs but also at the feelings I have. Then, I knew absolutely nothing about men or their desires and passions. I have since asked myself is such complete ignorance a good thing? My answer is both yes and no.

How many new wives are terrified of their wedding night, whether they love their new husband or not? Why are men congratulated when they sow their wild oats while women are castigated as being whores if they do the same thing? Will men and women always be so unequal?

Perhaps I should put any thoughts of marriage out of my head and abstain altogether.

Isobel Stevens

She got up and walked around the library. If only she could talk to Mrs Harvey, but that was out of the question. She stopped and glanced back at the letter on the desk. Was she putting poor Will under pressure to stop her from straying, as he had put it? Probably, but who else could she talk to?

Thank goodness. Will closed the front door after receiving Isobel's message via Jimmy. Thank goodness, thank goodness, thank goodness. He went to the stairs and climbed the first few steps but stopped and gasped with shock at the now excruciating pain in his side. What on earth was this? He felt a cold sweat break out on his forehead and he was forced to sit on the stairs, gripping his small oil lamp with both hands. Suddenly his stomach heaved and he had to ignore the pain and leap from the stairs, run along the hall, and into the kitchen.

The oil lamp went onto the table with a bang and he only just made it to the sink in time. He retched and retched and even when no more vomit would come up the retching just would not stop. He could hardly stand for the pain in his side and he had to hold onto the sink for dear life. What in God's Name was wrong with him?

He forced himself to think rationally. Cramp followed by pain in his side for some weeks. Now nausea. Intense pain and nausea. Christ, he had typhlitis! His cecum, part of the large intestine was inflamed. He needed his father. He needed a surgeon. He needed to get to Merrion Square somehow.

He pushed himself away from the sink, still retching. Each retch would send another agonising stab of pain down his side. By the time he reached the front door he was shaking violently. Or was he shivering? One second he was hot, the next freezing. He pulled his overcoat on over his morning coat and opened and closed the door behind him. On the step, he began to panic. In this state, he would never walk all the way to Merrion Square. He needed a cab – a cart – anything.

He staggered along the dimly-lit street like a drunkard, turned right and right again onto Cork Street. On Cork Street, he began to retch uncontrollably, and he sank to his knees in despair.

"That you, Doctor?" He heard a female voice but could barely raise his head. "Doctor, what is it?" It was young Elizabeth Millar. Her brother, George, was a cabman and lived locally. "Dr Fitzgerald?" She crouched down beside him and gently tilted his head up. "Tell me?"

He pulled air into his lungs. "I urgently need to get to number 67 Merrion Square. To my father. I'm ill. It's an emergency."

"George?" She rose and raced along the pavement away from him. "George, quickly. It's Dr Fitzgerald, he's ill."

"What?" He heard the doubt and confusion in her brother's voice as if it were a medical impossibility for a doctor to fall ill. "Where?"

"Down there at the corner. Get the cab, he needs to get to 67 Merrion Square to his father. Now, George."

Will heard the horse and cab rattle towards him and groaned with relief.

Elizabeth ran back to him. "Let me help you inside," she said, and he cried out with pain as he slowly rose to his feet. "You'll have to help me, George, I can't lift him in on my own." He was half pushed, half pulled into the cab, and he moaned. "Should I come with you, Doctor?" she asked, sitting beside him.

"No, there's nothing you can do, but thank you."

Elizabeth nodded and jumped out of the cab. "Number 67 Merrion Square, George, hurry."

And George Millar did hurry. Will was thrown around the cab as it careered around corners, people having to leap out of its way, shouting and swearing at them. George Millar just kept on going. He might kill him in the process but George Millar was going to get Will to Merrion Square somehow.

The Harveys' arrived home from the dinner party, early for them, at half past eleven.

"A dreadful occasion," was Mrs Harvey's only comment as Isobel helped her undress.

Before going to bed, Isobel went downstairs to the kitchen to heat some milk on the still warm range for herself. To her surprise, she found Claire still up and mending a stocking beside the fire in the servants' hall. Claire would never forgive her for Will Fitzgerald and was only just being civil towards her but halfway across the kitchen Isobel stopped and went back to the door.

"Would you like some warm milk?"

"No, thank you," came the crisp reply.

Isobel shrugged and proceeded on to the larder. Emerging with the jug of milk, she saw Claire through the serving hatch stop sewing, look up and frown. She put the jug on the table then listened, hearing something rattling out on the street.

"What's that?"

"I'm not sure." Claire put her stocking to one side and got up. "It sounds like a cab or a carriage but it's going like the devil."

They both went to the kitchen window and looked up at the street through the railings.

"I can't see a thing." Isobel opened the door and went outside, hearing Claire follow her. They climbed up the areaway steps and went onto the pavement as a cab hurtled towards them. The cab passed them, stopped outside number 67, and the cabman jumped down.

"Quick," he roared. "A man's ill in here."

They ran to the cab as the cabman opened the door. To Isobel's horror, Will Fitzgerald fell out, and into the gutter.

"Will." She sank to her knees beside him.

"Typhlitis," he said. She wasn't sure if he recognised her. "Inflammation of the cecum. Get my father," he added, his voice sinking to a whisper.

"Claire? Get Dr Fitzgerald senior. Tell him Will has an inflammation of the cecum. Hurry."

Claire ran up the steps and hammered with her fists on the front door. It was an age before it was answered. Claire pushed whoever it was back inside and the door was slammed shut.

Isobel cradled Will's head in her lap as his eyes closed. The cecum? Where was that? Where ever it was, it meant an operation, didn't it?

"Will he be all right?" The cabman stood anxiously beside them while the poor horse wheezed and panted a short distance away.

"I don't know. I think he needs an operation."

"An operation?" The man's hat came off.

"He won't die."

The Fitzgeralds' front door opened, Will's father ran down the steps doing up the buttons of a waistcoat, and Claire ran out behind him.

"Will told me he has typh-something – an inflammation of the cecum," Isobel told him.

"Typhlitis." Dr Fitzgerald senior nodded then looked around for the cabman. "Help me carry him inside. Take his ankles."

Will was carried into the house and she got to her feet. Claire stood beside her, wringing her hands.

"What can we do?"

"I don't know," Isobel replied. "I'm going inside," she decided and followed them.

"Along here," John Fitzgerald instructed the cabman, and Will was carried along the hall, into the breakfast room and placed on the table. "Thank you. Now I need you to go to number 1 Ely Place Upper and fetch Duncan Simpson and his son, Fred. Tell them it is typhlitis – that it's an emergency. Ty-phil-itis. Got that? Hurry, man."

The cabman pushed past her and ran towards the front door.

"Is there anything I can do?" she asked.

Will's father shook his head. "I've never been afraid to perform an operation before. But this is my son and Duncan is the best surgeon I know."

"Could Will die?" she asked, despite herself.

Dr Fitzgerald senior opened his mouth, closed it, then opened it again. "I won't lie to you, Isobel. There is a very poor prognosis but, as I said, Duncan is the best surgeon I know."

"John?" They heard his wife's anxious voice in the hall.

"Could you stay with Will, please, while I speak with her?" he asked, Isobel nodded, and he hurried out of the room to Mrs Fitzgerald.

Isobel walked slowly across the breakfast room to Will. His unruly dark hair was stuck to his forehead and she smoothed it away. "Don't you dare die, Will Fitzgerald," she whispered shakily, bending and kissing his forehead. "Just don't you dare."

"There is something you can do for me, Isobel." Dr Fitzgerald senior returned a few minutes later. "Would you mind sitting with my wife? It could be a long wait."

"Yes, of course."

"He'll be in good hands, Isobel."

She nodded, turned, and left the room. About to knock and go into the morning room, the front door opened and two tall men came in, each carrying two medical bags. The first man had a moustache and was Fred Simpson. The second older and bearded man had to be his father but she stared at him in consternation. This was Duncan Simpson? In the brothel, he had been known as Dr Samuels. Thankfully, neither man looked at her as they passed and she knocked and went into the morning room.

"John?" Mrs Fitzgerald rose from an armchair, her brown hair in a long plait, and wearing a white cotton nightdress with a white woollen shawl around her shoulders. "Oh, Isobel."

"I was asked to…"

"Keep an eye on me?"

"No. Just to sit with you."

"I know. I'm sorry." Mrs Fitzgerald exhaled an uneven sigh. "Was that Duncan and Frederick Simpson just now?"

"Yes."

"What on earth happened?"

"I had waited up for Mrs Harvey – she and Mr Harvey had been at a dinner party. I'd gone downstairs to the kitchen to warm some milk and I heard the cab coming. It was very noisy because it was going so fast. I went outside and the cabman opened the door and Will fell out." She shuddered at the memory.

"Trust Will to leave it until it's an emergency. Please, sit down."

"Thank you." Isobel sat in an armchair opposite her.

"As a child, he was rarely ill."

"Oh."

"I'm sorry, would you like some tea?"

Isobel glanced around the room and spotted a clock on the mantelpiece. It was midnight and most of the servants would have gone to bed. "Thank you, no."

"Something stronger? I think I need a brandy."

"Yes, please," she replied, and Mrs Fitzgerald went to three decanters on a tray on a corner table. She lifted the cap off one of the decanters but almost let it fall and Isobel rushed across the room to her. "Let me."

"Oh… I… thank you." The cap was passed to her. "See Will, there." Mrs Fitzgerald pointed to a number of photographs on the writing desk before picking one up. "This is his first photographic portrait. It's when he left the Wesleyan Connexional School. It's now called Wesley College." Isobel put the cap down and took the photograph from her. At eighteen, Will had been very much still a boy. "And this is when he graduated from Trinity College."

Isobel took the second photograph and couldn't help but smile. This was the Will she knew, albeit with a rather arrogant smile, but that could just have been pride at qualifying as a doctor. Or, as Mrs Harvey had told her, it was his time in Brown Street which had taken away the arrogance leaving him the good man he was today. The smile quickly turned to tears and she put the two photographs down with a crash and covered her face.

"You love him, don't you?" Mrs Fitzgerald asked softly, and she nodded. "Then, why keep him at arm's length?"

"Because I'm frightened."

"Of what? Not of him, surely?"

"No, of me," she replied. "I've been hurt so much in the past that if he fell out of love with me, like he did with Cecilia, I don't think I could stand it."

"Cecilia threw him over and hurt him deeply. If you were to completely reject him now…"

"Mrs Fitzgerald, please."

"If he survives this operation and, if you love him, marry him." Mrs Fitzgerald smiled. "Be a good wife to him and have lots of children. Make him happy, unless you think that he could not make you happy, that you could not go and live in Brown Street?"

"He could make me very happy and I would be delighted to live there with him."

"Then, marry him. Shall we have those brandies now?"

Isobel poured two helpings of brandy and passed a glass to Mrs Fitzgerald. The older woman's hand shook as she raised the glass to her lips.

"Why don't you sit down?" Isobel suggested.

"Yes, thank you." Mrs Fitzgerald went back to her armchair. "Do you follow current events at all, Isobel?"

"I try to follow the tenant and landlord agitation in the west of Ireland and I read Mr Johnston's *Irish Times* when I get the chance," she replied and took a sip of brandy. "But I don't think he really approves of women reading newspapers – or discussing politics. My father certainly didn't allow my mother or I to read his newspapers, or to mention Mr Parnell and the Home Rulers, or the Land League."

"Your father?"

"Yes. He was very strict."

"You do not miss him?"

She shook her head. "No, but I miss my mother and brother very much and I hope they are safe."

"You have not been in contact with them since you left?"

"No." She took another sip of brandy.

"So your mother does not know where you are, or even if you are still alive?"

"No. But as far as my father is concerned I am dead. That is why I have not contacted her because she would not be able to keep it from him and after what he did to me—" She stopped abruptly and took a gulp of brandy which made her cough. "I'm sorry."

"After what he did to you?" Mrs Fitzgerald frowned.

"Telling me I was dead to him and throwing me out."

"I see. I'm sorry, Isobel. You've been very hard done by."

She shrugged. "He had spent a fortune on my education. I became pregnant. It ended any hope of his securing a good marriage for me."

"How would he view Will?" his mother asked.

She smiled wryly. "As being too good for me now."

"Well, that is nonsense."

"My father does not have a very high opinion of women," she said quietly and lifted the glass to her lips again.

The time passed excruciatingly slowly until both women heard a door close at just after four o'clock. They got up as the morning room door opened and Mrs Fitzgerald reached for Isobel's hand. It was as cold as her own. John Fitzgerald closed the door. He looked exhausted. Then he smiled.

"Will's vermiform appendix, which is located off the cecum – here," Fitzgerald laid the palm of his hand over his lower right side, "was inflamed. Duncan has successfully removed it and Will is going to make a full recovery."

His wife burst into tears of relief and rushed to her husband. Isobel stood marooned beside the armchair unable to move. Will is going to be fine, she told herself. Multicoloured dots began to dance in front of her eyes and she raised a hand to her forehead before everything went black.

She came to slowly. She was being carried in someone's arms and she could hear a voice.

"In here, John." It was Mrs Fitzgerald speaking.

She was lain down on a bed before she drifted off again.

Her next conscious moments were ones of hearing Dr Fitzgerald senior's shocked voice.

"Good grief, the girl's bleeding. Fetch me a bowl of warm water, Sarah."

The next involved someone examining her 'down below' as her mother had quaintly called the region.

"Well?" Mrs Fitzgerald was asking urgently. "Is it her monthly or not?"

"This bleeding is too heavy for her monthly. The girl's having a miscarriage, Sarah."

"She never mentioned being pregnant?"

"She might not have known. Pull down the bedcovers and lay out those towels while I lift her into the bed." She was picked up and laid down again. "Help me with her clothes. Do you have a nightdress for her?"

"Yes, I have. Oh, John, was the child Will's?"

"Who knows?" he answered wearily. "I'll hold her, you take the dress off."

Layer by layer, her clothes were removed until Isobel felt the chilly air of the bedroom on her skin.

"Wait a moment with the nightdress, Sarah." Fitzgerald sounded puzzled. "Good God, look at her back."

Isobel heard a sharp intake of breath. "But it goes right down from her shoulder to her waist." Poor Mrs Fitzgerald sounded horrified. "What on earth did that... oh."

"What?"

"Something she said earlier about what her father did to her... Her father did this, John."

"But a stick wouldn't do this."

"No," his wife replied. "But a whip would."

"A whip?"

"I once saw a horse that had been severely whipped. It had long raised scars like this. Oh, John, her father whipped her."

"Good God." Isobel felt fingers on her back. "It's completely healed but it's not too old a scar. You can put the nightdress on her now, Sarah."

She was helped into the nightdress, lain down again, and the covers pulled over her.

"What now?" Mrs Fitzgerald asked.

"Let nature take its course and let her sleep. She's exhausted."

"Don't be too hard on her, John. With what she's been through…"

"But she got herself pregnant again, Sarah. As if the first time wasn't lesson enough for her."

"I know. When do we tell her?"

"I'll see how she is in the morning. And, Sarah?" he added sharply.

"Yes?"

"Will must not know she is here. Nor of what has happened. Not until we know whether it was his child."

"Yes, John."

When Isobel woke, her head felt much less muddled. The previous night almost seemed like a dream.

"Isobel?" She jumped as Mrs Fitzgerald rose from a chair beside the bed. "How do you feel?"

"Rather strange," she murmured. "But relieved about Will."

"Good." Mrs Fitzgerald smoothed down the bedcovers. "Are you hungry?"

"A little. What happened to me?"

"You fainted."

"Where is Will? How is he?"

"He is in his old bedroom and woke about an hour ago. He is a little groggy but that will soon pass." His mother smiled. "Would you like some toast and Apricot marmalade?"

"But what time is it? I must get up. Mrs Harvey—"

"It's a quarter past eight in the morning and Mrs Harvey has been told where you are. Toast and marmalade?"

"Yes, please," she replied, and Mrs Fitzgerald left the bedroom.

A few moments later there was a knock at the door and Will's father came in.

"How do you feel this morning?" he asked, sitting down in the chair his wife had just vacated.

"Rather tired."

"Last night you fainted, Isobel," he told her. "Have you been feeling faint recently?"

She shook her head. She felt fine, apart from a little cramping in her stomach. "I've never fainted before in my life."

"I see. Isobel, I have some news for you."

Her heart pounded. "Is it Will?"

"Will is fine," his father assured her. "He will make a full recovery. No, it is you, Isobel."

"Me?"

"Last night when you were brought up here I noticed you were bleeding."

"Bleeding?"

"There is no easy way to say this," he went on. "Isobel, you are having a miscarriage. You are losing a child."

She stared at him, her thoughts returning to the snatches of conversation she had heard last night and the unusual sensations she could feel in her stomach. "A child?"

"Yes. You had not known?"

"No," she whispered.

"Was it Will's?" his father asked and she nodded. "Are you sure?"

"Yes."

"You wouldn't lie to me, would you, Isobel?" he added.

"No."

"So when was it that you and Will had sexual intercourse?"

"The beginning of last month," she replied.

"Last month? And if I ask Will?"

"He will tell you exactly the same. I had no idea I was pregnant. Why did it happen?" she asked.

"It could be any number of reasons. You do know I will have to tell Mrs Harvey you are miscarrying?"

Her heart sank. "Why?"

"Why?" Fitzgerald gave her such a scathing look that she flinched. "Because Mrs Harvey is your employer and she needs to know that her lady's maid led my son on while behind his back she was lifting her skirts to any footman who would have her."

"But – but," she stammered. "Dr Fitzgerald, I promise you the child was Will's—"

"And, sadly, I believe you. But I will not have it known that Will fathered a child with a servant already known to be a fallen woman. You are a trollop, Isobel," he said, his voice rising, and she cowered away from him. "And you always will be."

Isobel watched helplessly as he left the bedroom before covering her face with her hands and bursting into tears.

An hour later, Mrs Harvey came in and sat by the bed. Isobel's shoulders slumped when she saw her employer's grave expression.

"If it had been at any other time, I might have been able

to persuade John not to tell my husband, but he was also in the breakfast room and is furious. I am so sorry, Isobel, but you are the second of our maids to fall pregnant by a footman and my husband insists I dismiss you without a character reference."

Isobel nodded. It had been too much to hope she would be given another chance or at least a reference.

"I promise I will cause you, Mr Harvey, and the Fitzgeralds' the least possible embarrassment. I will collect my belongings and leave number 68 this afternoon. Thank you for everything you have done for me, Mrs Harvey."

"This afternoon?" Mrs Harvey echoed. "John said you needed a couple of days rest?"

"I really need to find myself a new position—"

"Which you can do on Monday. Rest here while you can, Isobel."

Will pulled up his nightshirt and peered curiously at the stitches in his side. He was impressed, they were very neat. According to his father, he had arrived in the nick of time. The vermiform appendix had been on the point of rupture. His right shoulder ached, thanks to his having fallen heavily out of the cab, but thank goodness for George Millar. What followed was hazy but he knew Isobel had cradled his head in her lap just before he passed out. Would Mrs Harvey allow her to come to see him? More to the point, would his father allow her to come to see him?

The bedroom door opened and his mother came in. "How do you feel?"

"Sore, but my head is a lot clearer. Would it be possible for Isobel to come and see me?"

His mother looked troubled. "Isobel? I'll have to ask your father."

"Is everything all right?"

"Fine. I'm just a little tired, that's all."

Reaching out, he squeezed her hand. "Mother, you were up all night, you must be exhausted. Go to your bedroom and lie down – doctor's orders."

All of a sudden she appeared close to tears. "We thought we were going to lose you," she whispered. "Poor Isobel—" She stopped abruptly.

"Isobel?" he asked. "She was here?"

Mrs Fitzgerald nodded. "Your father and the cabman carried you to the breakfast room and Isobel followed. Your father asked her to sit with me. We sat in the morning room until your father came in just after four o'clock and told us you were going to recover."

"I see."

"Would you like a cup of tea?" she asked brightly.

"Yes, please."

His mother went out and he felt comforted by the fact that Isobel had stayed.

His father then opened the door and came in. "How's the patient? Any discomfort from the stitches?"

"Yes, but that is to be expected. Would it be possible to speak to Isobel?"

"Why?"

"To thank her for staying with Mother last night."

"I'll see," his father replied, irritating Will. He wasn't ten years old anymore.

"What is happening?" he demanded.

"I beg your pardon?"

"Father, I've had my vermiform appendix removed, not my brain. There is something Mother and you aren't telling me. What is it?"

"Not now."

"Yes, now," he snapped.

His father rolled his eyes. "All right. Have you and Isobel had sexual intercourse?"

Will stared at his father in complete astonishment. "I beg your pardon?" he replied, trying to control a hot flush.

"You heard me, Will. Have you?"

His mind raced. His father couldn't have found out about Isobel and the brothel. He couldn't have. "Father—"

"Just answer the question. Have you had sexual intercourse with Isobel Stevens in the last two months?"

Will's mind immediately went back to the afternoon in Brown Street. How on earth did his father know about it? "Yes, I have," he replied quietly.

"When?"

"The beginning of last month. Why?"

His father sighed. "When I went to tell your mother and Isobel that the operation had been a success, Isobel fainted. I carried her upstairs and your mother and I undressed her. It was then I noticed the bleeding."

"Bleeding?" he asked stupidly.

"Isobel is having a miscarriage, Will."

"Miscarriage." He stared at his hands, frowning as he watched them shake. Slowly he raised his head. "Where is she now?"

"In the guest room."

"How is she?"

"In shock. She claims not to have known she was

pregnant. I have to ask you this, Will. Was the child yours?"

"What?" he croaked. "Of course it was. How dare you—"

"Will, if you burst those stitches…" his father said calmly and Will swore. "I had to ask."

"The child was mine. There was no-one else."

"I see."

"No, you don't," he snapped. "To you, she's a fallen woman and will always be a fallen woman."

"Will, she got herself pregnant for the second time."

"Then, blame me for that. The child was mine. Can I see her?" he asked.

"No."

"Why?"

"You need to rest…" His father tailed off again, hearing a voice calling him. He went out onto the landing and Will swore once more. A few moments later, he heard his father speaking to someone. "Search the house. If she's not here, go next door."

"What is it?" Will asked anxiously as his father returned.

His father grimaced. "Isobel's not in the guest room."

"What?" Will threw back the covers. "I need to look for her."

"Will, no." His father grabbed his shoulders. "Stay in bed. You're in no fit state. The house is being searched. If she's not here, then we will try next door. We will find her."

Will swore for the third time as his father closed the door behind him.

Chapter Six

For the second time, Isobel stood in front of Mr Johnston as he glared at her.

"How could you be so foolish? Mrs Black and I have had no complaints from Mrs Harvey regarding your work. You have disgraced both yourself and the household and…" He tailed off and sighed. "What will you do now?"

"I don't know. May I go and pack, Mr Johnston?"

"Yes. Come back here when you're finished."

She climbed the stairs to her room for the last time and sat on the bed. She felt weary but that was thanks to a paltry four hours sleep, not just the fact she was in the process of miscarrying Will Fitzgerald's child. She slid off the bed, went to the dressing table, and reached for the dainty nail scissors Edith had left behind. Lifting up the towel from beside the ewer and bowl, she cut it into narrow strips and placed two strips in her drawers to absorb the discharge. It took her less than five minutes to pack her belongings in her carpet bag, placing Will's letters carefully between the layers of clothing. The nail scissors, and two more towels from Claire and Bridget's bedroom, she placed on top. She left the books she had bought on the window sill.

Putting on her coat and hat, she returned to the butler's pantry where Mr Johnston passed her a small package.

"Some ham sandwiches for you from Mrs Gordon."

"Thank you."

"Will you try and get a position in the same way you got yours here?" he asked.

"By lying, you mean? Only if it's necessary. I will try and get some shop work."

"I can only wish you good luck, Isobel," he said.

"Thank you, Mr Johnston, you've been very kind."

She went out through the silent servants' hall, climbed the areaway steps, and walked away in the direction of the city centre.

Will turned as the bedroom door opened again and his father came in. Dr Fitzgerald senior's expression was sombre and Will's heart sank.

"Isobel left number 68 half an hour ago," his father told him. "Johnston doesn't know where she was going. All she said was that she would try for some shop work."

"But why leave altogether?" Will cried.

"She's clearly not thinking straight. I'm sorry, Will, I should have watched her more closely but she seemed so calm."

"She is utterly shocked. She's losing our child and no-one is being in the least bit sympathetic." He threw back the bedcovers. "I have to go and look for her."

"No, absolutely not." His father forced him back into the bed. "You are recovering from an emergency operation and I will not allow you to traipse up and down Grafton Street looking for her. I'm sorry, Will, but you are in no fit state."

Will swore viciously and his father's eyebrows rose. "I won't ask where you picked up that language from."

"Don't you dare criticise my language. What did you say to her?" he asked harshly. His father looked away and Will exhaled a shaky breath. "You drove her away."

His father turned back. "No, I did not."

"Yes, you did. You have never approved of her and you never will—"

"She's nothing more than a trollop. You can do so much better—"

"Did you call her a trollop?" Will demanded. "Did you?"

"Yes, I did," his father replied, and Will rolled his eyes.

"Isobel's father also called her a trollop after he stripped her, whipped her, and threw her out of the house – pregnant," he informed his father, who winced. "I love Isobel, and as soon as I am in a fit state, I will look for her, and when I find her I will marry her. In the meantime, could you bring me some notepaper, ink, and a pen? I need to write to Mrs Bell."

"You're not going to get her to go to Grafton Street, surely?"

"No, of course not," he retorted. "But the boy who is cannot read."

His father sighed. "Very well."

Within half an hour, a letter and three shillings – in case Jimmy needed to bribe someone for information – was on its way to either Brown Street or Mrs Bell's home, depending on where she had gone when she hadn't found him or a note at home that morning. Will lay back on the pillows and swore yet again. He hated feeling so absolutely helpless.

With no experience, Isobel knew she would have great difficulty in finding a position as a shop girl, so she would have to forge another character reference. Kneeling down at a bench in St Stephen's Green, she lifted a sheet of notepaper and an envelope, and a pen and a bottle of ink out of her carpet bag. Closing her eyes for a moment, in an effort to think clearly, she opened the bottle, dipped the nib into the ink, and wrote:

> *Reynolds General Merchants & Drapery Warehouse*
> *Ballybeg*
> *Co Galway*
>
> *To Whom It May Concern:*
> *Constance Maguire was a drapery assistant in my establishment from June 1876 to July 1880. During that time she proved to be a hard worker, good timekeeper and was always polite, tidy, courteous, and willing.*
> *I would have no hesitation in recommending Constance Maguire for any future drapery assistant position she may apply for.*
> *Peter Reynolds (Proprietor)*

Connie Byrne, Maisie's eldest sister, worked for ten years in Reynolds Drapery Warehouse in Ballybeg village. Connie left when she married Cornelius Maguire in 1878, and they emigrated to Australia a few months later. The Byrne surname couldn't be used a second time, so Maguire would have to do.

Isobel returned the bottle and pen to the carpet bag while waiting for the ink to dry. She then folded the reference and placed it in the envelope. She groaned as she got to her feet but sat on the bench and pinched colour into her cheeks before getting up and walking to Grafton Street.

"So you only have experience of country people's clothing?" she was asked umpteen times in one form or another once the character reference was read. "The customers in this establishment are considerably more discerning."

"I have experience of shirts and suits, hats, dresses, and gloves and I'm willing to learn."

"I'm sure you are, but I need someone who already has experience of a better class of customer."

Furious at herself for not using the name of a linen and woollen drapers in Cheltenham she frequented while at school, she decided to set her sights a little lower. She turned away from Grafton Street, acutely aware it was now late Saturday afternoon and the shops would soon be closing. Passing a photographer's studio, she turned back and went inside.

"I used to be a lady's maid," she announced, shoving the reference into her coat pocket. "I was wondering whether you needed someone to help with ladies clothes before they are photographed?"

"You used to be a lady's maid?" a tall bearded gentleman behind the wooden counter enquired. "Why did you leave? Were you dismissed?"

Isobel felt her face burn. "My employer was rather contrary. She—"

The gentleman raised an eyebrow and she couldn't help but stare. His overly long hair and his eyebrows were jet black but his beard was ginger, giving him a very odd but striking appearance.

"Was she now?" he asked. "Are you sure it wasn't your employer's husband who was the contrary one?"

"I beg your pardon?"

He laughed. "Wouldn't do what he wanted? Was that it? Or were you too eager? They don't really like that."

"Are you the photographer and do – do you need an assistant or not?" She found herself stammering.

"I am, and, possibly. But I'll tell you what I do want."

"What?" She was on the verge of walking out but asked despite herself.

"A model. You're a very pretty girl."

She rolled her eyes. "You want me to take my clothes off. Typical."

"Now did I say anything about you taking your clothes off?" he replied innocently. "But now you mention it…" He had to shout the last sentence as she walked to the door and opened it. "I pay well," he added. "Very well, if you're good."

Isobel went out and slammed the door behind her.

A reply arrived surprisingly quickly from Mrs Bell.

> *Dear Dr Fitzgerald,*
>
> *Thank you for your letter. I met young Elizabeth Millar this morning and she told me about seeing you last evening and the state you were in. I'm so releeved you are recuvring. I have put a notice on the door at Brown Street to say you are away for a cupple of days. I did not say you were ill becuse doctors are not supposed to get ill!*
>
> *Jimmy is on his way to Grafton Street with one*

shilling. If I had given him all the three shillings you sent then we would never have seen him again. Let's pray he finds Isobel.

Get well soon.

Mary Bell

Will sighed with relief. At last, something was being done.

Isobel sat down on what was becoming her spot on the grass near the lake in St Stephen's Green. She was still shaking with anger. A few deep breaths later she pulled an exasperated expression. Perhaps if she could just persuade the photographer that he needed an assistant only? She was very cold. Perhaps she should have stayed longer in bed, but Will would only have learned she was miscarrying and of her dismissal. He would have expected her to, not only go back to Brown Street with him but to marry him. She smiled bitterly. How could she marry him now his parents knew of a second pregnancy? One pregnancy had been bad enough, but two? She was a trollop. Her father had said so, and Will's father had reinforced the fact. She was not good enough for Will Fitzgerald and never ever would be.

She got to her feet and retraced her steps to the photographer's studio. She stood for a few moments on the opposite side of the street. *J. Fortuin & Son* was painted above the door. It looked respectable enough from the outside, although the window display needed urgent attention. She crossed the street and went inside.

"Well, well, well." The photographer grinned at her. "Look who's back."

"Would you consider me as an assistant only?" she asked.

"I've already got an assistant only."

"And I'll wager it's a man. You need a female assistant, too. Unless you don't get any female clients whatsoever?"

"Just what are you implying?" he demanded.

"Well, you obviously deal in erotic photographs. All aimed at men, I'd say."

"And since when have you been such an expert on the subject?"

"My former employer's husband has quite a large collection," she told him.

"Does he now?"

"And your window display." She nodded in its direction. "It's atrocious. The display should be examples of your work – your legitimate work, that is – not three dusty old cameras. Entice people – ladies – to come in and be photographed."

"Something tells me you aren't no lady."

"A lot tells me you aren't no gentleman, but I only got as far as lady's maid." She sighed. "Just tell me if I'm wasting my time?"

He laughed. "Not at all. Look." He went to the door and turned the Open/Closed sign around followed by the key in the lock. "Come with me and we'll have a chat. All right?"

She nodded and followed him through one of two doors at the back of the shop and into a small kitchen with the back door opposite her, a solid fuel range at one end, and a wooden open tread staircase at the other. A short brown-haired man in his mid-twenties was making a pot of tea at the kitchen table, which stood in the centre of the room, and nodded to her.

"My son, Lucius," the photographer told her. "Lucius, this is..?"

"Connie Maguire," she replied.

"Connie is looking for work as an assistant to our lady clients. Well, the lady clients Connie claims she can attract to the studio."

"Oh," Lucius replied simply, looking her up and down.

"Allow me to take your coat and hat, Connie."

"Thank you." She took them off and passed them over. "And your name is?"

"Johan." He hung her coat and hat on wooden hooks on the wall beside the door to the shop and she placed her carpet bag on the floor below them. "Our family was from somewhere out foreign way back. Please, sit down," he added, and she pulled a chair out from the table and sank down onto it. "So," he continued cheerfully. "Did you have sex with your former employer's husband?"

"No, I did not."

"So why were you dismissed?" he asked. "You must have had sex with someone?"

She got to her feet. "That is none of your business."

"All right. All right. Look, you're right, we do need a female assistant."

She sat down again and Lucius passed her a cup of tea.

"Sugar?" he asked.

"No, thank you."

"But I'll be blunt with you, Connie, like you were with me," Johan went on. "We do need a model, and you have a most excellent figure from what I can see of it. What we usually do is to hold our more intimate photographic sessions in the early evening, no longer than an hour or two, before it gets too cold."

"I see."

"Think about it."

"What are the wages?" she asked. "I take it I would be paid for a normal days' work as well as your more intimate photographic sessions?"

"Of course."

"And what about accommodation?" she added.

"That will be provided. There is a bedroom at the top of the house you can have."

She nodded, longing to lie down and go to sleep.

Do what Maggie from Sally Maher's brothel did, she told herself. Allow yourself to be photographed and save as much money as you can. Allow yourself to be photographed for a few weeks – perhaps a month – then leave Dublin and go somewhere no-one knows you and try and put Will behind you as well as this backward step you are taking.

"Well," she said with a little sigh. "I suppose you want to see me?"

Johan's jaw dropped. "Oh. I, er, yes – yes, please follow me to the studio."

She passed the untouched cup of tea back to Lucius and followed Johan into the shop and through the second door to the photographic studio. It was a surprisingly large, bright, and airy room with a raised area and painted backdrops leaning against a wall at one end and a dressing screen, wardrobe, and door at the other. She went behind the screen and began to undress. When she braced herself and emerged topless, Johan's dark eyes nearly popped out of his head.

"Mother of God."

"I do have a few conditions," she announced.

"Oh?"

"I want to wear a mask."

"A mask?" He frowned. "Why?"

"To add an air of mystery. Agreed?"

Johan reluctantly raised his eyes from her breasts. "Agreed."

"Good. Shall we discuss my wages now?"

Will had never known a Saturday to pass as slowly as this one. He was weary but too preoccupied to sleep. It was almost dark when he heard voices outside the bedroom and the door opened.

"Jimmy?"

"Hello, Dr Fitzgerald." The boy came into the room with his cap in his hands. "How are you?"

"On the mend, thank you. How did you get on?"

"I went to Grafton Street and asked in a load of posh shops there. Miss Isobel was in them asking for work but she weren't taken on because she'd never worked in a posh shop before. I wanted to try some other streets and shops that weren't really shops the nobs would go to but it was late and the shops were closing. Sorry, Doctor."

Will's heart sank. "Thanks for trying, Jimmy. Is there anywhere else you can think of?"

"Well." Jimmy grimaced. "Don't shout at me, will ya, for sayin' this, but…"

"What?"

"Well, if she can't get work and she's got no money for food. I know what other girls have done for money…"

Will stared at the boy. She wouldn't go back to a brothel? Surely not? "Yes. So what do you suggest?"

"Well, I know of most of the kips in the Liberties and

there's Monto o' course. I can find out about others for you?"

Will hesitated before replying. He couldn't afford to pay Jimmy. He'd had three shillings and some small change in his trouser pocket when he left Brown Street. Jimmy now had one of the shillings for bribes and Mrs Bell had the other two in reserve. "Yes, please, but it's just that I don't—"

"Will." His father stood at the bedroom door. "A shilling a day and a package of sandwiches. How does that sound, Jimmy?"

Jimmy grinned at him. "Thank you, sir."

"Good. When can you begin?"

"Now, sir. There's no point in starting in the morning when all the girls are sleeping."

"Good lad. I'll get someone to make those sandwiches for you."

Will watched his father go then turned to the boy. "What about your mother?"

"Ah, she'll be grand when I show her the money I got."

"Be careful, won't you?" Will warned him.

"I will." Jimmy nodded and went out.

A few minutes later, Will's father returned with a cup of tea for him. "He's gone."

"Thank you, Father."

"Isobel wouldn't be so stupid as to prostitute herself, would she?" his father asked, and Will could detect a hint of anxiety in his voice.

"Why?" Will demanded. "Just because she had sexual intercourse with me? Are you finally feeling guilty for driving her away?"

"Will," his father replied calmly. "All I'm trying to say is that she obviously isn't thinking clearly so just be aware of where the boy might find her."

"Where could be worse than a brothel? The bottom of the Liffey?"

"Be prepared, Will."

The bedroom at the top of the house was very small and contained only a single bed and a chest of drawers, but at least Isobel had it to herself. Johan had stared at her as if he had never seen a topless woman before in his entire life, which he clearly had, so it was a little odd. Lucius didn't say a word all evening, she mused as she made the bed, but she was too tired to care. She got undressed, pulled her nightdress on, then placed two clean strips of towel in her drawers. Gazing around the room with the bloodied strips in her hand, she saw she had no choice but to hide them under her bed beside the chamber pot until she could burn them in secret. She got into bed, turned down the oil lamp, and slept.

She woke with a jump, hearing voices on the landing, and a rather hesitant tapping at the bedroom door.

"It's eight o'clock, Connie," Johan told her. "I'm leaving a bowl of warm water on the floor here."

"Thank you."

She got out of bed and went to the window but the view was a dirty yard at the rear of the building. She turned away, retrieved the bowl of water from just outside the door, and stripped naked. The stomach cramps, probably associated with the miscarriage, were finally gone. She washed herself, then reached for the nail scissors and one of the towels she had taken from Claire and Bridget's bedroom and cut it into strips. The bleeding had reduced to spotting, and would hopefully stop soon, but she needed to find a doctor and get herself examined. Her sorrow at losing Will's child, she forced to the back of her mind.

When she went downstairs to the kitchen, Lucius was at the solid fuel range stirring a saucepan full of porridge.

"Good morning," she said, wondering if he would reply.

"Sleep well?" he asked, and she smiled, she'd slept like the dead.

"Yes, I did, thank you."

"Good morning." Johan came in from the backyard and beamed at her. "Hungry?"

"Very."

"Good. Maybe you'd like to tackle the window display this morning? Then, this afternoon, we will discuss some photographs with you. Think about how you would like to pose, yes?"

"Yes."

"Good. We have clients coming in this morning—"

"But it's Sunday?" she interrupted in surprise.

"For some people, Connie, Sunday is the only day they are free."

She spent all morning in the shop window, scrubbing it clean, and placing suitably framed photographs on stands.

"Ah, yes." Johan was surveying the new display when she returned to the shop after changing the two strips of towel in her drawers. "Very respectable."

"Thank you."

"And I managed to find you this." He handed her a large mask which would hide the top three-quarters of her face. "Black velvet. It's beautiful, isn't it?"

"Very," she replied, running her fingers over the velvet.

"Yes, Hugh thought so when he called."

"Hugh?" she enquired.

"He sells my photographs."

"I see. Where exactly?"

"Hugh takes them to the gentlemen's clubs," Johan explained. "The nobs love a good pair o' tits."

"Do they."

"They'll adore you, Connie. And with the mask…" Johan gave a delighted laugh and headed for the kitchen.

The clients were a father and son, and a young man just graduated from Trinity College. Johan got through them quickly enough and she sensed he couldn't wait until the afternoon.

"So," he began over luncheon. "How will you pose?"

"Do you have other models?" she asked instead of replying.

"Oh, yes. Four others who pose regularly. And we have others who come when their pockets fall empty."

"I see."

"I have an idea for a pose." He smiled. "Your breasts just tumbling out of a corset. And you doing an 'oops!' expression? Yes? No?"

"Yes. But my corsets aren't—"

"I have suitable corsets, don't worry," he assured her. "I will dress you to perfection."

While Lucius set up the backdrop, Johan brought her a black satin corset, black drawers with lace at the knee, and black shoes with a high heel.

"These will go with the mask. Go behind the dressing screen and put them on, pin your hair loosely on the top of your head, and I will apply some cosmetics."

When she walked out in front of a backdrop of a four poster bed fifteen minutes later, Lucius gasped, and Johan shook his head.

"You are an angel, my dear," Johan declared, carrying a wooden camera out of the small darkroom at the far end of the studio, and placing it on its stand.

"Where shall I stand?" she asked, feeling considerably under, yet overdressed as he went back to the darkroom and returned with a box of photographic plates.

"A little to the right. There. Now, if I can loosen the corset a little... good. Hold it while I see to the camera." She stood awkwardly, holding the corset against her breasts, while a plate was inserted. "Now, lean forward a little and hold the pose for the ten seconds exposure time." She did, and the inevitable happened. She gasped as her breasts tumbled out and both men roared with laughter. "Perfect. Don't move."

She just managed to hold the pose and her facial expression. "Can I please straighten up now?" she asked.

"Yes, yes." A new glass plate was inserted. "Now, take off the corset and look as though you are going to drop it in disgust. Hold it away from you, arm stretched, and look in the opposite direction. Yes. Good. Now, hands on hips and glare at it angrily. Excellent. Now, down on your knees. Take the corset, and pretend to rip it apart. Kneel facing the camera, that's it. Good. Now, you couldn't rip it so just sit back on your heels, throw your head back, and laugh. Excellent."

"Was it?" she asked curiously.

"My dear, you are perfection," Johan assured her as he

passed all the plates to Lucius, who brought them to the darkroom. "Other girls just push their tits and bits towards the camera. Your poses are elegant, and you have such an expression-filled face – even with the mysterious mask – and having to hold the pose and expression for the required ten seconds. Men will demand to know who you are."

"I don't want them to know who I am," she told him firmly.

"Exactly. You will never reveal your face but they won't know that and will continue to buy the photographs."

"I see," she replied, bending to pick up the corset.

"Wait. Your back? Turn around." Reluctantly, she did so and felt his eyes on her scar. "What on earth happened to you?" he asked.

"I don't discuss it. Nor do I want it photographed."

"I'm not surprised. But don't worry, most people will be more interested in your front than your back."

"That's a relief," she replied dryly. "I'll go and get dressed."

Will was just about to tuck into breakfast in bed when the bedroom door opened and Jimmy was shown in. The poor lad looked exhausted.

"I been all around the kips in the Liberties, Dr Fitzgerald, and they haven't heard of a woman like Miss Isobel. I'm sorry, Doctor. I'll go up to Monto tonight."

"No."

"No?" Jimmy frowned.

"Leave Monto until last," he told the boy, not wanting Sally Maher to hear Isobel's description and realise 'Rose Green' wasn't dead. "Try the kips in the city centre tonight."

"Yes, Doctor."

Will nodded. "Thanks, Jimmy. Here." He held out a plate. "Have some toast and marmalade."

"Thanks, Doctor." He lifted the slice of toast from the plate. "You feeling better?"

"Much better," he lied, as Jimmy bit into the toast. His spirits had just plummeted. "I'll probably be up and about today. Take the toast with you and go home to bed."

"I will," Jimmy replied with his mouth full. "Thanks, Doctor. I'll be back tomorrow morning."

The door closed and Will swore, feeling disappointed yet relieved.

Shortly before luncheon, he slowly and carefully washed, shaved, and dressed, and went downstairs to the morning room. His mother stared at him in astonishment.

"Will, if you think for one moment that you are returning to Brown Street."

"No, I'm not. I just had to get out of bed."

"How did the boy get on?" she asked.

"Nothing."

"No news is good news."

"I suppose so. I'm going out to the garden for some air."

Outside, he stretched, feeling the stitches protest. He wandered to the end of the long and narrow garden then turned and glanced up at the house, jumping when he heard a shout.

"Will?" Jim Harvey was leaning out of his library window, his grey hair falling over his forehead in the breeze. "How are you?"

"On the mend," he called back.

"Doing anything?"

"No, nothing."

"Come for a chat?" Jim asked, and Will raised a hand in assent before going next door. Jim Harvey met him at the door to his library. "Gave us all a shock when we heard about you." Jim shook his hand and brought him into the room.

"Gave myself a shock, too."

"Drink?" Jim offered and Will hesitated. "It's Sunday," Jim snorted, making his bushy moustache quiver. "Go on."

"I will, then. A very small whiskey, please."

"Sit down."

"Thank you." He sat in a brown leather armchair and watched Jim at the decanters. It was only a quarter to one and the older man was already rather tipsy. "How are you keeping?"

"Oh, can't complain. Was at the club last night. Didn't get back until all hours. Harriett heard me staggering up the stairs and wasn't pleased so I've taken refuge in here with my new friends."

Will shrugged. "Your new friends..?"

Jim laughed and passed Will a glass of whiskey. "Hot off the presses, or whatever it is with photographs." Jim went to the writing desk and opened a large book. "Are you, er, how shall I put this... broad-minded, Will?"

"Well, I, er—" Will's mind raced. "Yes, I think I am."

"That's all right, then. Take a look at these."

Will put the glass to one side and took the book with photographs glued to the pages from Jim. His rather humiliating excursion to the photographers came flooding back as he stared at naked bodies of varying shapes and sizes.

"I think I've disgusted you, Will." Jim chuckled at his reaction.

"No, not at all. Naked bodies are nothing new to me. Not in this context, of course. Where did you get these from?"

"The club. A chap called Hugh Lombard." Jim frowned suddenly. "Surely you're not interested? I thought this sort of thing would only interest an old codger like me and not a young chap like you."

"I'm full of surprises," he murmured.

Jim's eyebrows shot up at that. "I don't go with them, you understand. What would happen if I caught something?" He laughed. "Of course you know, you're a doctor."

"Yes." Will went through the photographs again. This time more slowly. None were of Isobel, thank goodness.

"Like any of them?" Jim asked as Will's eyes rested on one picture. A girl with large breasts but her jet black hair colour clearly came from a bottle. Jim leant over and nodded. "Yes, she's very nice. Look, er, if you're interested…"

"Yes, I'd like to meet this Hugh Lombard, if it's all right with you?"

"Of course. I'll probably be heading to the club again this evening if you're up to it?"

Will nodded and leafed through the photographs again. "I am quite particular, though."

"So is Hugh. He only has the best."

"Good. Women haven't exactly been queuing up of late."

"No. I'm sorry about Isobel Stevens. One maid who got herself pregnant was bad enough, but two? Both Harriett and I were furious. She and the girl used to talk about all sorts. It must be terrible for you, but girls like that just can't be trusted. God knows who the child's father was. No, Will, you're better off without girls like that. I dare say you'll find a girl far more suitable."

Will put the book of photographs down and reached for his glass of whiskey. He drank it in one go, feeling the alcohol travel all the way down and settle in his almost empty stomach. "I dare say," he replied flatly.

"Another whiskey?"

"No, thank you." He must keep a clear head for that evening. "Have you any more photographs?"

Jim grinned. "Lots more."

"All of them have come from this Hugh Lombard?"

"All the recent ones, yes. I first began acquiring them from a photographers on the north side of the city, but Hugh's are of far superior quality. Here." Jim passed him a box.

"Mrs Harvey never comes in here, I take it?"

"Never, but then she started allowing the girl, Isobel, to read in here when we'd go out. Honestly. It's my library. She liked a 'good book' apparently. Well, if you can call *Emma* a good book. Imagine if she'd found this?" Jim laid a hand on the book of photographs and roared with laughter.

Will managed to smile politely and glanced through the photographs in the box until his stomach began to churn. He quickly returned the box to Jim. "These are a bit too extreme for my liking."

Jim pulled an 'each to his own tastes' expression and returned the box to its shelf. "More into 'arty' poses, then, are you?"

I know more about the human body than you will ever know, Will thought angrily. "The body is a beautiful instrument which should be valued, not abused."

"That's you the doctor speaking. What about Will Fitzgerald the man? Wish you could have 'entertained' Isobel first?"

It took all of Will's willpower not to jump up and punch Jim hard on the nose. Instead, he clenched his fists.

"Something like that."

"Go on. Of course you do."

Will shrugged. "It's too late now."

Jim nodded. "Beautiful girl. Wonderful figure. Just couldn't be trusted not to lift her skirts to all and sundry."

Will got to his feet as fast as the stitches would allow. "What time shall I meet you here this evening?"

"Eight?"

"Eight it is." Will went to the door and let himself out.

At half past eight, Will and Jim Harvey were seated in brown leather armchairs in the Trinity Club overlooking St Stephen's Green waiting for two brandies.

"Ever been here before?" Jim asked. "With your father?"

"No, never."

"Well, you're entitled to join, you are a Trinity College man."

"I'll think about it," Will lied. "Is Hugh Lombard a member?"

"No, but he makes it well worth the club's while to grant him access."

"Oh," Will replied and Jim moved awkwardly in his chair, making the leather squeak.

"Look, Will. If I offended you earlier with those photographs, then, I'm sorry. I was still rather drunk. I've drunk about a gallon of coffee this afternoon."

Will returned a weak smile then glanced over Jim's shoulder as a tall dark-haired man in his forties wearing a frock coat similar to Jim's walked into the room. Was this Hugh Lombard?

"James?"

Jim sat up and twisted around. "Hugh. Sit yourself down."

"Thank you." Mr Lombard sat down on a sofa and glanced curiously at Will. "Will, Hugh Lombard. Hugh, Will Fitzgerald."

"Pleased to meet you, Will." Mr Lombard held out a hand which Will shook reluctantly.

"And you."

"I was showing Will some of your photographs this afternoon."

"I see." Mr Lombard eyed Will with more interest. "And?"

"Do you have any more with you?" Will asked.

"I do." He reached down and patted a leather satchel at his feet. "We need to retire to a more private room, though."

"Of course," Jim replied. "When our brandies arrive, you lead the way."

Five minutes later, Will followed the two older men down a long corridor and into a room at the far end. Mr Lombard closed the door and turned the key in the lock then brought the satchel across the room to a table. Will took a gulp of brandy and joined them. Mr Lombard passed Jim about fifty photographs then did likewise to Will. Will brought his to an armchair and, struggling to hide his revulsion, he began to go through them. No Isobel. He sighed with relief and looked up as Jim held his bundle out and beckoned him to swap.

"I've made my selection from these."

"Oh? Can I see?"

Jim shrugged, passed them over, and Will found himself staring at a masked Isobel. His heart pounded before plummeting.

"Beautiful, isn't she?" Hugh asked. "Completely natural. Doesn't even look like she's posing for the camera."

"No," Will croaked before clearing his throat. "What's her name?"

"Connie. She's new. That's all I know but I'll definitely find out more about her." Will felt Mr Lombard stare at him. "You like her, don't you, Will? I don't blame you. I'm going to have to obtain a lot more photographs of her. The velvet mask does it for me. Adds a certain something, don't you think?"

"Yes. Do you have more of these?"

"I certainly do." Mr Lombard went back to his satchel. "Just look at this one." He handed the photograph to Will. Isobel was seated naked on a chair, leaning forward with her elbows resting loosely on her thighs and her hands clasped, gazing into the distance. "Extraordinary. As Johan was telling me, she's completely natural."

"Johan?"

"The photographer. This one's my favourite, though." He passed Will a photograph of Isobel's breasts tumbling out of her corset. Will felt his heart pounding again and he took another gulp of brandy before draining the glass. Both men laughed, irritating him. "You need to find yourself a woman, Will. This one's available." Will was handed the picture of the girl whose black hair colour came from a bottle he had seen earlier in Jim's library.

"Not Connie?"

"No. Apparently, she's quite specific as to what she does and does not do."

"I see."

"Look, you can have this photograph." Mr Lombard pointed to the girl with bottle-black hair. "But I'm afraid that I'll have to charge you for Connie. Five shillings per photograph."

"I don't want any of them."

"No?" Mr Lombard was astonished. "I know five shillings is a lot of money, Will, but these are the best you'll find anywhere in Dublin."

"I know. Connie's beautiful. But I don't want photographs of her."

"And I've just told you she won't have sex with you."

"I don't want sex," Will snapped.

"Well, in that case, I don't know what you want, sonny."

"Will's been ill." Jim intervened. His eyes were begging Will not to ruin things for him so Will bit his tongue, passed the photographs back and turned away. "I'll take all of these, Hugh."

"Right."

Will went to the window while Jim paid Mr Lombard. Isobel was Connie and was being photographed by a man called Johan. There can't be very many Johan's in Dublin. If Johan was his real name, that was.

"I can get photographs of men and boys, if you're interested, Will?" Mr Lombard called across the room.

Will slowly turned back. "No, thank you," he managed to reply politely. Mr Lombard just shrugged and rolled his eyes at Jim.

"Same time next week, James?" Mr Lombard asked cheerfully. "I'll have more of Connie for you."

"Ideal. Thanks, Hugh."

Will watched silently as Mr Lombard closed his satchel, went to the door, and let himself out.

Jim immediately hurried across the room to him. "You could have told me you were strapped for cash."

"You could have told me you were a fucking pervert."

Jim took a step backwards. "These are art, Will. Just because photography isn't recognised as such just yet."

"Art?" Will snapped in disgust.

"Yes. Look at the girl, Connie, compared to this other girl. As Hugh said, Connie acts completely naturally. She barely notices the camera. Look at the other girl thrusting desperately towards it. This is rubbish." Jim ripped the photograph in two and dropped it into the fire. "But these photographs of Connie are art and I'm happy to pay more for them. Take this." He held out the photograph of Isobel's breasts tumbling out of her corset. "Take it and try and remind yourself what a real woman is."

Will took the photograph from Jim and, without looking at it again, crumpled it up and threw it into the fire.

It was inevitable, Isobel supposed, that she should find herself posing for more photographs than any paying client. The new window display brought in one client first thing on Monday morning but Johan dealt with the man in such a desultory way it was little wonder legitimate business was slow. The next hour was given over to a more intimate session with Isobel meeting the other models, both female and male.

Esther was petite with red hair and appealed to those who favoured the nice but very naughty. Katy had the most enormous breasts Isobel had ever seen but had mousy brown hair which she dyed black regularly. Martin boasted of the largest penis in Dublin and when Isobel saw it, she couldn't disagree, even though it reminded her of an elephant's trunk.

She met Hugh Lombard in the photographic studio after returning from visiting a doctor. To her relief, the doctor had deemed her recovered from the miscarriage and saw no medical reason why she had lost the baby, or why she shouldn't conceive again in the future and carry the baby to full term. The miscarriage was just, 'one of those things,' he'd told her.

"I sell you," Mr Lombard informed her with a smile.

"I see. And do I sell?"

He laughed. "You do. I sell you to the more discerning customer willing to pay handsomely for the pleasure of viewing your body. One customer, in particular, is very taken with you, so I've asked Johan to take more photographs of you today and I've brought you these to wear."

She took the items of lingerie from him and held them up. They were a black lace corset, a pair of black drawers – the ends of which only reached the top of her thighs – and black stockings. "The corset is far too small."

"Of course it is. Martin is to stand behind you and try and contain your breasts and lace it up. But with great difficulty."

"I see."

"Off you go, then, and put them on. I'll wait over here."

"You're staying?" she asked.

"Connie, I have to be able to tell my clients something about you."

"What have you told them so far?"

"That you're a woman of mystery," he replied and gave her a grin.

"Shouldn't it stay that way?"

"Yes, but you can't blame me and my clients for being curious."

She got changed and joined Martin in front of the camera. The last man she had been this close to had been Will. He had never held her breasts in his hands like this, though, and she felt a pang of regret. She had tried so hard not to think about him but today, with first her visit to the doctor and now this, her mind was full of him. How was he recovering from the operation? How was he coping with her disappearance and the knowledge that she had been carrying his child but had lost it? What would he say – or do – if he could see her now? Sighing, she turned to Martin.

"Talk to me," she instructed him. "About anything. Anything at all. Just talk."

"All right. I want you to come home with me tonight," he whispered.

It was tempting. She missed Will. She closed her eyes for a moment, remembering him lifting her onto his writing desk then pushing her petticoat out of the way. They had created a child that afternoon. And she had lost it. She shook her head. "No."

"Why not?" Martin asked. "I can feel you trembling. I won't hurt you, I promise. I know you've been hurt before because of the scar."

"I don't talk about the scar," she snapped, making

Martin jump, and everyone stare at her. "Ever."

"Martin – shut up," Johan ordered. "Just do as I say. Concentrate."

"Martin propositioned you earlier, didn't he?" Mr Lombard had followed her into the kitchen when the photographic session ended and she jumped violently, pulling her black silk robe around her. "I'm sorry," he added, closing the door. "Did I startle you?"

"Yes."

"I can't say I'm surprised at him, though. You are the loveliest creature I've ever seen."

"What do you want?" she asked.

"To ask you about the mask. You demanded it, Johan tells me. Why?"

She shrugged. "To add an air of mystery."

"Not to hide from someone?" he suggested.

She tensed. "No."

"You're lying. Who is it? Husband? Father?"

"No-one."

"What if I were to search your room?"

"My room is private."

"Private?" He roared with laughter. "You show your body off to us all day and you talk to me about privacy."

"It's my room," she protested.

"It's my house."

Her eyes widened. "What?"

"I own this house," he told her. "Johan and Lucius are my tenants. As are you. Have you not wondered how they can get away with such a small legitimate clientele? They work primarily for me. As do you."

"In that case, I'm leaving."

"If you leave, Connie – if that is your name – you will never find work with a photographer or a madam in Dublin not indebted to me." Reaching out, he pulled her robe open. "You have an extraordinary body. I'd hate for you to have to whore yourself on the streets and let it go to waste."

"I wouldn't do that," she replied, pulling the robe closed.

"No?" he asked, yanking the robe off her shoulders and throwing it onto the kitchen table, leaving her naked. "Where exactly would you go? Where have you come from, Connie Maguire? You turn up here out of the blue and have absolutely no qualms in stripping off. Someone's mistress, were you?"

"No." Using one arm and her other hand, she attempted to cover herself.

"I don't quite believe that," he murmured, walking her backwards until her behind touched the table. "Though, no doubt I'll find out soon."

"What?"

"One of my clients in the gentlemen's clubs will recognise you sooner or later."

"They won't."

"Wasn't a gentleman, was he?" Mr Lombard smiled. "Well, neither am I, but I would consider it an honour if you would dine with me this evening. And as I am not a gentleman and you are not a lady, I shall expect the meal to be only the beginning of the evening."

She gave him a humourless smile. "I'd rather be Johan or Lucius' mistress, not yours."

Mr Lombard spat out a laugh. "That's hardly likely – they're sodomites – I most certainly am not."

"But?" She shot a glance towards the photographic studio. She'd had no idea.

"You thought they were father and son?" Mr Lombard inquired. "Brothers? Gentlemanly enough not to pester you?"

"I – I," she stammered. "I don't know."

"Dinner?" he asked lightly.

"I'd rather starve."

"Go on, then, sell yourself down at the quays."

"Well, it will be preferable to being your whore," she retorted and cried out when he hit her.

The door from the shop burst open, Johan came to her and tilted her face upwards. "Hugh, for God's sake," he cried, as she touched the skin around her left eye – her face was swelling already. "I won't be able to photograph her for days now."

"She wears that blasted mask."

"The skin around her eye will be visibly bruised," Johan protested.

"Well, no-one will want to fuck her now either." Mr Lombard leant towards her. "Except me."

Chapter Seven

When Will returned to number 67 from the club, he went straight to the bookcase in the morning room and pulled out the latest edition of *Thom's Directory*. His mother got up from the sofa and followed him across the room.

"Are you all right?"

"I'm tired."

"Your father and I warned you not to overdo things."

"I'm tired, that's all." He set the commercial and street directory down on the writing desk and flipped through the pages until he came to the list of nobility, gentry, merchants, and traders in Dublin. No Johan's... yes, there. *Fortuin, Johan, photographer, 5 Back Street*. He picked up the heavy book to return it to the shelf and winced as the stitches stretched.

"Will?" His mother darted forward, prepared to grab the book in case he dropped it.

Her shout brought his father running down the stairs and into the room. "What is it?"

"I'm fine," Will insisted, placing the book back on the shelf.

"You look awful," his father told him bluntly. "Stop

acting like a fool and go to bed and rest. Whose idiotic idea was it to go to the club? Yours or Jim's?"

"Both of ours."

"Well, it was far too soon for you to go out. Now, go to bed."

"Father…"

"Will – bed."

Angrily, he trudged up the stairs to his old bedroom, feeling like a ten-year-old boy again.

He slept deeply for almost twelve hours and woke at five minutes to eleven, having to remind himself it was now Monday morning and he was in number 67 not Brown Street. He quickly got washed and dressed, didn't bother about shaving, and went straight to the drawing room. Sitting down at the writing desk, he wrote Isobel a short letter, and put it in his morning coat's inside pocket. Downstairs in the hall, he met Tess carrying a breakfast tray.

"Good morning, Dr Fitzgerald. Mrs Fitzgerald asked me to bring this tray up to you."

He glanced at the tea, porridge, toast and marmalade, hoping his stomach wouldn't rumble. "I'm sorry, Tess, but I have to go out."

"Yes, Dr Fitzgerald."

"Oh, and if Jimmy calls, could you thank him for all he has done but I won't be needing his help anymore. I'll explain why the next time I see him." Delving into the pocket of his trousers, he brought out two pennies and a ha'penny. "Could you also give him these, please?" He put the coins on the tray. "And give him some breakfast? He'll have been out all night."

"Of course, Dr Fitzgerald."

"Thank you, Tess."

He put on his hat, let himself out of the house, and walked to Back Street. Number 5 looked respectable enough with an elaborate photographic display in the window. It just shows how appearances can be so deceptive, he thought. He walked to the end of the street and back down an alleyway at the rear, counting the houses until he found number 5 again. A wooden gate led into a dirty yard. He inched his way around the perimeter until he came to the door of an outbuilding. The privy, by the smell of it. A little further along, he reached the back door. Bending down carefully, he pushed the letter under the door, before leaving the yard without looking back.

Isobel recognised Will's handwriting immediately. She snatched the envelope with *CONNIE* printed on the front from the flag-stone floor at the back door and held it in the folds of her skirt before Johan saw it. How on earth had Will found her?

"Is your eye still paining you?" Johan asked from the solid fuel range, where he was shovelling coal into the firebox before starting to prepare their luncheon.

"A little," she lied. She'd held a cloth soaked in cold water to her eye for the past hour to bring down the swelling and to try and relieve the pain. The swelling had eased but she'd shuddered at her reflection in the bedroom mirror. The skin surrounding her eye was purple, the eye itself was bloodshot, and it ached dreadfully.

"Hugh won't give up, you know?" he told her, and she grimaced. "And being his mistress wouldn't be so bad. He's well-to-do, lives on Fitzwilliam Square, and you'd be well-dressed and well-cared for."

"Until he tires of me and finds another mistress."

Johan sighed and threw the small shovel into the coal bucket. "All I can do is advise you to do as he wants. He isn't a pleasant man when he is angered – as you now know."

"Very well," she said quietly. "It looks as though I have no choice."

"I'll send a note to Hugh." Johan gave her a relieved smile. "He'll be delighted."

Holding the envelope against her stomach, she ran upstairs to her bedroom. Tearing the envelope open, she pulled out a sheet of notepaper.

Isobel,

Perhaps you can imagine my feelings when my father told me you were miscarrying our child and then had to tell me you had disappeared. Perhaps you can imagine my feelings when I saw intimate photographs of yourself in Jim Harvey's club being sold by a 'gentleman' named Hugh Lombard. What are you trying to do to me, Isobel? How many times do I have to tell you I love you and I want you to become my wife?

Nevertheless, I would like to thank you for staying with my mother on the night of my operation even though I cannot help but wonder that if you had not, you would now still be carrying our child and not be all but lost to me.

Sincerely yours,
Will Fitzgerald

Poor Will. She was lost to him. Isobel put the letter down on the bed and gazed at her reflection again in the mirror hanging over the fireplace. Apart from the purple skin around her bloodshot eye, her face was devoid of colour. You need to leave this place, she told herself. But if you leave looking like this, not only will you attract unwanted attention, no boarding house owner will rent a room to you – an unmarried woman who clearly has been beaten – and do you really want to sleep in a doorway again? You will simply have to resign yourself to being mistress to a violent man for however long it takes for your eye to heal and the bruise to fade.

Covering her face with her hands, she sobbed, but her tears made her bloodshot eye sting, so she pulled a handkerchief from her sleeve and gently wiped the tears away. Turning back to the bed, she hid Will's letter in her bible and went downstairs to the kitchen.

A cab arrived for her at seven o'clock that evening, the cabman telling her she was being brought to Fitzwilliam Square. She climbed inside, wearing her black coat over her navy blue dress with the square neck and buttons up the front. It was the only respectable dress she still owned and she certainly wasn't going to arrive wearing one of her parlourmaid's uniforms. The cab stopped outside a Georgian terraced townhouse, not unlike those on Merrion Square. As she got out, a man in his sixties and dressed identically to Mr Johnston, opened the front door.

"I am Dwyer, the butler," he announced. "Please come inside, Miss Maguire."

They went into the hall, where a middle-aged woman dressed in black and a maid aged about thirty, were waiting at the foot of the stairs.

"I am Mrs Clarke, the housekeeper," the woman

declared, her dark eyes resting briefly on Isobel's bruised face. "This," she indicated the maid, "is Susan. Susan will escort you upstairs to the guest room and will dress you for Mr Lombard. Dinner will be served shortly."

She was brought to a bedroom on the second floor and told to remove her clothes. Susan then lifted a dress out of the wardrobe and helped Isobel into it. The silk satin dress was bright red and, as Susan did up the buttons, Isobel stared at herself in a long mirror. The short-sleeved dress was cut indecently low across her breasts. It seemed she was to be Hugh Lombard's scarlet woman in more ways than one.

"Beautiful." Susan stood back from her and smiled. "I'll escort you to Mr Lombard now. He is waiting for you in the dining room."

She followed the maid down the stairs to the first floor and was shown into a dining room dominated by a huge table and eight chairs. The table was covered with a white linen table cloth but was only set for two. The door was closed behind her and Hugh Lombard, dressed in white tie and tails, got up from the head of the table.

"I knew you'd see sense in the end." He looked her up and down and she fought an urge to cover her cleavage. "I hope you like your dress."

"I've never worn scarlet before."

"You surprise me," he said, holding her chair as she sat down at the opposite end of the table from him. "I expect you're hungry?"

"I have an appetite," she lied, and he smiled before returning to his seat.

A clear soup had just been served when the butler was called from the dining room. A couple of minutes later,

Dwyer returned and walked to the head of the table.

"I have shown Mr Duncan Simpson into the drawing room, sir," the butler said in a low voice. "I did explain you are dining with a guest, but he wishes to speak with you on a matter of urgency."

Mr Lombard swore under his breath and rose from his seat. "I won't be long," he told her, and the two men went out, leaving her alone in the room.

Duncan Simpson? Pushing her chair back from the table, she went to the double doors to the drawing room and peered through a gap of about an inch. She couldn't see Mr Lombard or Mr Simpson, but she could hear a heated whispered discussion then a punch as one man hit the other, followed by a thump as one of them fell to the floor. Duncan Simpson strode past the double doors and she heard a door open but not close. Opening the double doors a little, she could see Mr Lombard's shoes. Pushing the doors open further, she saw him unconscious on the floor, lying flat on his back on the colourful rug.

She ran through the drawing room and onto the landing. Hitching up the red dress, she ran up the stairs to the second floor two steps at a time. At the top of the stairs, she halted. Which bedroom were her clothes in? Opening the first door on the landing, she saw her black coat and navy blue dress lying across a chair. Grabbing them, she went back out onto the landing and froze, hearing someone running along the first floor landing and giving a little cry. It was a woman, and she peered over the banisters as Susan ran downstairs to the ground floor and out of sight. She went slowly down the stairs, hoping she wouldn't meet anyone, saw the front door was wide open and ran out of the house.

Clutching her clothes to her chest, she ran to a corner of the square before stopping. Where was she? Was Merrion Square nearby? In the dark, all the Georgian townhouses looked the same. Backing into the shadows away from a gas lamp, she fought to think clearly. She had to change out of this horrid scarlet dress and then just keep walking until she reached somewhere familiar.

She began to walk, not knowing if she was going in the right direction until she saw an alleyway. It was pitch-black and secluded, so she changed her clothes there, leaving the red dress on the ground. She walked on, keeping to the wider well-lit streets, wondering if she should dare ask for directions if she met anyone.

She had walked for about five minutes when she stopped beside a pillar post box near a street lamp. About to carry on, she frowned. The top layer of red paint was beginning to flake off in places, like on the post box she had used on the west side of Merrion Square. Surely not? She retraced her steps for a few yards then crossed the street to railing surrounding what must be private gardens. When she reached the corner, she clapped a hand to her mouth. Despite the darkness, she recognised the street and the houses, she'd walked along this pavement often enough. Along there were number 67 and number 68 – this was Merrion Square!

Now she knew where she was, she turned around and hurried on, reaching Back Street twenty minutes later. She crept into the backyard and peered in the kitchen window. Johan was alone in the room and fast asleep in a chair beside the solid fuel range. She tiptoed inside without waking him, and up the stairs to her bedroom. Closing the door, she burst into tears of relief.

Three days passed with no reply to his letter so Will wrote another letter and went to Back Street in the early morning with it. Pushing open the wooden gate to the backyard, he saw the privy door opening, and he only just managed to duck out of the yard and behind a wall without being seen. He heard a door close and pulled an exasperated expression. What now?

After a few moments deliberation, he went into the yard again and pushed the envelope under the back door. He crept out of the yard and walked to Brown Street for some money, then thanked and paid George Millar, before returning exhausted to Merrion Square.

He spent the next week regaining his strength at number 67 and growing a beard. His mother for one hated it.

"Will, you know I don't like beards and it makes you look like your grandfather. Please think about shaving it off?"

"I will. Just not yet."

Mrs Fitzgerald's eyes narrowed suspiciously. "What are you up to, Will? You're not in any kind of trouble? Your father can always lend you..?"

"I'm not in trouble of any kind, Mother, I promise. I need a beard because I'm going to search for Isobel. I don't know where I might have to search, but I won't stop searching until I've found her."

On the afternoon of the seventh day, he stood in his old bedroom staring at his beard and centre-parted hair in the freestanding mirror. Never mind his late maternal grandfather, he looked more like Mr Parnell, leader of the Home Rulers and president of the Land League. He donned the trousers, waistcoat, morning coat, and hat, purchased that morning at a second-hand clothes stall and grimaced at his appearance. He was a complete and utter sight, but this was for Isobel – last resort – shock tactics.

The shop doorbell jangled as it opened and closed and, behind the counter, Isobel jumped and peered up at the customer. Each time the shop door opened, she expected Mr Lombard to walk in and hit her again for not staying to continue with the dinner and the evening's main purpose. It had been over a week now, and his non-appearance was worrying her. He had been intent on making her his mistress, so why hadn't he come looking for her?

This couldn't continue, her nerves were in shreds. She would leave Dublin tomorrow, she decided, abandoning her intention to go once she had been paid her next wages. Her bruise had faded, her bloodshot eye had healed, and she was as well as could be expected. It was time she moved on.

You will be moving on and moving on for the rest of your life. Do you really want that?

Forcing Will's words from her mind, she began to plan her future. She had enough money put by to get her to London and to spend a week – perhaps two – in a cheap but respectable boarding house while she looked for suitable employment. She would start again – and she would do it properly this time.

Good grief. She did a double take at the customer. What on earth was this? The bearded man's check suit looked to have come from one of the many second-hand clothes markets scattered across the city.

"Good afternoon." Johan hailed the man cheerfully. "How may we help you?"

"Afternoon," the man replied in a broad Dublin accent and removed his bowler hat. Isobel did another double take and her heart somersaulted. It was Will. She'd recognise his brown eyes anywhere. "I was thinkin' o' havin' me picture taken. How much would it be?"

"Would you like to come through to the studio, sir, and we can have a chat about what you're after."

Will followed Johan without once looking in her direction and Isobel slumped over the counter, rubbing her forehead as it began to throb painfully with both horror and relief that he was there. It was a week since she had found his second letter pushed under the back door.

> *Isobel,*
>
> *I am stubborn as well as demanding and I will not give up on you. You may have lost our child but you will never lose me. I have tried to reason as to why you ran away from me.*
>
> *I know my father spoke harshly to you. I have assured him the child was mine and that when I find you, I will marry you, and we will live quietly in Brown Street. Nothing he, nor anyone else, says will have any effect on my feelings for you or lessen my determination to make you my wife.*
>
> *Another reason may be that you are afraid you may never be able to carry a child to term. I wish I could reassure you but I cannot. Your next pregnancy may pass without incident, but if you do miscarry again, then we will adopt a child. The child may not have been made by us, but he or she will still be ours.*

For now, however, all I want is you, and I know you also want me.
Will Fitzgerald

She pushed herself up off the counter and went into the studio. Johan and Will were at the costume wardrobe which stood along the back wall.

"Surely you want to look your best?" Johan was asking.

"Ah, sure what's wrong with me clothes?" Will protested, running his hands down the dark brown check morning coat he wore. It was so greasy the material shone.

"Well." Johan clearly didn't know where to begin. "Surely, you would want your family, and your children and grandchildren eventually, to see you at your best?" he asked, and Will stared straight at her, and she felt her cheeks burn. Johan turned to her with a smile. "Connie, what do you think?"

She braced herself and walked across the studio to Will with a polite smile, eying the creased and shiny morning coat. It looked as though he had slept in it, and the centre-parted hair and full beard were horrendous, putting years on him. "I could iron your coat and trousers for you, sir? Make them nice and smart?"

"Would you?" Will grinned stupidly, and she cringed.

"I would be glad to, sir. I'll just go and warm the iron."

She fled to the kitchen and put the iron on the solid fuel range's hotplate to heat up. To her horror, Will, dressed in one of the robes Martin favoured, came in shortly afterwards, followed by Johan.

"We'll have a cup of tea while we wait," Johan said, passing her the coat and trousers, before placing the kettle on the hotplate beside the iron.

When the doorbell jangled again, her heart thumped as Johan went out to the shop, leaving her alone with Will.

"What are you doing here?" she demanded.

"Being stubborn and demanding," he replied simply. "I love you, Isobel."

"You mustn't. I lost your child. I'll never be good enough for you. Your parents know I'll never be good enough for you. Soon everyone will know. And why. Just forget about me and find someone worthy of you. Please, Will?"

He shook his head. "I can't. I love you."

"Please go home, Will."

"Just what do I have to do to make you believe me?"

"What do you mean?" she asked, before quickly turning away as the door to the shop opened and Johan returned. "The iron will be a while yet, I'll just…" She tailed off and left the kitchen.

She paced up and down the shop floor for a few moments before halting outside the kitchen door.

"Beautiful girl," Will was commenting. "Your wife, is she?"

Johan laughed kindly. "No, Connie is just an assistant."

"You should photograph her, she's wasted as an assistant."

There was a long silence then she heard the sound of a chair being pulled out from the table and someone sitting down.

"Are you married..?" Johan asked.

"Sean," Will replied. "And, no, I'm not. It's not for the want of trying, though."

"Like women, do you?"

"Depends on the woman. My landlady now, a right dragon. Her now, Connie, that's a real woman."

"Ever been with a woman like her?" Johan asked casually, and Isobel's jaw dropped.

"Jaysis, no." Will laughed. "No-one as beautiful as her."

"So you wouldn't be all that experienced then?"

"What're you sayin'?" Will retorted angrily. "I been with women, you know. It's just that beggars can't be choosy, you know? But I been with women all right. What're you sayin'? Is this some sort of kip?"

"No, it bloody well isn't."

"Well, what, then?" Will demanded.

"I take photographs."

"I know."

"The sort you wouldn't want your mammy to see," Johan replied patiently. "Are you getting me, Sean?"

Another long silence followed before Will replied slowly, "I am. I can't afford to buy any off of you, though."

"That's all right, Sean. I was just wondering that as you're a big, strong lad..?"

"You want me to be in dirty photographs?" Will asked, sounding astonished.

"Not dirty photographs, Sean, artistic photographs. People don't quite yet appreciate how photographs can be seen as art in the same way paintings can."

"How much would you pay me?"

"Well, we could come to an arrangement? I would do your portrait free of charge, of course."

"And what would I have to do for these other photographs?"

"Various poses with Connie," Johan told him, and Isobel's eyes closed.

"Connie? Jaysis."

"Just poses, Sean. Nothing more. If you want more you can feck off to Monto."

"When do we start?" Will asked.

"Now, if you'll agree?"

"That's fine with me."

"Good. I'll just go and talk to Connie."

Isobel was polishing the counter when Johan walked through the door.

"Connie," he began hesitantly. "You know I sometimes get – how shall I put it – people who aren't models, to pose for photographs?"

"Yes?"

"Well, I've just managed to get Sean back there to agree to pose with you. I know you've only posed with Martin before but I'd say this Sean is a big lad, too."

"Oh."

"And if he tries anything he'll be out the door on his arse."

"What had you in mind for the photographs?" she asked.

"How old are you?"

"I'll be twenty-three next month. Why?"

"Well, I'd say Sean must be getting on for forty, so I was thinking of… here, I'll explain it to you both. Come through to the kitchen."

Reluctantly, she followed him. Getting on for forty. She rolled her eyes. Will was only around thirty.

"Sean." Johan gave Will a grin. "I'll just explain to you and Connie what I was thinking of for the photographs. Connie will dress you up all smart and you'll be Connie's employer. We'll have you sitting at a desk and Connie will be your maid. Naturally, you want your wicked way with her but you're too shy. What you don't know is that she wants her wicked way with you as well."

Will gave a delighted laugh and Isobel glared at him but he refused to look at her.

"So, Connie, you iron Sean's coat and trousers, while I nip outside to the privy."

The door to the backyard closed behind him and she leant over the kitchen table. "Please don't do this, Will."

"Why not? You do it."

"Yes, but—"

"Yes, but what?" he asked in a light but firm tone.

"Please, go home, Will. Don't—"

The back door opened and Johan returned. "Is that iron hot yet?"

"Yes, I think so," she replied.

"Then, do Sean's clothes, please. There's a maid's uniform and corset in the wardrobe. You can wear the corset loose-ish underneath."

"And the mask."

"Mask?" Will echoed.

Johan smiled. "Connie's trademark. Adds a certain mystery."

"Do I not get one?" Will asked.

"You?" Johan shook his head. "Sorry, but we've only the one mask."

Isobel ironed Will's coat and trousers, feeling him watch her every move. Silently, she passed them to him, then went to the studio to change her clothes. Just how far would she have to go before he realised she would never be good enough for him?

Will put on the trousers and coat and followed Johan to the studio. Isobel emerged from behind the dressing screen, a feather duster in her hand, and he stared. Apart from the loosely pinned up hair and mask, she looked as she had done back in Merion Square. He began to feel uncomfortable. Just how far did he have to go with all this? A box of photographic plates stood on the floor beside the large wooden camera, a rather battered desk had been placed on a raised area at the far end of the room, and Johan was putting a chair behind it.

"Now," Johan called. "Are we ready? You come and sit here Sean, and you, Connie, stand here across the desk from him. Good."

The chair creaked under Will's weight as he sat down and his heart started to thump.

"Now, the way I tend to work these days is to photograph a series of poses which tell a story," Johan explained. "Just try and relax, Sean."

"I'll try me best."

"Good. Now, Connie, you've come into the study to dust thinking the room's empty." Johan hauled a background showing a door and part of a window onto the raised area behind them. "Right, stand in front of the door. You're closing the door behind you and spotting Sean here. Look surprised and embarrassed – that's it. Sean, you're reading a newspaper," one was found and tossed onto the desk, "and you look up in surprise and embarrassment when Connie comes in. Excellent. Hold that pose for the ten seconds exposure time."

Johan hurried to the camera and a few moments later Will heard him count to ten.

"Good. Now, as Connie goes to leave the room, you get up and grab her arm, Sean, and persuade her to stay. That's it. Now, look embarrassed, Sean, like you've really overstepped the mark. Good. Connie, you smile and reach up and touch his face…"

Will watched Isobel swallow before slowly reaching up and touching his beard.

"Wonderful," Johan cried before Will heard him counting to ten in a murmur. "Now," Johan continued. "Kiss her, Sean. Turn a little to the left so I can see you."

Slowly, Will bent his head and touched her lips with his. Immediately, she backed away rubbing her mouth.

"Sorry," she gasped. "The beard."

"Try it again," Johan instructed, and Will bent his head and saw her brace herself. He touched her lips with his and he heard Johan count to ten. She broke away and rubbed her mouth again. "Good. Now, reach for the buttons on his coat, Connie, and you reach for her uniform buttons, Sean."

"Surely if they want each other they'll find the quickest way of doing it?" Will asked, and heard Isobel gasp angrily, no doubt remembering their afternoon in Brown Street.

"True, but the customers want to see you both, so buttons, please. Undo about half of them."

"I'll do my own," Isobel informed him.

"Fine," he replied and took off his tie and collar before undoing the buttons on his coat, waistcoat, and the top two buttons of his shirt.

"Reach for each other's buttons, please," Johan commanded. "That's it. Now, take the maid's uniform off please, Connie. You take all off except the shirt, Sean."

All except the shirt? Will grimaced and caught Isobel

frowning desperately at him, begging him not to do it. He stood back and undressed, throwing the clothes over the back of the chair. Turning back, he saw first the maid's uniform on the desk, then the corset she was wearing. It was too small for her and her breasts were all but falling out of it. He took a deep breath. Control yourself, Will, he warned himself.

"Sit on the desk, please, Connie," Johan continued. "Sean, you stand between her legs. Good. You are kissing her neck and trying to undo her corset at the same time. Connie, your hands are in his hair and you're arching your back towards him."

Will felt her tense then slowly relax as his beard touched the side of her neck. He began to fumble with the corset, feeling her fingers on his scalp. He exhaled and felt her shiver.

"Sorry," he whispered.

"Shut up," she whispered back, as Johan counted to ten again.

"Good. Are you sure you've never done this before, Sean?"

Will straightened up with a weak smile. "I think I'd have remembered."

Johan laughed. "Right, off with the corset, Connie, and off with that shirt, Sean."

"This is your last chance," Isobel begged. "Don't do it, please?"

Will hesitated for a moment then shook his head and threw off the shirt. Isobel sighed and took off the corset.

"Wait, Sean," Johan bellowed. "What is that?" He pointed to the scar.

"That," Will exclaimed proudly. "Is a scar from when I had some of me guts cut out. I had the stitches taken out yesterday."

Isobel peered curiously at the scar then saw him stare at her breasts and flushed, turning away.

"Your guts? Jaysis, we'll have to keep that out of the pictures… Right, Connie, back up on the desk. You get on it, too, Sean, and kneel between her legs. Good. Connie, lower your left leg a little to show more of Sean. That's it, good."

"Will, please don't do this?" Isobel whispered.

"You are exquisite," he replied, and lowered his lips to her breasts, hearing her sigh. "And I love you. I will always love you." Feeling her hands slide down his back to his buttocks, his control began to slip. "I know you love me, too."

Somewhere in the background Johan was shouting instructions, counting to ten, and changing plates. Below Will, Isobel moaned softly at first, then more and more loudly as he licked and pulled noisily at her nipples. The sounds echoed around the studio.

"Connie, I said we would calm down a little," Johan said, a little hesitantly, walking towards them. "Sean, that'll be all for now." Will just ignored him and kissed Isobel hungrily. "Sean?" An angry sigh followed. "Connie? Connie, I can go for a constable..?"

Isobel turned her head. "I'd like you to go away, please," she said. "Now."

Johan swore then left the studio, slamming the door and then the main shop door behind him.

Will pushed into her as she turned her head back to him.

The desk began to creak alarmingly under them and he was forced to slow down and thrust slowly. He came with a grunt and Isobel dug her fingernails into his back as she cried out.

Patting the desk, he climbed down from it, silently thanking it for just about coping with both their weights. He lifted her down, went to the dressing screen for her clothes, then laid them and his clothes across the desk.

"Get dressed," he said simply. "I'm taking you home."

It was no use. Will loved her. He would do anything for her. Absolutely anything. He was beyond shocking now. And she loved him with all her heart. Covering her face with her hands, Isobel sank to her knees and wept with shame at what he'd had to do to prove it.

"I'm sorry," she sobbed. "You've gone from being a good and decent man to… this…"

"I'll destroy the photographic plates and any photographs I find of you before we leave."

"Will, I'm sorry."

"Stop saying sorry, Isobel, and put your clothes on," he said, stepping into his drawers and trousers and buttoning them up. "We need to leave here as quickly as possible in case Johan does go for a constable."

"But I've ruined you, too," she protested, as she got to her feet and began to get dressed.

"No," he replied firmly, shrugging on his shirt, waistcoat, and then the awful coat, stuffing his collar and tie into the pockets. "You've opened my eyes, that's all."

"Johan must think I'm mad. I think I was mad, though… It's just that I didn't even know I was pregnant. I was carrying your child and I didn't even know."

"I'll look after you from now on," he told her, pulling on his socks, and slipping his feet into his shoes. "I won't allow anyone to say a word against you, and we will have a child of our own one day, whether we make it or not."

"Look at you," she whispered, taking his bearded face in her hands, and gently kissing his lips.

"My mother hates it."

"She's seen your beard?" she asked. "What was your excuse?"

"That I was going to search for you, that I didn't know where I might have to search, but I wouldn't stop searching until I found you."

She kissed him again. "I'll pack my belongings, then you can take me home."

Leaving behind a pile of neatly stacked but completely useless photographic plates in the darkroom, and five bundles of photographs of her in various poses reduced to ashes in the range, they left Back Street for the last time and walked home to Brown Street.

"What time is it?" she asked as he closed the front door.

"My pocket watch is with my clothes at number 67. I didn't want to wear it with these," he added, giving the tatty morning coat and trousers a disgusted look. Taking her hand, he led her upstairs. "It's a quarter past seven," he told her after putting his head around the parlour door. "Tired?"

"Yes, I am," she replied, following him into the bedroom, suddenly feeling fit to drop and overwhelmed with relief. "Will you please hold me while I sleep?"

"Of course I will," he said softly. He put her carpet bag down, lit the oil lamp, and closed the curtains. "Welcome home," he added, and she moved forward into his arms, tears streaming down her cheeks.

It was bright outside when she opened her eyes, hearing horses' hooves and people laughing on the street outside.

She looked down and saw that the bedcovers had been lowered. Will reached out and cupped one of her breasts in his hand. What he was thinking, she wondered. He knows the human body inside out. He ran a thumb over the nipple and it hardened. He smiled and he raised his eyes to hers.

"It's such a giveaway. All I had to do yesterday was to touch it lightly with my lips and I knew you loved me."

"It might have been your beard," she teased, but he shook his head. "All right." She laughed. "It wasn't the beard."

"I'm shaving it off, anyway. Kiss me?"

He closed his eyes as she moved across the bed and straddled him, his hands cupping her buttocks. She bent down and kissed his scar, then his chest, moving slowly upwards to his lips. He groaned and she laughed softly, straightening up. Then the front door slammed. His eyes flew open and he sat bolt upright, clasping her to him. The sound of someone singing wafted up the stairs and in the open door.

"Mrs Bell." He sighed and loosened his grip on her. "She knows how to pick her moments."

"Is she to know I'm here?" Isobel asked, reluctantly climbing off his lap.

"Yes, of course."

"But I'm in your bed, Will."

"I'll put a pillow and a rug on the sofa in the parlour," he said with a smile. "Once we've eaten, we'll go for a walk."

"A walk?"

He nodded. "I need to speak to you without being overheard." Getting out of bed, he went to the wardrobe and lifted out a frock coat, waistcoat, trousers, shirt, collar, and cravat. He quickly got dressed before grabbing a pillow and a rug, went into the next room, then came back out again. "Mrs Bell?" he called down the stairs.

"Oh, Dr Fitzgerald?" She heard Mrs Bell hurry into the hall. "Oh, Jaysis, Dr Fitzgerald, I didn't know you were back."

"Only since last night. How are you?"

"Me? Sure, I'm grand. How about you? Such a beard."

"I'm well on the mend, Mrs Bell, thank you. The beard's going, don't worry. I'm sleeping in the parlour, Mrs Bell," he added.

"Oh?"

"Isobel is sleeping in my bed," he explained.

Isobel bit her lip and smiled.

"Oh, Dr Fitzgerald, where did you find her?"

"Working in a milliner's. Now, shall I light the range for you?"

It was almost mid-day before Will emerged from the bedroom and came into the parlour where she'd been waiting.

"Better?" he asked.

"Better." She crossed the room and kissed both his clean-shaven cheeks.

"Good. Let's go for that walk."

Taking his arm, they strolled along Brown Street.

"No-one will ever know where I found you," he began. "Not Mrs Bell – not my parents – no-one."

"Thank you. I'll never be able to thank you enough," she said, and he shook his head dismissively. "I won't," she persisted. "But at the same time, I'm sad."

"Oh?"

"I feel there's nothing I can do that will ever shock you again."

"Well, isn't that a good thing?" he asked with a smile.

"No, it isn't. I know I'm damaged because of what I've been through – the things I've done – but you were a good, kind man…"

"And now I'm not?"

"Yes, you are, but I feel I have corrupted you and that makes me feel terrible."

"Listen." Halting, he tilted her face up. "Where did we meet?"

"I know, but you didn't want to be there, did you?"

"I still had sex with you. I could have left. I didn't. I had sex with you. In fact, I know now that I've done nothing but have sex with you, and that makes me feel terrible. But when we get home…" She flushed and he kissed her lips. "When shall we get married?"

"You choose."

"Soon?"

She nodded. "Soon. Because…" She tailed off.

"If you fall pregnant again, I will take responsibility for both you and the child. And if you don't, then we will adopt a child. Either way, we will have a family, and make a home for ourselves here."

"I did go and see a doctor," she told him. "He told me there was no explanation for the miscarriage and he saw no reason why I shouldn't carry another child to full term."

"I'm glad you did. And he's right. I'm afraid it's just one of those things."

"Will the Harveys' have told all and sundry why I was dismissed?" she asked.

"I don't know," he replied simply. "But I would think they wouldn't want it known why another of their maids was dismissed."

"That I was the second of their maids to fall pregnant, you mean?"

"Yes."

She nodded and gave him a sad little smile. "I'm a fallen woman twice over now – a scarlet woman."

"You are my fiancée. And anyone who makes any disparaging comments will answer to me." She slid her arms around his neck and felt his hands clasp her waist. "Just promise me one thing?" he whispered.

"If I can."

"Never run away again?"

She loosened her arms a little. His brown eyes were searching her face anxiously.

"I promise," she whispered, and his face broke into a grin. "Hold me?"

He tightened his grip on her. "On Monday, I begin work again. This evening, we'll go to Merrion Square and tell my parents. This afternoon, I make love to you."

And he did. She was led upstairs to the bedroom, undressed, and laid on the bed while he pulled off his clothes. He climbed onto the bed and went to kiss her but she turned her head away.

"What?"

"If this ever becomes a chore." She looked back at him and his eyebrows rose in incredulity but she continued. "If it does and if you feel that all you are doing is servicing me, you will tell me? Promise you'll tell me?"

"Servicing you?" he echoed.

"Please, Will?"

"Don't be silly." He lowered his lips to a breast.

"Will." She scrambled off the bed and he stared at her in astonishment. "Please."

"Just what do I have to do to prove to you how much I love you?"

"I'm not talking about now, I'm talking about ten or twenty years from now. I can't help being scared," she admitted. "My parents loved each other very much at first, I've been told. Then, as the years went on…"

"I'm not your father, Isobel. I will never be your father."

"Just promise me, Will."

He pulled a resigned expression. "Very well, I promise."

"Thank you." She returned to the bed and sat on the edge. "You were the only man not to be horrified by my scar. Some men had horrific scars themselves but I think they expected me to be perfect. They were paying, so the goods had to be faultless. You didn't pay, and you kissed the entire length of my scar even though you were very drunk." He flushed and she smiled. "Would you kiss it again?"

"Lie down and turn over," he instructed, and he bent over her. She felt his lips travel down the length of the scar then all the way up again.

"Thank you. Let me see yours properly." He smiled, rolled onto his back, and she leant over him. "It's healing very well."

"Thank you, nurse."

She gently kissed his scar then couldn't help but laugh. "Gosh, Will, you're eager."

"I can't help it," he told her frankly. "Never mind me servicing you, you might end up servicing me in the years to come."

"Now who's being silly," she replied, and straddled him.

"Let's just both be very, very silly," he whispered, his hands sliding down her back and to her hips, pulling her down onto him.

That evening, Maura admitted them to number 67. Both his parents got up from their seats in the morning room as Isobel walked in with him, gripping his hand tightly.

"Will, thank goodness. And Isobel." His mother rushed forward and kissed both her cheeks. "Oh, Isobel, I'm so relieved to see you. Wherever did you go to?"

"A milliner's."

"A milliner's?"

"On High Street," Will added. "After Jimmy had searched Grafton Street and said the shops there wouldn't take Isobel on, I remembered something she had mentioned in one of her letters about buying new ribbon for her hat and getting a bargain. It was a long shot, but I tried every milliner's I could think of, and one proprietor mentioned that a young woman had been in asking for work. He didn't have any work for her but had directed her to a milliner's on High Street. I went there, and there Isobel was."

"We were so worried but Will was—"

Isobel turned and gave him a smile. "I know."

"I'm so glad you have done away with that awful beard, Will." His mother kissed his cheek.

"I may have had to search in some less than respectable areas," he explained. "So I thought it would be better if I changed my appearance. Luckily, the milliner's was more than respectable," he added and gave Isobel's hand a little squeeze.

"I'm sorry for running away and causing you so much worry," she said. "I didn't know I was expecting a child, or that I was losing it. It was awful and I wasn't thinking clearly and I'm sorry."

"Come and sit down and tell us how you are." His mother ushered them to the sofa and they all sat down.

"I'm very well, Mrs Fitzgerald, thank you. It's as if I'm waking up from a very bad dream. I'm so grateful to Will for finding me, I'm glad it's over, and I'm looking forward to starting a new life with him."

"You are getting married, then?" his father asked them in a resigned tone and Will nodded. "When?"

"Soon," he replied simply, and his father pursed his lips but said nothing further.

"Congratulations." Mrs Fitzgerald reached out and squeezed their hands. "All's well that ends well. There is, of course, a home for you here, Isobel, until the wedding," she continued, and Will's heart sank. He should have known his parents would bring this up.

"I'm afraid I don't understand?" Isobel frowned.

"You cannot… how can I put it? You cannot live together under the same roof before the wedding, Isobel."

"I am sleeping in the parlour, Mother," Will informed her.

"The parlour?"

"There are no beds in the bedrooms on the second floor," he explained.

"Your mother is right," his father told him. "If you insist on marrying Isobel, you must go about it properly."

"But – but—" he stuttered, grabbing her hands, horrified at the thought of losing her again.

"Listen to me, Will," his father snapped. "Your mother and I are doing our best to ensure it doesn't become common knowledge that Isobel miscarried your child, so I insist you do this properly. Isobel will live here until the wedding and that is final."

Will glanced at her and she gave him a little shrug. They had no choice.

"Very well," he said quietly.

"Good. You will return to Brown Street by cab. Isobel will collect her belongings, and she will return here in it. Is that clear?"

"Yes." Will conceded defeat.

"Good. Will, you live in a rented house and you pay a housekeeper. Soon you will have a wife. And a family." There was an awkward pause before his father continued; "The practice needs more young blood. Two morning surgeries per week, that is all."

Will sighed. His father was right of course, he would need the extra money. But what about his practice in Brown Street? Would his patients feel as though he were abandoning them?

"I will have to discuss it with Isobel."

His father nodded. "At least you haven't turned me down flat."

"I will discuss it with Isobel, Father."

"Which church will you marry in?" Mrs Fitzgerald asked brightly.

Will looked at Isobel again and she returned a blank stare. "We don't know yet, Mother."

"You have a lot to discuss, then." His father got up and went to the drinks tray. "A drink to celebrate. Isobel, a sherry?"

"Thank you."

"Whiskey, Will?"

"Yes, thank you."

Two hours later, as they travelled back to Brown Street by cab, Will swore under his breath. "My father has wanted to organise my life from the very beginning."

"It's only two mornings per week."

"For now. And I'm losing you until the wedding."

"No, you're not," she replied. "I will visit Brown Street as often as I can and you will come to Merrion Square, I hope?" She raised an eyebrow suggestively, and he laughed and kissed her. "And I can't help but be grateful to your parents for trying to keep what happened a secret."

He helped her to pack her meagre belongings before following her downstairs. "You think I should join Father's practice?"

"If you don't want to, I will look for work. I can't cook but I am a good seamstress and I can take in sewing. I don't mind."

"Well, I do." He sighed. "I'll do it. Two mornings, no more. I'll call to number 67 tomorrow and tell him."

"And see me?"

"Of course." Taking her face in his hands, he kissed her, then opened the front door and helped her into the waiting cab. "And when I can't, I will write."

She smiled and he waved as the cab took her away.

The following afternoon, he walked to number 67 and Tess informed him that Dr Fitzgerald senior was having a breath of air in the garden. Will went outside and his father failed to hide his surprise on hearing Will agree to start working at the practice again.

"I fully expected you to say no. Thank you, Will. Which days would you prefer?"

"Wednesdays and Fridays?" he suggested, his father nodded, and Will went inside to the morning room.

His mother was alone, seated on the sofa with a book, and his heart began to pound with anxiety.

"Where's Isobel?"

"Upstairs in the drawing room. Will." Mrs Fitzgerald closed the book and put it to one side. "Isobel has hardly spoken two words since she arrived yesterday. She has only picked at her meals, and I don't think she slept at all last night."

"Mother, she needs to get used to being here and not in next door's servants' quarters. She also needs to recover from the miscarriage. She lost a child she didn't even know she was carrying. It's a lot for her to come to terms with."

"And for you as well," his mother said softly, and he nodded. "Go to her and tell her she needs to eat. Find out what her favourite meals are and I will ask Mrs Rogers to cook them for her."

He found a pale and wide-eyed Isobel in a corner of the drawing room.

"I'm sorry, I should have knocked," he said and kissed her lips. "Did I startle you?"

"A little. I didn't hear you come in. I'm tired. I woke up in the middle of the night and it took me a few moments to remember where I was. And I was so relieved."

"Did you get back to sleep?" he asked, and she shook her head.

"No. So I sat at the window and looked out over the square like I used to do next door. Except." She gave him a little smile. "The window in my bedroom here isn't draughty and I don't have to get up at six in the morning."

"Ask for some warm milk this evening. It will help you sleep through the night."

"Yes. It will just take me some time to adjust to not being… there… Anyway," she continued brightly. "Your mother said I could explore the house. Have you spoken to your father?"

"Yes, I have. My surgery is on Wednesday and Friday mornings. You will adjust, Isobel. Take all the time you need. Explore the Merrion Square gardens, too."

"Your mother suggested that and I did while your parents were at church but, coming back, I met Mr and Mrs Harvey and Claire on the front steps. Mrs Harvey said she was extremely relieved you had found me, that she was delighted to see me looking so well, and she has asked me to call on her. Mr Harvey didn't seem too happy at that prospect, but he said nothing. I don't think he wants me to set foot inside number 68 ever again."

"Will you call on Mrs Harvey?" he asked, and she shrugged.

"I don't know. To go from being her lady's maid to calling on her and drinking tea with her is a very big step. As well as that, I don't know if I could have Claire serve tea to me, even though she treated me like a stranger today, and called me Miss Stevens." She spread her hands helplessly. "I suppose I should have expected it, considering what I did, but it still hurt."

"You aren't a servant anymore," he said softly. "And you will be treated as such."

"Mr Johnston told me once that I belonged neither

upstairs nor downstairs. I seem to belong upstairs now and it will take a little getting used to."

He kissed her forehead again. "Mother is worried that you are not eating and wants to know what your favourite meals are so she can ask Mrs Rogers—."

"There is no need to go to the trouble of cooking my favourite meals, Will. It's just that I used to chat and gossip with Maura and Tess. Now, they serve me my meals, call me Miss Stevens, and try not to stare at me. Like I said, it will take a little getting used to, and I will have an appetite for dinner this evening."

"Good." He smiled. "We need to decide about the wedding. When and where."

"Soon, but I don't know where. What Church of Ireland parish is Brown Street in?"

"It's in the united Parish of St Nicholas Without and St Luke."

"Without?" she repeated.

"It means it was outside the walls of Dublin," he explained. "Out in the Liberties, where the rules within the city walls didn't apply."

"What's the church like?"

"I'll show you. It's St Luke's, situated just off the Coombe. Come on."

He waited in the hall while she went for her coat and hat, then they walked to the large, plain church.

"Well?" he asked as they stood at the door.

She smiled. "I like it. But your parents won't. They'll expect somewhere fashionable like St Peter's."

"We're the ones who are getting married, not them," he said and held her hands. "Shall we get married here?" he asked, and she nodded.

The commencement of Dr William Fitzgerald's surgery at the Merrion Street Upper practice was announced in *The Irish Times*. But his engagement was not, and Will hoped Isobel wasn't disappointed.

"I'm not upset," she told him. "We are going to have a quiet engagement and wedding and we don't need everyone to know. Has your father allocated you any patients yet?"

"So far I have the grand total of three."

"Well, this announcement will certainly help." She passed the newspaper back to him across the morning room's writing desk. "William," she mused. "It's strange, isn't it? That I've never called you William?"

"William is reserved by my mother for when she is very angry."

"Let's hope I shall never have to call you William, then."

On Wednesday morning, he opened the door to the practice house, feeling strangely nervous.

"Good morning, Dr Fitzgerald." Eva, practice secretary for the past twenty years and wearing a dress in the deepest of reds, came forward to take his overcoat and hat.

"Good morning, Eva. I hope there were some responses to the newspaper announcement?"

Eva smiled. "There were. You will see four patients today and four on Friday, Dr Fitzgerald."

"In which surgery?"

"In your former surgery, Dr Fitzgerald. If there is anything you require, please inform me."

"I shall."

"Your first patient is a Mrs Henderson, who is relatively new to Dublin. I will send her upstairs to your surgery presently."

"Thank you."

"Will?" He heard his father's voice and turned to see him and Fred coming down the stairs. "I thought I heard you. I just wanted to wish you luck."

"Thank you, Father."

"Fred." He shook his friend's hand. "Eight patients to my name so far."

"That will change soon," Fred replied with a grin. "I thought I'd never see you here again, Will."

"Never say never," Will replied simply, and went upstairs.

He rose from behind the leather-topped desk in his surgery as the door opened and a handsome dark-haired woman in her mid-to-late forties came in. "Mrs Henderson?"

"Good gracious me." She stared up at him in surprise as he went to the door and closed it. "I didn't realise you would be quite so young."

"I hope it's not a problem?" he asked with a polite smile.

"Oh, no, not at all. It just makes me feel very old."

"Please sit down." He held the chair as she sat down then seated himself back behind the desk. "Do you live locally?"

"Fitzwilliam Square. Actually, my son and I have only recently moved there. I'm newly married."

"Congratulations."

"Thank you. It's my second marriage," she explained. "I was widowed in February this year. My son and I moved to Dublin for a fresh start, and I met Ronald almost immediately. My new husband is a solicitor."

"Have you been in good health, Mrs Henderson?" he asked.

"Well, I… generally… yes." She smoothed a hand down the skirt of her russet-coloured dress then began to fiddle with her black gloves. "Unfortunately, I suffer from nerves. My first husband was not an easy man to live with and it will take a while for those nerves to leave me. My second husband is a kind man."

"Have you spoken to him about your first husband?"

"Yes, a little, but what I did not tell him was that my first husband was a violent man."

"Was he violent towards you?" Will asked her gently.

"No, never. All he ever needed to do was to raise his voice and… no, but he was violent towards our children. We had a son and a daughter."

"You had?"

"Yes." Mrs Henderson peered down at her hands. "But I'm afraid my daughter is no longer with me."

"I'm so sorry—" Will began, but Mrs Henderson's head jerked up.

"She is not dead, Dr Fitzgerald. Well, at least I believe she is not dead."

"I do beg your pardon." He frowned. "But I don't understand?"

"She was thrown out."

"Thrown out?" he echoed.

"Yes. You see, she was seduced by a neighbour's son who would not stand by her. Her father, naturally, was furious but he—" Her voice shook. "I do apologise."

"Not at all. Take your time. Would you like a glass of water?"

"No, thank you. My first husband was a clergyman but he had a cruel and violent temper. When he found out our daughter was expecting a child, he whipped her."

Will caught his breath and clapped a hand to his mouth, coughing. "I'm so sorry, do forgive me."

"Yes, it's dreadful. Poor Isobel was stripped, whipped, disowned, then thrown out of the house. I have not seen her since. Poor Alfie, her brother, has never forgiven himself. James, the neighbour's son, was his friend, you see."

"How long ago did this happen?"

"January," she replied. "I refuse to believe she is dead. She could have gone anywhere, but I did think Dublin. There are certain places, are there not, Dr Fitzgerald?"

Will gave her a blank stare. "Places?"

"For unmarried mothers?"

"Oh. Oh, yes, there are. Mrs Henderson, does your husband know all of this?"

"He knows all except for the violence. Poor Isobel, her poor back. Then, poor Alfie was beaten black and blue."

"And you, Mrs Henderson?" he asked, despite what she had told him earlier, and her shoulders slumped.

"Yes. My first husband beat me also."

"Did he whip you?"

"No. Once he saw what he had done to poor Isobel's back, I think even he was shocked. So you see, my poor nerves…"

"Does your son also live in Dublin now?" he asked, trying to remember what she had told him to begin with.

"Oh, yes. Alfie is studying medicine at Trinity College."

Will smiled. "That's where I studied."

"His father wanted Alfie to follow him into the church but Alfie bravely refused. Now he has the chance to pursue his ambition at long last."

"How do you feel now, Mrs Henderson? Now you've told me all?"

"Oh." She sighed. "Well… relieved… do you think I should tell my husband all?"

"Perhaps. Although it isn't wise to go into a marriage with secrets."

"No. Are you married, Dr Fitzgerald?" she asked.

"Engaged to be married," he told her. "Soon to be married."

"I hope you will be very happy."

"Thank you," he replied with a weak smile.

"You are right. It isn't wise to keep things hidden. Thank you, Dr Fitzgerald, for listening."

"Not at all." He smiled and they stood up.

"Good gracious." She stared up at him. "You are tall. Do you think I should enquire after my daughter at those institutions for unmarried mothers?"

Will hesitated. "I would be honest with your husband first, Mrs Henderson. Take one step at a time. If you need a list of institutions, I will provide you with one."

She smiled. "Thank you. You've been so kind, even if I did horrify you a little."

"Not at all." He went to the door and opened it for her. "Good morning, Mrs Henderson," he added, standing at the door watching her go down the stairs.

"Will?" His father hailed him from along the landing. "What is it?"

"I need to speak with you later. Here, not at number 67."

"You're not leaving are you?" his father asked.

"What? No."

When his last patient had left, Will went to the window,

hearing a knock at the door. "Come in," he called and turned around.

"What is so important?" His father came in and closed the door.

"My first patient. She's a Mrs Henderson." He sighed. "She's Isobel's mother."

His father's eyes bulged. "What? Are you sure?"

"Positive."

"Did you tell her?"

He shook his head. "Oh, I wish she hadn't been the first. I could hardly concentrate on the others. They probably won't come back."

"Don't worry about that for now. Are you going to tell Isobel?"

Will turned back to the window. "What if she runs away again? What if her mother is horrified by what's happened, where I live and refuses to give her consent to the marriage?"

"I'm afraid there is only one way to find out. But Isobel is over twenty-one, isn't she?"

Will nodded. "Yes, she is."

"Go back to number 67 and tell her. And ask Eva for Mrs Henderson's address."

"Yes."

"And, Will?"

He slowly turned around. "Yes?"

"Good luck."

Tess admitted him to the house and informed him that Miss Isobel was in the drawing room. He climbed the stairs, braced himself, and went in.

"Well?" Isobel was standing at the writing desk with a book in her hands and snapped the book shut. "How was it?"

She was so beautiful and, for a moment, he contemplated not telling her before giving her a little smile. "It went quite well."

"Only quite well?"

"My first patient was a Mrs Henderson… Isobel, could you sit down, please?" he asked, and she frowned.

"What's the matter?"

"Please?" he insisted, and she put the book on the desk, went to the walnut sofa with cream silk upholstery, and sat down. "Thank you. Mrs Henderson is in her mid-to-late forties and newly-married. Her first husband was a clergyman. She has two children but she lost contact with her daughter in January this year…" He tailed off. Isobel was staring up at him in disbelief. "Mrs Henderson's daughter had become pregnant by a neighbour's son," he went on. "Mrs Henderson's first husband stripped her daughter, whipped her, disowned her, and threw her out of the house."

"Oh, Will," Isobel croaked. "Is she really my..?"

"Yes, she is your mother. She mentioned you by name. Your brother is here in Dublin, too, studying medicine at Trinity."

She burst into tears and covered her face with her hands. He went and knelt beside her, kissing the top of her head.

"Did you tell her?" she whispered, dragging her fingers down her cheeks.

"No. But I have her address. Write to her?"

She nodded. "So my father is dead?"

"Yes. He died in February."

"And my new step-father?"

"A solicitor. Your mother says he's a kind man."

Pulling a handkerchief from her sleeve, she wiped her

eyes. "Thank you for telling me. It must have been a shock for you."

"It was," he admitted. "But it's much more of a shock for you."

"Mother must never know about any of—" she cried suddenly.

"Of course not – no-one will," he promised her, clasping her hands, and kissing them. "Shall I ring for tea?"

She shook her head. "No, I'm quite all right. I must write to her."

There was one envelope but no notepaper in the writing desk, so he went downstairs and met his mother in the hall.

"Is everything all right?" Mrs Fitzgerald asked anxiously. "I could hear raised voices."

"My first patient this morning – she was Isobel's mother."

It was a long time since he had seen his mother look quite so astonished. "But... how?"

"Isobel's father died early this year. Her mother has remarried, now lives on Fitzwilliam Square, and her brother is now studying medicine at Trinity."

"Is Isobel all right?" Mrs Fitzgerald whispered. "It must be a great shock."

"She wants to write a letter to her mother. May she have some notepaper? There is none left upstairs."

"Of course." His mother hurried to the morning room and came into the drawing room a couple of minutes later with several sheets of notepaper and an envelope. "Oh, Isobel."

Isobel smiled and took them from her. "Thank you."

"We'll leave Isobel in peace to write her letter. Will?"

"I'll be all right," she assured him.

He nodded, and followed his mother out of the room, not envying Isobel's task one bit.

Chapter Eight

Isobel stared at the sheets of notepaper before bringing them to the writing desk at the window and sitting down. Taking a deep breath, she opened the bottle of ink then picked up the pen. Dipping the nib into the ink, she paused for a moment before writing *67 Merrion Square, Dublin*, at the top of the sheet. If she planned the letter she would never get it written, so she continued:

Dear Mother,

I do not know how or where to start so please forgive me if this letter is a mass of jumbled words.

Dr William Fitzgerald, whom you met this morning, is my fiancé. Please forgive him for not telling you he knows me but he wished to tell me first that he met you. He has been so kind to me. I miscarried James' child soon after I arrived in Dublin and then I met Will and he set me on the road to recovery.

I found a position as a parlourmaid and later as a lady's maid in the house next door, it turned out, to Will's parents. Will was emerging from a broken engagement and neither of us was looking to fall in love but it happened!

It was not without incident. When I found I was miscarrying a child, Will's child, I was dismissed from my position as lady's maid and Will and I lost contact for a while. Somehow, Will found me again and we are to be married soon.

Will works in two medical practices. He takes surgeries twice per week in the Merrion Street Upper practice and he also has his own practice located on Brown Street, which is where he lives and where we will live after we are married. His parents live on Merrion Square, which is where I am living until the wedding.

I would be dishonest if I wrote of my sadness at hearing the news of Father's death. I do hope you are happy now in your second marriage. And I am sure Alfie is delighted to be a medical student at long last! Will studied medicine at Trinity College also.

I will close now. I chose to write to you so as to save you from the shock of our possibly meeting on the street or at the Merrion Street practice house. Please, can we meet soon?

All my love,
Isobel

She folded the letter and put it in the envelope as soon as the ink was dry and went downstairs to the morning room with it, the pen, and the ink. Will got up from the sofa and she held up the envelope.

"It is probably incoherent. But it is written. All I need now is her address, Will."

"I have a stamp." Mrs Fitzgerald went to a drawer in the morning room writing desk, took one out, and passed it to her.

"Thank you." Isobel moistened the stamp and placed it on the envelope. "Will?"

"Yes. It's number 55 Fitzwilliam Square," he told her, and her stomach constricted in horror. Hugh Lombard lived at number 30, but it was Fitzwilliam Square all the same.

"Fitzwilliam Square," she repeated, trying to hide her shock as she scribbled the address on the envelope. "There. I must go and post it. When I come back, could I have some tea, please?"

"Of course," Mrs Fitzgerald replied.

"I'll come with you, Isobel." Will followed her out of the morning room. "Isobel?" he added, sounding anxious as she stood for a moment in the hall staring at the address.

"I'm quite well." Taking his hand, she gave it a squeeze, and they left the house. "It is the official version in the letter, don't worry," she told him quietly. "I miscarried James' child, I met you, I found a position next door, we fell in love, I miscarried your child, we lost contact for a while, but we are now reunited and will be married. Rather a lot to take in but my mother is stronger than she appears."

"And you?" he asked as they walked along the pavement. "Tell me the truth now?" he added when they crossed the street and stopped at the post box.

She was going to have to tell him about Hugh Lombard. But not yet. "My mother must never find out where we really met. That would kill her."

"She won't find out from me and no-one else knows."

She nodded and posted the letter. "There."

"Will she write or will she come straight here, do you think?" he asked as they retraced their steps back to the house. All she could do was shrug.

She slept badly that night and, with her stomach in knots, could only manage a little tea and toast at breakfast. Will was to come to number 67 as soon as his house calls were completed but eleven o'clock came and went and no-one had called. She went out into the garden for some air and for something to do. Had she put too much in the letter? Had her mother disowned her, too?

"Isobel?" It was Will's voice and she spun around. He came down the steps to her and kissed her lips. "Your mother's here," he told her gently, and her heart began to thump. "We arrived at the same time. She's been shown into the morning room. My mother has gone next door so you can have as much time as you need."

She nodded. "Where will you be?"

"Upstairs in the drawing room. Come on."

They went inside and he kissed her again outside the morning room door before going up the stairs. Taking a shaky deep breath, she went into the room.

Her mother was standing at the window and turned. Both women stared at each other for a few moments before her mother gave a little cry and ran to her.

"Oh, Isobel." They clung to each other until her mother broke down in tears and pulled a handkerchief from the sleeve of her mauve dress. "I knew you were still alive."

"Come and sit down."

They went to the sofa and sat facing each other. Tears were still pouring down her mother's face. "You look well."

"And you."

"I recognised your handwriting immediately," her mother croaked, wiping her eyes. "I was almost in hysterics. Poor Ronald wanted to call a doctor until I showed him your letter."

"He knew about me?" Isobel asked.

"Yes, but not all. So I told him all."

"And?" she added anxiously.

"The poor man was horrified but is looking forward to meeting his step-daughter."

"Are you happy?"

"Oh, yes." Her mother smiled through her tears. "I suppose I married him before a proper length of time had elapsed since your father's death, but Ronald is such a good man. And you? Are you happy?"

"I haven't been this happy for a very long time," she told her mother truthfully.

"You were a parlourmaid?" her mother asked sadly.

"I had to work," she whispered.

"Of course."

"And I am marrying a doctor soon." Isobel smiled.

"Yes. My new young doctor is your fiancé." Her mother did not return her smile. "Isobel, I have asked where Brown Street is. It is in a slum."

"Brown Street is not in a slum," Isobel replied firmly. "The house there is very respectable. You do not like Will, do you, Mother?"

"He is a very pleasant young man. I just wish—"

"I love Will, Mother," she interrupted. "I do not know what I would have done without him. Just because he does not have a 'good' address."

"You also miscarried his child."

"Yes," she whispered.

"A respectable man would not have—"

"If Will is not respectable, what does that make me?" she interrupted again, her voice rising. "Two babies by two different men."

"Oh, Isobel, don't."

"Mother." She fought to calm herself. "I would be lying to you if I told you that what has happened to me has not left me damaged. James seduced and abandoned me. Father whipped and disowned me. Will has done none of those things. In fact, I have often treated him terribly, believing I was not good enough for him. But he has shown me beyond doubt that he loves me. And I will marry him, even if I have to drag two witnesses into the church off the street."

Her mother stared at her. "Oh, how you have changed…"

"Of course I have changed," she replied. "How could I not have changed? But I am still your daughter, aren't I?"

"Of course you are." Her mother clasped her face in her hands and kissed her forehead. "Of course you are."

"Will is in the drawing room. May I introduce him to you properly?"

"Yes, you may."

She hurried up the stairs, went into the room, and Will immediately got up from the sofa.

"Well?" he asked.

She smiled. "I want to introduce you properly." Taking his hand, she led him back to the morning room. "Mother, this is Will. Will, this is my mother."

"Mrs Henderson." He put out a hand and her mother shook it.

"May I call you Will?"

He laughed. "Of course."

"You love my daughter?"

"More than anything else in the world," he replied quietly.

"You live on Brown Street, however."

He nodded. "Yes, I do."

"Isobel has informed me it is not a slum, however, I have to confess I am uneasy when I learn that you will continue to live there after your marriage."

"It is not Merrion Square, Mrs Henderson. But the house is respectable, I can assure you."

"But the area is not."

"Mother—" she began but Will put a hand on her arm.

"I'm afraid I have to disagree. I would not bring Isobel to live there as my wife if I did not feel the neighbourhood was respectable. You are most welcome to visit the house and, if you will allow, Isobel and I can show you some of the neighbourhood and the church we are to be married in."

"Thank you, I shall."

"Tea?" he offered.

"Yes, thank you."

Will rang for a servant and they sat down.

"Can I ask what Father died of?" Isobel asked. "Then, I will never mention him again."

"A heart attack. Everyone was scandalised as, only two weeks after the funeral, Alfie and I were on the train to Dublin."

"And now you are happily married and Alfie is a medical student at long last."

"Yes." Her mother exhaled a delighted laugh.

"Does he know about me yet?"

"Yes, but he said I should come here alone. Can you come to Fitzwilliam Square for luncheon at one o'clock? Alfie is eager to see you again and Ronald also wishes to meet you. Both you and Will, of course."

Isobel looked at Will, who smiled and nodded. "We would be delighted to."

Half an hour later, after seeing her mother out, Isobel brought Will upstairs to the drawing room and closed the door.

"What is it?" he asked as she paced up and down for a few moments. "Do you not want to go to Fitzwilliam Square?"

"Yes, of course I do. But there's something I need to tell you first. And you're not going to like it."

He tensed. "Go on."

"Johan and Lucius' landlord is a man called Hugh Lombard. He also sells the photographs—"

"I know," Will interrupted. "I've met him."

"What?"

"It was through Jim Harvey and his collection of photographs," he explained. "He brought me to his club and he bought more there from Mr Lombard, including one of you, which he paid five shillings for. He gave it to me and I burned it."

She shuddered with relief. "Well, Mr Lombard turned up at the photographic studio and—" She rubbed her forehead. "And he wanted me to become his mistress." She paused and breathed deeply in and out to calm herself. "I said no, but Johan told me Mr Lombard would never give up pursuing me. So I went to his house." Will gasped but she went on. "His house on Fitzwilliam Square."

"What number?"

"Thirty."

"That's across the square from where your mother lives now," he told her. "Did you have sexual intercourse with him?"

"No," she assured him. "No, I didn't, Will, I promise. When I arrived, I was brought upstairs to a bedroom and dressed in a horrible scarlet dress cut so low it was indecent. I went downstairs to the dining room, where Mr Lombard was waiting for me, and the soup had just been served when the butler was called from the room."

"The butler?" he echoed then shook his head. "Sorry, go on."

"The butler returned a couple of minutes later and told Mr Lombard he had shown Mr Duncan Simpson into the drawing room and that Mr Simpson wanted to speak to him urgently."

"What?" Will's eyes narrowed.

"It was Fred's father. I recognised him from the night of your operation and—" She took another deep breath. "From Sally Maher's."

Will raised a hand to his forehead, clearly struggling to understand. "Fred's father was at the brothel?"

"Yes. Except, there, he was known as Dr Samuels. And," she went on, her voice shaking, "he was the doctor who carried out my abortion."

"Did he recognise you?"

"No, he didn't see me at all. He and Mr Lombard were arguing in the drawing room and I went to the double doors, which were open a little. I heard a punch and someone fall to the floor. Then, Mr Simpson walked past the double doors without seeing me. I opened the doors further and I saw Mr Lombard lying flat on his back unconscious on the rug. I panicked. I ran upstairs for my dress and coat then ran downstairs and out of the house. I got dressed in an alleyway and I managed to make my way back to Back Street. I expected Mr Lombard to come to Back Street looking for me but I haven't seen him since and I don't know why."

Will exhaled a long breath. "If Fred's father hadn't arrived, would you have stayed with Mr Lombard?"

"I don't know," she replied truthfully. "I was in such a state, and he had already hit me."

"He hit you?" Will cried. "When?"

"When he asked me to be his mistress and I said no. He hit me, bruising the skin around my eye, and making my eye bloodshot. I couldn't be photographed for about a week. By then my nerves were in shreds, but my bruise and bloodshot eye were healed. I had saved a sufficient amount of money and I decided to leave Dublin for London. But then you arrived. And I was horrified. But I was so relieved, too."

"Oh, Isobel." Will held her tightly as she cried.

"When we go to Fitzwilliam Square, I can't go anywhere near number 30. I can't risk Mr Lombard seeing me."

"We won't, I promise."

"Are you angry?" she whispered.

"About Mr Lombard and what he did to you – yes. About Fred's father… I don't know what to think."

"I saw Mr Simpson at Sally's a few times. I didn't have sex with him, I swear. In fact," she added, "he didn't have sex with any of the girls."

"I see."

"I'm sorry," she whispered. "But you needed to know."

"Duncan Simpson is one of the best surgeons in Dublin. I'm glad it was he who attended to you."

"And he saved your life."

"Yes, he did. Would he recognise you if he saw you again?" Will asked.

"I don't know. It was back in January. And I was probably one of many, so I doubt it."

Will nodded. "I hope you're right."

An hour later, Isobel and Will walked to Fitzwilliam Square and a butler admitted them to her mother's new home. They were shown into a morning room with cream walls and curtains, an enormous sofa upholstered in gold-coloured velvet and two matching armchairs, four side tables, and a writing desk at the window. The new Mrs Henderson rose from one of the armchairs and kissed them both before turning to a stocky man with greying receding hair.

"Isobel, Will, this is my husband, Ronald. Ronald, this is my daughter, Isobel, and her fiancé, Dr William Fitzgerald."

Isobel's stomach constricted when her step-father came forward but she put a hand out and he shook it warmly.

"I'm delighted to meet you, my dear. And you, Dr Fitzgerald," he added, shaking Will's hand.

"Will," he said. "I'm delighted to meet you, too."

She couldn't help but burst into tears when she spotted Alfie standing in a corner, and tears rolled down his cheeks as they embraced tightly.

"I'm so sorry," he whispered. "James was my best friend."

"It's forgotten," she said, pulling a white handkerchief out of the breast pocket of his black morning coat, and drying his tears. "Come and meet Will. Will, this is Alfie. Alfie, this is Will."

"'Good to meet a fellow medical man." Will shook his hand.

"Better late than never." Alfie smiled.

"True."

"When is your wedding?" Alfie asked her.

"Soon. It will be a very quiet affair."

A huge luncheon of mushroom soup, roast chicken and vegetables, and trifle was served and eaten in a bright breakfast room decorated in pale yellow. When Isobel put her desert spoon down, her mother reached for her hand.

"I have discussed it with Ronald, and we would very much like you to live here with us until the wedding."

Isobel stared at her in consternation. To live across the square from Hugh Lombard's home was the last thing she wanted. "Oh, I see. It's just that Will's parents—"

"I shall, of course, discuss it with them. But it would be better that you live here, don't you think?"

"Well, yes, I suppose so…"

"Good." Mrs Henderson beamed at her in delight.

"How soon can we get married without it seeming indecent?" Was the first thing she asked Will as they walked out of Fitzwilliam Square.

"It all depends on how long it takes for a Common Licence to be granted."

"Isobel? Isobel, wait." She turned, hearing Alfie's voice. Her brother was running along the pavement towards them. "You dropped one of your gloves," he said, sweeping his brown hair back off his forehead with one hand, and passing the black glove to her with the other.

"Thank you. I don't usually wear gloves anymore."

"I'm sorry, Isobel. Mother shouldn't have pressurised you into coming to live here."

"She wants to be with me as much as she can before the wedding. It's quite understandable."

"The square isn't such a dull place," he told her with a smile. "Quite scandalous, actually."

"Oh?" Will enquired.

"A gentleman across the square was found dead in his drawing room not too long ago. But don't let that put you off."

"What was his name?" she asked, trying to sound indifferent.

"Something foreign-sounding... Lombard – that's it. It appeared as though he had been involved in a fight but that's about as far as the police got with their investigation. He doesn't seem to have had any close family so the house is standing empty at present. Well, I can't stand here gossiping, I have studying to do." Alfie kissed her cheek and shook Will's hand. "See you both soon."

Exhaling a long relieved breath, she watched him walk away before turning to Will, who was gazing across the square.

"We don't get involved," he murmured.

"No, of course not. But all I heard was the sound of Mr Simpson punching Mr Lombard and Mr Lombard falling to the floor. How could one punch have killed him?"

"Mr Lombard may have hit his head when he fell. He may have had some underlying medical condition which was exacerbated by the punch or fall. Just be grateful that Mr Lombard is dead – that he will never find you now."

"I am grateful – of course I am – but Mr Simpson killed him," she protested.

"We know nothing about it, Isobel, do you hear me? Absolutely nothing."

"Yes."

"Now tell me how you know Ronald Henderson?" he added.

She grimaced. Had it been so obvious she knew him? "He owns Sally Maher's brothel."

"What?" Will cried.

"The landlord, a Mr Henderson, was mentioned a lot when I went there first. He'd raised the rent and he came in person to discuss it with Sally. He also knows Mr Simpson, as they arrived together one day."

"Did you have sex with Mr Henderson?" Will asked, and she heard the dread in his voice.

"No, I didn't." She was going to have to tell him and sighed. "Mr Henderson had sex with Mr Simpson."

Will's eyes widened. "Are you absolutely sure?"

"Yes, I'm positive. Sally used to provide a room for them. Once, sometimes twice, a week – and always at different times – probably so none of their friends or family would suspect anything. I'm so sorry, Will, I realise you know Mr Simpson well."

"Not at all well, it seems. I don't believe it." He grimaced and rubbed his forehead. "He's Fred's father and my godfather, and I just don't believe it."

"Sally used to rent a room out to quite a few gentlemen. Sally's is well known as a brothel – for men having sex with women – I mean. That it is also used as somewhere men can have sex with other men, is not as well known – for obvious reasons."

"But she could extort money from these gentlemen?"

"If Sally tries to extort money from Mr Henderson and Mr Simpson, Mr Henderson will simply evict her," she said.

"He has already threatened to when they discussed the raising of the rent. Sally doesn't want to move, she's put a lot of work into that house, believe it or not."

"Do you think your mother married Mr Henderson for love?" Will asked, and she shrugged.

"With what my father put my mother through, she will crave and be thankful for any type of affection. But affection doesn't equal love, and I won't see how Mr Henderson generally acts towards her until I move here. One thing is for certain, my poor innocent mother will not be able to comprehend that a man can love and have sex with another man. It is possible Mr Henderson does love her, and he just happens to like men, too. But the fact that he didn't have sex with Sally – or any of her girls – makes me conclude…" She tailed off and Will nodded.

"Will you tell Alfie?"

"Certainly not yet. I need to speak with him and try and find out what it was like at home after I left. Home," she added, giving him a sad little smile. "It's not my home anymore."

"We will make a home for ourselves in Brown Street," he said and kissed her hand.

"I was almost as innocent as my mother when I first came to Dublin. In some ways, innocence is a blessing but mostly it is a curse. Especially for women. The things I saw at Sally's – the things I heard and learned – I used to just sit in my room and shake. Then Maggie took me under her wing. I learned a lot from her. I had to, I would never have survived there, otherwise. Poor Maggie, I don't think she was ever innocent, but she was terrified of Mr Henderson. I think her family must have been evicted from their home because whenever Mr Henderson turned up at Sally's, Maggie was convinced we were all going to be thrown out onto the street."

"Mr Henderson didn't seem to recognise you. Or, if he did, he hid it well."

"I use to see him coming into Sally's from the top of the stairs but he never saw me. Please, can we get married as soon as possible?" she begged.

"I'll try my best," he said and kissed her hand.

Isobel moved into number 55 Fitzwilliam Square the next morning and her mother brought her to a large bedroom decorated in grey-blue on the second floor overlooking the rear garden. By five o'clock, she was feeling stifled. It was understandable her mother would want to spend time with her but, so far, she hadn't left her alone for five minutes.

"I'm going to write to Will now," she announced, getting up from beside her mother on the sofa in the morning room.

"Write to him?"

"I enjoy writing to him and I need a little time to myself," she explained. "I want to write to him now and put the letter in the post before the last collection."

"Very well. There are notepaper and envelopes in the writing desk."

"Thank you," she replied politely. "But I have notepaper and envelopes of my own in my bedroom."

And with that, she left the morning room. Out in the hall, she put her hands on her hips and sighed.

"Isobel?"

She jumped, hearing Alfie's voice, not having heard him follow her. "I'm sorry, I just needed—"

"I know. Look, fetch a coat and hat, and we'll go across the street to the gardens before it gets dark."

She gave him a grateful smile and hurried upstairs.

"I'm so glad you are happy now," Alfie told her as they sat down on a bench. "After what Father did—"

"Let's not talk about Father," she interrupted softly. "Except, I must ask – did he ever show any remorse over what he did to me?"

Alfie shook his head. "We weren't even allowed to mention your name."

That saddened but didn't surprise her. "Did he beat you and Mother?"

"Isobel…"

"Please, Alfie?"

"Yes." He sighed. "Yes, he did."

She reached out and squeezed his hands. "I'm sorry."

"Oh, Isobel, it wasn't your fault. I shouldn't have trusted James."

"Have you heard anything from him?" she asked.

"Not a word."

"That doesn't surprise me. But, yes, I am happy now. Will and I have decided to marry as soon as possible."

Alfie's eyes widened in surprise. "Why?"

"Why wait? We love each other."

"You miscarried his child."

"Yes, I did," she replied, peering down at her hands. "You're shocked, aren't you? That we had sexual intercourse before marriage?"

"A little, I suppose."

"Mother must be horrified, though, she hides it well. Has Mr Henderson mentioned it?" she asked, raising her head.

"Mr Henderson?" Alfie echoed. "Hasn't he asked you to call him Ronald?"

"He hasn't had a chance," she replied with a wry smile.

"Well, I did overhear Mother and Ronald speaking about you, and he did sound quite shocked, but I think he was pleasantly surprised when he met you."

"What do you know about him?"

"He's a solicitor, and Mother loves him dearly."

You really don't know much about him at all, do you, she thought. "Where did they marry?"

"St Peter's. I gave her away, which was rather odd but in a good way. Who do you want to give you away?"

She stared at him, not having given it any thought. "You."

"You don't have—" he began.

"I know, but I don't know Mr Henderson at all, and you're my brother. You won't trip me up, though, will you?"

She was relieved to see him laugh. "No, I won't. I promise."

When they returned to the house, she went straight upstairs to her bedroom and wrote to Will.

Dear Will,

Just a quick note to tell you I love you and I miss you.

Mother means well but she hasn't left me alone all day. Alfie and I managed to sneak out of the house and we went to the gardens in the centre of the square, where we talked and talked. He does not know much about Mr Henderson at all, except that he is a solicitor and loves Mother very much. I was dead to Father after he threw me out. Poor Mother and Alfie were not even allowed to mention my name.

When we marry, I have asked Alfie to give me away, and he has promised not to trip me up!

My bedroom is large, and so is my bed. I cannot wait to share your bed again.

All my love,

Isobel

Alfie brought her to the nearest post box. She posted the letter, and they returned to number 55.

At breakfast the next day, she broached the idea of a dress for the wedding.

"A wedding dress." Her mother put her tea cup down. "Yes, we must begin to consider some designs."

"Actually, I want something very simple and which can be made quickly. Will and I are marrying as soon as possible," she explained.

"But—" Her mother was horrified. "People will think—"

"Mother, people already know of my past. I don't care what they think of me now. All I want is to marry Will as soon as possible and look presentable doing so. You do have a dressmaker?"

"Yes, of course."

"May we go and see her?"

"Yes," Mrs Henderson replied faintly.

The dressmaker lived only ten minutes' walk away, but Isobel's mother wouldn't dream of walking there, so they travelled by cab. Isobel was measured, the dressmaker showed her some dress designs and Isobel scandalised her mother further by choosing the simplest one, with a v-shaped neckline and long sleeves, and asking that it be made quickly. Virginal white was also out of the question, so she chose cream silk satin and a lace veil which wouldn't cover her face, and she was to return for a fitting in a few days' time.

In the meantime, she needed to speak to Will about Mrs Bell. He hadn't mentioned whether he was going to keep his housekeeper on so, straight after Sunday luncheon the following afternoon, she managed to escape her mother and walked to Brown Street.

Will was carrying an enamel bucket of water from the pump in the backyard into the kitchen when he heard someone knock at the front door. He put the bucket down beside the sink and went to answer it. Opening the door, he found Isobel on the step.

"Hello." He smiled and she stepped into the hall. "You didn't say you were calling today?"

"I've called because I need to ask you about Mrs Bell. Are you going to keep her on? Because, if you're not, I need to learn how to cook – and how to cook on the solid fuel range."

"Well." He closed the front door and kissed her lips before going to the sink, pouring some of the water into a bowl, and washing his hands. "I was thinking of keeping her on. Not because she can cook and you can't, but because everyone around here knows her."

Isobel's face fell. "You mean, if I were here on my own, people wouldn't come to you?"

"It's possible," he admitted. "When I came here first, I

had no patients whatsoever for over a month. I was on the point of giving up when someone told me about Mrs Bell and her wonderful cooking. So I went to see her and, as I said, everyone knows her and by word of mouth alone I started getting patients."

"Oh. It's just that if I'm not going to be cooking and cleaning, I don't know what I'm going to do all day."

"What does your mother do all day?" he asked.

An exasperated expression crossed her face. "She never leaves me alone, that's what she does all day. I love her, and I am so happy we have found each other again, but she is suffocating me. I think she hopes to do as your mother does and make calls to acquaintances – except, Mother has no acquaintances yet. And." She shook her head. "I have no acquaintances here either. Will, I want so much to be your wife, but I'm scared, too."

He dried his hands then took her in his arms. How long had it been since she had lived a normal life? How long would it take for her to adjust?

"We'll speak to Mrs Bell and—" He stopped, hearing someone hammering with a fist on the front door. He kissed Isobel's forehead before going to answer it. Opening the door, he found a young maid wearing neither coat nor hat, on the step gasping for breath. "Catch your breath," he told her and she nodded, patting her chest until she could speak.

"Are you Dr Fitzgerald?" she asked.

"Yes, I am."

"Is Miss Isobel here? I've come from Fitzwilliam Square."

"I'm here," Isobel answered from behind him. "It's Dora, isn't it?"

"Yes, Miss. Mr Alfie sent me to find you. The police were

at the house. It's the master, Miss. He's dead."

Will shot a glance at Isobel, whose lips were parting in horror. "Dead?" he asked the maid. "Why were the police involved?"

"Because." The maid began to examine her hands. "I overheard that—"

"Yes?" he prompted.

"The master died in a brothel, Dr Fitzgerald. A brothel on Montgomery Street that he owned."

Behind him, he heard Isobel clap a hand to her face.

Think clearly, Will, he ordered himself. "Thank you, Dora. Let me find my hat and overcoat, and we'll take a cab back to Fitzwilliam Square."

"Me as well, Doctor?"

"Yes, of course. Just one moment." He led Isobel into the kitchen and closed the door.

"Mother is going to be in hysterics," she whispered.

"I'm going to bring my medical bag," he told her. "Just in case I may have to sedate her."

"Yes. Oh, God, why did he have to die? And in Sally's, too?"

"Isobel." He clasped her face in his hands. "We have to act as though we knew nothing about Mr Henderson – nothing at all."

"I know."

"Good." He kissed her lips and brought her back out to the hall. He shrugged on his overcoat, put on his hat, and retrieved his medical bag from the surgery. Dora was waiting on the pavement when they left the house. "We need to walk to Cork Street. We've more chance of finding a cab there." Taking Isobel's arm, and with Dora walking behind them, he hailed the first cab which came along. "Fitzwilliam Square," he told the cabman, while helping first Isobel, and then Dora inside. "Number 55," he added, before climbing in himself. What would Mr Henderson's death mean for Isobel and himself now?

The cab stopped outside number 55 and Dora hurried down the areaway steps while Will paid the cabman then followed Isobel up the steps to the front door. She rang the doorbell, and Gorman, the butler, admitted them to the house.

"Thank God, you've come too, Will." Alfie came out of the morning room and into the hall. "Mother is utterly distraught."

"Is she in there?" he asked.

"Yes. According to the police, Ronald died in a—" Alfie threw a hesitant glance at Isobel, "a brothel which he owned."

"Did you know he owned a brothel and used it?" she asked.

"No, I didn't. Mother and I knew he owned properties north of the Liffey but we thought they were boarding houses – perhaps some are – I simply don't know."

He followed Isobel into the large room. Mrs Henderson was seated on the huge sofa, hugging herself, and rocking backwards and forwards. Isobel sat beside her, attempted to stop the rocking, but couldn't. He put his medical bag down on the rug and sat on Mrs Henderson's other side.

"Mrs Henderson, it's Will Fitzgerald," he told her. "Isobel and Alfie are here, too." The rocking continued, so he reached for her wrist and felt for her pulse. Mrs Henderson's pulse was racing, her breathing rapid, and he laid a palm on her forehead, finding it clammy. "Isobel. Alfie." Getting up, he beckoned them to him. "She is in shock, so she needs to be brought to her bedroom, her clothes taken off – or her corset loosened at the very least – and she needs rest. Alfie, you and I will bring her upstairs. Isobel, find her lady's maid, and follow us."

Isobel nodded and left the room, while Alfie grabbed Will's arm.

"Do we have to carry her?"

"I don't think so. We'll each take an arm and guide her. Also, talk to her. Reassure her."

"Yes, Will."

"Mrs Henderson." He crouched down in front of her. "It's Will Fitzgerald again. You need to rest, so Alfie and I are going to help you upstairs, and Isobel has gone to fetch your maid. Alfie and I are going to take an arm each." Straightening up, he nodded to Alfie, and they helped Mrs Henderson to her feet. Slowly, they guided her out of the morning room and began to climb the stairs, Isobel and the maid hurrying past them when they reached the first floor landing. "Isobel is waiting for us, Mrs Henderson, you are doing very well."

An age later, they reached the second floor landing, and Isobel kissed her mother's cheek.

"It's Isobel, Mother. May and I are going to help you undress and, once you are in bed, Will is going to take another look at you before you rest."

Will and Alfie guided Mrs Henderson into a bedroom and sat her down on the bed before retreating back onto the landing and the door was closed.

"It's like she is in a trance," Alfie murmured.

"Severe shock. Once she's in bed, I'll see if she goes to sleep naturally, as I don't particularly want to sedate her. What happened this morning?"

"Mother had her breakfast in bed, and Isobel and I had breakfast together. Ronald was out, and we assumed he had gone to church. Gorman told me he had shown Ronald out of the house at eight o'clock this morning and assumed, like us, that he was going to church. We were a little puzzled when he didn't return home for luncheon, but he was winding down – as he called it – towards retirement, and he did go to his office at odd times to catch up on paperwork and to bring client files up to date. Isobel went out straight after luncheon and, shortly afterwards, two police detectives were shown in."

"What did the police say?"

Alfie grimaced. "That Ronald…" he began and tailed off.

"…Was dead after having sexual intercourse in his brothel," Will finished.

"Yes. But not with a girl."

"Do the police know the identity of the other man?"

"No."

"So, how did the police know it was a man?" Good God, it was like getting blood out of a stone.

"Because he—" Alfie shuffled awkwardly. "The man – he left items of clothing behind."

"I see."

"You don't seem shocked."

"Alfie," he began patiently. "I've been a doctor long enough to have seen some things I will never forget. And if you are intent on becoming a doctor as well, you are going to have to become a lot more worldly," he added, feeling as if he were Alfie's grandfather.

"I suppose so."

There is no suppose about it, Will told him silently. "What do you know of Mr Henderson's family?"

"He had no family."

"None at all?" he tried to clarify as the bedroom door opened and Isobel came out.

"Mother is undressed and in bed."

"I'll be downstairs," Alfie told him, and he nodded.

"Thank you, Isobel." He went inside and found Mrs Henderson in a white cotton nightdress lying back against some pillows. Her eyes were open but they stared right through him. "It's Will Fitzgerald again, Mrs Henderson," he said, reaching for her wrist. Her pulse had slowed a little and he looked around for the maid, who was hanging up Mrs Henderson's pale blue dress in the wardrobe. "May, I'd like you to sit here and keep an eye on her. She has calmed a little but needs rest."

"Yes, Dr Fitzgerald."

"Try and sleep," he advised Mrs Henderson softly but received no response. "I'll come back up in half an hour," he told the maid. "If she isn't asleep, I'll sedate her."

He brought Isobel out onto the landing and closed the door behind them.

"Can't you sedate her now?" she asked.

"I don't like sedating anyone. I'll examine her again in half an hour."

"Very well," she conceded.

"Alfie has told me that Mr Henderson had no relatives."

She pulled a puzzled expression and shrugged. "I don't know anything about his background. But I do know we aren't going to be able to marry as soon as possible."

She was right and his heart sank then pounded as they heard a wail from inside the bedroom. After another loud wail, the door opened and May ran out onto the landing, almost colliding with them.

"Oh, Doctor, the mistress just started crying all of a sudden."

"It's all right, May, it's a good sign."

He followed Isobel and May into the bedroom. Isobel sat on the bed and held her mother as Mrs Henderson sobbed.

"He's dead."

"I know." Isobel stroked her mother's hair. "I'm so sorry."

"He died in a – in a—" Mrs Henderson couldn't bring herself to even say the word brothel. "And he owned it."

"We know. Alfie told us."

"But he was with—" She gasped. "A man."

"You need to let Will examine you, Mother, and then you need to rest."

"But you don't understand," Mrs Henderson protested. "Ronald was with a man this morning."

"We know. Alfie told us. Let Will examine you."

Isobel made room for him as he took the older woman's pulse again. It was rapid but not racing.

"Do you think you will sleep?" he asked her.

"I don't know," she whispered. "My husband is dead and he was a—" She shuddered. "One of those."

"Is there anything Isobel or I can get for you?"

"No."

"Is there anyone who needs to be told of Mr Henderson's death?" Isobel asked. "Any of his family?"

"His brother died five years ago. There is no family left to tell."

"Very well." Isobel kissed her cheek. "I know it's difficult, but try and rest."

"How can I?" her mother asked. "Soon everyone will know where and how my husband died."

"I'm sure the police will be discreet," Will told her, but Mrs Henderson didn't seem at all convinced. "Try and sleep." To his relief, she lay down, and Isobel pulled the bedcovers over her.

"May will sit with you, Mother, and we will be just downstairs."

They went onto the landing and Will closed the door.

"I need to speak to Alfie," he told her.

"Why?" she asked.

"Come downstairs." He took her hand and they went into the morning room. Aflie was standing at the window but turned around as they went in. "Your mother is resting," he said, and Alfie nodded. "When did the police say they would be back?"

"I don't know, they weren't specific. Why?"

"Mr Henderson had no surviving family, so we will have to arrange his funeral. Is there a partner in the law practice we can speak to? We need to know if Mr Henderson had any specific wishes for his funeral and burial before we begin."

"Yes, there is – James Ellison. Would it help if I went and spoke to him? I'll ask Gorman where he lives."

"Yes, please," he replied. Alfie was Mr Henderson's step-son and more likely to be given the information.

"I'll go now."

Alfie left the room and Will took Isobel in his arms. "I hope the police are discreet," he murmured. "And that the body is released for burial soon."

"Released for burial?"

"Because of the circumstances of Mr Henderson's death, a post-mortem will have to be carried out," he explained. "The body might not be released for a day or two. That will give us time to either follow Mr Henderson's instructions, if he made any, or find undertakers and arrange the funeral ourselves."

"Do you know any undertakers?" she asked.

"Dalton and Sons were the undertakers used when my paternal grandparents died. Father knows Mr Dalton well."

"I can't believe this has happened," she said with a sigh. "I thought Mother was happy at last and we could be married soon. I should have learned by now never to take anything for granted."

"We will be married, Isobel, I promise. It won't be as soon as we had hoped, but it will happen."

"I hope so. I need to speak to the servants, Will. They deserve to know some of what is happening."

"Yes, of course."

They went down the steps to the servants' hall, where the servants all got to their feet.

"This is my fiancé, Dr Will Fitzgerald," she began. "You probably know by now that Mr Henderson has died suddenly and in unfortunate circumstances," she went on, and they nodded. "My brother has gone to speak with Mr Henderson's business partner, Mr Ellison, to see if there are any instructions for Mr Henderson's funeral and burial. If there are none, Will, Alfie, and I will arrange for the funeral to take place as soon as possible. My mother is, naturally, very upset and is resting. May is sitting with her so I'd be grateful if a cup of tea could be brought upstairs to her."

"Of course," Gorman replied, and turned to one of the maids, who went into the kitchen.

"There is also the possibility that journalists may call," Will added. "Please do not admit them, nor make any comment."

"No, Dr Fitzgerald."

"And that, I'm afraid, is all I can tell you for now," she concluded.

"Thank you for taking the time to speak to us, Miss Stevens."

They returned to the morning room to wait for Alfie and they heard voices in the hall about an hour later. The door opened and he came in with a tall man in his fifties with greying hair.

"This is James Ellison," Alfie told them. "James, this is my sister, Isobel Stevens, and her fiancé, Dr Will Fitzgerald."

"I am sorry we are meeting under such sad circumstances," Mr Ellison said, shaking their hands. "How is Mrs Henderson?"

"Deeply shocked at, not only her husband's death but the circumstances," Will replied. "And is not receiving any visitors."

"I understand. I worked with Ronald for over thirty years and I knew nothing about his sexual proclivities." Mr Ellison sighed. "Alfie and I have just come from Ronald's office, where I went through Ronald's private papers, and there are no instructions as to his funeral or burial."

"I see." Will's heart sank. "In that case, we will have to arrange the funeral ourselves. Dalton and Sons are my family's undertakers."

"A good firm. Would you like me to liase with the police

regarding the post-mortem and release of the body for burial and then call on Mr Dalton and the clergyman at St Peter's?"

"That would be very helpful, thank you. We also need to write a death notice for the newspapers."

"I hope you don't mind, but Alfie and I have drafted one." Mr Ellison pulled a sheet of notepaper out of the inside pocket of his frock coat, unfolded it, and passed it to Will. The words 'suddenly' and 'deeply regretted' jumped out at him, and he handed it to Isobel. "If it is acceptable, I shall have it published in tomorrow's editions."

Isobel read the notice and nodded at Will.

"Yes, it is," he said. "Thank you, Mr Ellison."

"It's the least I can do, Dr Fitzgerald." Mr Ellison took the sheet of notepaper from Isobel, folded it, and returned it to his coat pocket. "I knew Ronald for a long time but, today, I sadly feel as if I didn't know him at all."

"Are you the executor of his will?"

"Yes, I am," Mr Ellison replied. "The reading will take place a day or so after the funeral when, I hope, Mrs Henderson will be able to attend."

"Yes, I hope so, too," Will replied.

"I shall be in contact with you all when I have spoken to the police and been to Daltons and St Peter's."

"Thank you."

Alfie saw Mr Ellison out and returned to the morning room a few moments later. "I thought it would be better if I brought him here to meet you both."

"Thank you, Alfie. And I'm relieved he's dealing with the police." As it helps us to keep our distance, he added silently. "I will look in on Mrs Henderson again and then I need to return to Brown Street."

Picking up his medical bag, he followed Isobel up the stairs, and she quietly opened the door to her mother's bedroom. May held a finger to her lips and, to his relief, Will saw that Mrs Henderson was fast asleep. He beckoned May out onto the landing and closed the door.

"I'm glad she went to sleep naturally," he said. "I don't like sedating anyone. Let her sleep for as long as possible. Then, try and get her to eat and drink. I will be back tomorrow."

"Yes, Dr Fitzgerald."

"And, May?" he added, as the maid went to return to the bedroom. "Don't forget to eat and drink and get some rest yourself. Arrange something with the other maids that each of you sits with Mrs Henderson for only a few hours at a time."

"Yes, Doctor."

Taking Isobel's hand, they went downstairs to the hall, where Gorman handed him his overcoat and hat.

"Thank you, Gorman. Isobel." He kissed her hand, wishing he could kiss her lips, but the butler was waiting to show him out. "I will be back tomorrow," he said, and she nodded.

He released her hand, left the house, and walked to number 67 in search of his father.

Dr Fitzgerald senior was alone in the morning room reading a newspaper. He went upstairs with Will to the more private drawing room and listened without interruption before walking to the window.

"And Mr Henderson owned the brothel he died in?"

"Yes," Will replied. "Alfie says he and his mother knew Mr Henderson owned properties north of the Liffey but assumed they were boarding houses. Did you know Ronald Henderson at all?"

"Not really," his father replied. "I met him a few times but that is all. I know James Ellison a little better. Ronald Henderson always struck me as a man who kept himself to himself. Let James Ellison deal with everything, the less contact you have with the police the better."

"I agree." Will sighed. "Just when I thought Isobel and I could finally get married."

"How has she taken this?"

"She barely knew Mr Henderson but is concerned for her mother."

"Do you think Mrs Henderson had any inkling her husband had sex with men?"

"No," Will replied at once. "None whatsoever. I would say she had little or no comprehension of the fact that a man could have sex with another man until now. Even James Ellison, who worked with Mr Henderson for thirty years, didn't know he had sex with men."

His father shook his head. "And what about Isobel's brother? Did he know?"

"No. And considering he is a year older than Isobel, Alfie is surprisingly innocent."

"I remember when you were surprisingly innocent. You are anything but now."

"Older and wiser as well, I hope?" Will asked.

His father turned away from the window and gave him a little smile. "Yes. Let James Ellison deal with it all, Will. Allow the dust to settle. Then quietly marry Isobel."

"I shall. I also wanted to ask you if you would take over as Mrs Henderson's doctor. It's not best practice for me to be doctor to my future mother-in-law."

"Of course I will. Have you spoken to her about it?"

"Not yet, I wanted to wait until after the funeral and speak to you first. Thank you, Father. Well, I'd better go. I want to speak to Mother before I go back to Brown Street."

His mother was coming down the stairs from the second floor as he left the room and he asked that she join him in the drawing room while his father went downstairs to the ground floor.

"You seem troubled," Mrs Fitzgerald commented as they sat down. "Is it Isobel?"

"No. It's her step-father, Mr Henderson. I'm afraid he's dead."

"Goodness," she exclaimed. "Was it a heart attack?"

"I don't know. Mother, I've told Father what I'm about to tell you, but it must not go any further."

"Of course."

"Mr Henderson was found dead in a brothel," he explained. "A brothel he owned. And he had been with a man."

"A man?" his mother echoed slowly.

"Yes."

"I see," she replied. "And how is Mrs Henderson?"

"Deeply shocked. She didn't know her husband…" He tailed off deliberately and his mother nodded. "I have spoken with Mr Henderson's business partner, Mr Ellison, and he is going to deal with the police, the undertakers, and the funeral. But I am worried about Mrs Henderson. She hasn't lived in Dublin for very long and now her husband is dead."

"You would like me to befriend her?" Mrs Fitzgerald asked.

"If you would, Mother, please? And introduce her to your friends and acquaintances in due course."

"Yes, of course. I met her when we discussed Isobel's move to Fitzwilliam Square and she seemed a very pleasant person. Please let me know when and where the funeral will take place as I will attend."

"Thank you, Mother." He reached out and squeezed her hands gratefully.

"How is Isobel?"

"Concerned for her mother. And this also means we will not be able to marry as soon as we had hoped, so she is disappointed as well."

"Yes, I can imagine. Good gracious me." His mother shook her head. "What an ignominious way to die. Try and allow Mr Ellison to deal with as much as possible."

"That's what Father said, and I shall. I actually thought you would be more shocked," he added, giving her a little smile.

"I do know it is possible for a man to love another man. And of the need to keep that love secret. I am not a complete innocent."

"Well, I'm afraid Mrs Henderson is. Or was." He corrected himself. "Hence her shock. And Alfie is surprisingly innocent, too."

"Perhaps you should befriend him. Bring him to Brown Street and allow him to observe your work there."

"Yes, I will. Thank you, Mother."

Will bought an evening newspaper on his way home, brought it upstairs to the parlour, and stood at the window in the fading light. On first glance there was no mention of Mr Henderson's death but, on closer inspection, he found a paragraph at the bottom of page three on the death of a man in a brothel but which mentioned no names. He closed the paper, sat down on the sofa, and shut his eyes in relief.

Chapter Nine

Mrs Henderson slept right through the night to eight o'clock the following morning, and Isobel went into her bedroom before going downstairs to breakfast. Her mother was sitting up in bed with a breakfast tray on her lap. The two slices of toast were untouched.

"Try and eat something," Isobel said softly. "May has just told me you have a particular fancy for this lemon marmalade."

"I'm not hungry."

"Some tea, then?" she suggested. "You must be thirsty?"

Mrs Henderson pulled an indecisive expression before nodding. "Very well."

"Good." Isobel poured her some tea and added milk.

"Have you eaten?"

"Not yet. I wanted to see how you were."

"What am I going to do?" her mother asked quietly.

"Take one day at a time. Alfie didn't want to go to his lectures today but I told him last night that he should, so I shall be here, and Will said he would call to see you."

"You won't be able to marry Will as soon as you hoped."

"I know," she replied as neutrally as she could. "And I

will let the dressmaker know. Do you think you'll get up today?"

"Perhaps."

"Good. Drink your tea and eat some toast and marmalade. I will come back once I've eaten."

"Isobel?" Her mother clasped her hand tightly. "Will everyone know about Ronald?"

"Mr Ellison was here yesterday. He is going to liase with the police and the clergyman at St Peter's. He is also going to the undertakers Will suggested, and he's written the death notice for the newspapers. I'm sure he will do his best to keep the circumstances of Mr Henderson's death confined to as few people as possible."

"That is a relief." Her mother selected a slice of toast from the rack and bit into it.

"Let me add some marmalade." Isobel took the triangle of toast from her, added butter and the lemon marmalade, before passing it back. "There."

"Thank you. Who are the undertakers?"

"Dalton and Sons. They buried Will's grandparents, and Will's father knows Mr Dalton well."

Mrs Henderson nodded and Isobel kissed her cheek.

Alfie was seated at the table when she walked into the breakfast room, went to the sideboard, and helped herself to some scrambled egg.

"There's a small article in *The Irish Times* but Ronald isn't mentioned," he told her, folding and putting the newspaper down. "And the death notice has been printed."

"Good." She poured herself some coffee and brought her plate, cup, and saucer to the table. "Mother might get up today. She's eating some toast and marmalade."

"I'm glad. I still feel that I shouldn't—"

"Go to your lectures, Alfie. Don't fall behind."

He got to his feet, gave her a quick hug, and left the room. She retrieved the newspaper from beside his plate and brought it to her seat. She glanced at the death notice before scanning the rest of the newspaper for the article and finding it on page four. Thankfully, Sally Maher wasn't mentioned either and she closed the newspaper and began to eat.

When she had eaten, she went back upstairs and opened her mother's bedroom door. Mrs Henderson was fast asleep, her breakfast tray gone. Isobel closed the door, wondering what to do to keep herself occupied. Retrieving her hat and coat from her bedroom, she walked to the dressmaker to reluctantly tell her that the wedding dress would now not have to be ready as quickly as she had asked.

Returning to number 55, and finding her mother still asleep, she decided to explore Mr Henderson's library. Like Mr Harvey's, this library had been created when the large drawing room was split in two. It also smelled of a mixture of leather and pipe tobacco. She went to his desk and tried to open both the drawers. One opened, and she saw a bottle of ink, a pen, and notepaper, while the other was locked.

Wandering around the room, she noticed how Mr Henderson had liked works by Charles Dickens, George Eliot, the Bronte sisters, and Sir Walter Scott, but what was in the locked drawer? Returning to the desk, she opened the other drawer again and searched it, but couldn't find a key. Getting down on her knees and running her hand over the underside of the desk, she smiled as her fingers touched something on a ledge and it fell to the floor. She picked the key up and unlocked and opened the drawer.

The drawer was full of photographs, and she lifted some out onto the desk. The first few she glanced at were of young men having sexual intercourse and she recognised Martin in two of them. Oh, God, she wasn't in any of them, was she? Lifting out all the photographs, she quickly went through them, but they were all of young men and boys. Some of the boys were no more than ten years old and she quickly threw those photographs into the drawer in disgust. All of these were going to have to be burned.

Hearing voices downstairs in the hall, she shoved the remainder of the photographs back into the drawer, closed it and locked it. Replacing the key on the ledge under the desk, she left the library, went down the stairs, and found Mr Ellison in the hall handing his hat to the butler.

"Miss Stevens."

"Mr Ellison, good morning. Please come into the morning room."

"Thank you."

"Please sit down." She sat on the sofa and extended a hand to one of the armchairs. "I'm afraid my mother is not receiving callers and my brother is attending lectures," she told him as he sat down. "So it is just myself here today."

"That is quite all right. I simply called to tell you that I have been to the police. There is no need for an inquest and Ronald's body will be released for burial this evening. I then went to St Peter's Church, and to Dalton and Sons. The funeral will take place tomorrow afternoon at three o'clock, with the burial immediately afterwards in Mount Jerome Cemetery. The hearse and a carriage from Daltons will arrive here at half past two."

That was a relief. "Thank you, Mr Ellison, you have been

very kind and helpful. And thank you for somehow managing to keep Mr Henderson's name out of the newspapers."

Mr Ellison gave her a sad little smile. "I knew Ronald for thirty years and I am happy to do what I can for him to ensure his reputation is damaged as little as possible."

"I knew him very little, unfortunately, but he has been very kind to my mother, Alfie, and now myself."

"You are to marry Dr Fitzgerald junior?" he asked.

"Yes. Now not as soon as we had hoped, but we will marry."

"I am acquainted with his father."

"Will's parents have been very good to me. Others would not have been so kind."

Mr Ellison nodded. "I must admit that Ronald did mention you to me when your mother received your letter."

"My past is no secret," she said matter-of-factly. "But I am looking forward to a life with Will."

"I hope you will be very happy, Miss Stevens."

"Thank you," she replied gratefully. "Can I ask you something about Mr Henderson?"

"Yes, of course."

"Why do you think he married my mother?" she asked. "I can understand why my mother married him, she had a very unhappy marriage to my father and probably craved affection and companionship. But if Mr Henderson preferred men, why did he not marry years ago to disguise this fact?"

Mr Ellison seemed taken aback at such a question from a woman but recovered quickly. "Perhaps Ronald had no place in his life for a wife until now. He had hoped to retire soon, and I can only presume he wanted companionship for when he did stop working."

"Yes, I expect so. But the sad thing is that my mother seems to have loved him very much."

"Please give her my deepest condolences."

"I will. Thank you again for all you have done."

They got up and she showed Mr Ellison out herself.

"Miss Isobel?" She turned and saw May standing at the top of the steps which led down to the servants' hall. "Mrs Henderson has decided to get up. She asks that you come upstairs to her."

"I'm glad. Thank you, May."

She hurried up the stairs and opened the door to her mother's bedroom. Mrs Henderson was seated at her dressing table in a black silk taffeta gown trimmed with crepe.

"Isobel. Could you help me with this locket?"

"Of course." She lifted up the gold heart-shaped locket and fastened the chain around her mother's neck. "I'm glad you have got up."

"I did not take to my bed when your father died, Isobel, and I will not do it now."

"Mr Ellison called. Mr Henderson's funeral will take place tomorrow at three o'clock."

"I see."

"Somehow, he has managed to keep Mr Henderson's name out of a tiny article in the newspaper," she added. "The death notice only says 'suddenly'. No-one knows the full details except us, Mother."

"Truly?" her mother asked.

"Truly," she confirmed. "Mr Ellison has been very kind. Will you attend the funeral?"

"I—" Mrs Henderson seemed indecisive for a moment before nodding. "I attended your father's funeral and my presence was frowned upon. But he was my husband, and so was Ronald. Yes, I would like to attend."

"Good. I'm afraid I shall have to borrow a mourning dress from you," she said, and her mother glanced at Isobel's plain black cotton dress, once part of her parlourmaid's uniform.

"I have three similar to this dress you may choose from. You certainly cannot wear that."

"Thank you, Mother. Come downstairs, and I will ring for some tea."

"No." Her mother stood up. "Not tea. I would prefer coffee."

Isobel smiled. "Coffee it is."

Will was shown into the morning room just after midday and was delighted to see that her mother was downstairs and seated in one of the armchairs.

"Will." Mrs Henderson beckoned him to her and kissed his cheek. "Thank you for looking after me so well."

"It was nothing."

"I don't think it was nothing." She gave him a little smile. "I don't remember a thing from when the policemen were shown out until I started to cry and found myself upstairs, undressed and in bed, with May not knowing what to do. When Isobel's father died, my then doctor sedated me. Thank you for not doing the same."

"You are very welcome."

"Mr Ellison was here," Isobel told him. "The funeral is tomorrow at three o'clock. A carriage will be here at half past two."

"I will be here in plenty of time."

"I think I will go and lie down and read in my room until luncheon," Mrs Henderson announced, getting to her feet.

"Let me help you," Will began but she shook her head.

"Thank you, but there is no need."

"Very well." He opened the door, Mrs Henderson went out, and he closed it after her. "What else did Mr Ellison say?"

"Mr Henderson's body will be released for burial this evening. There was no need for an inquest. Mr Ellison arranged the funeral at St Peter's Church, then with the undertakers and the cemetery."

"Will your mother attend?"

"Yes," she replied simply.

"What's the matter?" He frowned. "There's something else."

"I went to the library this morning and I unlocked one of the desk drawers," she explained. "It is full of photographs of young men and boys having sexual intercourse. Many of the boys are very young," she added, and he pulled a disgusted expression.

"Where is the key?" he asked.

"Back where I found it, on a ledge under the desk. The photographs need to be destroyed, but I don't want the servants here thinking we are burning his private papers."

"I'll bring them back to Brown Street and burn them in the range."

"Thank you. Come with me."

He lifted his medical bag from the hall table and she brought him upstairs to the library. Retrieving the key from the ledge, she unlocked and opened the drawer.

"Don't look at the photographs, Will, they are disgusting. Just burn them as soon as possible."

"Are they all of men and boys?" he asked, shoving the photographs into his bag. "Are there none of any women or girls?"

She shook her head. "None."

"Have you found anything else?"

"No, nothing. I don't dare go into his bedroom, but I doubt very much if he would keep anything incriminating in there."

"No." He closed the bag. "I'll burn these as soon as I get home. How are you?" he added softly.

"Bored," she admitted. "I hate having nothing to do. And I miss you."

"I miss you, too." He leant over the desk and kissed her lips. "I've asked my mother to take your mother under her wing. My mother has umpteen friends and acquaintances she can introduce to yours."

"Thank you. And, then, can we decide when to get married?"

He nodded. "Yes. And now I must go. I will be here before half past two tomorrow."

In Brown Street, Will closed the front door and hung up his hat. On opening the door to the kitchen, he found Mrs Bell mixing ingredients in a bowl on the table with her hands.

"I thought I'd bake some soda bread," she said with a smile. "You have only half a loaf left."

"Oh. Good," he replied, his medical bag suddenly feeling very heavy.

"Been busy?"

"Yes, very. I'm afraid Isobel's step-father has died."

Mrs Bell crossed herself. "Her poor mother. They were married no length, weren't they?"

"Only a few months. The funeral is tomorrow afternoon, so I'm cancelling tomorrow's surgery, but I'll be doing house calls as usual in the morning before attending it."

"I'll let people know. Give Isobel my sympathies."

"I will. Thank you, Mrs Bell."

He went back out to the hall and glanced down at his medical bag. He had to hide the blasted photographs. But where? Carrying the bag upstairs, he stood on the landing. His desk in the parlour was out of the question because the drawers didn't lock. Glancing towards his bedroom, he nodded to himself. He went inside, closed the door, and opened his bag. Taking out the photographs, he put them under the double mattress as Mrs Bell was unable to lift it. As a boy, he had hidden books, pamphlets, and bad poetry under his mattress at number 67, only to have his collection uncovered in a most embarrassing fashion the next time the mattress was turned.

When he saw the last patient out after surgery three hours later, Mrs Bell was gone, but two loaves of soda bread stood cooling on wire racks on the kitchen table with a clean dishcloth laid over them. The fire in the range was still lit so he went upstairs, retrieved the photographs, and brought them down to the kitchen. Despite Isobel's warning, he glanced through some of them, his stomach churning. These were little boys, no more than ten years old, and they were committing the most disgusting sex acts. He threw some into the range's firebox, watching as they smouldered before bursting into flames. He spent the next fifteen minutes disposing of the photographs before rattling the ashes with the poker and shovelling in some coal.

He made house calls in the morning before returning to Brown Street for a meal. He then walked to Fitzwilliam Square, arriving there at a quarter past two. As Gorman admitted him to number 55, Isobel was coming down the stairs. She was wearing a black silk taffeta dress with a high neck and jet buttons down the front and was securing a small black tricorn hat to her hair with a pin.

"I have no suitable mourning attire, so I had to borrow this dress and hat from Mother," she explained, running her hands lightly over her stomach, waist and hips. "Mother will join us in a few minutes."

When the butler left the hall, Will kissed her lips. "I burned the photographs," he then whispered.

"Good. Oh, here she is now," she added as her mother came down the stairs, dressed from head to toe in black, and with a black lace veil obscuring her face.

"Mrs Henderson." Will nodded to her and then to Alfie, who came running down the stairs behind her, doing up his frock coat buttons. "Alfie."

"Hello, Will."

The front doorbell rang and the butler walked past them and opened the door. John Dalton, the undertaker, was standing on the step and Will went forward.

"Mr Dalton."

"Dr Fitzgerald." They shook hands. "The hearse and carriage are here."

"Thank you." Will stepped to one side as Alfie took his mother's arm and they went outside and down the steps to the carriage. "Isobel." He held out a hand, she clasped it, and they followed.

Mr Ellison was waiting outside the gates to St Peter's Church on Aungier Street when the hearse and carriage stopped outside.

"May I have a quiet word with you at some point?" Will whispered as they got out of the carriage.

"Yes, of course," Mr Ellison replied, and Will nodded as the coffin was lifted out of the hearse and borne into the church with Mrs Henderson and Alfie, Will and Isobel, and Mr Ellison following it.

Will spotted his mother and father seated half way down the church as he sat beside Isobel in the front pew, and was glad they were both in attendance.

The funeral service was proceeding blandly, Mr Ellison clearly having been careful to choose hymns such as 'Abide With Me' and psalms such as 'The Lord is My Shepherd' until there was a shout of "Fuck God" from the rear of the church during its reading. Isobel jumped violently and grabbed his hand, and Will longed to turn around as someone opened the church door and went out, slamming it behind them. The congregation shuffled and he heard some murmuring but the clergyman continued with barely a pause.

While Will was leaving the pew at the end of the service, he caught his father's eye and nodded gratitude to him for attending. His father nodded in reply but seemed preoccupied. Had he seen who had made the outburst, Will wondered.

His parents attended the burial service in Mount Jerome Cemetery as well, but he saw them leave as soon as it ended as he left Isobel's side and went to Mr Ellison.

"Thank you for all you have done." Will shook his hand warmly.

"It was the least I could do for a friend and colleague of thirty years standing."

"May I come and see you tomorrow?" he asked.

"Of course, but I hadn't planned on reading the will—"

"It isn't about the will."

"Oh. Well, yes, of course. Shall we say half past twelve?"

"Half past twelve," Will confirmed and returned to Isobel.

He was shown into Mr Ellison's wood-panelled office at half past twelve on the dot the following afternoon.

"Thank you again for all you've done."

"Not at all," Mr Ellison replied. "Please take a seat."

"Thank you." Will sat down. "I'll come straight to the point – may I see the post-mortem report on Ronald Henderson?"

Mr Ellison's eyebrows rose. "Why?"

"You do have it, then?"

"Yes." Mr Ellison sounded cautious. "Why do you want to see it?"

"Ronald Henderson died following sexual intercourse with a man. I want to know if there is anything that I, as his widow's doctor, should be aware of."

"Such as?"

"Sexually transmitted diseases. Who knows how many other men Mr Henderson had sexual intercourse with."

Mr Ellison winced before reaching for a key and unlocking one of the drawers in his desk. He opened it and lifted out a file. Taking out some sheets of paper, he silently passed them to Will.

Reading the post-mortem report, Will's heart sank. Numerous ulcers in the epidermis. Cardiovascular lesions causing inflammation in the supracardiac portion of the aorta. Lesions also present in the stomach wall, liver, and brain. A significant degree of softening in the tissue of the cerebel cortex. The subject had been in the tertiary stage of syphilis for quite some time. Will grimaced and put the report on the desk.

"Advanced syphilis."

"Yes," Mr Ellison replied simply.

"Had you noticed a change in him?" Will asked. "In his behaviour? Emotionally? Physically?"

Mr Ellison pursed his lips as he considered the question. "He had become quite short tempered. He had passed some clients on to me, but I thought it was because of his impending retirement. What will this mean for his widow?"

"That all depends on whether they had full sexual relations. Who was his doctor?"

"I don't believe Ronald was registered with a doctor. When he was ill, which was rare, he would consult an acquaintance – Duncan Simpson, the surgeon."

Will's stomach constricted. "I see. Thank you."

"What will you do now?"

"Go to Mercer's Hospital and see Duncan Simpson."

Duncan was with a patient and Will was asked to wait. He sat down, hearing raised voices from inside the consulting room, and a couple of moments later the door opened and a young man stormed out. Nervously, Will got up and went inside.

"Will." Duncan greeted him shortly, getting up from his chair behind his desk, and shaking his hand.

"Duncan. Awkward patient?" he asked lightly as they sat down.

"Doesn't know what's bloody good for him. What can I do for you?"

"I wanted to thank you for operating on me and—"

"It was nothing," Duncan interrupted, waving a hand dismissively. "I don't get to operate on a breakfast room table very often these days, so I enjoyed the procedure. Is that all?"

"No, it isn't. I believe you attended to the late Ronald Henderson if he was ill?"

Duncan's eyes narrowed momentarily before he nodded. "Those occasions were rare but, yes, I did. What of it?"

"I am his widow's doctor," Will explained. "And James Ellison permitted me to read Mr Henderson's post-mortem report."

"I see. And?"

"The post-mortem revealed Mr Henderson had been in the tertiary stage of syphilis," Will told him, and Duncan closed his eyes for a moment. "Do you know whether he had sexual intercourse with his wife?"

"That is absolutely none of your business," Duncan snapped.

"It is when it concerns the woman who is going to be my mother-in-law. Did he?"

"I would have thought you'd have known that a person in the tertiary stage of syphilis is not usually infectious."

"Please answer my question," Will persisted. "Did Ronald Henderson have sexual intercourse with his wife?"

"Yes," Duncan replied quietly, and Will grimaced. "But only once. On their wedding night. But Ronald came to me and asked how they could have sexual intercourse without any possibility of him infecting her. I advised him to use a condom or two."

"And did he?"

Duncan cringed. "Will, for God's sake."

"Did Ronald Henderson use a condom, Duncan?"

"Yes. I obtained and provided him with a box of condoms and he told me he used two," Duncan replied, and Will nodded.

"Good. Thank you, Duncan."

"Is it wise to be your future mother-in-law's doctor?" Duncan asked.

"No. So I am passing her care on to my father."

"Good. Well." Duncan got up. "If that is all?"

"It is. Thank you." Will got to his feet and left the consulting room.

He walked to the practice house and went up the stairs to his father's surgery, relieved to find him still there.

"Father, I need to tell you that Ronald Henderson was in the tertiary stage of syphilis. Duncan Simpson was his doctor and I've just come from speaking with him because I needed to know if Mr Henderson and Isobel's mother had sexual intercourse."

"And?" his father asked. "If he was in the tertiary stage, Mr Henderson may not have been infectious."

Will nodded. "I'm aware of that, but I still wanted to know. And they did – on their wedding night. But Mr Henderson was wearing two condoms on Duncan's advice."

"Do you believe Duncan?"

"I don't know. He wasn't in very good humour and he didn't appreciate me questioning him."

"I'm not surprised."

"Why?" Will asked.

His father sighed. "Because I questioned Duncan myself

earlier today and we didn't part on good terms. Will, it was Duncan who swore and stormed out in the middle of the funeral service. Luckily, he was seated at the very back near the door, but I'm sure some of the mourners must have recognised him."

"Duncan has syphilis as well, doesn't he?"

"Yes," his father replied. "And it was passed to him by Ronald Henderson."

"Duncan operated on me," Will said, hoping his voice wasn't shaking. And Isobel, too, he added silently.

"There were no lesions or ulcers on Duncan's hands that night, Will. In fact, I have never seen any on his hands. Fred and I would never have proceeded with the operation if there were."

"How long have you known?"

"Only since mid-day today," his father replied, and Will pulled an incredulous expression. "Duncan has always been secretive, but I never knew until now that he was attracted to men as well as women – not even a suspicion. I thought his behaviour at the funeral was due to a mental breakdown but, no, Duncan admitted to me that he and Ronald Henderson had been lovers for many years and that Ronald Henderson had passed syphilis to him."

"Has he told anyone else?" Will asked, and his father shook his head. "Not Mrs Simpson, or Fred?" he added, and his father shook his head again. "Well, his wife must be told. Did you tell him he must not continue to perform surgery?"

"No, but I must. I'll demand that Maria is told and examined, and I must ask Duncan if he will consent to me being his physician for however long he has left or whether he wishes to be admitted to an institution." His father sounded reluctant and Will didn't envy him questioning his oldest friend on the subject. "In the meantime, one of us will have to ask Mrs Henderson if she noticed that her new husband was wearing two condoms."

Will rolled his eyes. "I doubt very much if Mrs Henderson knows what a condom is, never mind what one looks like, but I'll speak to her this evening."

"Are you sure?"

"Yes," he replied, sounding far more confident than he felt. "As well as that, I need to speak to her about you becoming her doctor."

"Very well."

"I'm sorry, Father. Today must have been a terrible shock for you."

"It was," his father admitted. "I've known Duncan for sixty years, but now I feel I don't know him at all."

"If there is anything I can do..?" he offered.

"Thank you, Will."

"I shall see you tomorrow, Father."

His stomach was in knots when Gorman showed him into number 55's morning room. Isobel and her mother were seated in the armchairs reading and glanced at him in surprise.

"Will?" Isobel smiled and closed her book. "I wasn't expecting you to call this evening."

"No." He waited until the butler shut the door. "But this couldn't wait until tomorrow. Would you mind very much coming with me to somewhere more private, Mrs Henderson?"

"Private?"

"Somewhere the servants will not walk in," he explained and picked up an oil lamp from a side table. "I'm afraid I need to ask you something as a doctor."

"I see. Very well. The drawing room?" she suggested, getting to her feet.

"Yes." He opened the door for her, followed her up the stairs to the first floor, and into the chilly drawing room. Closing the door, he placed the oil lamp on a side table beside the sofa, then waited for her to sit down. On his walk to Fitzwilliam Square, he had tried to formulate how he would even begin to question her but it had come to nothing. "Mrs Henderson, as you know, when someone dies suddenly or in suspicious circumstances, a post-mortem is carried out on the body to try and determine the cause of death."

"Yes, I was aware of that."

"Well, today, I read your late husband's post-mortem report. I'm afraid it made for disturbing reading."

"Oh?" Mrs Henderson replied hesitantly.

"It concluded that Mr Henderson was in an advanced stage of syphilis. Syphilis is—"

"I have heard of syphilis, Will."

That was a relief. "It is spread through contact with syphilis sores, generally through sexual intercourse. People who are in the tertiary stage of syphilis are not usually infectious, but I feel I have to ask you this – did you and your husband have sexual intercourse?"

Mrs Henderson looked down at her hands and two pink spots appeared in her cheeks. "Yes, we did. Once. On our wedding night."

"I see. I also need to ask you whether you noticed your husband wearing what is known as a condom on his penis?"

Isobel's mother raised a shaking hand to her forehead and Will cringed with sympathy for her.

"Yes. I, er, yes. I have not yet gone through the change, so Ronald suggested he use two condoms. I must admit I had never seen one before, never mind two, but he did assure me that he would clean them thoroughly before he used them again."

"I hate to have to ask you this, but was it vaginal intercourse only?"

"Yes," she whispered. "Was that wrong?"

"No, not at all."

"Has Ronald given me syphilis, Will?" she asked, her voice shaking. "I have not noticed any sores on my body."

"As I said, it is likely he was not infectious and, by using two condoms, I am confident he has not. But as your doctor I had to ask these questions, you do understand?"

"Yes."

"There is something else I need to discuss with you."

"Oh?"

"At some point in the not too distant future, I will be your son-in-law, and I think it would be more appropriate if someone else were your doctor. Can I suggest my father?"

She nodded. "Yes. Thank you for all you have done for me, Will. You are a kind and conscientious doctor and a good man."

"You are very welcome."

"Shall we rejoin Isobel and tell her that I am quite well? I'm sure she must be wondering what the matter is."

They returned to the morning room and Isobel listened in first shock and then relief.

"And Mother has definitely not been infected?"

"I am as sure as I can be that she has not," Will assured her.

"I think we deserve a small drink," Mrs Henderson

announced. "A sherry for myself and Isobel, and help yourself to a whiskey, Will."

"Thank you." He went to the drinks tray on a small table in a corner of the room. He poured two sherries and passed the glasses to Isobel and her mother, before pouring his own whiskey, and holding up his glass. "What shall we drink to?"

"The future?" Mrs Henderson suggested, and they clinked glasses. "I know Isobel and yourself hoped to marry very soon. Might I suggest in a month's time?"

"A month?" Isobel echoed. "Mother, are you sure?"

"Well, you weren't planning a large wedding, so I see little point in delaying it."

Will gave Isobel a smile and she smiled back. "I will go and see the clergyman at St Luke's tomorrow."

"Go together," Mrs Henderson advised.

"We will," he promised.

Half an hour later, Isobel went with him to the hall to see him out herself. Once he closed the morning room door, she grabbed his arm.

"What about Mr Simpson?" she whispered. "He has operated on both of us."

Will grimaced. "He does have syphilis, yes," he replied, and Isobel's eyes widened in horror. "But Father didn't see any lesions or ulcers on Duncan's hands on the night of my operation – he has never seen any on Duncan's hands. We are both well, and you would have noticed by now if you had been infected. I would never lie to you, Isobel," he added, bending his head and kissing her lips.

At a quarter to five the next afternoon, they walked back to Brown Street from their meeting with the clergyman at St

Luke's Church with a wedding date thirty days from then.

"A month." She smiled in delight. "I can't believe it. I thought once Mr Henderson died, it would be six months or a year. Take me upstairs?"

"To the parlour?" he teased.

She just laughed, led him upstairs to the bedroom herself, and undressed him. She took off her own clothes while he lay on the bed watching her.

"Where do you want me?" she asked, throwing her corset onto the pile of clothes on the chair in the corner.

"Just in my bed," he murmured. "It's been too long since you've been in my bed."

Climbing onto the bed, she straddled him before walking forward on her knees and sinking down. Yes, it had been too long. Her eyes closed as she took all of him inside her and began to rock her hips back and forth, her pace slow but steady, eager to prolong their time together.

She rose up then felt Will's hands slide up her thighs and grip her waist firmly as he thrusted into her, clearly having other ideas. Her eyes shot open as he continued to thrust and she gripped his arms to steady herself. Oh, God, she'd wanted to hold off but he kept driving up into her, making her gasp, and she was so close now. His right hand cupped her left breast and he closed his lips around her nipple. He sucked her nipple hard and her back arched, forcing her breast against his mouth. She watched him as he moved to her other breast and pulled at that nipple. The pleasure shot through her and she hugged him close as she cried out. Her orgasm was intense as it spread across her body and she held on to him for dear life as the waves took over.

She didn't know what it was but, as Will kissed her lips,

she became aware all of a sudden that they weren't alone in the room and glanced at the door. Duncan Simpson was leaning against the door frame watching them with his arms folded and her heart leapt into her mouth.

"Duncan." Will clasped her to him. "This is my house. What do you want?"

"Just to satisfy my curiosity. Sally Maher's kip." He gave her an icy smile and her heart sank like a stone. "I saw you at the funeral with Ronald's widow and I thought your face was familiar. Then, I saw you on Fitzwilliam Square earlier and I followed you."

"You went to Fitzwilliam Square and you followed me?" She fought to keep her voice steady. "There was no need to follow me."

"I wanted to satisfy my curiosity. And as for that scar on your back – how could I forget that scar? I've carried out countless abortions but preparing you for the procedure, I've never seen a scar like yours before or since. And this." Reaching into his frock coat's inside pocket, he extracted something and unfolded it. Laying it on the bed, he stood back, and they stared at a photograph of Isobel holding a too-small corset away from her in disgust. "Connie Maguire, the mysterious masked beauty. No wonder you love fucking her, Will, she is stunning."

"Give me that." Will tried to grab the photograph but Mr Simpson snatched it back.

"Oh, no, you don't. This is mine. And the only copy I have. Photographs of Connie Maguire are, sadly, now as scarce as hen's teeth. Any idea where Johan and Lucius have disappeared to?" he asked her.

They'd disappeared? "No."

"That's a pity. And I've heard Hugh Lombard is dead, so I had better value this dearly." He folded the photograph and placed it back in his frock coat's inside pocket. "Hugh told me he was looking forward to making you his mistress. Did he get that far?" Isobel didn't reply and Mr Simpson chuckled. "No? Poor Hugh. You're a lucky man, Will. What I would give to be in your position."

"All right, that's enough. Get out."

"You are fucking a whore, Will. A whore whose bastard child I aborted. A whore who posed for erotic photographs." Mr Simpson laughed. "Just wait until this is common knowledge – just wait until I tell all of Dublin who Connie Maguire really is."

"You really expect anyone is going to believe the rantings of a man who has syphilis?" Will retorted.

Mr Simpson backed away from the bed. "Don't be ridiculous."

"You have syphilis, Duncan."

"No."

"Yes," Will replied firmly. "Because you admitted it to my father and he told me. Allow my father to help you, Duncan, because if you don't it will soon be obvious to everyone that you are ill. Swearing and walking out of Ronald Henderson's funeral certainly didn't help. Now, get out of my house."

Without another word, Mr Simpson turned and left the bedroom. A couple of moments later, she heard feet running down the stairs, and the front door opening and closing.

"Oh, Will." She began to shake and he held her tightly. "I never thought he'd recognise me."

"I need to go to Ely Place Upper and speak to Fred

immediately." She could feel him shaking, too, but suspected it was through anger rather than fear. "Are you all right?" Smoothing wisps of hair off her forehead, he kissed it. "He said some awful things but put them down to the illness."

"I've never been spoken about like that before," she admitted.

"That will be the first and last time, I promise. Get dressed and I'll walk you back to Fitzwilliam Square before I go to see Fred."

"Do you think Fred knows his father is ill?" she asked, climbing off him, and sliding off the bed.

"Father said Duncan hasn't told anyone else, but Fred must have noticed a change in his father's behaviour," Will replied, getting off the bed.

"I didn't realise syphilis causes..."

"Insanity," he said, as they both got dressed. "Yes, I'm afraid it does. It's a truly horrible disease."

Will walked Isobel back to number 55 and kissed her hand on the steps. "Please don't go out alone," he told her. "Promise me?"

"I promise."

"Good. I will be back as soon as I can, but it may not be until tomorrow." She nodded and he kissed her hand again before ringing the front doorbell. When Gorman opened the door, Isobel went inside, but Will beckoned the butler outside. "I'm not coming in," he explained. "I also want to warn you that a Duncan Simpson may call. He is extremely unwell, so please do not admit him."

"No, Dr Fitzgerald."

"Thank you," Will replied, turning away, not relishing the conversation he was about to have with his friend.

When he was shown into the drawing room of the Simpson residence on Ely Place Upper, Fred got up from the writing desk in some surprise.

"Will? It's good to see you." He pointed to an armchair upholstered in silver-grey silk. "Sit down."

"I'd rather stand. This isn't a social visit."

"Oh?"

"Have you noticed any changes in your father, Fred?" he asked.

"Changes?"

"In his behaviour," Will elaborated. "Both mentally and physically."

Fred stared at him. "What are you trying to tell me, Will?"

"Your father has syphilis, Fred."

"You're talking absolute rubbish," Fred snapped. "There is nothing wrong with my father."

"No? Then, perhaps, you'd like to ask him why he followed Isobel from Fitzwilliam Square all the way to St Luke's Church, then to Brown Street, into the house and up the stairs to my bedroom, where he watched us in bed together." Fred's jaw dropped, and Will poked him hard in the chest. "Isobel is my fiancée and I will not allow your father to frighten her like this. Do you hear me, Fred? I will not allow it."

"Yes, of course," Fred croaked.

"Good." Will stood back from him. "In that case, I would like to examine him, and I would like you to be present."

"You want to examine him?"

"Or my father could do it? Your father admitted to my father that he has syphilis."

"Christ," Fred whispered. "But how can we get Father to agree to an examination?"

"That is up to you, Fred. Duncan is your father and he is ill. He is becoming not only a danger to himself, but to others now, too. Your father swore at Ronald Henderson's funeral and walked out. If he hadn't been sitting at the very back of the church, everyone would have seen him. His outburst and his behaviour towards Isobel are probably only just the beginning." Fred looked wretched and Will relented. "Your father saved my life, Fred. I just want to try and repay him a little by keeping this matter between as few people as possible and preserving his reputation as one of the best surgeons in Dublin, if not the whole of Ireland. Feel free to speak to my father, if you'd prefer, and contact either or both of us with a time and a place when Duncan has agreed to be examined."

"Yes," Fred whispered.

"If he refuses, I will have no choice but to report him to the authorities. He cannot continue to work now and, if his behaviour worsens, he will have to be confined in an institution."

"Oh, God." Fred sank down onto the chair at the desk with his head in his hands.

"And, Fred?" he added, and Fred's head jerked up. "Have your mother examined by a doctor, too."

"Christ." Fred covered his face with his hands.

"I'm sorry," Will told him softly. He squeezed Fred's shoulder before leaving the house and walking to number 67.

Will's father was alone in the morning room seated on the sofa and jumped as Maura showed Will into the room.

"What's happened now?" he asked and Will waited for the maid to close the door after her.

"Duncan Simpson followed Isobel to Brown Street. He came into the house, used utterly foul language, and terrified her. I escorted her back to Fitzwilliam Square and went to see Fred."

"Did Fred know his father is ill?"

Will nodded. "He did, but he refused to acknowledge it at first. I told him that either you or I would examine his father but I think it probably should be you."

"Yes. Did Duncan hurt Isobel?"

"No, but she's extremely shaken. Duncan followed her all the way from Fitzwilliam Square. He is attracted to her, and I am terrified he will rape her. I've told her not to go out alone."

"Quite right." His father got to his feet. "I've been putting it off, but I will go and see Duncan now. Come with me."

Isobel went upstairs to her bedroom and sat on the bed, finding herself shaking again. Mr Simpson may be ill but what if he repeated those things about her in public? She jumped as the door opened and her mother looked in at her.

"Isobel? Did you set a date?"

"Yes." She just managed a smile. "Thirty days from now."

Mrs Henderson frowned. "You don't seem very happy?"

"I'm just a little overwhelmed. I was beginning to think it would never happen."

"Come to the morning room and I will ring for tea."

Isobel nodded and got off the bed. "I think I will find another book to read, too."

Her mother went downstairs and she went into the library. Her mother would be shocked to see her reading anything by Dickens, so she scanned the shelves for something more suited to a 'lady'. *Wuthering Heights* caught her eye. She hadn't finished Will's copy, so she pulled it out, not caring what her mother would say.

She went down the stairs to the ground floor and Gorman passed her on his way to the front door. Was that Will back already? She watched as the butler opened the front door, only to be pushed out of the way by Duncan Simpson. She ran into the breakfast room but he had seen her and she attempted to close the door on him. He was too strong and she staggered backwards, almost tripping over her dress, as he came into the room and slammed the door in Gorman's face.

"I want to fuck you, whore," he told her almost conversationally, wedging a chair under the door handle. "Then, I'm going to tell everyone I know that you begged me to fuck you."

Throwing the book onto the table, she began to search for something she could use to defend herself. On the sideboard, she found a butter knife. It was ridiculously small, the blade was only about four inches long, but it was all she had.

"Keep away from me," she warned, pointing it at him.

"That's an ironic thing for a whore to say. Sally Maher told me she suspected you liked being fucked a little too much. I can't imagine Will Fitzgerald satisfies you. Lift that dress and let a real man inside you."

"Will Fitzgerald satisfies me more than you will ever know," she said, moving to her left so the table was between them.

"I find that very hard to believe."

"I don't care what you believe." She moved again as he walked around the head of the table.

"I could teach Will a thing or two, but I doubt if he'd let me."

"He knows enough already, thank you all the same."

"Taught him well, did you?" Mr Simpson asked as they circled the table. "I wanted to share you with Hugh Lombard but he wouldn't let me, the selfish bastard. He wanted you all to himself. We even fought over you." Mr Simpson smiled. "He had stopped selling the photographs of you, but there was a rumour you were still being photographed, and I wanted to find out where that was. Hugh wouldn't tell me so I had to find out for myself. By the time I found Johan's photographic studio it was deserted, so I couldn't believe my luck when I happened to see you on Fitzwilliam Square and then in Will Fitzgerald's bed."

"Mr Simpson." She fought to keep her voice steady and low, hoping Gorman couldn't hear what was being said. "You are ill and you need help."

"I need to fuck you, whore."

"Do you?" she demanded. "I thought men were more to your liking? Such as a certain Mr Henderson?"

Mr Simpson's mouth opened but no words came out.

"I know you were his lover," she continued. "Once or twice a week Sally Maher set a bedroom aside for you both. Did Mr Henderson give you syphilis, or did you give it to him? Not that it really matters. He's dead, and you soon will be. If you rape me, you'll die a horrible death in gaol. If you let me go, Will, his father, and Fred will do their best for you and you will die in your own home and in your own bed with your reputation intact. Which would you prefer?"

"I loved Ronald," Mr Simpson whispered. "And I have told no-one but John Fitzgerald. Who have you told?"

"Only Will. Let me go, and he will look after you. Whatever you might say will go no further." Slowly, she began moving away from the table and towards the door. She pulled the chair away and opened the door, Gorman, Alfie, and the footman, all rushing into the room. "I'm all right," she assured them. "But Mr Simpson is extremely ill. Sit him down, pour him a large whiskey, and don't let him out of your sight."

With that, she walked out into the hall on shaky legs, and almost collided with her mother.

"Oh, Isobel." Mrs Henderson clasped her shoulders, tears pouring down her cheeks. "Did that man hurt you?"

"No."

"May has gone to find Will. Alfie gave her money for a cab."

"Good."

"Isobel." Hearing Alfie's voice, she turned around. "You can let the knife go now." She looked down. Sure enough, she was still holding the butter knife. She passed it over, noting the red marks on her fingers from gripping it as tightly as she could. "Are you all right?"

"I think so. He's very ill, please take no notice of what he says."

"What is wrong with him?"

"May I have a glass of brandy?" she asked instead of answering.

"Yes, of course," her mother replied. "Alfie, go and watch him until Will arrives." They went into the morning room, Mrs Henderson poured her some brandy, and she gulped it down. "More?"

Isobel shook her head. "No, thank you."

"What did he say to you?"

"Most of it was filth, so I'd rather not repeat it."

"Where do you know him from?"

"Mr Simpson is a surgeon," she explained. "His son, Fred, is a friend of Will's. He also carried out Will's operation."

"But why do this? What is wrong with him?" Her mother's eyes widened suddenly. "He has syphilis, doesn't he?"

"Yes, he does, but there were no lesions or ulcers on his hands when he operated on Will and Will is perfectly well. Mother, please don't tell anyone Mr Simpson is ill, or what he has done here today. Allow Will to deal with him?"

"Of course I won't tell anyone," Mrs Henderson replied as they heard a smack from the next room.

Isobel put her glass down and ran out of the morning room, ignoring her mother's protests. The breakfast room door was open and she steeled herself before going inside. Alfie was lying flat on his back on the rug in front of the fireplace and both the butler and footman were pinning Mr Simpson to the chair at the head of the table.

"Alfie, are you all right?" she asked, and he nodded as he sat up, clutching his jaw. "I thought I told you to pour him a glass of whiskey. Go and calm Mother down," she added, and approached the table slowly, Mr Simpson watching her every move. "Whiskey?" she asked.

"Yes."

She gave him a nod then returned to the morning room. Ignoring her mother and brother, she poured a large helping into a glass and brought it to the breakfast room.

"Let him go," she instructed Gorman and the footman. "But stay where you are. I want you to drink this whiskey," she advised Mr Simpson, silently begging him not to call her a whore in front of them. "Someone has been sent to find Will and he will take care of you."

"I want to fuck you," Mr Simpson stated, and the butler gasped.

"No, you don't," she replied calmly, holding up a hand to quieten Gorman. "Just drink this whiskey." She held the glass out to him, hoping he wouldn't just smack it out of her hand and onto the floor. To her relief, he accepted it and threw the contents down his throat in two gulps. "Better?"

"Yes. But I still want to fuck you."

"Well, you can't." Where on earth was Will? "Do you like reading?" she asked rather desperately, glancing at the book on the table.

"I like fucking."

"You must have some time to read? I started *Wuthering Heights* a few months ago, I must try and finish it. Think, Mr Simpson," she urged. "What books do you like? Have you read *Wuthering Heights*?"

"Yes. I think Heathcliff liked fucking."

"Yes, I think he did, too," she replied, hearing the sound of someone hammering with a fist on the front door. "Alfie will answer that," she told the butler before turning back to Mr Simpson. "I think it may be Will."

And, to her great relief, it was. Both Will and his father hurried into the breakfast room. Will came straight to her, while his father went to Mr Simpson.

"Are you all right?" Will asked, kissing her lips and cheeks.

"A bit shaken. Please see to Mr Simpson, he is extremely disturbed."

"We're going to bring him home and examine him. I don't know how long that will take."

"It doesn't matter. Just please take him away from here."

Will nodded, kissed her lips again, and helped his father lead Mr Simpson out of the room. When the front door closed after them, she sighed with relief and turned to Gorman and the footman.

"Did he hurt either of you?" she asked anxiously.

"No, Miss Isobel," Gorman replied.

"Good. Thank you for your help, and I'm sorry you had to hear all that foul language."

"I am sorry I couldn't keep him out." The butler wrung his hands. "I am terribly sorry."

"I'm glad no-one was seriously hurt. I'd better go and see if Alfie is all right."

"Would you like some tea?" Gorman offered.

"Thank you, but I'm going to have something considerably stronger. Do you have whiskey or brandy in the servants' hall?"

"We do."

"Then, have a large glass of whatever takes your fancy."

The two men smiled. "We will."

She went into the morning room, where Alfie and her mother got up from the sofa.

"That man is mad," Mrs Henderson declared in a shaky voice as she hugged her.

"How is your jaw?" Isobel asked Alfie, noting how it was red but not swollen.

"I'll live. It was more of a smack than a punch. A sherry?"

"No. A brandy, please."

"How did you manage to calm him?" Alfie asked as he went to the drinks tray.

"By asking him whether he had ever read *Wuthering Heights*. Thankfully, he had."

"You asked him about what he liked to read?" Mrs Henderson squeaked.

"I couldn't think of anything else. Thank you." She accepted the glass of brandy from Alfie and drank it in two gulps. Putting the glass down, she caught them both staring at her in astonishment. "I needed that."

"Are you quite all right?" her mother asked. "Truly?"

"Yes," she lied. "Please excuse me, I'm going to the garden. I need some fresh air."

She went out into the garden at the rear of the house and sat on the steps. An urge to cry almost overwhelmed her but, holding her head in her hands, she took some deep breaths and it passed. Mr Simpson was so ill there was no filter between what was in his head and what came out of his mouth. It was only a matter of time before he gave her away.

Chapter Ten

Will caught his father eyeing him angrily as they sat squashed on either side of Duncan Simpson in the cab Mrs Henderson's lady's maid had travelled to Merrion Square in. They had been about to leave the house and if May had been a couple of minutes later she would have missed them. Duncan was demanding over and over again that Will be his doctor and Will's father was clearly put out by this.

They brought Duncan to his home on Ely Place Upper, up the stairs, and into his bedroom. Fred pushed his way into the bedroom after them a moment or two later.

"You can fuck off now, John," Duncan informed Will's father in a matter-of-fact tone. "You, too, Fred. I only want Will to stay."

"I'm your oldest friend and I want to be the one helping you, you bloody fool," Will's father retorted.

"Didn't you hear me, John? I said fuck off."

"Will." His father turned to him. "I'll be downstairs, just in case you need assistance. Come on, Fred."

With that, Will's father opened the door and they went out, closing it with a bit of a bang.

Rather nervously, Will placed his hat and medical bag on

top of the chest of drawers then turned towards Duncan, who was watching him calmly.

"Why me?" he asked. "My father has known you for sixty years."

"I want you to be my doctor."

"I know, but why?"

"Because you're not my oldest friend, and you know."

Will's mind raced. "Know..?"

"Your whore told me she told you about Ronald and I."

Will tensed. "Her name is Isobel."

"She's still a whore."

"In that case." Will reached for his hat.

"Wait," Duncan commanded, and Will turned.

"Duncan, I will not have you speak about Isobel in that way."

Duncan shrugged. "She is what she is."

"And you are what you are."

"Which is?" Duncan smiled.

"An extremely ill patient."

"I wanted to fuck her but for some reason, she prefers you inside her. Oh, and she enjoys reading *Wuthering Heights*. We mustn't forget *Wuthering Heights*."

Will's mind went back to the afternoon in Brown Street when Isobel had read half the novel. Just what had Isobel and Duncan said to each other?

"I won't forget *Wuthering Heights*. Could you get undressed please, Duncan, so I can examine you?"

"No."

Will only just kept his temper. "Duncan, I have to examine you."

"There's no point. I'm dying."

"Yes, you are, but I still need to examine you."

Duncan shrugged. "You're stubborn."

"Yes, I am. Please get undressed."

Will fought to hide his revulsion as Fred's father took off his clothes. Duncan's body was dotted with ulcerated lesions, especially on his chest and legs.

"You're disgusted, aren't you?" Duncan gave him a little smile.

"Allow me to—" Will began.

"No." Duncan shrank away from him. "Don't touch them. I clean them myself. When I remember to."

"Then, what do you want from me?" Will asked.

"I can tend to myself. When I remember to. What I cannot do is control what I say. I know most of it is vile. I am very much afraid that I am going to give Ronald and myself away to a stranger. I want you to be on hand to attend to me until I die. I know I haven't got long left. I can go for hours – if not days – and not remember where I've been, what I was doing, or what I said."

"Duncan, I cannot be your gaoler."

"I'll pay you well."

Will flushed with a mixture of anger and embarrassment. "That is not what I meant. I have two practices to attend to now."

"I need someone I can trust."

"Employ a nurse?" Will suggested.

"No."

"Will?" He heard Fred's voice on the landing, followed by a hesitant knock at the bedroom door.

"Not now."

"Yes. Now."

"See what he wants," Duncan told him, and Will nodded and left the bedroom.

"What is it?"

"There is a boy at the front door called Jimmy," Fred explained. "He's been sent by Mrs Bell. You're needed. A breech birth by the sound of it."

Will ran down the stairs and he and Fred went out onto the steps. Jimmy was red-faced and panting on the pavement.

"Jimmy, don't tell me you've run all the way here."

"Yes, Doctor. First to Merrion Square, then Fitzwilliam Square, and then here. Mrs Bell said to tell you that it's Mary Healy, Doctor. The baby's coming feet first and can you come quickly."

"Yes, of course. Wait there, my medical bag is upstairs, and we'll get a cab."

He ran back up the stairs, wondering how to tell Duncan he was going to have leave him and attend to the birth. Pushing open the bedroom door, he stopped dead. The room was empty. Turning, he ran into each of the other bedrooms but they were empty too, and he clutched his head.

"Fred?" he roared over the banisters. "Your father's gone."

"What's this?" Will's father came out of the morning room.

"Duncan's not up here, search the rest of the house."

"Doctor?" Jimmy came to the foot of the stairs and spoke up bravely. "Mrs Bell said to hurry."

Grabbing his hat and medical bag from Duncan's bedroom, Will ran down the stairs. "Father, Fred and I will look for Duncan. Please, could you go with Jimmy and attend to a breech birth?" His father threw a glance at the small boy now standing at the front door. "Please, Father?"

"Very well." His father picked up his medical bag from the hall table. "Find Duncan," he ordered.

Will saw Fred heading for the servants' hall and followed him. Fred went into the servants' hall while Will carried on. The back door was wide open and he shouted for Fred before running out onto a pitch-black laneway which ran parallel to the house. There, he had to stop and think for a moment. Duncan was naked. Where could he have gone in the dark in his bare feet? Would it have mattered? Would he have cared? Will's heart then turned over. Isobel.

"Will?" Fred gasped as he ran into him. "What now?"

"I'm going to Fitzwilliam Square," he said. "You go to Mercer's Hospital," he added. "Yes, try his consulting room."

Will ran along the lane and out onto Ely Place Upper, his hat in one hand, his bulky and heavy medical bag in the other. Having to keep to well-lit streets, it took him ten minutes to reach number 55. He banged on the front door with his fist, gasping for breath.

"Who is it?" the butler asked from inside.

"Will Fitzgerald," he wheezed, and the door opened, Gorman staring at him in surprise. "Is Duncan Simpson here?"

"No."

"Where's Isobel?"

"In the morning room."

Will pushed past him and opened the door, Mrs Henderson and Alfie turning to him in surprise. Isobel wasn't with them.

"Where's Isobel?" he demanded.

"In the garden," Alfie replied. "She said—"

Will didn't wait to listen. He ran through the house and opened the door to the garden. Isobel was seated on the steps in the light from the kitchen window and twisted around to look up at him. Dropping his hat and medical bag, he pulled her to her feet, and into his arms.

"Will? What is it?" she asked. "What's happened?"

"Duncan Simpson is missing. I thought he had come here again."

"Missing? How?"

"He escaped from the house." Will kissed her forehead and picked up his medical bag and hat. "You need to come with me, so we'll fetch your coat and hat. I'm not letting you out of my sight until he's found." Taking her hand, he brought her into the house, meeting Alfie in the hall. "Duncan Simpson is missing," he told Alfie as he and Isobel went upstairs. "He may come here. Do not let him in."

"No, of course not. Where are you going?" Alfie called after them.

"To find him, and I'm bringing Isobel with me."

In her bedroom, he helped her on with her coat and hat, and they went downstairs.

"Is this wise?" Alfie asked him.

"Yes. It is. Do not admit Duncan Simpson, do you hear me?" he insisted.

"Yes."

"Good." Will opened the front door and they went out.

"Where are we going?" Isobel asked as they hurried out of Fitzwilliam Square.

"I sent Fred to Duncan's consulting room at Mercer's Hospital. We'll go there, too."

"Tell me what happened."

"We brought him back to Ely Place Upper and into his bedroom. He was demanding that I be his doctor and no-one else. I managed to get him to undress so I could examine him. He wanted me to attend to him until he died because he didn't want my father to do it and I knew about him and Mr Henderson." Will sighed. "And I said no, I couldn't. Then Fred called me out of the room. Mrs Bell had sent Jimmy to look for me to attend to a breech birth. While we were speaking to Jimmy, Duncan escaped. I shouldn't have left him alone."

He was beginning to wilt when they reached Duncan's consulting room. It was locked and Will swore under his breath.

"Now where?" he said aloud.

"The Liffey," she said simply.

Will steeled himself, and he and Isobel walked to and along the quays, following the river downstream. At first glance, all seemed as it should be. Despite the late hour, cabs and carts were making their way up and down the quays, and goods were being off-loaded from ships onto the quayside. Then, Isobel grabbed his arm.

"There," she said, pointing along City Quay to where Fred was struggling with his father. "Give me your medical bag and hat."

Gratefully, he passed them to her and ran to the two men. "Duncan, it's Will Fitzgerald," he told him, taking hold of his arm, and the older man peered curiously at him. "Let's take you home."

"No." Duncan began to struggle again and Will tightened his grip on him. "I want to fuck – I want to fuck her," he added as Isobel approached.

"No, you don't," Fred ordered. "We're taking you home."

"I want to fuck you." Duncan made a lunge for Isobel and Will almost lost his grip on him.

"You must be cold." Isobel put the hat and medical bag down and began to unbutton her long black coat.

While Duncan's eyes were following her fingers, Will nodded to Fred, who quickly shrugged off his frock coat and helped his father into it. Isobel then put her coat around Duncan, tying the arms around his waist, disguising his lack of trousers.

"Lift your skirts now," Duncan ordered. "And let me inside you."

"We're taking you home," Fred repeated, and they escorted Duncan off the quay, Isobel walking behind them with the medical bag and hat.

Trying to attract as little attention as possible, they walked at a slow but steady pace back to Ely Place Upper. Maria Simpson burst into tears in the hall when she saw the condition her husband was in. Margaret, her daughter-in-law, quickly put an arm around her and guided her into the morning room. Bringing Duncan upstairs to his bedroom, Will took his medical bag from Isobel and gave her a quick kiss.

"I'll wait downstairs with his wife and Margaret," she told him and he nodded, closing the door.

Miraculously, Duncan was uninjured, except for a few deep cuts on the soles of his feet.

"Get the girl in here," he kept repeating. "And let me fuck her."

"No," Will replied, cleaning Duncan's feet. "She's spoken for."

"What about you, then?" Duncan asked him suddenly, and Fred gasped. "I like you. Ever been with a man?"

"No, I haven't."

"Want to?" Duncan offered.

"No, thank you."

"Pity. It's been a long time since I fucked someone as young and handsome as you."

"Will, I want you to sedate him immediately," Fred ordered. "He doesn't know who we are and if he escapes again, he won't even know where he lives."

"And then what?" Will snapped. "Keep him permanently sedated from now on?"

"You've never liked sedating anyone, have you?"

"No, because most of the time it isn't necessary."

"Well, it is now. Unless you like him propositioning you and speaking about your fiancée like that?"

Will didn't, so they helped Duncan to bed and Will sedated him.

"How did you find him?" Will asked as they cleaned their hands.

"He was outside Mercer's Hospital when I got there," Fred replied. "I made the mistake of shouting his name and he looked at he and I realised he didn't recognise me. He ran away from me and made a beeline for the quays. I chased him from Crampton Quay all the way to City Quay. If he hadn't trodden on something sharp, I'd never have caught him. Christ." Fred closed his eyes for a moment. "I was chasing my naked father along the quays and I didn't see one police constable."

"Be grateful for that," Will said and Fred nodded. "I'll call here first thing in the morning," he said, closing his medical bag, then picking it up, putting Isobel's coat over his arm and walking to the door.

"Did you know my father is sexually attracted to men as well as women?" Fred asked, and Will froze.

"Yes. Your father told my father, and my father told me."

"And you didn't think to tell your best friend?"

"No," he replied, turning around, and seeing Fred close to tears. "I wanted to spare you. I thought it was enough that syphilis is killing him."

"And was it because you knew that he wanted you as his doctor?"

"Yes. He admitted he was afraid of what he might say to a stranger. He wanted to protect you and your mother, Fred, so please try not to be angry."

"I don't know what to tell Mother," Fred whispered.

"Would you like me to speak to her?" Will offered, and Fred shook his head. "Very well. I need to bring Isobel home then go to number 67 and see if my father has returned."

Fred nodded and Will opened the door. They went downstairs and Fred went into the morning room. A few moments later, Isobel came out, and Will gave her a little smile.

"I'll bring you home," he said. "Don't wear this coat again until it's been thoroughly laundered," he added, putting it over her arm.

"I won't."

"Duncan is under sedation," he went on, taking her hand as they left the house.

"I have to admit I'm relieved," she said, passing him his hat.

"And Fred knows his father is attracted to men as well as women."

"How?" she asked.

"Because." He sighed. "Duncan propositioned me in front of him."

She stopped and stared at him, her mouth opening a little in shock. "Fred isn't going to tell his mother, is he?"

"I don't know. I offered to speak to her but he wouldn't let me. I hope he won't."

They walked to Fitzwilliam Square in silence and on the steps of number 55, he lifted her hand and kissed it.

"You look exhausted," she whispered, running a thumb across his lips.

"I feel exhausted," he admitted. "But I need to find my father. Then, I'll go home and go to bed."

"When do you call to see Mr Simpson again?" she asked as he rang the front doorbell.

"First thing in the morning."

"And he'll stay sedated until then?" she added, her voice sounding a little desperate.

"Yes, he will," he replied, raising both her hands to his lips.

"Good. I know he's ill, but…" She tailed off as someone inside loudly cleared their throat.

"May I have your name, please?" the butler called.

"Will Fitzgerald and Isobel Stevens," he said, and the front door opened. He kissed her hands again and watched her go inside. "I can't promise I'll see you tomorrow but I'll try."

Tess admitted him to number 67.

"Is my father here?" he asked, passing her his hat, and putting his medical bag on the hall table.

"He has only just returned from attending to a birth, Dr Fitzgerald, and has gone to change his clothes."

Will ran up the stairs and along the landing to his father's bedroom. "Father?" He knocked at the door, and it opened a moment later. "We found Duncan," Will told him, and his father closed his eyes for a moment.

"Thank God. Where?"

"City Quay. I'm afraid he is no longer lucid and is aggressive and violent, so I had to sedate him. I'll examine him again in the morning."

"He didn't recognise you?"

Will shook his head. "Or Fred."

"Christ," his father whispered.

"Was the birth a success?"

"Yes. I thought I might have to perform a caesarean but we got there in the end. A boy."

"Good. That's her third son. Thank you, Father."

"Did you deliver the previous two?" his father asked.

"Yes, I did."

"In that tiny room?"

"That tiny room is Mary's home," he said, and his father nodded and began to unbutton his blood-splattered shirt. "Father, I must go. I'm exhausted and I need some sleep."

"You can't be on both sides of the city at the same time, Will. The next time, you might not be able to find someone to take your place, and then what will you do? You have to decide which side of the city needs you most."

"Father—" He was too tired to argue this now.

"You live in a rented house. You pay a housekeeper. Soon you will have a wife and family. You simply cannot afford to treat patients who pay you in pig's trotters."

Will's eyebrows shot up. "Pig's trotters?"

"I was presented with four pig's trotters wrapped in a copy of the *Freeman's Journal*. I went to Pimlico and left them with Mrs Bell. She was delighted. She's going to pickle them in brine for you, apparently."

"Oh," he murmured, not relishing the prospect of the end result one bit.

"Will." His father caught his arm. "Come back and live here and join Fred and I in the practice full time. You can build up your own patient list and support whatever charities take your fancy in your spare time."

"I need to go, Father, I'll speak to you tomorrow."

He left the house and went straight to see Mary Healy to apologise for not being able to attend to the birth himself. On the second floor landing of the tenement house, he was puzzled to find the local 'handywoman' washing her hands in a bucket of bloody water.

"Mrs Connell." He greeted her politely.

"You're too late," she snapped, and Will frowned.

"I'm sorry, I don't understand?"

"You feckin'-well should be sorry. The other doctor left her far too soon and she bled. A babby and two little boys have no mammy now."

Will pushed past her and went into the room. Mary was lying in the centre of the double bed, the covers pulled up to her chin. The baby boy, tucked up in a drawer, was wailing along with his two brothers sitting on the floor beside him. Mary's husband, Gerry, was seated on a stool beside the bed frozen in shock. Will lowered the bedcovers a little and felt Mary's neck for a pulse. Nothing. His heart sank like a stone. How the hell could this have happened?

"Gerry," he began, but the door opened.

"We'd prefer it if you left now, Dr Fitzgerald," Mrs Connell told him in a stiff tone.

"Yes," he replied quietly. "Yes, of course." He left the room and went down the stairs. Outside, it had begun to rain and he put on his hat. "Christ," he whispered as he walked away.

In Brown Street, he let himself into the house and slammed the door.

"That you, Dr Fitzgerald?" Mrs Bell's voice called from the kitchen. The door opened and she watched as he put his medical bag on the floor and hung up his hat. "You look terrible," she told him with her usual bluntness.

"Mary Healy's dead."

Mrs Bell crossed herself. "But how? Your father brought the pig's trotters to Pimlico and he said she was fine when he left her."

"I don't know what happened, but she bled. I spoke with my father and he gave no indication that anything was wrong." He rubbed his forehead. "I should have been there."

"You can't be in two places at once."

"No."

"Let me make you a cup of tea?" she offered. "The fire's still lit, I came here to cook the trotters."

"Thank you, but I'm almost asleep on my feet. I'm going straight to bed."

He went upstairs, into his bedroom, and closed the door. He sat on the bed in the dark for a few moments before curling up on it fully clothed and falling fast asleep.

He slept for eight hours but woke up wishing he could just turn over and sleep for eight more. The fire in the range had gone out, so he took off his clothes and washed and shaved in some cold water. Lifting a clean shirt and collar off a shelf in the wardrobe, he got dressed, his stomach rumbling. Unable to make tea, he drank a mug of milk and ate four slices of soda bread and marmalade before leaving the house.

Twenty minutes later, he was admitted to the Simpson residence on Ely Place Upper. To his relief, Fred was still in bed, so he went upstairs to Duncan's bedroom alone.

The bedroom was dark, so he opened the curtains first before turning to the bed. Something wasn't right, it was too quiet, and Will leant over Duncan before jerking back in shock. Duncan wasn't breathing. For the second time in almost nine hours, Will felt for a pulse and found nothing. No. No. No. He clutched his head. Duncan couldn't be dead. He'd only been sedated.

Will pulled the bedcovers down and lifted up an arm. The body was cold and rigor mortis was evident, telling him Duncan had been dead for a number of hours. Opening Duncan's mouth, he checked for any obstructions but found none. He lifted one eyelid, then the other, and noted how the pupils were pinpoint small. Oh, God, no. Abnormally constricted pupils suggested opiate overdose but the amount of morphine he had used to sedate Duncan would not have caused this reaction. A stroke would, though, and Will grimaced. Was this death natural or had Duncan been helped on his way?

Will replaced the bedcovers, picked up his medical bag,

then put it down again. This might be his only chance. Going to the wardrobe, he searched the pockets of all the coats hanging up inside before finding the folded-up photograph of Isobel. He placed it in his frock coat's inside pocket before picking up his medical bag, walking to the door, and taking the key out of the lock. He went onto the landing, locked the door behind him, and put the key in his frock coat's inside pocket beside the photograph. Glancing at his pocket watch, he saw it was almost half past eight, and went downstairs. In the hall, he met a housemaid carrying a breakfast tray.

"Could I speak to the butler, please?"

"Yes, sir. Just one moment."

Putting the tray on the hall table, she hurried down the steps to the servants' hall and a few moments later returned with the butler.

"I need someone to ask my father to come here at once. It is urgent."

"Of course, Dr Fitzgerald. I'll send the footman."

"Thank you."

He went into the morning room, put his medical bag down on a side table, and went to the window. Surely Fred wouldn't have..? Will shook his head, not wanting to even begin to contemplate that possibility.

"Will?" Hearing Fred's voice, he jumped and turned around. Fred was standing in the doorway and seemed more angry than concerned. "Why is Father's bedroom door locked?"

"Come in and close the door."

"Why?"

"Just do it, Fred," Will snapped, and Fred closed the

door. "There's no easy way to say this," he began, watching his friend closely. "But your father is dead."

Fred gave him a blank stare. "Dead?"

"Yes. And has been for some hours."

"Dead?" Fred repeated.

"I'm sorry, Fred."

"Why have you locked the door?"

"So the servants don't go in," Will lied. "When did you last check on your father?"

"Just before I went to bed at about midnight. There was no change from when we left him earlier. I suppose this is a blessing in disguise."

"Is it?" Will asked.

"Yes, of course. It's better that he die peacefully in his sleep rather than linger on…"

"…As an embarrassment?"

Fred frowned. "What are you trying to say?"

"I examined him and I noticed his pinpoint pupils. Can you remember what that suggests, Fred? Or was it one of the many lectures you slipped out of?"

"I don't have to listen to this." Fred turned, opened the door, and went into the hall as the butler walked past him towards the front door.

"Dr Fitzgerald." Will heard the butler greet his father. "It's good to see you again. Did you happen to meet Kilby? He was sent to ask that you call here urgently."

"Yes, I met him on Hume Street. Your umbrella."

Will walked to the door and saw his father hand the butler a large black umbrella.

"Thank you, Dr Fitzgerald. I'm glad to see the weather has improved since you were here last night."

Last night? Oh, no. Will met his father's eyes for a split-second then backed into the morning room, clutching his head as his father and Fred followed him.

"Will," his father began, but Will held up a hand to quieten him.

"Which of you was it?" he demanded savagely, and the door was quickly closed. "Or did you and Fred administer the overdose together? No," he decided. "Don't tell me, I don't want to know." Picking up his medical bag, he made for the door, but his father blocked his way. "Please don't make me have to move you, Father."

"Duncan was my oldest friend, Will."

"Duncan was my patient," Will snapped. "And he was put to sleep as if he were a dog. If you're expecting me to certify his death, you can think again."

"I wasn't."

"And if you're expecting me at surgery this morning, you can think again, too. I will never work with either of you again and if you had any decency, Father, you'd retire from practising medicine right away and never go near a patient ever again."

"Please don't do anything hasty, Will."

"Hasty?" he repeated in disgust. "Mary Healy is dead because you couldn't wait to get out of the tiny room she lives in. She bled to death. A baby and two little boys are now without a mother. All because of your haste. Here." Dropping his medical bag, he pulled Duncan's bedroom door key from his frock coat's inside pocket. He lifted his father's hand and pressed the key hard into the palm. "Now, get out of my way."

Silently, his father stepped aside, and Will picked up his

medical bag again and opened the door. He walked along the hall and lifted his overcoat and hat from the stand before opening the front door and leaving the house. Turning into Hume Street, he began to run. Reaching St Stephen's Green, he darted behind a tree and vomited onto the ground. He wiped his mouth with shaking hands, feeling tears on his cheeks, so he pulled a handkerchief out of his trouser pocket and wiped his eyes as well.

He walked on, and ten minutes later he was in Fitzwilliam Square being shown into number 55's morning room. When the door closed after the butler, Will put his medical bag on a side table and went to the fireplace. Pulling the photograph of Isobel out of his frock coat's inside pocket, he dropped it into the flames. He watched it burn then turned as she came into the room.

"I'm sorry, Will, we're still at breakfast." She kissed his cheek then drew back. "You've been crying. What's happened?"

"Duncan Simpson is dead."

Her eyes widened. "Dead? I don't understand. I thou—"

"Promise me you won't tell anyone what I'm about to say."

"Of course, I promise."

"My father – or Fred – or both of them – gave Duncan an overdose of morphine," he told her, and she clapped a hand to her mouth. "I've refused to certify the death, and I've resigned from Father's practice. I can no longer trust either him or Fred."

"Oh, Will…"

"As well as that, the patient I asked Father to attend to, died. So." He gave a little shrug. "I need to rebuild my reputation in the Brown Street practice. I don't want people thinking I casually pass my patients over to someone who doesn't care."

"Have you had anything to eat?"

"Some bread and marmalade and a mug of milk."

"Would you like something a bit more substantial?" she offered.

"A cup of coffee would be very welcome."

"Come next door," she said, holding out a hand.

He shook his head. "I'd prefer it in here if you don't mind."

"Of course not. I won't be long."

She left the room and he went to the sofa and sat down. The gold-coloured sofa was almost the size of a single bed, and he wished he could lie down on it, block everything out and just go to sleep.

Isobel returned with two cups and saucers and passed one to him.

"Thank you."

"Is there anything I can do?" she asked, sitting down beside him.

"No, not really, but thank you for asking." He sipped the coffee then exhaled a long sigh. "I'm worn out and it's only nine o'clock."

"Will, I would be lying if I said I was anything but relieved Mr Simpson is dead. He terrified me and, from what I have read on the disease, his behaviour would have become more and more erratic as the disease progressed. But I can't believe two doctors have hastened his death. What are you going to do?"

"What can I do?" he asked bitterly. "They are my father

and my best friend. But they can clean up the mess they made, it's no longer anything to do with me. So," he added, taking another sip of the delicious coffee. "Have you anything planned for today?"

She nodded. "Mother, Alfie, and I have to be at Mr Ellison's office at eleven o'clock for the reading of Mr Henderson's will. I can't wait for it to be over so Mother can begin her life again."

"How is she?"

"Bearing up. She's stronger than we give her credit for."

"And you?" he asked softly. "I am so sorry that Duncan terrified you."

"Which is why I cannot be sorry he is dead. Who knows what else he may have said? I just want to look forward to our wedding."

Will gave her as bright a smile as he could manage. With only the Brown Street practice now and his reputation there most likely in tatters, could they afford to get married? He would need to work hard to ensure they could. He finished the coffee, put the cup and saucer down on the side table beside his medical bag, and got up.

"I have to go," he said, reaching for the bag. "But I'll call and see you soon, I promise."

"Will." She put her cup and saucer beside his and got to her feet. "If there is anything I can do to help, tell me? Anything at all."

"I will."

"I love you."

"And I love you, too." Bending his head, he kissed her, and she saw him out herself.

Retrieving the cups and saucers, Isobel returned to the breakfast room and placed them on the sideboard before retaking her seat at the table.

"Has Will gone?" her mother asked.

"Yes. He came to tell me Mr Simpson died last night," she said, and there was a shocked silence. "I told Will I couldn't help but be relieved."

"Yes, after what that man did," Mrs Henderson replied. "But, having said that, Will knew him well, didn't he? He must be very saddened."

"He was Will's godfather. And Mr Simpson was his father's oldest friend, so it is a big loss for them both," she added diplomatically, then steered the conversation away from the subject of death for the time being.

At just before eleven o'clock, they were shown into Mr Ellison's office. He rose from his chair behind the desk, greeted them warmly, and shook their hands.

"Shall we begin?" he said, and they sat down. "Ronald liked to keep his will up to date, and he updated it very recently to include you, Miss Stevens. I shall read the will aloud," he added, picking up a sheet of paper from the desk.

"'I, Ronald Henderson, of Fitzwilliam Square in the city of Dublin, do hereby revoke all former wills and testamentary depositions made by me and declare this to be my final will and testament. I bequeath to my wife, Martha Henderson, my residence and contents on Fitzwilliam Square. I bequeath to my wife, Martha Henderson, my house and contents on Fitzwilliam Square, and my house on the Rathmines Road, and also to receive the rents and profits from the said houses. I bequeath to my wife, Martha Henderson, the sum of five thousand pounds. I bequeath to my step-children, Alfred Stevens and Isobel Stevens, my house on Montgomery Street, my house on Purdon Street, and my house on Westland Row, the rents and profits to be divided equally between them. I bequeath to my step-children, Alfred Stevens and Isobel Stevens, the sum of five hundred pounds each. I hereby appoint James Ellison to be the trustee of my will. Signed Ronald Henderson.'"

Mrs Henderson spoke first. "Ronald owned a second house on Fitzwilliam Square?"

"Yes, he did." Mr Ellison flipped through some papers. "Yes. Number 30," he said, and Isobel's heart pounded. "It is currently unoccupied."

"I also didn't know of the house on Westland Row or the house on the Rathmines Road," Mrs Henderson continued.

"Ronald acquired them just over a month ago so he would have a pension, so to speak, when he retired," Mr Ellison told her. "Now, there are some papers I need you all to sign."

The papers signed, her mother and Alfie got up to leave, but Isobel remained seated.

"I would like to speak to Mr Ellison in private," she explained. "I won't be long." After giving her puzzled glances, they went out. When the door closed, Isobel leant forward. "Mr Ellison," she said in a low voice. "I'd like to know if the houses other than the one on Montgomery

Street are respectable? I am going to suggest to Alfie that the house on Montgomery Street should be sold."

"That would be best. And I would advise selling the Purdon Street house, too. It is also a brothel."

Her heart sank. "Oh. Well, I'll definitely try and persuade Alfie to sell it as well, then."

"But the others are all respectable houses, Miss Stevens, and will provide excellent rental income."

"Thank you, Mr Ellison," she replied gratefully. "And thank you again for all you've done. I know this must have been difficult for you."

"You're very welcome." Mr Ellison smiled as they rose from their chairs, shook hands, and he held the door open for her as she went out.

"I wanted his advice on two of the properties," she explained as they travelled back to number 55 in a cab.

Getting out of the cab, she glanced across Fitzwilliam Square towards number 30. So Mr Henderson had been Hugh Lombard's landlord. And she was now Sally Maher's landlady. Life was certainly unpredictable.

While Mrs Henderson went upstairs to her bedroom with May, Isobel went into the morning room with Alfie.

"Alfie, I have a suggestion to make," she began immediately. "The properties on Montgomery Street and Purdon Street are the only two north of the Liffey and, according to Mr Ellison, both are brothels. I propose that we sell them as soon as possible, be rid of them, and invest the money in a property elsewhere. A rental property in a better area and the house on Westland Row will provide a far higher rental income for us. We both need the money. Being a medical student at Trinity must be costly, and Will and I are getting married soon."

"I agree," Alfie replied. "We'll sell the Montgomery Street and Purdon Street properties."

"Good." She gave him a relieved smile. "Then, we'll go and see Mr Ellison soon."

Will had one patient for surgery that afternoon. He showed the elderly woman out at a quarter to four – fifteen minutes before surgery was due to end – and glanced down the hall as he closed the front door. It was empty, apart from Mrs Bell standing at the kitchen door.

"I'm sorry, Dr Fitzgerald."

"It's not your fault. It's mine."

"The kettle's on the boil. I'll make a pot of tea."

"Thank you."

He had just re-taken his seat at the desk in the surgery when he heard a knock at the front door. Getting up, he quickly went to open it, only to find his father on the step.

"Father."

"May I come in?" his father asked, and Will stood aside as his father came into the hall. "Will, Duncan was going to get progressively worse—"

"Mrs Bell is making a pot of tea," he interrupted. "Go into the surgery." His father went into the room, Will closed the door, and walked along the hall to the kitchen. "My father is here," he told her.

Dr Fitzgerald senior rarely came to Brown Street, and Mrs Bell nodded, clearly knowing his visit must be an important one. "I'll go, then. I've made the tea, and there are scones in the larder."

"Thank you." They went into the hall, and he helped her with her coat before opening the front door. "See you tomorrow." He closed the door after her and opened the surgery door. "Tea?" His father followed him to the kitchen and Will felt him watching as he poured two cups. "I'm not rescinding my resignation," he said, putting the teapot down and adding milk to the cups.

"Will, come back. There has been a Fitzgerald in the practice for the past one hundred years."

"Give me one good reason why I should work with a doctor whom I can never trust again?" he demanded.

"Because you wouldn't have to. I'm doing what you want and retiring from practising medicine."

Will didn't know how to respond. He was sure his father was going to ignore what he had said, or simply refuse. Despite being sixty-six, his father was still a fit and active man. This news was quite a shock.

"Last night, I did something I thought I would never do," his father continued. "Yes, it was me. I administered the overdose. Fred said goodbye to his father and I sat with Duncan until he was dead. We didn't tell you because we knew you would refuse to do it. You're a good doctor, Will, and it is because you came here to Brown Street, even though I hate to admit it. Whether or not you and Fred can work together is up to the two of you, but I am retiring, and I want you to take over the practice from me."

Will picked up his cup of tea, hoping his hand wasn't shaking and drank half the contents. "I need to think about it."

"Do you?" his father asked. "How many patients presented at surgery today?"

"One. Thanks to you."

"I'm sorry."

"Are you?" Will snapped, setting the cup back in its saucer with a crash. "You never wanted me to come here, and the, 'You're a good doctor and it is because you came here to Brown Street,' flattery isn't going to wash with me now."

"It wasn't flattery. I meant what I said. The offer is there. I hope you will take it."

"When do you want an answer?" Will asked.

"As soon as possible. I retire at the end of next week."

"What will you do?"

"I've been offered the position of editor of the *Journal of Irish Medicine*. There are also a number of medical papers I've always wanted to write but I've never had the time."

"I see." The *Journal of Irish Medicine* was a prestigious periodical and there would probably be speeches and lectures, too. His father certainly wouldn't be left out of pocket by retiring from practising medicine. "Congratulations, but I need to speak to Isobel."

"Of course. I hope she can make you see sense."

"I never thought you'd decide to retire."

His father took a sip of tea then put his cup down. "I never thought I would hasten a friend's death. Or retire. I don't want to see you struggle, Will, and have nothing to show for all your hard work when you retire. Come back with me now in a cab and I'll get it to bring you to Fitzwilliam Square."

"No, I'm going to wait here until four o'clock in case someone does present for surgery."

His father's eyebrows rose in defeat. "You're stubborn."

"I've always been stubborn," Will replied. "I'll speak to Isobel as soon as I can. It was the reading of Ronald Henderson's will this morning."

"I see. Well, I hope you'll say yes."

Will followed his father to the front door. "This is only the third time you've been here in almost five years."

"It's not every day you retire and ask your son to take your place. Think carefully, Will. Soon you will have a wife and family to support."

Will saw him out and returned to the kitchen. Pouring himself another cup of tea and adding milk, he left it untouched. He needed to speak to Isobel now. He went to the front door again, put on his hat and overcoat, and left the house. He strode down Brown Street so lost in thought that he walked straight into someone and grabbed their shoulders.

"Will?" It was Isobel, and he pulled her into his arms. "Whatever is the matter?"

"I was on my way to see you. Father has just been here." He kissed her forehead and took her hand. "Come to the house, I have to discuss something with you."

"I have lots to tell you, too."

"There's tea," he said as they went into the house and he closed the door. "But it's probably stewed by now."

"No, thank you."

"Come upstairs, then." They hung up their coats and hats, went upstairs, and into the parlour. "Ladies first," he said, as they sat down facing each other on the sofa and she smiled.

"Mr Henderson left number 55 and some money to Mother, which wasn't a surprise. What was a surprise is that he was also the owner of number 30 Fitzwilliam Square, and he also left that house to her, along with a house on the Rathmines Road."

"Mr Henderson owned Mr Lombard's house?"

"Yes. And Alfie and I were left Sally Maher's brothel, plus another brothel on Purdon Street, a house on Westland Row, and five hundred pounds each."

"You and Alfie now own two brothels?" he clarified incredulously.

She grimaced and nodded. "But we're going to sell them. The fact that I own half of Sally Maher's brothel makes me shudder. In the next couple of days, we're going back to Mr Ellison to ask him to have them valued and sold. I just want rid of them as soon as possible. Now, what did your father want?"

"He admitted it was he who gave Duncan the overdose. He also came to tell me he is retiring and he has asked me to take over the practice from him."

"Do you want that?" she asked.

"I want to discuss it with you. It's a valuable practice but, at the same time, I'm reluctant to leave here. Even though…" He tailed off and shook his head.

"Even though?" she prompted softly.

"Only one patient presented for surgery today," he told her. "One. My father has killed my practice here in one fell swoop."

Getting up, she sat on his lap, resting her cheek on the top of his head. He slid his arms around her and held her tightly.

"Do you think your father neglected the patient on purpose?" she asked.

Will sighed. "That had crossed my mind but, no, I don't think he did. Where Mary Healy lived simply disgusted him and he left her too early. There's just such a huge difference between his practice and here. The reason I came here in the first place was to escape rich hypochondriacs and I don't know if I can go back to all that. But—" He grimaced. "I have to be realistic. My practice here is dead, and it's too good an offer to turn down. I'll take over the practice from Father," he decided. "Yes?"

"Yes," she replied. "Where will we live?"

"You choose."

"No, Will, we must choose our home together, but there's the house on Westland Row, or we could rent the house on the Rathmines Road from Mother?"

"We'll go and see them both?" he suggested.

"Yes."

"That's decided, then," he said. "And now," he added, sliding her off his lap, then getting up and holding out a hand. "I need to make love to you."

Taking his hand, she allowed him to lead her into the bedroom. Slowly, he undressed her, clearly relishing every button and every hook and eye. When she was naked, all he could do was shake his head.

"Each time I see you naked, it astonishes me how beautiful you are."

She smiled. "Let me undress you."

He stood watching her fingers as she undid his cravat and collar and then the buttons of his frock coat, waistcoat, and shirt. She eased his clothes off his shoulders, her breasts rubbing against the hair on his chest. Undoing the buttons on his trousers, she pushed the trousers and drawers down, and he stepped out of them.

They climbed onto the bed and she lay spread-eagled as

he kissed his way up her body. When he licked a hard nipple, she moaned. When he sucked on it, she groaned. When he nibbled it, she gasped.

He kissed her and she pushed her tongue into his mouth. She wanted to feel him inside her and moved back further onto the bed. She needed him inside her now and he raised himself up over her with a little smile.

As he slipped into her, she arched her back to meet his thrust. He held himself deep inside her for a moment, as if to savour it. Then, he started to thrust with long, slow strokes. She spread her legs as wide as she could, wanting him deeper. Slowly, he picked up the pace, thrusting a little harder and faster. She closed her eyes as he pounded into her, giving into the pleasure. Moans and groans of bliss escaped her mouth and she didn't care who heard her. She felt her orgasm building, and she cried out as he continued to drive into her, carrying her on continuous waves of pleasure.

"Yes. Yes. Yes," she chanted over and over again.

Opening her eyes, she gazed into his. He was thrusting more slowly into her now but hadn't come yet. She wrapped her legs around him, pulling him into her, and he moaned as he came inside her, jerking hard. He collapsed on top of her, his face buried between her breasts.

She held him tightly as they fought to catch their breaths. He raised his head a little, kissed her breasts, then reached up and kissed her lips.

"I needed you," he whispered. "When I make love to you, everything else goes away. I want us to share a bedroom. I don't care if anyone finds that shocking. You'll be my wife and I want us to share a bedroom and a bed."

"I'm glad." Clasping his face in her hands, she kissed him. "I didn't want to be in a bedroom along the landing from yours, wondering if I should go to you, or if you'll come to me. My mother and father had bedrooms which were the furthest away from each other in the house. It didn't matter as their marriage disintegrated, but in the beginning, it must have been awkward to have to creep past my bedroom and Alfie's."

"My parents' bedrooms are beside each other. Edward and I never heard anything. Come to think of it, even Fred and his wife Margaret have separate bedrooms."

"Is Fred faithful to her?" she asked bluntly. "He brought you and your friend to a brothel the night before his wedding."

"I don't know. Fred's never mentioned anything to me and I've never asked," he added, rolling his eyes. "So I really shouldn't be so surprised that my father didn't know Duncan liked men as well as women. I have to go and speak to Fred about whether we can continue to work together at the Merrion Street practice. I'm not looking forward to it. I all but accused him of killing his father."

He rolled onto his back and she leant over him. "Is he a good doctor?" she asked.

"Yes, he is. But, like my father, he would not be happy attending to a breech birth in a tiny tenement room. I would like us to work together but we might just be too different now."

"Be patient with him. You have much more experience than him now. I have to be very patient with Mother and Alfie. Their naivety either astonishes or irritates me."

"What would they say if they saw us now?" he teased,

running a hand down her back then letting it rest on her buttocks.

She couldn't help but laugh. "They would be horrified and speechless." She kissed and pulled at his lips, hearing the clock in the parlour chiming five times, then Will swearing under his breath.

"It can't be five o'clock already?" she asked in dismay.

He nodded. "And I have to speak to my father and to Fred. We need to get dressed," he said and, reluctantly, she slid off the bed.

They got dressed and went downstairs, where he helped her with her coat, and she put on her hat.

"Let me kiss you before we go outside." He tilted her face up and kissed her lips before putting his overcoat and hat on. "I love you."

"I know. I love you, too."

He walked her back to Fitzwilliam Square and kissed her hand on the steps of number 55 before ringing the front doorbell.

"I'll see you soon," he told her and walked away.

Chapter Eleven

Will went first to Merrion Square and met his mother as she was leaving the Harveys' house. Mrs Fitzgerald was delighted to see him and brought him into the morning room.

"Your father will be home soon. He's at the Simpsons'. Isn't it awful about poor Duncan?"

"Yes," he replied simply, wondering what his father had told her if anything.

"Tea?"

"No, thank you."

"How is Isobel?" Mrs Fitzgerald asked as they sat down.

"Very well, thank you. I saw her this afternoon. It was the reading of Ronald Henderson's will this morning."

"Oh, I see. How is her poor mother?"

"Bearing up." He shot a glance at the clock on the mantelpiece. How much longer was his father going to be? "So, how are you?"

His mother smiled. "I'm very well. Will, I do know your father has asked you to take over the practice."

"Oh."

"Duncan's death has shaken him up greatly, so we sat down and I put it to him that perhaps he should retire from practising medicine and make the most of all he has worked so hard for. And who better to take over the practice than his son?"

"Mother, I have made a decision but—"

"You want to tell your father first." Mrs Fitzgerald nodded as they heard voices in the hall. "I completely understand. That must be him now."

Will got up as the door opened and his father came in.

"Will."

"Father. Can I speak to you in private?"

"Come into the breakfast room."

"Excuse me, Mother," he said, followed his father out of the room, and down the hall. He closed the breakfast room door behind him and saw his father waiting expectantly at the head of the table. "I've discussed it with Isobel, and I will take over the practice."

His father closed his eyes for a moment in relief. "I'm so glad."

"I have two conditions," Will added.

"Which are?"

"I will run the practice the way I see fit with no interference from you. And you will leave the practice with immediate effect. As from now, you no longer run the practice or practise medicine."

"Very well."

"I will resume my Wednesday and Friday surgeries but I cannot start at the practice on a full-time basis just yet, so a locum will be engaged," Will continued. "I have to give notice on the house in Brown Street, pack, and move my belongings out. As well as that, Isobel and I must find somewhere to live after we are married."

"Yourself and Isobel can live here."

Will shook his head. "I want Isobel and myself to live in our own home. She and her brother have been left some houses in Mr Henderson's will. We will be going to look at one of them, and also to a house left to her mother."

"Where?"

"One house is on Westland Row and the other is on the Rathmines Road."

His father nodded. "When you move from Brown Street, you can live here until you choose a house."

"Thank you."

"What is the date of your wedding?"

"It was the beginning of next month," he replied. "But now I'm moving from Brown Street and looking for somewhere else to live, I will have to cancel the date."

"You'd better not get Isobel pregnant again, then."

"We will be getting married soon, whether she is pregnant or not," he replied icily. "Now, shall we tell Mother?"

"Just a moment. Duncan's funeral is on Monday at eleven o'clock. Will you attend?"

"Yes. I take it Mother thinks he died of natural causes?" he queried.

"Of course. And that I took her suggestion to retire."

Will exhaled a humourless smile and looked away. "Anything else?"

"No."

"Good. You can tell Mother now."

Will returned to the morning room, hearing his father follow him.

"Well?" Mrs Fitzgerald asked, getting to her feet.

"Will has agreed to take over the practice," her husband told her.

"Oh, Will." She kissed him on both cheeks. "I am so pleased. Your father was worried you'd say no." His mother went to the drinks tray and reached for a decanter. "Let's have a drink to celebrate."

"Mother, no," he called after her. "Thank you, but I have to speak to Fred, and I'd rather not do it with whiskey on my breath. The next time I'm here?" he suggested, seeing her face fall.

"Very well."

"And I must go now," he said, crossing the room and kissing her cheek. Otherwise, I'll never do it, he added silently. "I will call again soon and we will have that celebratory drink."

At the Simpson residence on Ely Place Upper, he passed his overcoat and hat to the butler, was brought upstairs and shown into the drawing room. Fred was smoking a cigarette lying on the silver-grey sofa with his feet up on one of the arms.

"My father has admitted to administering the overdose," Will began, deciding to come straight to the point. "He has left the practice and he has retired from practising medicine. I have taken over the practice from him."

Fred swung his legs down from the sofa arm and stubbed the cigarette out in an ashtray. "You're leaving Brown Street?"

"Yes, I am."

Fred whistled in amazement, irritating him. "I never thought I'd see the day."

"Will we be able to work together?"

"I don't know," Fred replied, meeting his eyes, and Will

saw how bleary they were. Was he drunk? "The last time we spoke, you as good as accused me of killing my father."

"You were present when my father administered the morphine. You knew exactly what he was doing because the two of you had discussed it behind my back." Will's voice rose and he sighed. "Father has told me the funeral is on Monday," he added in a calmer tone.

"Yes. Eleven o'clock at St Peter's. Will you come?"

"He was my godfather. I would like to be there."

Fred nodded. "Good."

"How is your mother?" Will asked.

"How do you think?" Fred snapped then groaned. "I'm sorry. Margaret is with her in the morning room. I needed a few minutes to myself up here. Want a whiskey?"

"No, thank you. And I think you've had enough, don't you?"

Fred exhaled a humourless laugh. "You think I'm drunk? I'm anything but drunk. I'm bloody exhausted, that's what's wrong with me. I haven't slept and, to top it all, Margaret is expecting a child. Marvellous timing, don't you agree? I've just lost a parent but I'm gaining a child."

"Congratulations," Will said, not quite sure if he meant it. Isobel had been carrying his child and he hadn't known until after she miscarried.

"It's early days but it hasn't sunk in yet. In fact, none of it has. It just goes around and around my head. I don't regret what was done, I just wish…" Fred tailed off and squeezed his eyes shut for a moment. "He was my father, he had such a brilliant mind, and he was reduced to running through the streets naked and propositioning my best friend for sex."

"Don't remember him like that," Will told him.

"Remember him throwing questions at us while we were studying for our finals, trying to catch us out. Remember all the people whose lives he saved, including mine."

"How can I not remember him like that?" Tears began to spill down Fred's cheeks. "The disgusting things he was saying and doing – I'll never be able to forget him like that." He made a useless attempt to wipe the tears away. "I'm so bloody tired. I've been the one hiding his mistakes and behaviour from people and I'm so tired." Covering his face with his hands, Fred wept.

"Come here." Will held Fred's arms as he sobbed on his shoulder. "How long has it been going on for?"

"The best part of a year." Fred pulled a handkerchief out of his trouser pocket and wiped his eyes before blowing his nose. "He was starting to make mistakes – silly little mistakes – like forgetting he took sugar in coffee and not in tea. Then they started getting bigger. He was getting bad tempered – swearing a lot – using language I didn't even know he knew. And then I discovered he was having sex with men."

"How?" Will asked.

"I followed him one night. He had told Mother he was going to a meeting at the College of Surgeons but I knew there was no meeting there that evening. He went to Sally Maher's brothel in Monto – the same brothel I took you and Jerry to. He met a man outside – a well-dressed man – and they kissed and went inside." Fred winced. "My father – kissing another man on the street."

"Did you recognise the other man?" Will asked and, to his relief, Fred shook his head.

"No. It was dark. But it was there – standing on Montgomery Street – that I realised what was wrong with

Father – and I simply didn't know what to do. Shortly afterwards, his mistakes started to affect his patients. He would forget surgeries and surgical appointments. He closed up a patient after an operation one day and left a scalpel inside. After that incident, I suggested he retire. It didn't go down well and he punched me, but I swore he wouldn't operate on anyone again. Then." Fred gave him a wry smile. "He was called to Merrion Square late one night."

"My operation?" Will asked and Fred nodded.

"I almost panicked. But I insisted that I accompany him and be on hand to assist, as well as your father because you are my best friend. Somehow, I had to keep his mind on where he was and what he was doing without your father noticing. I just about managed it, and the operation went smoothly, but you were his last ever surgical case."

Will exhaled a long breath. "I wish you had told me all this."

"He was my father, Will, and he had syphilis. I was ashamed of him, and I hate myself for that."

"What have you told your mother?" Will asked.

"Only that he was losing his memory, which was true. What I didn't, and will never tell her, is why."

"But—" Will began.

"Mother and Father hadn't shared a bed for years," Fred interrupted. "And now I know why – Father was having sexual intercourse with a man in Sally Maher's kip instead."

"All the same, Fred…"

Fred winced. "Very well. I'll speak to her before she moves."

"Moves?"

"She has decided to go and live with her sister, Diana

Wingfield, and will be moving on Tuesday. I shall speak to her before then."

"Good." Will didn't envy him the task.

"Will, I'm sorry I reacted the way I did when you questioned me, but I need to know if you're going to report your father and I for what we did?"

"My father will never practise medicine again and I am satisfied with that. As for you, I came here to ask whether we can work together, whether I can trust you never to go behind my back in such a way again. Can I?"

"Something had to be done, Will, and it is something I will never be part of again, I swear."

"If I ever find that you have, I will report you, and you will not only never practice medicine again, you will also be deprived of your freedom. I mean it, Fred."

Fred stared at him. "You've changed."

"I've had to change. Now, shake my hand, and we can announce that Doctors Fitzgerald and Simpson will be in general practice together." Will held out his hand and Fred shook it.

"When do you start?" Fred asked.

"I will continue with my Wednesday and Friday surgeries," Will replied. "But I have to move from Brown Street and Isobel and I must find a home for ourselves. A locum will be engaged until I can start at the practice full-time."

"When is the wedding?"

"We're not sure yet, but soon."

"So you'll be looking for a best man?"

"I might be." Will gave him a sudden grin and Fred smiled then yawned. "Go to bed and get a good night's sleep," he added, and Fred took out his pocket watch and looked at it. "Now," Will insisted. "Doctor's orders."

"Very well." Fred yawned again, as he put his watch away.

"A father, eh?" Will commented as they walked to the door. "So you and Margaret will be looking for godparents?"

"We might be." Fred laughed and opened the door. "I never thought you'd leave Brown Street."

"I'll have a wife soon, and then children, we hope. I've enjoyed my years there, but it's time to move on."

His last call of the day was to Mrs Bell's rooms on Pimlico. In the almost five years he had lived in Brown Street, he had only been to her home twice. There had been no need, she was in his home almost every day.

She opened the door to his knock and smiled at him in surprise. "Good Lord, Dr Fitzgerald."

"Is this an inconvenient time?" he asked.

"No, come in and sit down."

"Thank you." He waited for her to sit down at the kitchen table before sitting opposite her. She gave him a nervous little smile, knowing this visit, like that of his father, must be important. "My father came to tell me he's decided to retire from practising medicine," he told her, coming straight to the point again.

"Retire?" she repeated. "How old is he?"

"He's sixty-six. His oldest friend has died and he will now edit a medical journal and enjoy everything he's worked so hard for. I have to admit, I never expected him to retire."

"I hope he asked you to take over from him at the practice?"

"Yes, he did. And I've accepted."

"I'm so glad," she said with a wide smile.

"You are?" he asked. "I expected you to tell me I was giving up here far too soon."

She shook her head. "No. I remember the first few weeks you were in Brown Street when you had next to no patients and you didn't give up. You're a good doctor, and everyone knows you're a good doctor. I'm afraid it was your father who let you down badly."

"Yes," he replied quietly. "And we've had words about it."

"If Mary hadn't died, it might not have been so bad, but she did."

"Yes, and she shouldn't have, and there are no excuses."

"When are you leaving?" she asked.

"Soon. I need to give notice on the house, but I wanted to speak to you first and ask you something. Isobel and I are going to look at a house on Westland Row and another on the Rathmines Road, and she's admitted it herself that she can't cook, so I'd like to ask you if you'd consider being our housekeeper?"

Mrs Bell reached across the table and squeezed his hand. "Thank you for asking, but no," she said, and his heart sank. "I've lived in the Liberties all my life and I can't leave now. I'm sorry."

"Please don't be sorry," he said, putting his other hand on top of hers. "I can never thank you enough for all you've done for me. I came to Brown Street completely wet behind the ears and I wouldn't have survived five minutes, never mind almost five years, if it wasn't for you."

"Nonsense." She chuckled in embarrassment.

"I mean it," he told her softly. "And I hope you'll come

to the wedding? I don't know when or where it will be yet, but I'd very much like you to be there."

"I'd be delighted to. I'll buy meself a new hat."

He laughed with relief. "Good."

He left her rooms feeling understandably sad at her decision yet relieved they wouldn't be losing touch. He put on his hat and walked away from the tenement house in search of his landlord.

On Sunday evening, Isobel and Alfie left their mother reading in the morning room, and went upstairs to the library. Lifting a map of Dublin down from a shelf, Alfie opened it out on the desk and he used coins from his trouser pockets to mark where the houses they had been left were situated.

"Shall we go and see Mr Ellison sometime tomorrow?" she asked. "And ask him to start the process of selling the two properties north of the Liffey as soon as he is able to?"

"I can't, I'm afraid. I have lectures all day tomorrow."

"Well, I can go?" she suggested. "And I can also ask him to seek out a suitable property we can then purchase with the proceeds."

"Do you mind going on your own?"

She shook her head. "No, not at all."

"Very well, then," he replied and she smiled.

"How are you liking Trinity College?"

"I love it." He gave her a grin. "When I think back to when—" He stopped and pulled an awkward expression. "I'm sorry."

"No, Alfie, don't be," she assured him. "We've all been through a lot and we deserve to be happy now. And I hope Mother will be soon, too."

After breakfast, she excused herself and went upstairs to her bedroom. She took off her plain black cotton dress and put on the black silk taffeta dress and hat she had worn to Mr Henderson's funeral. She was halfway down the stairs, pulling on a pair of black gloves when the morning room door opened and her mother came out into the hall.

"Isobel?"

"I'm going out."

"I can see that." Mrs Henderson's eyes took in the black dress, gloves, and hat. "Not to Mr Simpson's funeral, surely?"

"After I've been to see Mr Ellison, yes."

"After what that man did? Why?"

"Mr Simpson was Will's godfather," she explained. "And I am Will's fiancée."

Her mother pulled an exasperated expression. "Very well. Invite Will to luncheon or, at least ask him to escort you home. I wish to speak to you both."

"Yes, Mother."

She went to Mr Ellison's law practice and was speaking to his clerk when the solicitor's office door opened and he came out.

"Miss Stevens."

"Mr Ellison. I was just enquiring whether I needed to make an appointment to see you."

"I'm free for a few minutes." He extended a hand into the office. "Please come inside."

She went into the office and he held a chair for her as she sat down before seating himself behind his desk.

"I hope you are well?" he asked. "And your mother and brother?"

"We're all very well, thank you. Alfie and I have agreed to have the two properties north of the Liffey valued and sold. We would be grateful if you could begin that process as soon as you are legally in a position to, and also to look for a suitable rental property we can purchase with the proceeds."

He nodded. "Of course."

"Thank you, Mr Ellison. Well." She got up and he rose to his feet. "I must go. I expect you heard that Mr Duncan Simpson, the surgeon, died a few days ago. His funeral is this morning. He was Will's godfather, so I feel I should be there, too."

She walked to St Peter's Church on Aungier Street and went inside looking for Will. Spotting his dark head three pews from the front, she approached him and tapped his shoulder. He jumped and glanced up at her.

"Isobel?"

"I felt I should come," she said, and he got to his feet and stepped out into the aisle. "You don't mind?" she added, as she went past him into the pew.

"No, not at all," he replied, and she sat down next to his parents, who nodded to her. "I didn't ask because I didn't want you to feel you had to come."

"Thank you." She gave his hand a grateful squeeze as he sat down then released it before his father saw.

When the coffin was carried in, she couldn't help but tense. Will clasped her hand and held on to it, hiding their hands in the folds of her dress, until the congregation sat down and he had to let her go.

"I'm reading the next lesson," he whispered in her ear in the middle of a hymn. "Then, Father is giving the eulogy," he added, and she nodded.

He read the lesson in a calm, clear voice, unlike the previous nervous reader, and returned to the pew as his father got up and took his place at the lectern.

Glancing at Will, she saw him examining his hands rather than looking at his father. Had their relationship completely broken down, she wondered and reached for his hand. She held it in the folds of her dress again until the congregation rose to sing another hymn and she had to let him go.

They filed out of the church a few minutes later and she took his arm.

"Will you come to the cemetery?" he asked.

"Yes, of course," she replied, and they went to hail a cab.

When the burial service in Mount Jerome Cemetery was over, they joined the other mourners on the walk along the Main Avenue to the gates and their waiting cab.

"Will?" a male voice called, and they both turned as Will's father approached them. "Will you share a cab with your mother and I?" he asked.

"No, thank you. I'm bringing Isobel home, then going on to Brown Street," Will told him.

"Isobel." His father raised his hat to her before walking away.

"I know it's easier said than done," she began. "But try not to fall out with your father permanently."

Will grimaced. "It is easier said than done after what he did, but when I spoke to him on Friday evening, he agreed to retire from practising medicine and to give up the running of the practice with immediate effect. I went to see Eva the practice secretary this morning and I told her my father would not be returning and that I now run the practice. I will resume my Wednesday and Friday surgeries and I have advertised for a locum until I can begin to work there full-time."

"Is Fred remaining at the practice?" she asked and Will nodded.

"After I spoke to Father, I went to see Fred. He now knows where he stands and we will continue to work together. He and Margaret are coming over to us," he added, and she turned to see Fred and his wife slowly walk towards them. "Fred. Margaret."

"Thank you for coming, Will." Fred shook his hand.

"Not at all. Now, I know you have already met briefly, but may I introduce Isobel to you properly? Margaret, Fred, this is Isobel Stevens. Isobel, this is Margaret and Fred Simpson."

"I'm very pleased to meet you," she said, shaking their hands. "And you have my condolences."

"Thank you," Fred replied. "Have you set a wedding date yet?"

"No," Will replied. "But we must."

"Come to tea soon?" Margaret asked them. "I'd very much like us all to get to know each other."

"Thank you, we shall." Isobel smiled, and they moved away. She watched them go to a cab before turning to Will. "Margaret is pregnant, isn't she?"

"Yes."

"I thought so," she murmured. "Fred's holding her arm as if it's made of glass."

"It's very early days yet."

"Did you tell him about my miscarriage?"

"No, I didn't. And I won't if you don't want me to."

"I'd rather you didn't," she replied, and he kissed her hand. "I suppose Margaret would be horrified if she did know."

"I'm afraid she would be, yes. But don't let that put you off making her acquaintance. She is quite direct, like you, and she also has a good sense of humour." He shrugged. "She'd need to have, being married to Fred."

She smiled. "You're invited to luncheon. Mother wants to speak to us about something."

"Let's go to our cab, then."

Outside the cemetery gates, they climbed into the cab and she saw him rest his head back, closing his eyes for a moment.

"Glad it's over?" she asked gently, as the cab set off, and he nodded.

"It's over in Brown Street, too. I move out on Saturday and I went to St Luke's and cancelled the wedding there."

Taking his hand, she kissed the palm. "I'll help you pack. And we'll choose a home."

"And when and where to get married," he added. "Because I've had enough. I want you to be my wife. I want you in my bed. I just want you."

"Kiss me?"

He leant over and kissed her as the cab went around a corner and they began to slide off the seat. Grabbing her arms, he hauled her onto his lap, and they began to laugh.

"We need our own home," he declared. "And soon."

"Yes, we do."

"Why did you really come to the funeral?" he asked, and she flushed.

"You'll think it's ridiculous."

"No, I won't," he said softly. "Tell me."

"Mr Henderson and Mr Simpson loved each other. And no-one could know. Mr Henderson is dead, but I'm his step-daughter. And I knew."

"So you came to represent him," Will finished, and she nodded. "It's not ridiculous at all."

At Fitzwilliam Square, she rang the front doorbell while he paid the cabman, and they were admitted to number 55. Gorman showed them straight into the breakfast room, where Mrs Henderson was sitting down at the head of the table.

"Was it a big funeral?"

"Yes, it was," Isobel told her. "I'm glad I went. What was it you wished to speak to us about?"

"You'll see after we've eaten, Isobel."

Half an hour later, they followed her mother into the morning room. Mrs Henderson went to the writing desk near the window and opened a drawer. "I asked you to be here too, Will, because there is something I would like to give you both." She lifted out an envelope and passed it to him. "Open it."

Puzzled, Isobel went to Will's side as he opened the envelope and pulled out a sheet of notepaper. It was a letter authorising Mr Ellison to transfer the deed of number 30 Fitzwilliam Square to William Fitzgerald.

"Mother," she began, but Mrs Henderson held up a hand to stop her.

"It has to be in Will's name when you marry, but number 30 is my wedding gift to you both. With Will starting in general practice nearby, you will need a good address. It is also a rather selfish gift, as I don't want you too far away."

"It is far too much." Will both looked and sounded utterly shocked.

"No, Will. Ronald has left me well provided for. Alfie will continue to live here and shall inherit this house when the time comes. I want Isobel and you to have number 30. I went to see Mr Ellison when you were both at the funeral and I informed him of my decision. I also asked him how long it will take for probate to be granted. He assures me it will be granted soon and he will then deal with Ronald's assets and the deed of number 30 as swiftly as possible. We then viewed number 30. It needs decorating but, apart from that, it is a beautiful house and will make a more than suitable family home."

"I don't know what to say… thank you." Will kissed her cheek.

Isobel was frozen to the spot. Number 30 had been Hugh Lombard's home. How on earth could it ever be hers?

"Isobel?" Will prompted her and she forced a smile.

"Thank you, Mother," she said, but was unable to keep the dismay out of her voice and her mother's shoulders slumped.

"You know, don't you?" Mrs Henderson asked quietly.

"Know?"

"About the tenant who died recently in the house."

"Yes, I'm afraid I do."

"Isobel." Her mother squeezed her hands. "Please do not allow it to deter you. Mr Ellison told me the tenant – a Mr Lombard – was attacked by an intruder and he assured me it is an extremely rare occurrence. I have asked Mr Ellison to arrange to have all Mr Lombard's possessions removed from the house and the locks changed and that will be done when probate is granted. The furniture which belongs to the house will remain, however, and it is your choice whether to keep it or sell it all and start afresh. I also asked Mr Ellison if you could view the house and he agreed, provided the key is returned to him afterwards. The key to the front door is in the envelope. Go and view your new home then bring the key and my letter to Mr Ellison, he will be expecting you."

Will took her hand and led her from the morning room. In the hall, she opened her mouth to speak, but he held a finger to her lips.

"Let's just go and see the house."

They walked around the gardens and Will extracted the key from the envelope. He unlocked and opened the front door and they went into the hall. The house smelled musty and unlived in and she waited for him to close the door before speaking.

"This was Hugh Lombard's home."

"With fresh paint, new wallpaper, some new furniture, and new rugs on the floors, we can make it ours."

"But I came here to be his mistress."

"But you didn't become his mistress," Will told her softly. "Here, you will be my wife and mistress of this house."

"I simply don't know if I can be mistress of a house like this," she said, glancing around the hall at the fanlight over the front door, the decorative plasterwork, and the carved banister rails which had been painted white.

"How long did you spend in this house that evening?" Will asked, and she pondered his question for a few moments.

"Half an hour at most," she replied.

"And how many rooms were you in?"

"Three. A bedroom, the dining room, and I ran through the drawing room. It sounds so little," she admitted. "But I don't think I will ever be able to forget that evening."

"Isobel, think of this house as the rented residence of a man you were briefly acquainted with. That man is now dead, and the man who killed him is dead now, too. We will own this house, we will transform this house into our home, and we will live and raise a family in it. Yes?" he asked a little tentatively.

"Yes," she agreed quietly, and he lifted her hands and kissed them. "But can we afford to run a house of this size?" she asked as she sat down on the stairs and he sat beside her.

"With my income from the Merrion Street practice, yes. Provided we don't have more than ten children." That finally made her laugh, and he put an arm around her. "We will transform this house into our home – our family home." Getting up, he held out a hand. "Come and walk through the house with me."

She got up and clasped his hand and he opened the door to the morning room. All the furniture was covered in dust sheets. Unlike her mother's, this morning room was rather gloomy and badly needed to be decorated in brighter colours. But with some effort, it would be a lovely room, and just right for everyday use. The brighter breakfast room next to it, faced onto an overgrown rear garden.

Upstairs on the first floor, they went into the huge drawing room. It was cold, the furniture was covered in dust sheets, and the rug was gone from the floor. Next door was the dining room, and she walked to the double doors which had been left open. The table and chairs were also covered in dust sheets and bore little resemblance to what she remembered of the barely-touched meal she had sat down to.

Climbing the stairs to the second floor, they walked into the bedroom she had been dressed in, and she shuddered.

"We will transform this house," Will reminded her softly and led her out onto the landing. "Choose a bedroom for us."

Worried she would choose a bedroom and then discover it had been Mr Lombard's, she was relieved to discover all the bedrooms were as bare and impersonal as those in a hotel. Had Mr Lombard slept in this house at all? Or had his personal effects been stolen by his servants? They went from bedroom to bedroom until she led Will back to one with a window overlooking the rear garden. It was the bedroom furthest from the stairs and, she smiled, the most private.

"This one," she said. "Unless our bedroom needs to be at the front?"

"No," he replied. "The footman we will employ will have a bedroom downstairs. If I'm needed somewhere at night, he will hear the front doorbell and call me. It worked without fail for my father."

"This one, then?"

Will went to the window and she joined him, slipping an arm around his waist.

"This one," he said and kissed her forehead. "Let's go outside."

They made their way downstairs to the long and narrow garden which ran between the house and the mews. It was neglected and overgrown but, in a corner, she found a rose bush struggling grow through the weeds.

"We had white and yellow roses in the garden in Ballybeg," she told him. "And daffodils in spring. Alfie and I even had a little vegetable patch and chickens for a while."

"Well, this garden is big enough for a vegetable patch."

"And a bench," she decided.

"A bench?" Will smiled. "Where?"

She glanced around the garden before pointing. "There, on the lawn."

He took her hand, they returned to the hall and sat on the stairs again. "This house is close to your mother and Alfie, near to my parents, and within walking distance of the practice house. The morning room and breakfast room we will use for everyday purposes, and the drawing room and dining room upstairs if we ever have guests. It's perfect."

"Yes," she said, resting her head on his shoulder. "We'll transform it – the whole house – decorate it from top to bottom – have gas lighting installed – it will be perfect for us."

"Marry me soon."

"Tell me where and when and I'll be there."

"I know." He sat up suddenly, startling her. "Trinity College Chapel. I've been to a couple of services there. It's lovely – not too big – quite intimate, really."

"Is it allowed?" she asked.

"I'm a Trinity graduate so, yes. I'll bring you to see it, come on."

"Now?" She laughed as he jumped down from the stairs and pulled her to her feet.

"Yes."

"But we're both dressed in black," she protested, then laughed again. "Oh, what does it matter?"

"Not a bit." They left the house and he locked the front door behind them. "Soon, we will have our home, let's find somewhere to get married."

They walked to Trinity College, Will mentally kicking himself for not having thought of the chapel before. The door was open and they made their way slowly towards the altar, Isobel glancing at the oak pews which faced the aisle, then up at the ornate plasterwork on the ceiling. They climbed the steps then turned and surveyed the chapel. Isobel, he was relieved to see, had a smile on her lips.

"Well?" he asked.

"How soon can we get married here?"

"Can I help you?" a male voice called from the door, and they turned as a clergyman came in and closed the door behind him.

"Are you the chaplain?" Will asked.

"Yes, I am."

"Would it be possible to speak to you about a wedding?"

"Of course." The chaplain walked up the aisle. "It for yourselves?"

"It is."

"Are you a former student?"

"Yes. I'm Dr Will Fitzgerald." He put out a hand and the chaplain shook it.

"James Wilson."

"And this is my fiancée, Isobel Stevens."

"Stevens?" Wilson echoed as they shook hands. "Anything to Canon Edmund Stevens?"

Will felt Isobel tense. "I'm his daughter."

"He was a very fine man."

"Yes," she replied simply in a flat tone.

"Come with me and we can discuss a date." He brought them to an office and bade them sit down before sitting down himself. Taking a diary out of a desk drawer, he flipped through it. "I have a Saturday three months from now."

"Is there nothing sooner?" Will asked.

"How much sooner?"

"As soon as possible. We have already had to cancel one date."

"I see." Wilson flipped back through the pages. "And where was the marriage to have taken place?"

"St Luke's. I live in the parish but I am about to move from there to begin in general practice on Merrion Street Upper so we need to find somewhere else to marry."

"Where do you live, Miss Stevens?"

"Fitzwilliam Square," she replied.

"Which is in the parish of St Peter."

"Yes, but I have been to two recent funerals there and I now rather associate that church with death."

"Due to the death of Isobel's step-father, ours is going to be a small wedding," Will explained. "We would both very much like it to take place here."

Wilson nodded. "Ah, here we are. Saturday the 4th of December at eleven in the morning?"

"Yes," Will replied immediately.

"Are you sure?" Wilson frowned. "It is rather short notice and a special licence will be required."

"We are."

"Very well, I will see to the licence at once." Wilson wrote their names into the diary. "I will need both your baptism and confirmation certificates as soon as possible."

"Of course. Thank you for accommodating us."

Outside, he pulled Isobel into a quick hug, and they hurried back to number 55.

"Well?" Mrs Henderson asked as they sat down on the sofa.

"The house is perfect, Mother," Isobel replied with a wide smile. "Thank you."

"We also have some other news," Will added. "Isobel and I are to be married by special licence on Saturday the 4th of December in the chapel in Trinity College."

Mrs Henderson's eyes filled with tears. "I am so happy for you. I attended a service there many years ago with Isobel's father. It is a beautiful chapel."

"It is." Will got to his feet. "I'm sorry, but I must go. I need to tell my parents, call to Mr Ellison with the letter and key, go back to the chaplain with our baptism and confirmation certificates, and start packing in Brown Street. I cannot thank you enough for the house."

"You are very welcome, Will."

Isobel gave him her certificates, he went straight to number 67 and was shown into the morning room. He came straight to the point and his parents were astonished.

"Isobel's mother has given you a house on Fitzwilliam Square?" his mother gasped.

"Yes. Number 30. Isobel and I viewed it this afternoon. It needs decorating, but it will be perfect for us."

"I don't believe it."

"I can hardly believe it either," he admitted. "I also want you to clear your diaries for Saturday the 4th of December. Isobel and I are getting married in the chapel in Trinity College at eleven in the morning."

"Trinity?" his father echoed.

"Yes. We went to see the chaplain this afternoon."

"You have been busy. Trinity is a good choice, Will."

"Thank you."

"Will Fred be your best man?" his father asked.

"I hope so. I'd also like Jerry to attend."

"You'd better send him a telegram, then. A celebratory whiskey?"

"Yes, please," he said, and his father got up from the sofa and went to the drinks tray.

"Have you thought of where you will go on honeymoon?" his mother asked.

It hadn't even crossed his mind and he shook his head. "No, I haven't given it any thought at all."

"Well, your father and I would like to give you your honeymoon as a wedding gift," his mother said, taking a glass of sherry from his father. "So discuss it with Isobel."

"That's very kind." He accepted a glass of whiskey from his father. "Thank you."

"What shall we drink to?" his father asked, holding up his glass of whiskey. "The future?"

"The future," they chorused and drank from their glasses.

"I saw you speaking to Fred and Margaret Simpson at the cemetery," his father said, re-taking his seat on the sofa.

"Yes. Margaret has invited Isobel and I to tea. She would like us all to get to know each other."

"Good." His father nodded. "Yes, Margaret and Isobel should become acquainted."

"I agree." He sipped at his whiskey. "I move out of Brown Street on Saturday."

"I will have your room prepared," his mother told him.

"No," he replied a little too sharply, and he quickly smiled to reassure her. "Thank you, but if probate has been granted and if Isobel's mother allows it, I will move straight to number 30."

His mother's face fell. "But you said the house needs to be decorated?"

"It does, but it is not in an uninhabitable condition, and I want to be on hand to supervise."

His mother's eyebrows rose. "Very well."

Will engaged Mr Ellison as his solicitor and handed him the envelope containing Mrs Henderson's letter of authorisation and the key to number 30. He then sent a telegram to Jerry and returned to Brown Street for his baptism and confirmation certificates. After passing the four certificates to the Trinity College chaplain, and paying the fee for the special licence, he walked home via a grocer's with two tea chests. Carrying them upstairs, he began to pack.

Chapter Twelve

Isobel went to see the dressmaker that evening, her mother insisting she take a cab and not walk there in the dark. She apologised that her plans had changed again, then explained when the wedding was taking place. The wedding dress was ready for a fitting and she stood admiring the dress in a long mirror while the dressmaker added pins. It was over four weeks since the miscarriage, her monthly cycle hadn't returned, and her breasts felt tender. While it was far too soon to get her hopes up, she couldn't help but give her stomach a little pat. One final pin was added before the dressmaker stood back from her, nodding critically.

"It's beautiful, Miss Stevens, even though I say it myself. So many dresses are overly fussy, but the simpler the better, I say."

"Yes. I've never liked fuss, in a dress or otherwise."

"Come back next week for another fitting, Miss Stevens."

"It will be ready in time?" she asked anxiously.

"It will be, I promise."

Returning to Fitzwilliam Square, she got out of the cab outside number 30. She paid the cabman, then stared up at the Georgian townhouse. She and Will would make this house their home and she would never have cause to be reminded of Mr Lombard again. She gave the house a determined nod before turning away.

She called to Brown Street the following morning. Two tea chests full of books were standing in the hall.

"I thought I'd make a start." Will kissed her lips. "But I need a lot more tea chests. You seem pleased about something?"

"I am pleased – I'm delighted, in fact." She smiled. "Probate has been granted. Mother, Alfie, and I received letters from Mr Ellison this morning asking us to call to his office this afternoon. Mr Lombard's belongings are currently being removed from number 30 and the locks are being changed. Mother says she is going to present me with the new key there and then."

"That's wonderful." Will grinned and kissed her lips again. "I hoped probate wouldn't take long because I've decided to move from here straight into number 30. I'd rather the house didn't stand empty anymore, and I want to be there while the gas lighting is installed, the decorating is carried out, and so we can interview potential servants."

Servants. Her heart began to thump nervously. She had been a servant herself, and soon she would be in charge of some.

"Should we begin to advertise for servants?"

"I'm going to ask Mrs Bell and the servants in number 67 if they can recommend anyone," he said. "You should ask your mother's servants, too."

"I will, and I'm going to lodge the five hundred pounds Mr Henderson left me to my bank account so we will have money to begin work immediately on number 30. Mother has recommended a company of painters, paperhangers, and decorators and another company who install gas lighting. After I've been to the bank, I'm going to call to the decorators and ask for some wallpaper samples and then call to the gas lighting company."

"Good. You can bring the samples straight to number 30."

"What items of furniture do you own here?" she asked.

"The desk, chairs, and examination couch in the surgery. The writing desk, chair, and bookcase in the parlour. And my bed. I wasn't going to sleep in the bed which was here, so I treated myself to a new one."

So he owned the bed, that was a relief. "I like your bed."

"I was wondering whether to buy a new one."

"No," she told him. "I want it to be our bed. It's big enough."

He nodded. "I wanted a bed I could stretch out in."

"We'll have to find someone to transport it all to number 30."

"I know a local man with a cart – Pat Byrne."

"I don't know if I like the thought of you all alone in that huge house," she said softly, sliding her arms around him.

"It will only be for a week or so. And I was hoping you would visit me?" He raised an eyebrow suggestively and she laughed.

"I must visit you before you move from here, too. In the meantime, shall we find some more tea chests?"

They spent the rest of the morning packing a further four tea chests and leaving them in the hall.

"Mrs Bell has made vegetable soup," he said. "There's enough for us both."

She heated the soup on the solid fuel range while he cut some soda bread. "We don't need many servants, do we?" she asked. "Surely just enough to keep up appearances? And certainly not a butler?"

"A cook-housekeeper, a kitchenmaid, two house-parlourmaids and a footman?" he suggested.

"Yes. We had a cook-housekeeper and one house-parlourmaid in Ballybeg, but the house was smaller."

"We'll see how they cope."

"Yes. I'm sorry." She rested the wooden spoon against the side of the saucepan. "I can't help but be nervous. I grew up in a house with servants, then I was a servant myself, but I have never run a house before."

Will put the bread knife down and held her in his arms. "You took charge when Mr Henderson died and your mother was in shock and you coped wonderfully."

"I want to be your wife so much," she murmured into his chest. "But I'm so afraid I'm going to let you down."

"You will never let me down," he whispered fiercely. "We will employ competent servants and the house will run itself. Both of us will be starting afresh and we will learn together and any mistakes we make, we will make together."

At two o'clock that afternoon, she collected a bank draft for five hundred pounds from Mr Ellison. Her mother then presented her with two keys to the front door of number 30, two keys to the back door and another to the mews. Asking if she could remain behind as she needed Mr Ellison's advice, she waited for her mother and Alfie to leave the office before speaking.

"May I ask you something about number 30 Fitzwilliam Square?" she asked.

"Yes, of course."

"The man who died there – my mother said his name was Mr Lombard and that he was attacked by an intruder – do you know what really happened to him?"

"What I told your mother was the truth. I admit that it was not all the information I had acquired, but it was the truth."

"Mr Ellison, if I am to live there, I would like to know it all. If you please."

"Very well," he conceded. "The tenant's name was Hugh Lombard and he was a bachelor aged forty-five." Then Mr Ellison sighed and Isobel's heart began to thump. "As far as I could ascertain, he rented the house in order to pass himself off as a gentleman. He did own property, however, a photographic studio on Back Street. It was outwardly respectable but the vast majority of its income came from the producing and selling of so-called erotic photographs, which Mr Lombard sold in various gentlemen's clubs across the city."

"Erotic photographs," she managed to repeat casually. "I see."

"And your mother does not know this, Miss Stevens, but once I discovered how Mr Lombard made a living I went to number 30 and searched it myself. I was glad I did, as I found umpteen bundles of photographs wrapped in brown paper and tied with string in one of the bedrooms. I brought them all downstairs to the servants' hall and burned every last photograph in the range. Some I had the misfortune to see were of the most repulsive kind."

"Thank you," she replied, fighting to hide her relief. "And what do you know of the circumstances surrounding

Mr Lombard's death? A disgruntled customer, perhaps?"

"I honestly don't know," Mr Ellison replied. "All I could obtain from the police was that Mr Lombard was found dead on the drawing room floor by a neighbour who had noticed the house was unusually quiet, called at the house, and discovered the front door was unlocked. Mr Lombard had been dead for at least a week. The post-mortem revealed there was evidence he had been involved in a fight and that he died of a fracture to the base of his skull which caused severe bruising and bleeding to his brain."

Isobel winced. She had heard Hugh Lombard fall like a stone when Duncan Simpson punched him.

"According to his neighbours," Mr Ellison continued. "Mr Lombard had employed a butler, a cook-housekeeper, a kitchenmaid, two house-parlourmaids, and a footman. They have all disappeared. As have the tenants in the photographic studio – a Johan Fortuin and Lucius de Bruijn. Whether any of them were implicated in or knew who was implicated in Mr Lombard's death, no-one seems to know. The police investigation has ground to a complete halt."

"Thank you for being honest with me, Mr Ellison," she said.

"Please don't allow Mr Lombard's death to overshadow your mother's gift of the house. It will make a wonderful home for yourself and Dr Fitzgerald."

"Yes." She smiled. "It will."

She went straight to her bank, the former Irish Houses of Parliament on College Green, with the bank draft. The bank was busy and she joined a queue. Glancing along the counters at the customers and clerks, she did a double take. It was unusual to be a woman in a bank, and she rarely saw another. The woman at the counter was wearing a gaudy dress – purple with vertical yellow stripes – and Isobel couldn't help but stare. Then the woman turned towards her and Isobel's heart somersaulted. It was Sally Maher.

Isobel tried to tug her hat down to hide her face but the hat pins held it secure, so she pulled a handkerchief from her sleeve and pretended to blow her nose. Sally walked straight past her, passing within three feet of her. Lowering the handkerchief, Isobel saw her hands shaking as she returned it to her sleeve. Breathing deeply in and out, she fought to control herself and walked to the counter on unsteady legs. She lodged the bank draft to her account, then went to the bank's entrance, glancing up and down the street to make sure Sally had gone.

Leaving the bank, she turned in the direction of Dame Street and hid behind one of the grand building's many pillars until her breathing slowed. She needed to be more careful, more observant. Extracting the hat pins, she re-positioned her hat so it was lower over her face, and pushed the pins back in. That done, she peered out from behind the pillar, before hurrying back to the safety of Fitzwilliam Square.

Will had just acquired two more tea chests and was carrying them down Brown Street when he heard a shout.

"Will?"

Fred was getting out of a cab and Will put the tea chests down. Fred paid the cabman then joined him on the pavement.

"This is an honour." Will smiled and shook his hand.

"Packing already?" Fred asked, nodding at the tea chests.

"I move out on Saturday."

"That soon?" Fred picked one of them up.

"There's no point in continuing to pay rent here anymore." Will lifted up the other chest. "Come to the house, I've something to tell you."

"So have I."

Leaving the tea chests in the increasingly full hall, they went upstairs to the parlour.

"I haven't packed the whiskey and glasses yet." Will held up the bottle and Fred nodded. "You're not going to believe this," he said as he poured them each a helping. "But Isobel's mother has given us a house on Fitzwilliam Square as a wedding gift – number 30."

Fred's eyes widened. "That is quite a gift. What condition is it in?"

"It needs decorating, gas lighting installed, and some new furniture." He picked up the two glasses and passed Fred one. "I also want to tell you that Isobel and I will be getting married on Saturday two weeks in Trinity College Chapel at eleven in the morning. I'd like you to be my best man."

Fred touched Will's glass with his and smiled. "It would be an honour. Trinity Chapel, eh?"

"I can't believe I didn't think of it before. Margaret is also welcome, and I've sent Jerry a telegram."

"Good. I hope he can come over."

"Now you can tell me what brings you here." Fred looked troubled and Will began to feel uncomfortable. "It's not Margaret, is it?"

"No, she's absolutely fine. I met Cecilia's father this morning."

"Oh?"

"Will, there's no easy way to say this, but Clive Ashlinn is dead and Cecilia is badly injured."

Blood drained from Will's face. "What happened?"

"They were travelling home in a cab from a dinner party two nights ago. Something frightened the horse, it bolted, and the cab turned over."

Will put his whiskey glass down. "Will she live?"

"It's touch and go. She's been unconscious ever since."

"I see," he replied quietly.

"I came here to tell you because I didn't want you hearing it from a stranger or reading it in the newspapers. I wanted you to hear it from a friend."

"I haven't had time to read a newspaper recently. Thank you."

"Drink your whiskey," Fred advised him softly, and Will picked up the glass and took a sip. "Are you all right?"

"I don't know," he admitted. "I haven't loved Cecilia for a long time, but I did love her very much once. I hope she pulls through."

"Yes, because she's also expecting a baby."

Will grimaced. "Thank you for telling me, Fred. Please let me know if..?"

Fred nodded then slapped his shoulder. "So, an address on Fitzwilliam Square, eh?"

"Number 30. Isobel is a little daunted at the prospect. And, I must admit, I am, too. Number 67 was always going to be Edward's and I never expected to own – or even rent – a house of its size."

"You'll need servants."

"Yes. You don't know of a good cook-housekeeper, do you?" he asked.

"No, but I'll ask Margaret."

Will nodded. "I'm moving from here straight to number 30. There was little point in me moving to number 67 and from there to number 30 a week or so later."

"No, I suppose not. But I'd hate to see you and your father fall out completely."

"I can't help being angry. And disappointed. At you, as well, not just at my father. But we all know where we stand now, so there's little point going over it all again."

"No," Fred replied, then added in a brighter tone, "Where are you going on honeymoon?"

"Mother asked me that and I don't know. I need to discuss it with Isobel, but probably somewhere in Ireland. I don't want to waste too much time travelling."

"No?" Fred raised an eyebrow comically and Will smiled.

"No. And we won't be doing a lot of sight-seeing either."

"So, a gaggle of children are on the cards, then?"

"We hope so." He nodded. "I love her, Fred. I thought I loved Cecilia, but that love was nothing compared to what I feel for Isobel."

"I'm happy for you, Will. When Cecilia ended your engagement, I thought you'd never find anyone else."

When Will closed the front door after Fred, he ran a hand over his jaw. Cecilia was widowed and pregnant. If she did pull through, he hoped she would be strong enough to cope.

It was dusk, and Isobel was seated on a bench in the Fitzwilliam Square gardens still shaking a little when a cab stopped outside number 55 and Will jumped out. She hurried to the gate and left the gardens, locking the gate behind her.

"Will?" she called as he went up the steps and he turned. "Go to number 30, I have the keys."

He waved in reply, got back into the cab, and she followed it around the gardens. As she approached, he was reaching into the cab and lifting out a tea chest and then another. He paid the cabman, carried the first tea chest up the steps to the front door, and she joined him as he was carrying the second tea chest to the door.

"I thought I'd make a start on my move here," he explained and kissed her lips. "Did you get the samples?"

The wallpaper samples and the gas lighting hadn't even crossed her mind. She had meant to call to both companies once she had been to the bank.

"No." Taking one of the front door keys from her handbag, she unlocked and opened the front door, and they carried the tea chests into the hall. "I got a terrible fright in the bank," she continued and closed the door. "Sally Maher was there."

"Did Sally see you?"

She shook her head. "I covered most of my face with a handkerchief, but she was as close to me as you are now," she went on, clenching her fists to try and stop the trembling. "I got such a fright, I came straight back here."

Clasping her hands, he raised them to his lips and kissed her fingers. "I'm sorry."

"I hoped I would never see her again. I'm usually the only woman in the bank when I go there, so when I saw another woman, I couldn't help but stare. And it was her." She closed her eyes for a moment. "If only Dublin wasn't so small."

"You were just unlucky. It's highly likely you will never see her again."

"Yes," she conceded. "I hope so. I also asked Mr Ellison about Mr Lombard's death."

"Was that wise?" he asked.

"I told him if I was going to live here I needed to know. Will, according to the post-mortem, Mr Lombard died of a fracture to the base of his skull which caused severe bruising and bleeding to his brain." Will sighed but she continued. "He had been dead for at least a week when he was found and, in the meantime, Johan and Lucius and all his servants disappeared. Mr Ellison confirmed that the police got nowhere with the investigation."

"I see."

"And once he discovered what Mr Lombard did for a living, Mr Ellison searched this house and found and burned hundreds of photographs."

Will rolled his eyes in clear relief. "Mr Ellison is worth his weight in gold."

"Yes, he is. I can do nothing about the photographs already in circulation, but the fact that hundreds more have been destroyed is a huge weight off my mind. And I had to find out about Mr Lombard, Will, otherwise, I'd never have stopped wondering."

"I know. Fred came to see me, I asked him to be my best man, and he accepted."

"Good."

"He also told me Cecilia's husband is dead and she is badly injured."

Isobel's jaw dropped. "How?"

"A cab they were travelling in turned over. I have to admit, it was a shock."

"Will Cecilia live?" she asked.

"Fred said it is touch and go. And that she is also pregnant. I've asked him to let me know if she pulls through."

"How awful. Poor Cecilia," she replied quietly.

"Yes. She hurt me deeply but I would never have wished anything like this on her."

"She would have willingly lived in this house with you."

"Yes, but we would have made each other extremely unhappy. I have absolutely no regrets that she threw me over – none. You were willing to come and live in Brown Street and we would have been happy there. We will be just as happy in this house."

The following morning, they went to the gas lighting company to employ them. That done, they went to the decorators, selected wallpaper samples, and brought them back to number 30. By mid-afternoon, they had made their choices, returned to the company, and engaged them.

The day before Will was to move out of Brown Street, Isobel went there after luncheon with some chocolates.

"As it's the wrong time of year for flowers, I bought these for Mrs Bell from the two of us," she explained, squeezing between the rows of tea chests in the hall, and putting the box on the kitchen table. "To thank her for looking after you so well."

"She'll be delighted."

"Alfie and I received a letter from Mr Ellison this morning to inform us that a Sarah Maher has made an offer on both the Montgomery Street and Purdon Street properties. He has advised us to accept it. I've just called to see him and accepted the offer on behalf of Alfie and myself."

"Good." He kissed her lips. "That's the brothels dealt with."

"Yes, I'm so relieved Alfie and I are rid of them. Is everything packed?"

"All except the necessities," he said, leading her upstairs. "This is your last visit here. I remember the first time you called. I opened the front door and you were standing on the step with a cabbage in one hand and a cake tin in the other."

The bookcase in the parlour was empty and the writing desk free of photographs. Everywhere was bare and she hoped number 30 would be as homely as this house had been.

"Make love to me?" she asked. "For the last time here?" He smiled, began to lead her out of the room, but she stopped him. "On the desk first," she told him, taking both his hands, and walking backwards until they reached it. She unbuttoned his trousers, pushed them and his drawers down then slid a hand around the back of his neck, guiding his head down to her. "Kiss me."

Slowly, he licked her lips, and she closed her eyes as his tongue worked its way into her mouth. She felt his hands on her dress, raising the skirt, and lowering her drawers. She stepped out of them, and he lifted her onto the desk.

Parting her thighs, he slid into her, and she clasped his buttocks to hold him there for a few moments. He grunted, and she knew he needed to thrust. Sliding her hands up his back allowed him to pull out a little then slide back inside. Like that first night in the brothel, he thrusted into her with a slow and almost hypnotic rhythm, and she rested her forehead on his shoulder. He brought her to a moaning climax before holding himself inside her and coming with a series of satisfied grunts.

Suddenly, she felt herself moving. The desk wasn't

supporting her weight anymore. Instead, Will's arms were hooking around her thighs, his hands clasping her waist tightly as he lifted her off the desk.

Before she could say anything, he had thrust into her hard.

"Like that?" he whispered, his lips pulling at her earlobe. "Tell me you like that."

Again, just before she could speak, he started walking, carrying her in his arms. It took him only a few seconds to walk from the desk in the parlour to the bed in his bedroom, but by the time he laid her down on the mattress, she was ready to explode. The friction, caused by his movements, had turned her insides to liquid.

He covered her body with his, thrusting harder and deeper, with a rhythm which had her whimpering with each breath she forced into her lungs.

Her hips began to move with his, trying to match his rhythm. Just three more thrusts and she was coming hard, her fingernails digging into the shoulders of his morning coat as she let out what sounded like a million profanities and 'I love you's' all at once.

Will came right after her with a loud curse, holding himself deep inside her. He lay on top of her in a tangle of legs and clothes and she stroked his hair as they fought to catch their breaths.

"Where did you learn to do that?" she murmured.

"In my imagination," he replied, and she laughed softly.

"I hope there's a lot more where that came from?"

"There is, but I'm saving it for our house."

Our house. She smiled and kissed the top of his head.

In the morning, Will received a hand-delivered letter from Fred. It was the last letter addressed to him in Brown Street and brought good news.

> *Dear Will,*
>
> *Just to let you know that Cecilia regained consciousness yesterday. Apart from a broken humerus, both she and the baby appear to be fine.*
>
> *Clive's funeral is this afternoon at St Peter's with burial afterwards in Mount Jerome Cemetery. Margaret and I will be attending.*
>
> *I'll speak to you after you've moved.*
>
> *Fred*

Relieved, Will folded the letter and put it back in the envelope then went upstairs for a final walk through the house.

He stood in the empty bedroom, putting the envelope in the inside pocket of his morning coat, before walking into the parlour. It had been cosy and he would miss it. Going back down the stairs, he went into the kitchen. He did a circuit of the table, remembering all the chats he'd had with Mrs Bell. Walking the length of the hall, he went into the surgery and peered into what had been the dispensary.

Hearing a knock at the front door, he opened it and found Mrs Bell on the step.

"I couldn't let you leave without being here," she told him.

"Thank you. Come in." He stood aside and she came into the hall. "I was saying goodbye to the surgery, I'll miss it."

"It was an ideal room. I'll miss the range in the kitchen myself. It was great for baking."

"I'll miss your cooking."

"I'll miss our chats. You found a housekeeper?" she asked.

"Yes, Mrs Dillon, a cook-housekeeper. She comes highly recommended by Fred's wife. We also found a kitchenmaid, two house-parlourmaids, and a footman. They all arrive tomorrow and the decorators and gas lighting installers begin on Monday."

"Good. I hoped you wouldn't be stuck for servants."

"This—" He went to the kitchen, lifted the box of chocolates from the table, and passed it to her. "Is from Isobel and myself – a thank you gift for looking after me so well."

"I can't remember when I last had chocolate. Thank you, and thank Isobel for me?"

"I will." There was another knock at the front door and he gave her a sad smile. "Pat wants to go."

"The best of luck, Dr Fitzgerald."

"Thank you. Isobel and I will see you at the wedding," he said, shrugging on his overcoat and reaching for his hat.

"You will."

"And we'll keep in touch?" he added.

"We will."

"I can't thank you enough," he said, bending and kissing her cheek before they left the house, and he climbed up onto the cart beside Pat, the cart man. "See you at the wedding," he called as the cart moved off.

Mrs Bell stood on the pavement waving as the cart turned the corner at the end of the street.

Isobel was standing at the front door of number 30 when the cart arrived with the last of Will's furniture and belongings. Will jumped down, ran up the steps to her, and she kissed his lips.

"Let me help," she said and followed him to the cart.

"These aren't too heavy." He reached for the first of four wooden boxes. "But be careful, there are bottles of medicine inside."

Taking it from him, she carried the box into the house, and carefully set it down on the floor in the hall. She had to stand to one side as Will and Pat carried the bedstead and then the mattress inside and up the stairs. She brought the three other boxes inside then returned to the cart for his medical bag. She put it down on the pavement as Will and Pat came back outside and Will shook his hand.

"Thanks, Pat."

Will held her hand as Pat climbed up onto the cart and it moved off. Then, he picked up his medical bag and they went into the house, closing the front door behind them. He put the bag down on the hall floor before taking her face in his hands and kissing her.

"I will carry you over the threshold when we're married."

"Good." She smiled. "Let's go downstairs to the coal hole and get two buckets of coal so you can light a fire in the morning room and in our bedroom. I want you to have two warm rooms."

"Our bedroom." Holding her tightly, she felt his chin resting on the top of her head. "Our house."

"You are also eating with us at number 55 until Mrs Dillon arrives," she told him.

"Thank you."

They filled two buckets with coal, brought one upstairs, and she made the bed while he lit the fire.

"Let's wait for the room to heat up a bit." He gave her a broad wink as he placed the spark guard in front of the hearth and she laughed. "The fire in the morning room next."

While he lit the morning room fire, she went to the window and looked out over the square. A cab passed by and she turned back to Will. He was sitting on his heels watching as the fire took.

"Come back to number 55 while the rooms are warming up," she said. "And I'll ring for some coffee."

Nodding, he straightened up and stood the spark guard in front of the grate.

"I received a letter from Fred," he told her. "Cecilia is going to pull through."

"She didn't lose the baby?"

"No."

"I'm glad."

"Clive's funeral is today," he added. "Both Fred and Margaret are attending."

They walked around the gardens and were admitted to number 55 by Gorman, who took Will's hat and overcoat. The morning room was empty and she shrugged.

"Mother didn't say she was going out. I'll just go upstairs and see if she's all right."

She went up the stairs to the first floor and was about to continue on up to the bedrooms when she heard a thud from the generally unused drawing room. Puzzled, she pushed open the door and jumped, clapping a hand to her mouth. Alfie and a dark-haired young man with a beard were kissing in front of the fireplace, but broke apart and gaped at her in horror.

"I didn't see anything." She held her hands up and began to turn away.

"No, Isobel, wait," Alfie called after her. She turned back and he made a helpless gesture with his hands. "Isobel, this is David—" He stopped speaking as Will looked into the room over her shoulder.

"Is your mother in bed, Alfie?"

"No," Alfie replied. "Your mother called and insisted she accompany her back to Merrion Square for luncheon so they could become acquainted. Mother and I assumed you and Isobel would be in number 30 all day."

"I lit fires in two of the rooms and we thought we'd give them time to warm up."

Isobel saw Will glance at David with an expectant expression, clearly waiting to be introduced. "Come into the room," she said, and when Will did as he was asked, she closed the door.

Alfie sighed. "Isobel, Will," he began. "This is David Powell. He is my…" He tailed off and cringed.

"Lover," David finished, and Will's eyebrows shot up. "Alfie and I are lovers."

"Mother doesn't know, Isobel," Alfie added. "Please don't tell her."

"No, of course not, but you must be more careful than this. Will and I could have been any of the servants."

"I know," he replied quietly.

"Are you a medical student, too?" Will asked David, who shook his head.

"Not anymore, I recently graduated."

"Congratulations. Well, we'll give you some privacy."

"No, it's all right." Alfie gave them a weak smile. "Actually, I'm relieved you know now."

"Oh, Alfie." Crossing the room, she hugged him. "Will and I won't tell anyone."

"I didn't even know how to begin to tell you. Especially after what happened and you—" He stopped, clearly realising he had said too much.

"What happened..?" she repeated with a puzzled little shrug.

"To you."

"I don't understand, Alfie. Did Father know about you?"

"No. But James did."

Her stomach constricted. "How?"

"He caught me with his brother, Peter. He threatened to tell Father if…"

"If what?" she urged.

"If I didn't let him have you."

"Continue," she said as calmly as she could.

"It was clear you liked James," Alfie went on. "And I told him to call on one particular day as we would all be away from the house except you. James bragged about it afterwards. How naïve and innocent you were. How, when he asked to see Father's new mare, you brought him to the stables. How you blushed when he told you how beautiful you were. And how, when he kissed you, he put his tongue into your mouth and you sucked it, and allowed him to lift your skirts…"

"It was all because of you," she shrieked and lunged forward but Will grabbed her arms.

"Isobel – no."

"James ruined me and it was all because of you," she wailed. "It was all because of you."

"I'm so sorry," Alfie whispered.

"Come on." Will guided her out of the drawing room and down the stairs. "You're coming back to number 30 with me."

She was walked out of the house, around the gardens, and into number 30. He sat her down on the dust sheet-covered sofa in the morning room and went back out to the hall, returning with a box. He set it down on the floor then lifted out a bottle of whiskey and a glass and poured her some.

"Drink this," he instructed, sitting beside her, and touching the glass to her lips.

Holding the glass with both hands, she gulped the contents down. He took the glass from her and put it on the floor. Gently, he lifted her onto his lap, and she rested her head against his.

"'How naïve and innocent'," she murmured. "Three months later I was working in a brothel."

"What would your father have done if James had told him about Alfie?"

"Disowned him, like he disowned me. But—" She heaved a sigh. "Beaten him half to death, too. If not actually to death. Father wanted a large family, with lots of sons, but all he got was Alfie and me. If he had known Alfie preferred men then, yes, I think he would have killed him. Oh, God, poor Alfie."

"Had you no idea Alfie preferred men?"

"No. But we never ever spoke about things like that. Until I told him I was pregnant with James' child, that is.

He begged me not to tell Father, but what else could I do? James wasn't going to stand by me, he'd already got what he wanted. That was the last time Alfie and I spoke to one another for months. I need to speak to him now," she said, sliding off Will's lap.

They returned to number 55 and were shown into the morning room, where Alfie was standing alone at the window.

"I'm sorry," he said simply.

"I know." She ran across the room and hugged him. "I'm sorry, too. I'm disgusted at James and I took it out on you."

"I thought James was a friend, which just shows what a great judge of character I am."

"You were coerced." Will spoke up. "And it was a sordid thing for him to do."

"Yes, it was."

"Where's David?" she asked.

"Gone back his rooms. He told me to go and speak to you. I was standing here trying to pluck up the courage."

She squeezed his arm. "Please don't be afraid to speak to either myself or Will."

"Isobel's right," Will added. "If you need to speak to us about anything then do. Because…"

"We need to be much more careful," Alfie finished. "We know."

"Well, I am now resident in number 30," Will announced brightly. "All I need now is for my wife to join me."

"Will, your mother mentioned that you still haven't decided on a honeymoon destination," Alfie told him. "So I suggested Galway and I gave her the name of a hotel. She said she would send them a telegram. So if you'd rather not go to Galway in the month of December, you'd better go after her immediately."

"I've never been to Galway," Will replied. "But is the area safe at present? I haven't had the time to read a newspaper recently."

"It is safe," Alfie told him. "Just don't go anywhere up near Lough Mask. There was trouble on the Earl of Erne's estate with his land agent, Captain Boycott, refusing to lower rents and carrying out evictions. The trouble could still be rumbling on."

"Yes, I read about that. The locals did what Mr Parnell suggested at a Land League meeting back in September and they ostracised Boycott. You said there was trouble. Is Boycott now dead?" Will asked, and Alfie shook his head.

"No, Boycott and his family finally had enough, and they left the estate a few days ago. The papers have been full of it."

"If we go to Galway, could you return to Ballybeg?" Will turned and asked her softly and she nodded.

"I'd love to show you where I was born and grew up." Before it all went wrong, she added silently. "Yes, we'll go to Galway."

"That's settled, then, and we'll leave the arrangements to my mother."

Their servants arrived at number 30 one after the other the following morning. Isobel walked with Mrs Dillon through the house from the servants' bedrooms at the top of the house to the servants' hall in the basement. The cook-housekeeper was in her late forties with plaited brown hair wound into a bun at the nape of her neck. Although she was dressed in black, thankfully, Mrs Dillon's appearance wasn't as severe as that of Mrs Black, her counterpart at the Harvey residence.

"The rooms we'll be using most are the morning room and the breakfast room," Isobel explained. "So the majority of the new furniture will be going into those rooms and also into our bedroom."

"Your bedroom?" Mrs Dillon frowned. "You will be sharing a bedroom with your husband?"

"Yes, I will," Isobel replied, daring her to say anything.

"I see," was all the reply she got.

"Will and I will be living very quietly here, Mrs Dillon."

"Until you have children." Mrs Dillon gave her a kind smile. "Where did you grow up, Miss Stevens?"

"I was born and brought up just outside Ballybeg, Co Galway. My late father was a clergyman."

"Ballybeg?" Mrs Dillon echoed. "You don't have a Ballybeg accent."

"I was sent to school in England," she said. "But Will was born, brought up, and educated here in Dublin, and my brother is a medical student at Trinity College. Will and I are very lucky to have our families living close by."

"You are, and soon you and Dr Fitzgerald will have a beautiful home. Well, Miss Stevens, I'd better make sure the others are settling in."

"Well?" Will whispered in her ear as Mrs Dillon hurried upstairs.

"I think I shocked her when I said you and I would be sharing a bedroom but, other than that, I think we will get on well."

She went for her final dress fitting the morning before

the wedding. As promised, the dress was ready and she burst into tears when she viewed herself in the mirror.

"Beautiful," the dressmaker said simply, and all Isobel could do was nod. "I shall deliver the dress to Fitzwilliam Square this afternoon."

She ran her hands over her breasts and stomach. It was one day short of seven weeks since the miscarriage and she had been scrutinising herself like never before. Her monthly cycle still hadn't returned and her breasts had never been so tender for so long. She was pregnant. She would tell Will he was going to be a father when they were in Ballybeg.

That evening, she called to number 30. As she went up the steps, the front door was opened by a tall dark-haired stranger wearing an unbuttoned frock coat and holding a glass of whiskey.

"I saw you coming," he said. "You must be Isobel. I'm Jerry Hawley, fresh off the boat from Holyhead. Come in."

"You're not getting Will too drunk, are you?" she asked, stepping into the hall.

"No." Jerry smiled and closed the front door. "In fact, he's limiting himself to only three glasses."

"I see, but what size are the three glasses?"

Jerry just chuckled and opened the door to the newly-decorated morning room. The new reddish-brown leather sofa and two armchairs and the pale yellow wallpaper glowed in the light of the fire and gas lamps, and she nodded approvingly. The room looked wonderful.

"Isobel." Fred gave her a grin and held up his glass.

"Fred." She greeted him with a smile and glanced at Will, who got up off the sofa and put a small whiskey glass down on a side table. "I thought we'd acquired a butler for a moment."

Will laughed. "There you go, Jerry. If Harley Street doesn't work out for you, there'll be a position here for you as our butler." Jerry grinned and held up his glass in reply, and Will led her out of the room. "I won't get drunk, I promise."

"Good, and don't let Fred get too drunk, will you?"

"I won't. Nervous?" he asked softly.

"A little bit," she admitted. "Are you?"

"Yes, a little. I'm glad Jerry managed to come over. The three of us started at Wesley together and then went on to Trinity. We've been through a lot together. Fred and I need to get him up the aisle now."

"I'd better go. I just called to tell you I love you and I can't wait to be your wife."

"I love you and I can't wait to be your husband." He kissed her lips then opened the front door. "I'll walk you back to number 55."

"There's no need, Will, go back to Fred and Jerry. See you in the morning."

"Eleven o'clock," he said. "Or are you going to be fashionably late?"

She just laughed and went down the steps.

Will closed the front door and returned to the morning room. Staying in with a bottle of whiskey was a much better idea than traipsing around the majority of Dublin's pubs.

"You said Isobel was beautiful," Jerry began. "But not that she was that beautiful. Good God, Will, she is an angel."

"And, tomorrow, she will be my wife." Will gave him a grin as he sat down again. "She also doesn't want you getting too drunk, Frederick."

Fred snorted. "Got any coffee, then?"

"Yes. When you've finished that glass I'll fetch some for you."

"How are the new servants?"

Will shrugged. He hadn't had all that much to do with them yet. Isobel had called every day and was coping magnificently with them.

"Fine, as far as I know. Isobel has been dealing with them."

"And Dr Fitzgerald joins Dr Simpson full-time in the practice when?" Jerry asked.

"Monday week," Will replied. "Isobel and I are in Galway for five days, which gives us enough time to settle in here when we get back."

"I never thought your father would retire."

"Neither did I," Will admitted. "But Duncan's death shocked him, and editing the *Journal of Irish Medicine* leaves his evenings and weekends free for him to enjoy life so, why not?"

"I completely agree."

Will watched Fred knock back a glass of whiskey before getting up. "I'll go and ask for some coffee."

"Can't you ring for it?" Fred asked.

"Yes, but I'm feeling a little light-headed, so I'm going to have a breath of fresh air in the garden. I won't be long." He left the morning room, walked down the steps to the servants' hall, and knocked before he went in. Mrs Dillon and Annie, the kitchenmaid, were seated opposite Florrie and Mary, the two house-parlourmaids at the long dining table, while Gerald, the footman, was smoking a pipe beside the fire. All got to their feet. "I'm sorry to disturb you," he began. "But could I have a pot of coffee, please?"

"Of course, Dr Fitzgerald." Mrs Dillon nodded to Annie, who went into the kitchen.

"Thank you. It's not often that Fred, Jerry, and I get together these days, but we've had enough to drink now."

"Quite right," Mrs Dillon replied. "I've seen grooms at weddings looking quite the worse for wear."

"Well, I certainly don't want that," he replied. "Excuse me, I need a breath of air."

He opened the door to the garden and went out, closing it behind him. Walking into the centre of the freshly-cut lawn, he put his hands on his hips and breathed deeply in and out. Two glasses of whiskey and he could feel himself getting drunk. Hearing the back door open, he turned. Mrs Dillon was approaching him with something in her hand.

"An ashtray, Dr Fitzgerald."

"Thank you, Mrs Dillon, but I don't smoke."

"Oh, I'm sorry."

"Not at all." He smiled. "I just needed a few moments to myself."

"I'll leave you, then."

"No, I didn't mean to be rude, Mrs Dillon. I'm sorry. I'm just not used to more than one glass of whiskey these days," he explained. "Or, maybe, it's because I'm a little nervous."

"Marriage is a big step."

"Yes, it is, and I love Isobel very much. I'll just be relieved when it's all over."

"I was married for twenty-seven years," she told him.

"You were married?" he asked. "Oh, I do apologise, it's just that…"

"Many housekeepers say they are married, even when

they aren't," she finished with a sudden grin. "I was married at eighteen to the most wonderful man. My father and I walked to the church and Patrick walked me home."

"Do you have any children?"

"Two sons," she said. "And they're both in London. Terence is a police constable and Bernard is a solicitor's clerk."

"You must miss them?"

"I do, but I go to London once a year to see them, so they're not completely lost to me."

"I'm glad."

Mrs Dillon gave him a smile. "I have to admit that yourself and Miss Stevens aren't quite what I had expected. In a good way," she added quickly, and they both laughed.

"I have no airs and graces, I hope. And Isobel neither. We love each other very much."

"I can see that. And I wish you all the luck in the world, Dr Fitzgerald."

In the morning, he stood in front of the wardrobe mirror in his hired black frock coat, waistcoat, and trousers giving the silver-grey cravat a final adjustment. Fred was due to arrive at ten o'clock and they would travel to Trinity College Chapel together. He walked to a front window and peered out across the square, wondering if all was as calm as it seemed.

Downstairs in the hall, he found Fred wearing almost identical clothes to his and looking him up and down before nodding.

"You'll do."

"And you," he replied, trying to hide his relief. "I thought I'd have to go to Ely Place Upper and pull you out of bed."

"That pot of coffee last night did the trick. Are you ready?"

"You have the ring?"

"I do," Fred confirmed.

"Then, we're ready to go."

They travelled to Trinity College by cab and he and Fred walked into the chapel. Mrs Bell was seated near the door wearing a black hat adorned with white silk roses and he gave her a quick smile as he passed. His mother, seated with his father in the second pew back from the aisle, was wearing an ostentatious pale blue-feathered creation on her head and he fought back a laugh as he halted.

"Mother. Father."

"Nervous?" His mother clasped his hand.

"Not anymore," he replied as Isobel's mother walked up the aisle, wearing a silver-grey dress and hat trimmed with purple. They nodded to each other as she took her seat opposite them. "Isobel can't be too far behind," he said. "So I'd better take my place."

He was right. He had just shaken hands with Jerry and sat down in the front pew beside him and Fred when his mother tapped him on the shoulder.

"She's here."

He got to his feet, climbed the steps to the altar, then turned as the 'Wedding March' began.

Chapter Thirteen

Isobel stood in her bedroom, counting to ten. Her mother meant well, but she had chosen a simple wedding dress for a reason – no fuss.

"There." Mrs Henderson smiled after adjusting the veil for the umpteenth time. "You look wonderful."

"So do you." Her mother's silver-grey and purple dress and hat, both colours of mourning, were very stylish yet demure.

"It's time you left, Mother," Alfie called from outside the door.

"Very well. Isobel, I am so happy for you. Will is a good man."

"Yes, he is. Thank you for everything, Mother."

Mrs Henderson kissed her cheek then left the bedroom, leaving the door open.

Alfie came into the bedroom, doing up the buttons of a black frock coat, and gave her a grin. "She does fuss, but it is because she loves you."

"I counted to ten. Many times."

He laughed and held out an arm. "Ready, Miss Stevens?"

Miss Stevens. He would probably be the last person to

call her that. Moving forward, she took his arm, and they carefully walked down the stairs to the hall and out of the house. A carriage was waiting for them and Alfie helped her inside.

"How's David?" she asked as the carriage set off.

"Very well. He wishes he could see me dressed up like this."

She smiled. "Bring him to number 30 when Will and I are back from Galway. We'd like to get to know him."

"Thank you. I shall."

When the carriage stopped in Trinity College's Front Square, Alfie jumped down and helped her out.

"Ready?"

"Yes," she replied without hesitation and put her hand on his arm.

They entered the chapel and the 'Wedding March' began. Will and Fred were standing at the top of the steps and as Will turned she gave him a little smile. He had never looked more handsome and in a matter of minutes, he would be her husband. She climbed the steps, stopped beside him, and the chaplain began to speak.

The wedding service passed in a haze. Beside him, Isobel was a vision in a simple but stunning cream silk satin dress with long sleeves, a v-shaped neckline, and a lace veil which didn't cover her face. When Alfie gave her away and placed her hand on his, Will gave it a gentle squeeze. On being pronounced man and wife, he almost caught his breath as she lifted his hand to her mouth and kissed it. At long last, she was his wife.

After signing the marriage register, they stood at the door

to greet everyone as they left the chapel. Mrs Bell was one of the first to leave.

"You will come to number 55 for the wedding luncheon?" he asked.

"I won't, no," she replied. "I just wanted to see you and Isobel married."

"Keep in touch?"

"I will, Dr Fitzgerald, I promise."

"You next." He gave Jerry a grin as his friend congratulated them.

"Well, I'll see what I can do. I certainly didn't think I'd be the last of the three of us to remain unmarried."

His mother was in tears as she approached them and he bit back a groan. "You're supposed to be happy for us," he teased.

"I am. I'm just being silly." She kissed their cheeks then made way for his father, who held out a hand.

"Congratulations."

"Thank you, Father." Will shook it.

"Welcome to the family, Isobel," his father added in a neutral tone, and she replied with a little nod before he walked on.

Mrs Henderson was also in tears and Isobel reached out and wiped them away.

"I'm only going to be across the square, Mother. You'll probably see me every day."

"I know. It's just with everything that has happened—"

"We won't think of those things today," Isobel interrupted softly but firmly and gave her mother a smile as she moved on.

Will helped Isobel into the carriage before getting in and

sitting beside her. "May I kiss you, Mrs Fitzgerald?"

"Yes, you may." She smiled and he leant over and kissed her thoroughly.

"I'm glad we're spending our wedding night in number 30."

"Oh, why?" she asked with a twinkle in her eye.

"Because I want to wake up with you after our first night as husband and wife in our bed in our home."

That evening, they left number 55 as early as they dared, and hurried around the gardens to number 30. He opened the front door then swept Isobel off her feet and carried her inside, kicking the door closed with a foot. He kissed her then set her down.

"Welcome home."

"Oh." Mrs Dillon came up the steps from the servants' hall. "You're back. Congratulations, Doctor and Mrs Fitzgerald. I hope you had a wonderful day."

"Thank you, we did," Isobel replied. "I've asked May to bring over some wedding cake tomorrow for you all."

"That's very kind. Well, I'll say goodnight."

Discreetly, Mrs Dillon retraced her steps back to the servants' hall, and Will led Isobel upstairs.

When Will closed the door of their bedroom and turned the gas lamps down a little, Isobel heaved a sigh of relief. She had been looking forward to their wedding day for so long and it had thankfully passed without incident. Now, she and Will could unwind.

"Do you think our mothers are still crying?" he asked with a grin and she laughed.

"My mother was on the brink of tears from the moment

May brought me my breakfast tray at eight o'clock this morning."

"I think Mrs Dillon is a little shocked we're back so soon."

"It's our wedding night and we don't want to waste a moment." She turned her back on him. "Your wife needs some help to undress."

Feeling his lips on the side of her neck, she closed her eyes as he removed her veil. Turning her around to face him, he ran a thumb over her lips.

"My wife," he whispered and kissed them, the side of her neck again, before returning to her mouth.

He deepened the kiss and desire made her legs go weak. Her arms slid up around his neck, he pulled her more snugly against his body, and she felt a hard bulge in his trousers.

Her own need surfaced, then intensified with the touch of his hands on her breasts, smoothing over them and caressing them through her dress. He kissed the side of her neck yet again then he crushed her tender breasts together and she couldn't help herself and moaned.

Her fingers pulled at the buttons on his trousers then she pushed them and his drawers down and he grunted, resting his forehead against hers.

"Isobel." His deep groan ignited fires of want deep inside her. She reached up and kissed him, and he kissed her back, hard. She couldn't wait until she had undressed, she needed him at once. Lifting her skirts, she lowered her drawers and stepped out of them. He spun her around, bending her over the bed. His hands then clasped her waist and he thrust hard inside her.

"Oh, God." This was what she feared she would never

have – a husband who loved her and who could satisfy her, too. How lucky she was.

She clutched the bedcovers, gasping as he pumped into her – harder and harder – deeper and deeper. She pushed back against him with each stroke before she finally let go and allowed the waves of pleasure to claim her, screaming as Will thrusted, grunting and growling. His hands gripped her hips, pulling her onto him, until he released himself, crying out as he came.

She smiled as she lay on the bed, exhausted, but satisfied.

"Isobel." Lifting her up, they stood for a few moments, his arms tightly around her, as they caught their breaths. "I love you, Mrs Fitzgerald," he whispered.

"I know," she replied. "I love you, too, Dr Fitzgerald."

Will had never been west of Dublin. On the few occasions he had left the city, he had travelled east to London for Edward's wedding and to visit Jerry. He and Isobel arrived in Galway in the late afternoon of the following day and set about hiring a horse and trap, before returning to the hotel for dinner and an early night.

Despite intending to go to Ballybeg on their first day, it wasn't until their last morning that they set off in the horse and trap. Over the few days, he could sense Isobel's nervous reluctance and he didn't want to press her into going. But at the same time, if she didn't, he didn't want her to regret not visiting her birthplace and her father's grave.

Tethering the horse next to a water trough so it could drink, they walked out of the village. First, to be over and done with it, they went to the churchyard. The grave was near the church door and he read the inscription on the tall headstone:

IN LOVING MEMORY OF | CANON EDMUND
STEVENS, D.D. | RECTOR OF BALLYBEG | DIED
23rd FEBRUARY 1880 | AGED 58 YEARS

"'In Loving Memory'," Isobel read aloud. "That's ironic. Looking back, I remember little or no love between him and any of us."

"What would your father say if he saw you now, as my wife?" he asked.

"That you could have done better," she replied matter-of-factly.

Will exhaled a shocked breath. "That's nonsense."

"That was my father. I'm sorry, Will," she added quietly.

"Whatever for?"

"I so wanted to bring you to Ballybeg and show you where I was born and brought up, but once we arrived in Galway, I couldn't help but be nervous. Despite my father being the way he was, I was happy here as a little girl, and I was worried that it wouldn't be as I had remembered."

"It's beautiful here."

"Yes, it is." She finally smiled and glanced around the churchyard, bathed in December sunshine. "The Glebe House is only five minutes walk from here. Let me show it to you."

They left the churchyard and he closed the gate as a horse and cart trotted towards them. They let it pass before setting off along the road hand in hand, only to have someone shout after them.

"Isobel?"

Will felt her tense, heard feet running up behind them, and they turned around. A blonde man of about his own age peered curiously at her then laughed.

"Isobel Stevens, I thought it was you."

"James," she replied crisply and, this time, Will tensed. So, this was James. But why wasn't he in America?

"What are you doing back here?" James asked. "According to my father, your father disowned you and you vanished."

"Good afternoon, James." Isobel went to walk on, but he blocked her way.

"Alfie thought you were dead, but your mother refused to believe it. They went to live in Dublin, did you know that?"

"Yes, I did. Now, kindly step aside."

"Aren't you going to ask me how I am? You look well."

"You were supposed to have gone to America."

"I did, for a while," he told her. "Boston."

"Most people who emigrate don't come back."

"America wasn't for me. I missed Ballybeg."

Isobel looked sceptical. "I find that hard to believe."

"You'd believe anything at one time." James gave her a smug smile and Will clenched his fists. "In any case, Father discovered that Peter was... well, let's just say Father wrote Peter out of his will and he asked me to come back to Ireland and run the farm."

"Where is Peter now?" she asked.

"I have no idea," James replied airily and Will's stomach churned with disgust. Whatever had she seen in this man? "Aren't you going to introduce us?" he added, nodding towards Will.

"This is my husband, Dr Will Fitzgerald. Will, this is James Shawcross."

James put out a hand and Will shook it reluctantly.

"So you took her on, then, Will?" James asked. "The child, too?"

"The child died," Isobel said quietly.

"Ah, well. A blessing in disguise. No gentleman would want to take on another man's bastard." James grinned but Isobel gasped, slapped his cheek, and the grin vanished. "You—" James began, raising a hand to strike her.

Will punched him before he had finished speaking and James fell flat onto his back, clutching his jaw.

"That was for what you did to Alfie, to Isobel, and to your own brother," Will informed him, his voice shaking with fury.

"You've broken a fucking tooth," James wailed and spat it out.

"Good. No other woman will look twice at you now."

Taking Isobel's arm, they walked on until they turned a corner. There he stopped, shaking his hand, as it began to throb.

"Let me look at it," she insisted, and he held his hand out. His knuckles were starting to swell already. "There's a stream across the road from the Glebe House, you can bathe it in there."

She led him on until they reached the stream and he passed her his hat before crouching down, holding his hand in the icy-cold water, and massaging his knuckles with his other hand. His hand ached but he doubted if he had broken any bones. Even if he had, it would be well worth it, having wiped the arrogance off James' face.

"Thank you," she said simply.

He squinted up at her with a smile. "That's the first time I've punched anyone. I'm absolutely delighted it was him."

Laughing, she bent and kissed his lips. "I love you. How is it?" She nodded to his hand.

"Numb now." Straightening up, he shook his hands dry, and she handed him his hat.

"This is the Glebe House," she told him, pointing across the road to a large two-storey stone and slate house with a range of outbuildings to its rear. "I was born upstairs in the middle bedroom."

He put an arm around her waist and they walked to the garden gate. Despite it being December, the garden was tidy with the rose bushes growing on both sides of the path up to the front door seeming well cared for. He had been dreading finding the house deserted and the garden neglected and overgrown.

"When I was whipped and thrown out," she continued. "Father chased me out of the house, down the path, and through this gateway before throwing my clothes after me. I tripped and fell on the road and I had to crawl for a few yards on my hands and knees before getting to my feet again and grabbing my clothes and my bible." Feeling her shudder, he hugged her to him. "I got dressed in the churchyard, even though my back was in agony, and I could feel the blood trickling down my body. I ran into Ballybeg village and saw that the coach was leaving for Galway. I offered the driver a necklace I was wearing and he allowed me a seat."

"What did you do for money in Galway?"

"I pawned a ring. The money got me a train ticket to Dublin. I've never felt so alone as when I did as the train left the station in Galway. I didn't know what I was going to do. I was carrying James' child and I had no money left. A girl was standing outside the station in Dublin and I know now she was a prostitute but, in my innocence, I asked her if there was anywhere I could work in exchange for bed and board. She said, yes, and brought me to Sally Maher's."

Will kissed her forehead and they began to re-trace their steps back towards Ballybeg village. Half-expecting to find James still on the ground outside the churchyard gate, he was relieved to see the road empty. He never wanted Isobel to see James Shawcross again.

"Is there somewhere in the village we can have tea?" he asked.

"There's a hotel. It's where the Galway coach leaves from. But, before we go there, I need to tell you something, and I want to tell you here."

"Oh?" he said, stopping and frowning at her. "What is it?"

"Will, I'm pregnant."

He expelled a long breath. "You aren't ill in the mornings. When was your last monthly?"

"I haven't been ill in the mornings at all, but my breasts have been tender for weeks, and I haven't had a monthly since the miscarriage."

"At all? Not even some spotting?" he clarified and she shook her head.

"There's been nothing. I wanted to be sure before I told you. I didn't want to get your hopes up."

Pulling her gently to him, he kissed her, and she slid her arms around his neck.

"I love you, Mrs Fitzgerald."

Linking her hands at the back of his neck, she smiled at him. "I left here disowned by my father and carrying James' child. This time, I'm leaving here with you and carrying your child. And I'm so happy."

"I can hardly believe it."

"But you're happy?" she asked anxiously.

"Oh, yes," he whispered. "I have never been so happy."

"Let's not bother with tea. Can we go back to Dublin now so we can prepare for our first Christmas in number 30?"

"Our first and last Christmas just the two of us," he said, giving her a grin. "Yes. Let's go home."

THE END

About The Author

Lorna Peel is an author of historical fiction and mystery romance novels set in the UK and Ireland. Lorna was born in England and lived in North Wales until her family moved to Ireland to become farmers, which is a book in itself! She lives in rural Ireland, where she writes, researches her family history, and grows fruit and vegetables. She also keeps chickens and guinea hens.

Scan the QR code for other books by Lorna Peel, to sign up to Lorna's newsletter and to connect with Lorna on social media.

Printed in Great Britain
by Amazon

27527271R00223